Reluctant Warrior

George Chute (signature)

George Chute

greatunpublished.com
Title No. 669
2002

Reluctant Warrior

Thanks to good friends Tom, Will and Win for their interest in reading the manuscript, and for their comments and encouragement. Particular thanks to my wonderful wife Kathy, who believed in me and supported the lengthy effort from emerging idea to finished novel.

Author's Note

This story is set against a backdrop of the Vietnam War in the late 1960s and early 1970s. That was a time, unlike almost any other in American history, when our country was torn by disagreement and filled with misgivings over the decisions that had put us into a war we seemed to be incapable of winning. U.S. involvement by then had grown to well over a half million soldiers in Vietnam and hundreds of billions of dollars in military costs. The American public had become weary of unrelenting images of war, and many were fed up with the lies and duplicity coming from our elected officials.

Richard Nixon won the 1968 presidential election in part because of his promise to end the war. National opinion was leaning toward extricating this country from the Vietnam morass, under almost any conditions, even if faced with dishonor from a failed military effort. By 1969, diplomats from Hanoi, Saigon and the U.S. had gathered in Paris to debate an exit strategy, although the discussion was delayed for a time by bickering over an appropriate shape for the conference table around which they were to sit.

The U.S. Army at that time was also considerably different from almost any other era in our history. By the time in the Vietnam War this story takes place, the Army was largely made up of draftees, and those citizen-soldiers who marched off to Southeast Asia were a microcosm of the conflicted populace back home. They knew the war had little popular backing, and that they were being asked to fight it anyway. The policy of a one-year tour of duty created a constant demand for replacement troops, which often translated into a disturbingly low level of experience within combat units.

The ultimate outcome of a promised U.S. withdrawal was clear to Vietnam combat troops even as the exit strategy began. They could see that South Vietnam would not last for long without American military support on the ground. Hanoi would almost certainly prevail once the Americans were gone, and that realization contributed to low morale. Tens of thousands of soldiers had died fighting the war and more were still dying every day, apparently without purpose. Vietnam at that time felt like a mistake, and twenty-some years later Robert McNamara admitted that it had been a mistake.

I have attempted to capture in this story the character and feel of the Army during those few years late in the war. The Army depicted here may be one to which you can relate, or it may not. Several million men, and more than a few women, were volunteers and draftees during the Vietnam War, and I believe many of those who served toward the end of the war will find in the story descriptions and events that will strike a familiar chord, perhaps evoke a memory or two.

Some readers may see a negative perspective in how *Reluctant Warrior* depicts the Army and the war effort. Many, I hope, will find accuracy and even occasional amusement in the portrayal of a frequently inept venture. Others may believe it is a disrespectful characterization, particularly at a time such as the present day when America's armed forces have been called on to do yet another unpleasant job in a far corner of the world. No disrespect is intended for anyone who ever put on a uniform and made a commitment to defend this wonderful country. The list of sacrifices by our countrymen in uniform is a long one, and even includes the sacrifices made by those frequently unappreciated soldiers of Vietnam.

But it is an unavoidable fact that troops in Vietnam toward the end of the war were burdened by conditions that made the combat effort something less than completely effective. And the Army experience I knew was very much as I have described in my story.

Vietnam veterans were scorned as "baby-killers" and roundly disparaged for roles in a war that many found futile, even immoral. Yet the men I knew had a quiet pride at having done their part in this unpopular war. All of them answered their country's call—many in spite of personal doubts—and a good number of them made the ultimate sacrifice. I am honored to have known them.

Among the medals and service ribbons I earned while in the Army are a Combat Infantryman's Badge, an Army Commendation Medal, and two Bronze Stars. Notwithstanding the circumstances of a war largely abandoned and citizens who thought ill of those who went, I am proud of those decorations. The fact that I am willing to criticize and even poke fun at the Army that awarded the decorations does not lessen my pride.

Chapter One

There were no heroes.

At least not in the classical sense—the noble and selfless warrior who, heedless of his own safety and welfare, performs some courageous act for the sake of a greater good.

Real heroism is born of individual choices to subordinate ourselves and our well-being to some grand purpose that we consciously accept as more important than we are. Those choices usually have alternatives, often significantly more prudent and usually a lot healthier than the "heroic act".

By the time I arrived in Vietnam in 1969, there no longer were any illusions of a grand purpose. The United States was committed to a path of disengagement from the war, and public opinion had shifted toward ending our involvement any way possible.

It's not that we didn't do astonishing things over there. We did. I'll want to tell you about some of them. I haven't yet met a Vietnam vet who wasn't surprised at least one time to find himself performing physical or mental feats he never would have thought possible. Simply enduring the often unimaginable conditions was no small accomplishment for inexperienced young Americans who found themselves in unforgiving and terrifying circumstances.

But the operative notion here is choice. And we generally didn't have any. Nobody in his right mind willingly seeks out needless adversity. But overcoming uninvited peril does not make for heroism if there is simply nothing else to do but get on with it. Learn to cope. You can't really say, "Time out! I don't want to play any more!"

It's probably more accurate, then, for me to say that there were none who set out to be heroes. It was a time, not of moral certainty in the rightness of a war, but of increasing national self-doubt and political polarization. It was a time of disillusionment and, for some, open rebellion. The seeds had already been sown that would ultimately lead to National Guard soldiers gunning down protesting college students. The mood of the country didn't foster attitudes among those sent off to war that the mission was somehow more important than any individual soldier, which I had always thought was a principal ingredient for the quintessential military hero of history. Instead, the mood was one of resignation to the idea that the war would eventually be brought to a close—probably not a victorious one—and that soldiers who were daily paying the highest price were not accomplishing much with their sacrifices.

Vietnam wasn't at all what I had expected, although it's probably fair to say that I didn't really know what to expect. Wars never have been pretty, but we buy into their less appealing qualities more easily when we feel they are justified by a noble and glorious cause. I kept thinking, naively, that I would be swept up in some wonderfully energizing spirit of duty to my country. Sadly, this war didn't have such a worthy feel. I saw nothing noble or glorious in Vietnam.

It wasn't patriotism, or honor, or the threat of some distant menace to our way or life, or even the exciting promise of a role in a real-life war movie that made most of us go. It was the local Selective Service Board, harvesting the young men of their communities to fuel the needs of a huge and voracious war machine in Southeast Asia. It was the draft, conscripting armies of citizen-soldiers.

My name is Steve Jennings—Hobie to my friends—and this is my story. More appropriately, it is a story of so many unremarkable guys like me who were swept up in a life-altering event. I don't pretend that my experiences were necessarily representative, or that this is the definitive Vietnam tale; I don't think there is such a thing. This is instead an account of an era when hundreds of thousands of very ordinary people found themselves taken on an unpleasant journey to a place of killing half a world away from everything they knew and loved, and most not by choice.

Much has been written about the "John Wayne" Vietnam experience. Less has been recorded about the majority of us who obediently, but reluctantly, put our lives on hold and marched off to a war we didn't understand or completely believe in. Sights and sounds, emotions and impressions were deeply burned into the minds and memories of people like me who, for a time, were part of this place. The memories remain vivid, their refusal to fade demanding the telling of the story.

I think what struck me the most during my time in Vietnam is that everything always seemed just a little off balance, and that most of us didn't really know what was happening or what we should be doing. For grunts fighting on the ground, there never was any grand plan, any clear tactical strategy. The war was more a confusing mosaic of disconnected pieces, frequently illogical, and occasionally resulting in needless casualties. Actual combat was more often by accident than by design. For hapless troops out in the jungle, there was no feeling of purpose, no motivating reason to be there.

Absent purpose, our mission was simply survival.

Some might reasonably argue that there really was a thoughtful, detailed military plan and an artfully orchestrated war effort in Vietnam—that a low-level ground-pounder like me just wouldn't have noticed the big picture. It could be said that my impressions of chaos were the narrow experiences of one field unit in one limited area of operations. Perhaps that is so. But the story I have to tell is often punctuated by examples of bumbling and ineptitude, inconsistency and indifference, politics and private agendas. It is profoundly at odds with the image of an impressively trained, equipped, and motivated juggernaut that Washington insisted had been fielded in Vietnam.

It wasn't like all those Hollywood war movies. We were scared, sometimes bored, and often miserable. All of us had a single-minded focus on marking off the days of our tours of duty, staying alive, and waiting for a plane ride back to "The World".

During the early years of the Vietnam War, the period when U.S. involvement was escalating from a few advisors to a much larger field force, the Army was principally composed of career soldiers. Although the war effort against a guerilla enemy was handicapped by adherence to tactics left over from World War II and Korea, at least the troops in those early years were reasonably seasoned. Later in the war, about the time virtually everyone knew it was only a matter of time before it became an abandoned cause, lightly trained draftees and fresh-faced Officer Candidate School graduates dominated the incoming replacements. The resulting lack of experience, coupled with the spreading disillusionment over our presence in Vietnam and recognition that the war would end with something less than a victory, assured a degree of disarray that was almost unavoidable.

So, at any time during my two years in the Army, most of the people around me were a far cry from professional military men. We had nothing in common, and everything in common. We were white and black and Hispanic. We were high school dropouts and college graduates. Some were dirt-poor, while others were sons of comparatively affluent families. We came from every place in the U.S. that had young men with the rotten luck to be between the ages of 18 and 25 at a singularly poor time in our country's history. The vast majority of us were draftees, and most of us categorically did not want to be in Vietnam.

Many of the names have faded away as the years have gone by, but I think their faces, the events we shared, and most of all the feelings—that incredible palette of thoughts and senses brought about by events none of us could have imagined—will be with me all my life. Some of the names I never knew; there were lots of nicknames. And, there was a wordless understanding that you didn't get too friendly. That way, so we thought, it didn't hurt quite as much when your buddy got blown away.

My Vietnam tour began in 1969. Nixon had been saying for months that the war was winding down, that he was going to be the architect of a successful withdrawal of American troops and a transfer of military responsibility to the South Vietnamese government. And, every day bombs fell, bullets flew, and people died. To those of us out in the jungle, it didn't feel very much like the war was ending.

I was a "shake and bake", an "instant NCO". Those were among the more complimentary names describing graduates of the Non-Commissioned Officer Candidate School at Fort Benning, Georgia. Although I'm not sure I count it as one of my life's more notable accomplishments, I was second in my NCOCS class. That meant a promotion to staff sergeant E-6 after a whopping eleven months in the Army. Not surprisingly, career NCOs ("lifers" to us draftees) viewed guys like me with absolute disgust, as it took 20 years for some of them — particularly those with specialties other than combat arms — to get the same rank. On the other hand, most of the grunts that the Army was sending into the jungle at that point in the war were kids and not lifer types, so mass-produced NCOs like me who were wet behind the ears and expendable sort of fit right in.

The conditions that led me to the Army and NCO school were not all that uncommon in those days. Like many young people of the era, I had found it difficult to figure out what I wanted to do with my life. The Vietnam War had been hanging over us throughout our high school and college years. It was tough to focus on questions like, "What do I want to be when I grow up?" A lot of high school graduates went on to colleges and universities just to avoid the draft, with hopes that the war would somehow be over by the time they graduated. I had always figured on going to college, but preserving that precious student deferment took care of any doubts I might have had.

College was a journey on an unsettled ocean. It was a confusing time, marked by strident opinions on what was right or wrong with the United States and its role in Vietnam. Said Dylan, the times were a-changin'. Looking back, I think that the four years between 1964 and 1968 saw more transformation on the college scene than perhaps any comparable period in history. When I was a freshman, drugs were almost unheard of. By the time I graduated, they were endemic on campus and it was a rare student who hadn't at least experimented, if only with marijuana. I tried smoking grass a few times, and I even inhaled.

Obedient, quiet, and generally satisfied with their lives, the college kids of the early sixties usually presented no more serious disciplinary problems to the administrations of their schools than the occasional kegger party or panty raid on the girls' dorms. In a remarkably short few years, as I watched first-hand on campus, those harmless rites of passage gave way to far more purposeful activities like protest demonstrations, anti-war political activism, and the emergence of organizations such as the Students for a Democratic Society (most of which were viewed by our government as subversive).

Music was another measure of the shifting sentiments of the era. In 1964, the Beatles still only wanted to hold your hand and love you yeah, yeah, yeah. By the time I went to Vietnam, they had left that early innocence long behind for a much more psychedelic imagery. A lot of pop groups sang social commentary on drugs, the war, and in outcry against the increasingly repressive authoritarian response to voices critical of U.S. policy. Even The Association, those straight-arrow California guys with the lyrical love ballads and tight harmonies, dabbled with a few songs like "Along Comes Mary" and "Requiem" that cautiously reflected on the turbulent times.

San Francisco's flower children had been discovered by the media and the rest of the country, and clothing styles on campus quickly popularized this new, languid lifestyle. Posters celebrated the philosophers of the day, including a picture of alternative rocker Frank Zappa sitting on a toilet with the caption "Phi Zappa Crappa" that graced the institutional green enamel-painted cinder block walls of my dorm room.

I was a child of the late 40s and 50's who had grown up believing in the legitimacy of government and the wisdom and vision of our leaders. Those years were defined by the aftermath of World War II and our righteous victory over a Nazi tyrant and Japanese imperialism. It's hard now to think there ever was a time of such innocence, when most folks were predisposed to accept what politicians said and reluctant to believe they would ever misuse their power.

It was indicative of their strong feelings, then, for students brought up in such an environment to be taking to the streets in protest marches. Many of my close friends were angrily demonstrating against the Vietnam War, and even students who didn't join the protests admitted to be uneasy about the continued escalation of U.S. involvement. The more I learned about Vietnam, its history, and how the U.S. presence had grown, the more I too wondered about the path our country had chosen. Sure, I loved my country, and I still can get a tear in my eye hearing a rousing rendition of the Star Spangled Banner. But the Vietnam cause didn't inspire a mindless rush to arms among the majority of the population in those days.

Considering the times, it isn't surprising that my most vivid recollection of graduation day in 1968, as I stood there after the ceremony clutching my freshly minted bachelor degree, was thinking, "What the hell do I do now?" I had been a better than average student and had even enjoyed my college experience. But whatever satisfaction and stability university life had provided for four years had ended, and I was faced with both the loss of my student deferment and the real-life need to make a buck doing something—without a clue as to what that something would be. My focus in school, like that of many around me, had been more on avoidance of the Army and less on preparation for a grown-up life.

Graduation day also brought orders to report for a pre-induction physical. Coincidence perhaps, but the orders actually arrived in the mail on the day of my graduation ceremony. With them came a growing certainty that my days as a civilian were numbered, that I was soon going to have the privilege of defending my country from godless communist hordes in a far-off place which had been a staple feature on the TV news for as long as I could remember. I recall a feeling of helplessness, an inability to control my own destiny, like being a marker on some huge board game. The dice rolled, you were picked up and moved a certain number of places, and set back down. Sooner or later, you knew you had to land on the square marked "U.S. Army".

I did have other choices than waiting for the draft board to call. I could have enlisted, which would at least have offered the opportunity to pick a low-risk military occupational specialty in exchange for a longer commitment than the two-year draft obligation. Or I could have joined the reserves, although spots in reserve units were very hard to come by unless you were "connected". Finally, the draft could be avoided by an escape to Canada. I had always been a practical sort of guy, and somehow running away to Canada seemed a little extreme. It was a step once taken that would unequivocally alter the rest of your life. I wasn't sure I wanted to cut myself off from my own country. And, the famous capriciousness of the draft board offered hope that I might not get called. Most promising, the growing anti-war sentiment was causing changes in Washington. It was becoming clear that, one way or another, the U.S. would eventually pull out of Vietnam.

The months following college graduation went by quickly. Without any sense of what I really wanted to do, I half-heartedly took a management trainee position ("management trainee" was a popular entry-level job title in those days) with a large retail chain. I stood around with a nametag that said "supervisor" on it, surrounded by unfamiliar products and resentful commissioned salesmen, smiling sweetly to indifferent customers. I was marking time; waiting for my invitation to the party and hoping it wouldn't come.

Home was an apartment I shared with a guy I knew from college, who had dropped out after happily learning he had a medical condition that would keep him out of the Army. He was a big, friendly guy who chose not to be overly challenged by life, or to take much of anything too seriously. Bobby was as easy-going as anyone I knew, and was well suited to his chosen occupation of real estate sales (which he only worked at when he felt like it and needed some cash). He could charm anyone, made house sales effortlessly, and once even picked up a girl at a party to go on a blind date with me!

Bobby and I made an interesting pair, as I tended to be more introspective and quiet, while he could fill up a room all by himself. He was more the class clown type, where I was the kid who teachers had always called on for the answer. We were good buddies, though, and fit well together.

We partied hard and enjoyed our independence from school, parents, and most other former authority figures. I met some girls, one of whom I later married. Leaping into marriage was another fairly common occurrence in those days for guys on their way to Vietnam. It was a desperate attempt to create an emotional anchor to cling to, another reason to survive the war, a way to make sure there was someone waiting at home for you.

Those blurry few months after graduation ended when the party invitation arrived—Steve Jennings' orders to report for duty in the U.S. Army.

I was inducted in August of 1968. It was the first step on a road of new experiences for a kid who had grown up in suburbia (the Ozzie and Harriet version, with neat bungalows and neater lawns, all equipped with one-car garages and charcoal grills). I was a kid who wasn't terribly athletic, who had only fired a gun once or twice in his life, and who wasn't particularly amenable to mindlessness, intolerance, and unquestioned authority. The Army introduced me to all of that, and so much more.

First stop was basic training at Fort Knox, Kentucky. During an orientation session for my group of new recruits, I stupidly rose to ask a question of the lieutenant who was conducting the presentation. We were in a large room, much like a college lecture hall, and still in civilian clothes. I suppose that made me feel at ease to speak up. How proud I was to have recognized that the soldier was a lieutenant, and I demonstrated my keen powers of observation by addressing him as "Lieutenant". I never did get an answer to the question.

Instead I got an ass chewing for being too dim-witted to know that an enlisted man addressed officers as "Sir" and not by their rank.

From there we were ushered to platoon barracks where we met our drill sergeants. With a practiced and menacing style, they told us that "Your soul might belong to Jesus but your ass belongs to me". They assured us that, despite all of us being useless excuses for human beings, they were up to the task of turning most of us into real men. Drill sergeants were filled with witticisms—a legion of wannabe stand-up comics. None of the new conscripts laughed.

"And don't call me Sir. Call me Sergeant. I ain't an officer; I work for a living." I heard that line from every drill sergeant I ever met.

My platoon's drill sergeant was a stocky black guy named Boggs. He was built like a fireplug, the image enhanced by the Smoky Bear D.I. hat pushed low on his forehead, and was solid as a chuck of granite. Boggs was a staff sergeant E-6 with maybe 25 years in the Army. He had a weakness for bourbon. When he was drunk, which was more often than the company commander knew, he was like a large, friendly teddy bear, even to us low-life trainees. When he was sober, he was more like a grizzly bear. As soon as we caught on, the trainees in his platoon bought SSG Boggs a bottle of booze any time we had the money and access to the PX.

One of our first destinations was a building that housed a dozen barbers where we were treated to a skinhead haircut. The "barbers" undoubtedly learned their trade by shearing sheep. Each of us was in the chair less than a minute. We went in looking like civilians and came out bald.

The barbers used electric clippers, making long strokes that began at the forehead, went back over the top of the head and ended at the neckline. Any remaining stubble averaged less than an eighth of an inch long. Since 1968 was smack in the middle of an era when many folks wore long hair and said "groovy" a lot, there were some lengthy-locked flower types among the new recruits. And a few brothers sported the massive

"Mod Squad" afro whose wearers single-handedly filled up a doorway. It didn't matter—short or long, the hair was gone in seconds. The haircut so markedly changed the appearance of some guys that even those who had gotten to know each other had a hard time recognizing the newly bald as they exited the building.

Although a short haircut is really no big deal, it was a violating experience for some of the new troopers. It was all part of a coordinated effort to break down us trainees, to strip away individuality and replace it with military conformity. It was intended to be a bit intimidating, and it worked.

Once our heads were uniformly cue ball smooth, we visited a vast supply complex of clothing and equipment. The entire company of brand new privates was paraded through the warehouse at a double-time shuffle, with fatigues and khakis and belts and boots and caps heaped on us as we hobbled along. Size was determined by the eyeball estimate of disinterested supply clerks whose attitude was close is good enough. "Don't worry if they're a little tight, you'll be losing weight real soon."

The barracks building that housed my platoon was essentially a single large rectangular room accommodating 40 or so trainees, with bunk beds neatly lined along each long wall. At the end opposite the entrance was a doorway, which led into a gang latrine in two parts. One section was a shower stall with ten showerheads poking out of the wall. The second section had sinks down one side, and urinals and toilets without stalls down the other. The lack of walls around the toilets initially tended to induce constipation. The first time I found myself sitting on a toilet with guys a foot away on either side of me was just a little strange. True togetherness in this Army! Guys that take a dump together...hmm...might possibly be taking team-building a bit too far. Maybe that particular basic training latrine experience is why ground-pounding infantry soldiers are called "grunts".

There were lessons in housekeeping, like how to clean the latrines with a toothbrush. You even got to bring your own! Bunk beds with threadbare, thin mattresses had to be made with blankets stretched tight enough to bounce a quarter. We spent hours spit-shining our footgear with cotton balls, Kiwi shoe polish, lighter fluid, and of course lots of saliva.

High gloss shining wasn't just for combat boots and low-quarters; we did it to the floors, too. In fact, the entire center floor area of the cramped barracks was kept shined to a bright luster, and nobody was permitted to walk on it except the drill sergeant, who would intentionally tromp around to scuff it and then revile us for our sloppy housekeeping.

KP was always a memorable experience, from peeling potatoes, to washing pots and pans, to everybody's favorite, cleaning the accumulated gunk in the grease traps on the ovens. Although there was an official KP roster, trainees could find themselves picked for extra KP duty just by the bad luck of walking through the chow line at a time when the mess sergeant needed an extra pair of hands.

Other valuable lessons over the next eight weeks included painting rocks in the company street, digging holes and filling them back in, how to fold underwear and arrange it in a foot locker to Army standards, how to field-strip a cigarette butt. We were taught not to question, not to have an opinion.

The drill instructor cadre regularly reminded us that we were lower than pond scum, not worthy of the uniform, and at best suited for future cannon fodder. They fervently hoped that the majority of us would have the cojones to make it through their charge and emerge in eight weeks transformed into real men. And you know we were all tremendously excited at that prospect.

We learned how to stand at attention in the company street, ramrod straight, feet placed just so at a thirty degree angle. Parade rest was really another form of standing at attention, only not quite as rigid. Standing at ease was a little more forgiving. And of course we were taught to salute properly— never show your palm.

Push-ups were a way of life. We spent a lot of time in the "front-leaning rest position", which is simply holding yourself at the top of a push-up while the muscles in your arms turned into mush. Drill sergeants penalized the slightest shortcoming, real or contrived, with the order to "Drop and give me twenty". In the course of an average day, you might rack up a couple hundred push-ups, between PT (physical training) and penalties.

Running was popular, too. Combat boots back then were stiff, heavy leather jobs that defiantly refused to be broken in. We walked and ran and jogged in them, but they were no competition for Nikes. They were clunky and wearying—and to this day I hate running.

There were two hills at Fort Knox named "Agony" and "Misery". The drill sergeants loved to run training companies up them and back down again. It was a rare trainee who didn't blow lunch at least once running up and down those hated hills. You'd get a pain in your side like a knife had been stuck in your guts, and you couldn't get enough air no matter how fast you sucked it in. But you didn't dare stop to catch your breath; the D.I. would be all over you in seconds if you were unwise enough to fall out of the moving column.

We had long marches in formation with heavy loads and bleeding blisters. We were marched everywhere. Sometimes platoons of marching trainees created traffic jams at post intersections. The entire fort echoed with chants of "Hut, two, ee, ho. Gimme yo ell, eye, ell!'

Drill sergeants were masters of singsong cadence, and most had an inexhaustible supply of profane little ditties they would call out to keep us in step. We chanted cadences, and sang about killing and mayhem, and about some civilian guy named Jody who was supposedly back home screwing your girl. And of course we chanted how we wanted to become Airborne Rangers and get to Vietnam so we could kick the crap out of some Viet Cong we didn't even know.

Close order drill was practiced just about daily—"Right shoulder arms! Left shoulder arms! To the rear march! Port arms! Left face! Column right MARCH!" That "MARCH!" command always came out sounding like a bad cough, like someone trying to hack up a lung. Some guys never could get all this drill stuff. "No you dickhead, your *left* foot! Your *other* left foot!" It didn't matter too much; there weren't many parades in Vietnam.

Physical training, or PT, was another daily activity—sometimes twice a day. As with most things, the Army had made PT so programmatic that it became numbingly routine. There were a couple of "Army Drills", each consisting of a series of exercises to be performed to cadence. An instructor would holler out, "Army drill one, exercise number one. I will call the cadence, you will count the repetitions." Every single PT instructor talked exactly the same way. "Ready, begin. One, two, three...ONE! One, two, three...TWO! One, two, three...THREE!" And we did them, on and on and on, in a semi-conscious stupor, minds wandering to thoughts of home, until an instructor's boot in the ass reminded us where we were.

Fort Knox was the home of armor training. There were a lot of tanks around, and guys learning how to operate them. Several times we were trucked out to rifle ranges, and passed by tank ranges where we could see them firing. Pretty awesome, but I was to learn that tanks didn't fare all that well in choking jungle. In fact, I never even saw a tank in the part of Vietnam where I spent my tour.

One training exercise involved a lesson on, and a ride inside, an armored personnel carrier (APC). It was a tracked vehicle, used by armored cavalry troops, and it seemed to me at the time that duty on a track probably was a whole lot preferable to walking. But they had a negative side, too. They were metal sweatboxes that cooked in the sun, and they made wonderful targets for enemy soldiers with anti-armor weapons.

At meal times, trainees had to go through various drills before being allowed into the mess hall. Most typical was the overhead ladder, the monkey bars, which required a hand over hand trip down the length of the ladder, swinging between the rungs. Not too hard for the skinny guys, but it was particularly tough for the heavier guys who kept losing their grip and falling off. The drill sergeants were right there to torment their hapless victims with extra push-ups while the rest of us in the chow line slowly passed by, averting our eyes and glad not to be fat.

Inside the mess hall it was generally quiet. If you talked, the drill sergeants assumed you weren't hungry since you were using your mouth for something other than eating. They would give you 30 seconds to bolt down the rest of your chow and leave. The food wasn't half bad, what you might call rib-sticking. What it lacked in flavor, it made up for in heartiness. This was years before modern medical revelations about good cholesterol and bad cholesterol and free radicals and all that bullshit, so we scarfed down huge quantities of eggs, bacon, red meat, potatoes and similar fare. Many Army posts were in the south, and I'm convinced that *all* mess sergeants were from the south, so grits were accorded the status of an official food group.

While our bodies were being conditioned with lots of exercise and hearty chow, the docs made sure we were immunized against every ailment known to man. It was a rare week when the training company didn't have to line up with shirts off for some inoculation or other. They used those high-pressure guns that blasted the juice into your arm, no needles required. The assembly-line column of troops sometimes got two or three doses of different stuff as we shuffled past the medics. We were tested for TB, got drops for polio, and were injected for smallpox, yellow fever, cholera, tetanus, typhus, influenza, typhoid, and (honest) the plague. Bring on the germs of the world—we were invincible. And we had sore arms.

Although close quarter battles with fixed bayonets are more suited to wars long forgotten, we received regular instruction on fixing, thrusting, and parrying with bayonets. Human-shaped targets filled with straw took the brunt of our affected fury, thankfully minimizing wear and tear on the trainees. It wasn't enough to show appropriate zeal; the drill instructors demanded that we bellow "Kill" as we buried the blades in our targets.

A related exercise was fighting with "pugil sticks", six-foot long poles with padded ends the size of paint cans. Trainees were paired up and encouraged to pound the crap out of each other with the pugil sticks, while the rest of us stood around egging them on. Interestingly, I never saw either a bayonet or a pugil stick in Vietnam. But I suppose the training ensured that we would have suitably broad combat knowledge, preparing us for every contingency, in case we ever had to charge an enemy position armed with a pugil stick.

"Fire guard" was a rotating nightly duty, sort of a precursor to standing watch in Vietnam. Fire guard sentries were needed because the barracks were made of wood and so old that a fire would have turned them into instant death traps. In those days, lots of Army barracks were still heated by coal stoves, a few others by electric space heaters. That was a recipe for disaster, and necessitated overnight watchmen. After a day packed with physical activities, being awakened and unwillingly dragged back to consciousness in the middle of the night to stand fire guard felt like trying to swim up to the surface from the bottom of a very deep lake.

We learned about first aid, and how to use pressure bandages to stop blood flow. We learned about sucking chest wounds, arterial bleeding, traumatic amputations, and other medical byproducts of battle that were guaranteed to ruin your whole day.

Training also included sections on CBR—chemical, biological, and radiation warfare. We were sent wearing gas masks into a building filled with CS gas (a variety of tear gas), and then made to remove the masks. That wasn't any fun. Guys were stumbling around, tears pouring down their faces, groping in the CS haze for a way out of the building. For a half hour afterwards fumes kept rising out of our clothing, starting the waterworks all over again.

As a training postscript to the gas chamber (that's what they called it), we were shown some little needle-tipped toothpaste tubes of atropine. The stuff supposedly was a remedy to counter a nerve gas attack. The instructors kept threatening to make us inject ourselves with the tubes, but finally relented. It was mildly amusing to later learn that gas masks and atropine were not available items in most supply rooms in Vietnam.

Of course, all basic trainees had weapons training and had to qualify—which meant achieving a minimum acceptable score on a target range—with the M-14 semiautomatic carbine. The

M-14 had been around a long time, and was a decent military rifle. But it was no longer the primary infantry weapon, and had been replaced in Vietnam with the M-16 automatic rifle. The M-16 was in such short supply that I saw (but didn't fire) exactly one in the eight weeks of basic training.

A remarkable 98% of the troops in my basic training company were recent college graduates. We were probably a little less receptive to the unquestioning obedience demanded of us by the drill sergeants, many of whom had difficulty completing a sentence. I've heard that the burden of the Vietnam War fell disproportionately on less educated and economically disadvantaged folks who couldn't pull strings to either avoid service or to get cushy jobs in the reserves. I guess that's generally accepted as true, but in my narrow military experience it was not the case. There were a lot of middle class guys with college educations and bright prospects who didn't have any strings to pull, either.

The entire training company had come from Michigan, and the Detroit Tigers made it to the World Series that fall. The National League team was St. Louis, and guess where the company commander hailed from. He was a short, pimply 1st lieutenant with a Napoleon complex, and he was virtually the only person in the company who was rooting for St. Louis. Every game the Tigers won was followed by extra PT for the trainees, but we were so damn smug the CO's team got beat that we took it in stride.

Overall, basic training was mostly time to be endured. The purpose was ostensibly to break us down and rebuild us into the Army's vision of what a soldier should be. Most of us were better conditioned physically than we had been at the beginning, but otherwise pretty much unchanged after all was said and done.

We trained all day and went to sleep exhausted. Reveille always came too early, long before the sun rose, and was usually accompanied by Sergeant Boggs stomping through the barracks shouting, "Drop your cocks and grab your socks!" Then we scrambled into our fatigues in roughly 30 seconds, and assembled in ranks outside for a morning run. We ran around the company area in formation for fifteen or twenty minutes, tripping and stumbling and bumping into each other in the dark, hating every step we took. Then back to the barracks to get cleaned up for the day, and a trek to the mess hall for breakfast. All this before daylight.

Somewhere along the way I was designated a "platoon guide", kind of a trainee boss, which presumably meant I showed some signs of leadership. Or maybe it meant I was standing in the wrong place when Sergeant Boggs decided to appoint one. It was also a designation that was interchangeable with "gofer", someone whose principal function was often to make life easier for the good sergeant.

At the end of eight weeks, I could shoot a gun, could yell "Kill" while lunging with a bayonet, march around in step with a bunch of other guys, and was reasonably conditioned physically (I sure could do a lot of push-ups).

Our orders were posted on the company bulletin board two days before basic training ended. I was promoted to private E-2, which got me a single stripe for my formerly bare sleeves. I learned that my MOS (military occupational specialty) was to be "light weapons infantryman". What a surprise! Like maybe I was expecting "interior decorator", or "talk show host", or some other bullet-exempt specialty.

With my MOS designation came transfer orders assigning me to Fort Polk, Louisiana for infantry AIT (AIT is advanced individual training in a designated MOS). I think it might have been at that point in my military "career" that things really got serious.

Chapter Two

I have no idea what Fort Polk might be like in today's "modern" Army, but I can tell you that in 1968 it sucked—big time. Fort Polk, often dubbed "Fort Puke", had a fearsome reputation and lived up to it. Fort Polk was the training base best known for producing Vietnam-bound infantry soldiers. The advanced individual training regimen supposedly prepared raw recruits like us to step right into a jungle war. When my AIT class ended 10 weeks later and it was time to leave, I looked out the back window as the bus drove away and swore to myself that I would never set foot in that place again in my life.

And I haven't.

Fort Polk was a military installation where guard duty stations had to be manned by teams of two, because one alone might get mugged (I'm not kidding). You wore your steel pot— helmet to you civilians—even when you were in the enlisted men's club (on the rare occasion you were permitted to go there). Steel pots were de rigueur attire, not because the trainees were being taught discipline or exercising neck muscles. They were required because every now and then someone would get a bottle broken across his head.

Although some basic training was conducted at Fort Polk, the principal unit based there was the Tiger Brigade, the jungle infantry training outfit. The buses that brought us from Fort Knox ended our long journey in a section of Fort Polk called "Tigerland". As we pulled in, I saw a huge sign proclaiming, "Tigerland—Home Of The Vietnam Combat Soldier".

It wasn't an inspiring sight.

If anything, the facilities at Fort Polk were even older and more worn than those at Fort Knox. I found myself quickly assigned to an AIT training company and delivered to a dusty company street to stand around for an hour or so, waiting with the other early arrivals for the balance of the new trainees and the eventual sorting into platoons.

The company area was carved out of the Louisiana pine woods, and might have passed for a rustic summer camp to someone unfamiliar with its real function. While those of us who were among the first to arrive waited and endured the harassment of the drill sergeants, I glanced around at the aging barracks buildings that surrounded the company street. They were stark. Peeling paint, dirt-filmed windows and foot-worn wooden entranceways signaled their hard use. When platoon assignments were completed and we were sent inside to stow our gear, I wasn't surprised to see accommodations even more austere than we had in basic training. Much was familiar, though, including rows of narrow bunks, footlockers, the gang latrine, and the off-limits highly shined central floor area. So everybody crowded and crammed through the tight passageways between the bunks and the outer walls, laying claim to beds.

It was to be home for the next two and a half months.

Infantry training began bright and early the next day, and it was tough. Basic training had provided a broad foundation of military skills and knowledge, but not in any great depth. Infantry AIT was much more focused on the tools of war. The M-14 that had been our periodic marching and rifle range companion in basic training was replaced by the official rifle of the Vietnam War infantryman, the M-16. At Fort Polk, each soldier was assigned his own M-16, and we carried them around with us damn near everywhere except maybe in the shower. We marched with them, ran with them, crawled with them, slept with them, and ate with them. We field-stripped, zeroed, fired, cleaned, qualified, kissed, and completely mastered them.

The M-16 was radically different from any previous Army rifle. The stock and grip were made of a lightweight high-impact plastic, unlike the heavy wood of its M-14 predecessor, and so it had none of the heft you normally expect to feel in a rifle. It was jokingly called a Mattel gun, because it looked and felt like a toy. But nobody doubted its effectiveness once they had fired this toy. It had both a semi-automatic setting—one round for each trigger squeeze—and a full automatic setting. On "rock 'n roll", the full automatic mode, an M-16 emptied a magazine of 20 rounds in a couple of seconds.

M-16 bullets were little things, about the size of a .22 long rifle bullet. In fact, the caliber of the M-16 round was .223, almost indistinguishable from the .22. But the powder-packed shell behind the bullet was disproportionately large and produced an unusually high muzzle velocity. Because the round had such low mass, it had a tendency to tumble when it hit something and it was easily deflected by dense undergrowth, which caused critics to question its accuracy and usefulness. Still, that inclination to tumble also meant that it did lots of damage when it hit a live body, and it had a reputation for making huge exit wounds as the tumbling bullet tore its way through flesh.

In addition to living with an M-16, I learned to shoot, operate, detonate, throw, and service a truly formidable arsenal. There was the 45-caliber pistol, the M-79 grenade launcher, the M-60 7.62mm machine gun, the 50-caliber machine gun, the 81mm mortar, the LAW Light Anti-tank Weapon (the LAW was a shoulder fired self-contained single shot weapon with a plastic throw-away tube—think of a baby bazooka), the recoilless rifle (modern version of a bazooka), hand grenades, claymore mines, C-4 plastic explosive, booby trap detonators, Bangalore torpedoes (for blowing holes in concertina wire obstacles), and probably some other stuff I don't even remember.

Instructors loved to impress the trainees with descriptions of the mayhem the various weapons could create. The bullet from a 50-caliber machine gun was the size of a man's thumb, and could pass through the walls of a whole row of barracks buildings without losing much velocity. It could even pierce lightly armored vehicles. Even in 1968, a single 50-caliber round cost about 50 cents, so we weren't allowed to burn off a lot of ammo on the training ranges.

Hand grenades were remarkable killing devices. The old "pineapple" of World War II had been replaced by a newer, sleeker model. It was a little smaller, but deadlier. Under the smooth outer surface was an explosive core wrapped with tightly wound heavy gauge wire that was scored at intervals of about an eighth of an inch. When the grenade exploded, the wire broke into something like 1,000 small jagged pieces, propelled up to ten meters in all directions. The instructors told us that the effect of these shrapnel pieces on the human body was a lot like dragging a fork through spaghetti.

The M-79 was an interesting weapon. It fired a 40mm round from a stubby single-shot launcher that broke open like a shotgun to reload. The launcher had a weird report, more like a "floop" sound than a bang. M-79 rounds looked like caricatures of bullets, about 5 inches long and a little less than two inches diameter across the base. They came in three types: high explosive grenade, white phosphorous grenade, and a shotgun shell that was a handful of quarter inch ball bearings packed into a plastic sabot. The high explosive round was mostly like a hand grenade, except that it could be launched a lot farther than anyone could throw the hand version, up to 400 meters. The white phosphorous (known widely as "willie peter") exploded on impact in a blinding flash of hot burning phosphorous—nasty stuff that would stick to a target (euphemism for Viet Cong) while it burned. Lastly, the shotgun round did quite a number on targets at close range, even through foliage.

Claymore mines were uniquely suited to the Vietnam War. They were electronically detonated antipersonnel mines, and packed a deadly punch. Claymores were little more than blocks of explosive, imbedded with 700 steel balls. They were roughly a foot long and rectangular, gently curved around the long axis. Intended for perimeter protection, claymores were placed outside defensive positions. They sat on short metal legs, and were aimed at likely enemy approaches with the convex side of the claymore facing outward. (The Army helped out here, by putting the warning "Front toward enemy" on the claymore.)

You armed a claymore by inserting a detonator into the top, in a receptacle right next to the aiming hole. The detonator was attached to a long electrical cord that was trailed back to a trigger device at the defensive position. A properly placed claymore could be fired at an attacking enemy from a safe distance, sweeping the kill area like a volley of shotgun blasts. The balls sprayed in a 60-degree fan-shaped pattern that was lethal to a range of about 50 yards.

Then there was the LAW, the light anti-tank weapon. As its name suggests, it was intended for use against lightly armored vehicles. It fired a single round, then was discarded. The fiberglass launching tube telescoped, and came out of its shipping box in a collapsed state with waterproof covers over each end to keep the round inside dry. When it was time to fire the LAW, you popped the covers off the ends and pulled the telescoping tube open to its full length of about four feet. As the tube locked into its open position, a sighting device flipped up and a trigger mechanism covered by a rubber membrane became accessible right behind the sight.

The LAW round was a rocket-propelled shape charge, which focused and intensified the detonation to punch a small hole through armor. The molten metal and remaining force of the blast worked like a Cuisinart on anything inside the armored vehicle. I never personally saw any armor—friend or foe—in Vietnam, but the LAW was a useful weapon against bunkers and fortified positions, and it was mighty intimidating.

To fire the LAW, you placed it on your shoulder—again, think bazooka—laid your cheek on the barrel while sighting a target, and let fly. KABOOM! The rocket made a hell of roar coming out of the tube, and the backflash would roast anyone foolish enough to stand close behind. The blast of the round blowing out of the tube was followed a split second later by an explosion as it hit the target. A final LAW instruction was to smash the used fiberglass launching tube, because the Viet Cong were remarkably inventive and often modified intact tubes to fire their mortars at U.S. forces.

I suppose all this is more information about the Army's

armory of toys than you have an interest in knowing, but the fact is these were the tools of our trade. They were to be our primary companions and potentially the difference between living and dying, so a great deal of attention was focused on the details of knowing and mastering them.

Infantry AIT trainees visited any number of different ranges around Tigerland to observe or shoot quite an arsenal of weapons. Sometimes the exercises went well into the night, especially when range practice was followed by field-stripping and cleaning whatever the gun "du jour" had been.

On one such day on an M-60 machine gun range, I had my first experience being under fire. The 7.62mm M-60 was a principal element in an infantry company's arsenal, since it was sufficiently portable for grunts to carry around and was capable of delivering a whole lot of lead downrange. So it was an important lesson and the entire day was spent training and shooting.

Night had fallen, and most of the trainees were at ease in a company formation, waiting for the last unlucky "volunteers" to finish disassembling and cleaning the machine guns we had used on the range. About a dozen troops were working under open-walled sheds, sponging the barrels and firing mechanisms in vats of cleaning fluid. The rest of us were bored and hungry, smoking and joking on a nearby gravel-covered street.

Some idiot hadn't cleared his weapon, and some instructor had failed to perform an anti-idiot check. One lonely round left in the chamber of a half-assembled M-60, a retracted bolt suddenly released to hammer forward against the round, and "POW"—the bullet plowed into the ground.

Right in front of me.

I almost wet my pants.

I had a little cut on my forehead from flying gravel, but the bullet fortunately didn't hit anyone. It must have ricocheted straight up into the sky; otherwise it couldn't possibly have missed a whole company of trainees standing there. We were pretty shook, though. Somehow, all the shooting and training hadn't seemed quite real before. That wayward bullet brought it home—this stuff could really hurt you.

During basic training, the troops had normally worn helmet liners, the fiberglass inner part of a helmet. Helmet liners looked like helmets, but were considerably lighter than the complete rig because they lacked the heavy outer steel pot. Liners were smoother than the steel pot and could be dressed up with shiny unit decals and fancy paint jobs, which apparently appealed to the basic training cadre.

Infantry AIT training called for troops to wear the real combat helmet, a heavy steel pot covered by camouflage cloth and wedged tightly over that inner fiberglass helmet liner. For the first week or so, until we got used to the weight, trainees' neck muscles were pretty sore. New arrivals marching down the streets of Fort Polk were easy to spot. They were the ones whose heads bobbed around like puppets.

In addition to frequent weapons training, there was even more PT than we'd had in basic training. The Tigerland PT not only used the standard Army Drill exercises, we were also schooled in hand-to-hand combat. Some of the instructors were Rangers and at least one was a Green Beret, and they enlightened us infantry trainees on various ways to incapacitate or kill an opponent with nothing but bare hands.

This was definitely not stuff from the Marquis of Queensberry manual. It was down and dirty, "get him before he gets you" fighting. The techniques emphasized judo throws, punches to the throat, straight-fingered gouges into eyeballs, open-palmed slams to the side of the head (to bust eardrums), neck-breaking twists, and vicious kicks into insteps, testicles, and the heads of opponents who were foolish enough to be knocked down.

I suppose it was all intended to make us feel like tough guys. Didn't work.

The receptiveness of the cadre wasn't any better than it had been at Fort Knox. It was useless to ask why something was done a particular way, you just DID it. Don't ask questions, just memorize what we drill into you and quit wasting time with a stupid question like "Why?"

For whatever reason, trainees were put under a lot of

pressure to sign up for a savings bond payroll plan. Since Private E-2's, which was the rank most of us had achieved by then, were only paid about $140 a month, not many troops wanted to lose the cash. Still, the not too subtle squeeze was unremitting, and within a few weeks most of the company had succumbed.

I was one of the few stubborn ones; I just wouldn't do it. The company first sergeant, a dour, ignorant lifer who could have been a poster boy for the literacy council, kept hounding me to sign up, suggesting I was unpatriotic to refuse. At one point he told me if I didn't sign up he would personally tear off my head and shit down my neck. He really was a silver-tongued devil.

When he finally asked me why I didn't want bonds, I launched into a discussion of rates of return on different investment vehicles, and how savings bonds were uncompetitive alongside more attractive alternatives like equities. I could almost see the gears in his head freezing up. He walked away, muttering to himself about useless cock-sucking draftees, and never mentioned savings bonds to me again.

It was a rare and memorable day when a trainee prevailed against the establishment, even in such a small way. But I had so little money I simply wasn't going to be told how to spend it.

Infantry AIT at Fort Polk was well known in those days for a place called Peason Ridge. It was the site of a weeklong bivouac, a training exercise intended to simulate jungle warfare in Vietnam. Peason Ridge wasn't jungle, but it was heavily wooded and easily conjured up a feeling of jungle combat. Each training company had its own week to play war games, to go through endless exercises, and to live in squat two-man tents, rain or shine.

There were "aggressors", who were training staff and other permanent party at the base in the role of bad guys whose mission was to stalk and ambush elements of the training company. We tied brush to our helmets and smeared greasy brown and green sticks of camouflage gunk on our necks and faces to reduce reflective shine. There were ground assaults up defended hills, with live machine gun fire going over our heads.

We had low-crawls through barbed wire and mud, again with live machine gun fire overhead. There were sloppy wet foxholes and slit-trench latrines, cold meals of C-rations (more on them later) and sometimes warm meals of gray mystery meats and other unidentifiable substances, lectures on jungle warfare, compass and topographical map exercises, booby-trapped trails, and lots of blank ammunition to shoot.

It was cold, rainy, and generally miserable. December had arrived, and wet nights even in Louisiana could get mighty frigid. Fires weren't allowed; we were learning to be stealthy. At night we huddled in ponchos, enduring the rain and trying to stay warm. What I didn't appreciate at the time was how luxurious it all was compared with the real thing, half a world away.

On one particularly rotten night at Peason Ridge, my training company was set up in a roughly circular defensive perimeter—a number of foxhole positions located around a central company operations position. In Vietnam, I later learned this was called a night laager, and that setup was common practice for any overnight position of platoon size or larger. Since in a guerilla war you never know from what direction an attack might come, defensive positions had to anticipate a threat from any direction.

An unending cold drizzle stained the night, and the foxhole position I was in along with three other guys was muddy and foul. The temperature was around 40 degrees, and I remember that, soaked and lightly dressed, I felt colder than I ever had before in my life—colder even than during the long dark nights of a midwestern winter.

It was close to midnight, and sleep wasn't going to happen. We were bored, wet, uncomfortable and restless. About the only diversion was a PRC-25 radio assigned to our position, which one of us on watch had to use periodically to report back to the command position, to prove that someone was awake and standing guard.

The "prick 25" as it was called was a battery-powered and too-heavy chunk of outmoded technology, and incredibly was the primary communication tool for field units all throughout the Vietnam War. Civilian radios of twice the power and a quarter of the weight had long existed, but prick 25s were good enough for grunts.

Playing around with the radio's frequency dial, one of us discovered a previously unknown capability of the PRC-25 that night. We learned that it could receive the audio band of a few civilian television broadcasts. So, in between scheduled checkpoint reports to the command center, our intrepid little band of soggy soldiers was tuning into the Late Show With Johnny Carson on some local Louisiana TV station.

It didn't take long before we began to speculate about whether anything broadcast over the prick 25 on that frequency would wind up on the TV sets of anyone within range watching Johnny at home. Being close to Christmas and all, we felt it was appropriate to offer a heartfelt "seasons greetings" to all the fine Louisiana citizens unfortunate enough to live within radio range of Peason Ridge.

I don't recall all of the salutations we dreamed up that night, but "Santa blows dead reindeer" was a fairly representative example.

At the time, we had no idea whether our creative transmissions pushed their way through the Tonight Show laugh track on any local TV sets, but we had a good time imagining the scenes in a few bedrooms. "Did y'all hear what that feller just said on the TV Martha!?! He can't say that on TV!!"

It was a diversion, and the night was a little more endurable as a result.

A week or so after the exercise ended, everyone who had been at Peason Ridge that night received a stern warning about radio discipline, and a reminder about prohibited transmissions on Army communications equipment. Most guys had no idea what the heck the instructors were talking about, but the four of us had to keep from snickering, as the lecture was confirmation of the secondary capabilities we had discovered in that backbreaking hunk of radio.

Some of the training they gave us at Peason was on infantry

strategy. Unfortunately, much of that training was still based on tactics that had been successful in World War II and which often proved to be ineffective in Vietnam. Even though returning Vietnam veterans were trying to influence training content, there was still considerable narrow thinking about conventional infantry policy.

One example taught during bivouac week was an exercise in defending a front line. Unlike the night laager, this presumed that enemy attacks would predictably come from one direction, and a fortified front line of defense could be established to repel the attack. Part of that defensive tactic involved setting out "listening posts" a few hundred yards outside the main lines, to enable early detection of probing enemy forces.

I later learned that if you were to ask a GI in Vietnam to go sit in a listening post outside a defensive position at night, he would tell you to do something to yourself that would create a serious sexual identity problem.

Lucky me, I was one of the trainees chosen to man a listening post for a night mission that was to include an attack by a team of aggressors. The main line of friendlies was atop a ridgeline and the listening posts were located about 100 yards down the slope in front of that line, spread every 200 yards. Each listening post was a hole in the ground that held one guy, equipped with a wired field phone connected back to the main defensive line.

It was another crappy night, maybe our fifth of the bivouac. I was by then downright cruddy, and dying for a hot shower. It was getting to be more and more difficult to maintain a suitably military outlook about being in those godforsaken Louisiana woods in the middle of another cold December night playing soldier games and whispering on some stupid toy telephone.

You might reasonably ask what happens to people in forward listening posts when the bad guys start arriving. What's *supposed* to happen is a recall of all listening post personnel as soon as enemy probing is detected. Among other things, that helps avoid the little problem of troops on the main line shooting up the guys in the listening posts along with the approaching enemy.

To nobody's surprise, no recall order was given even after approaching aggressors had been reported by one of the listening posts. So I sat there in the dark, unmoving, watching barely visible shadowy bodies creeping up the hill, so close I couldn't even use the phone. Suddenly I heard a scraping noise behind me. I turned slowly, and could just make out a dim figure crawling back down the hill toward my position, following by touch the telltale landline to the field phone.

OK Mr. Aggressor, war games we're playing and your ass is mine. I held my breath, flipped the safety on my M-16 to rock 'n roll, and crouched in my hole in the darkness. He was no more than ten feet from me when I noisily lit him up with a burst of blanks. It absolutely scared the shit out of him, and he wasn't at all complimentary about my prowess, my relationship with my mother, or my ancestry. After all, us pussy trainees weren't supposed to blow away those tough seasoned aggressors.

The whole thing felt like a kid's game of cowboys and Indians, but real enough to provide an adrenaline rush. And it was just a little satisfying to be the winner.

At the end of our bivouac week, it was back to the barracks for a weekend pass and the most enjoyable shower I ever had—hosing and scrubbing off all those days of Louisiana mud and crud. We were all amazed at how good the beat-up old barracks looked after tents and foxholes.

Anyone who had the pleasure of a stay at Fort Polk undoubtedly remembers the other infamous training exercise for infantry AIT classes—the dreaded nighttime Escape and Evasion course. Trainees heard horror stories about Escape and Evasion weeks before actually going out to it. The course was several miles of dense woods, and troops were graded on how successfully they maneuvered their way through it in the dark, eluding capture.

The idea was to put trainees in the situation of being behind enemy lines (something of a ridiculous notion in a guerilla war). The mission was to avoid detection and safely get out of the area. We had M-16s, but no ammunition and no other provisions. Here's the kicker—the woods were full of aggressors, who reportedly captured luckless trainees and took them to an enemy base camp hidden somewhere on the course, where they did horrible things to them. The aggressors were supposedly all Vietnam veterans who got a kick out of terrorizing gullible trainees, tying them up and threatening all sorts of interesting torture. I'd guess they stopped short of actual physical harm, but you sure wouldn't know it from the rumors about stuff that went on at the aggressor camp.

I suppose there is some sort of appeal in sneaking around in the woods, trying to outwit or capture someone else. When the context is make-believe and nobody gets hurt, it's a big boy game, a macho thing. That's probably why some guys enjoy hunting, or smearing camouflage grease on their faces and heading off into the woods to play splatball. But most of us weren't too thrilled at the prospect of Escape and Evasion, and the cards appeared to be stacked in favor of the aggressors.

The exercise started at mid-day with classes on evasion techniques, and tips on living off the land like eating bugs and tree bark. When it was time for evening chow, one instructor demonstrated how to rip the head off a live chicken. I guess this was to prepare us in case we were to someday find ourselves behind enemy lines with a chicken and no knife, and feeling hungry. The little demonstration accomplished two things—nobody had much of an appetite, and everyone wondered whether that particular instructor doubled as an aggressor. We hoped he didn't.

At dusk, it was time to hit the course. The starting point was a shallow stream running perpendicular to the direction of the course. Groups of two or three trainees were sent out to follow the streambed for a few hundred yards, until a gunshot signaled each group to turn left and head into the woods. It was up to the small groups to decide whether to stay together or to split up and chance the course on their own. With luck, the trainees would exit the woods on the far side of the gauntlet after about three or four hours. Those less fortunate might expect to spend the night entertained by their aggressor hosts.

I found myself with two other guys who had even less

interest in this fun trip than I did. We splashed down the stream, heard the shot, and promptly turned right—the opposite direction from the course.

It was almost completely dark, and the woods were thick enough to keep our truancy from being noticed. We climbed out of the stream and continued in the wrong direction until we came to a main road, where we (true story) flagged down a taxi. I'm sure we made an interesting sight—three guys in fatigues and full web belts carrying M-16s. But the driver stopped for us anyhow. Could it be that we weren't the first clever trainees to elude the dreaded Escape and Evasion course via taxi?

We rode uneventfully to the other end of the course. There we found a place just inside the tree line to hide, and we smoked and joked for a few hours until the other trainees started coming out of the woods. We were pretty smug dudes as we blended in with the others walking off the course. Did we feel guilty, like we cheated or wimped out of a tough mission? Not a bit. What the hell—the point of the exercise was to teach resourcefulness. And what could be more resourceful than outfoxing this notoriously unpleasant event altogether!

It was during my Fort Polk infantry training that I first met "shake and bake" NCOs. These were sergeant E-5 graduates of Non-Commissioned Officer Candidate School, who were fulfilling the second component of the NCO school training—an assignment to an AIT training company for one cycle. The apprentice NCOs helped out with the training and harassment of us AIT trainees. This presumably honed the skills of these budding leaders to a finely tuned precision, so they would be ready to hop a plane to Vietnam and charge into battle. After completing the AIT duty assignment, these probationary almost-sergeants were accorded official rank and shipped off to war.

Several of us infantry trainees concluded that it could be a wise move to sign up for the NCO school training. Virtually all Fort Polk AIT graduates ("survivor" might be a better word than "graduate") were handed orders for Vietnam at the conclusion of training. A very few, perhaps one or two percent, were sent to Germany, and everyone prayed they would get those coveted orders.

NCO school candidates, on the other hand, assured themselves another six months of stateside duty by going through the two training components of the NCOCS course. If you believed Nixon, every day of delaying tactics improved the odds that the war would end before we would have to go. Half a year seemed like a lifetime, a reprieve from the all too real prospect of imminent departure from AIT to Vietnam. After all, the Paris peace talks had begun in May, and once the envoys got over arguing about the shape of the goddamn conference table, I thought there was at least some possibility they might actually agree to wind down the war.

It really was a roll of the dice, though. Because every single NCOCS graduate could count on Vietnam duty. There was no shortage of or need for NCOs stateside; the whole point of mass-produced NCO school graduates was to meet the need for canon fodder in sunny Southeast Asia. By signing up for the school, if the war didn't end soon, I virtually guaranteed myself a combat tour, without even the slim chance of orders for Germany. And, volunteering for NCO school meant another round of all the Mickey Mouse crap that inevitably accompanied *any* Army training.

It was a tough choice, but I opted for the extra six months of stateside training and put in a request for NCO school.

I was given 24 days of leave time between graduation from Fort Polk and the start of the next NCO school cycle at Fort Benning, Georgia. It was Christmas, and I enjoyed temporarily being a civilian again. I had been promoted to private first class E-3, had a few bucks, and had a 22 year old's ability to push unpleasant thoughts from my mind for a brief time.

A bunch of the guys I had met in basic training, all from Michigan like me, kept in touch during our various AIT assignments. One pal got an armor MOS and stayed at Fort Knox for training, a few others had been sent to Fort Sill, Oklahoma for artillery training—they were what we called "gun bunnies". Two others had been right down the road from me in

Tigerland. Most of the group had orders for Vietnam following their AIT training, and we planned to get together and raise a little hell while on leave. Not to be melodramatic, but we didn't really know if we would all see each other again when it was over.

It was time to party, spend some time with family, and catch up on girls.

Ah yes, girls. There had been a few weekend passes while I was at Fort Polk, but not much opportunity for any serious trolling unless you wanted to pay for her company. Leesville, a seedy little burg just outside the Fort Polk installation, was a real pit back then, consisting of one long arcade/bar/whorehouse running the entire length of the main drag. There were girls, but most were there to be bought and used.

I had visited Leesville a few times. It was a depressing place. The girls were hard and cynical, not at all like the soft and demure Donna Reed types with whom I grew up. I had always been partial to gentler sorts, and was naively dumbfounded at the underbelly of life I found in Leesville. My visits usually consisted of a few pitchers of beer in a quiet corner of a bar.

In my high school and college years, I had often found myself involved with girls who John D. MacDonald's character Travis McGee would have described as "broken birds", hurt in some way and vulnerable. Good old Hobie Jennings had a big shoulder to cry on, just like knight errant Travis McGee. Not many girls like that in Leesville. Another ugly lesson for a clean-faced college boy—I took one look and then stayed away.

Chapter Three

My leave ended much too quickly, and then it was back to reality. The days had zipped by, packed with family gatherings, Christmas celebrations, and too many hangovers from all-night parties. I kissed the girls goodbye, wished my basic training pals a safe tour of duty in Vietnam, and boarded a jetliner for an assignment that promised to be a bigger challenge than either basic training or AIT.

Fort Benning, Georgia was the home of the infantry school, and its motto "Follow me, I am the Infantry". Infantry Officer Candidate School was located there, as well as my Non-Commissioned Officer Candidate School destination. Some Ranger training and elements of airborne training were also conducted on the post. You could always count on a platoon of trainees from one or another of the classes jogging past singing cadence:

I wanna be an Airborne Ranger,
Live a life of death and danger.
I wanna go to Vietnam,
I wanna kill a Viet Cong.

The last leg of my journey from Detroit was a cab ride from the Columbus, Georgia airport to the post. The cab passed through neighborhoods of neat little homes and churches, and then cruised along streets closer to the installation that were filled with all the businesses that catered to a military presence — tattoo parlors, dim bars, bookie joints, roving girls in too-short skirts.

A depression settled over me as the cab entered the Fort Benning grounds. The driver knew where I needed to go (more than I could say), so I sat back and watched unhappily out the window as we passed group after group of green-clad soldiers in training. Some were marching, some exercising, some poised in the ever-popular front leaning rest position. Now that I had some idea of Army life, particularly as a trainee, I found I had no enthusiasm for the coming months of NCO school. My gloominess was especially keen coming off a leave where I had enjoyed a temporary return to civilian normalcy.

It was winter in Georgia, time for field jackets, coal stoves, and extra careful fire guards.

Although I had orders for NCOCS, no class openings existed right then and I was temporarily dumped in a basic training company. They put me to work as a clerk in the company orderly room. It was easy duty and, for the first time in the Army, the cadre actually treated me like a human being— like one of them. Quite a pleasant change it was, not being one of the trainees.

The work was mostly paper shuffling, some typing and filing, keeping a fire in the coal stove, and an occasional gofer errand to the headquarters of the training battalion. They also expected me to growl at the trainees from time to time, treating them the same way I had hated being treated in basic training. Fortunately, the opportunities for a clerk to harass trainees were infrequent.

I wasn't a terribly proficient typist, but my hunt and peck technique was all that was needed to get the job done. The company commander had to send a daily report to his superiors at battalion, and it almost always contained the same meaningless military double-talk. I got so I could type it up error-free from the previous day's report.

This temporary duty lasted about a month, and I didn't mind the delay one bit. It was further postponing my trip to the war, so who could complain. Besides, I was starting to hear stories about NCO school. It was rumored to be awfully rigorous, with a level of harassment a few notches higher than either basic training or infantry AIT. The prospect of six more months of that kind of training was causing me to rethink my decision to take the course, especially since I had found a place in the Army where I didn't mind being. Alas, just about the time I was going to ask the basic training company commander if he could get me assigned permanently as his clerk, an NCOCS class opened up and any wavering I was going through became moot.

NCO school truly did kick everything up a few steps. The quality of training and the variety of subjects was more demanding than basic or AIT. The caliber of trainees was generally higher, too, since there were some qualifications to be met—pre-induction test scores, performance in AIT, etc.—in order to be accepted at the school. NCO school trainees (we were called "candidates", as we were candidates for promotion to non-commissioned officer) wore no rank, but were paid as corporal E-4.

As much emphasis was placed on books and studying as on weapons training and physical skills. There were new areas of study geared toward soldiers who would have responsibility for other troops. Competency was required in navigation and topographical map reading, radio procedures, calling for artillery and air strikes and adjusting fire on targets, setting up ambushes, calling for dust-off medevac choppers, and any area of expertise that an NCO might reasonably need to know in order to keep himself and his team alive.

Some of the new training was really useful, and I was later glad to have gone through it. Unfortunately, much of the training was not as helpful, as it was based too rigidly on tactics and theory left over from World War II and wasn't very applicable to the jungles of Vietnam (kind of like the "listening post" fiasco from my bivouac week at AIT). A lot of weight was placed on battle planning that presumed a conventional enemy with territory to defend and objectives to be attacked and won. The stateside Army in the sixties still acted and trained like it had in 1949. Counterinsurgency warfare and its tactics were not well known, and the military still prepared for this new type of conflict with the same linear battle strategy Eisenhower employed in Germany.

Fighting guerillas wasn't like conquering Fortress Europe. Fighting guerillas was like fighting smoke.

Most striking, in retrospect, was the lack of real leadership training for us budding NCOs—skills on motivation, subordinate evaluation, delegation and so forth. Also absent was any depth on how to coordinate the battle efforts of a group. Oh sure, we learned how to set up interlocking zones of fire, which was great for fighting in a fixed defensive position. But there was precious little knowledge passed on to us sergeants-in-the-making about maximizing the efforts of a squad in a close jungle firefight.

I'm pretty sure the absence of leadership and coordination training was based on the assumption that newly minted NCOs would be performing job responsibilities just like it said in the TO&E, the Table of Operations and Equipment, one of the Army bibles. Meaning that a staff sergeant E-6 would be a squad leader in charge of eight to ten men. That squad would be part of a platoon normally consisting of three or four squads. Each squad would consist of two fire teams of four or five men, both headed by a team leader. The book said each team leader would be a buck sergeant (a sergeant E-5). And since almost all NCO school graduates were buck sergeants, it was reasonably presumed they wouldn't immediately be thrust into leadership roles any more taxing than team leader and consequently wouldn't need so much leadership training.

The book also said Army infantry platoons were supposed to have both a platoon leader (a 2nd lieutenant) and a platoon sergeant (a sergeant first class E-7) in addition to the lower ranking NCOs in charge of squads and fire teams. The platoon leader and platoon sergeant were first and second in command of the platoon, and would be expected to provide all the leadership and combat strategy the platoon might need. This made sense because the lieutenant would be fresh from Officer Candidate School where such leadership classes *were* taught, and because the platoon sergeant E-7 would be an experienced, grizzled military professional who had seen it all and could calmly direct the troops (and sometimes also the very inexperienced lieutenant) to do whatever was required.

Career infantry E-7s were a precious commodity, because of their amazing store of knowledge and experience. For that matter, infantry staff sergeant E-6 squad leaders were expected to be, at least in theory, almost as seasoned as the E-7s.

Not so. For a variety of reasons, there was a shortage at that time of experienced career NCOs. Why do you suppose the NCO school was churning out class after class of shake n' bake instant NCOs? A large factor contributing to the shortage was the Army's policy of a one-year Vietnam tour of duty. Unlike World War II and Korea, wars that committed soldiers to the duration of the conflict, assignments to Vietnam only lasted a year. Although many career NCOs had more than one tour of duty in Vietnam, the rotation of experienced leaders left big holes in the Army's ability to field effective fighting units. It was also true that some career soldiers found ways to escape subsequent tours, or ways to get rear area assignments with less exposure to bullets, bombs and booby traps.

For me, the impact was very personal. And I don't think my circumstances were at all unique. When I arrived in Vietnam as a staff sergeant E-6, I never spent a single minute as a squad leader—my TO&E expected assignment. Instead, I found myself a ranking NCO and was a platoon sergeant more than half the time I was in the jungle, a job for which my training was woefully inadequate. Even more frightening, the rest of my time was spent as an acting platoon leader, an officer's job. That made me responsible for the lives of 30 to 40 men, and it didn't take long for me to realize how much I didn't know.

The upshot of all this was that the people on the ground in Vietnam were, for the most part, incredibly young and very green—even those of us who were supposed to be leaders. In the late 60s and early 70s, Vietnam was a war fought mainly by drafted kids.

Back to the NCO school. Notwithstanding the greater depth of training in comparison to basic and AIT, this was still the Army and the harassment never ceased. The training company cadre were all over us, in their words, "like stink on shit" at least 17 hours a day, and sometimes longer. There were

demerits for the slightest real or contrived flaw or offense. The
demerit system was so pervasive that some instructors even
made candidates fill out demerit slips on each other. Not the
most effective way to build teamwork and trust among the
guys.

Candidates spent a lot of time in the front leaning rest
position. Sometime the entire company would get extra drill
because one guy screwed up. Some of the instructors took great
pride in how intimidating they could be, and it wasn't unusual
to see one of them right up in the face of some hapless trainee,
yelling and berating, spraying spit. And the candidates, braced
at attention, had to stand there and take whatever abuse the
instructors felt like dishing out.

Just like with basic training and AIT before, I understood
that the harassment was intended to break us down so we could
be "rebuilt into better men". But for many of us, the abusive
and degrading treatment only provoked resentment. It's been
said that the Army is one of the few places you can find young
men in their teens managing the lives of large numbers of other
people. Some of those young guys got caught up in the heady
power rush, feeling like the big shot they had never been before,
and their management styles were often rooted more in cruelty
than in motivation. I unfortunately found this also to be true in
some regular units after I left training behind.

Other familiar dimensions of NCO school were daily
physical training, regular close order drill (I guess it was
important for platoons of candidates to look smart while
marching from class to class), and long field marches with
web belts, packs, and rifles. On those long walks, I began to
discover an ability to shift my mind into some neutral gear,
where time didn't seem to matter as much and where I was
strangely disconnected from the discomfort by body felt. It was
an aptitude that later served me well on long days and nights in
the jungle.

Classroom lectures were mixed with field exercises. I went
on my first "eagle flight", riding into a simulated hot LZ (a
landing zone under fire from the bad guys) in the Georgia

woods aboard a Huey helicopter with door guns blazing. It was confusing and unsettling, and chaotic. I learned later that it was also realistic. The chopper swooped in for a quick touch-down surrounded by the sounds and smells of gunfire, you jumped off, and you didn't have the slightest damn idea where you were, where the bad guys were, and what direction you should go.

Although I suppose there are people who have the knack, I never was able to identify the direction from which gunfire was coming simply by listening to the reports. Oh sure, a single gunshot can usually be localized at least to a general compass direction. But fire off a number of different guns, maybe throw in some automatic weapons and an explosion or two, pick up a few echoes bouncing back from different directions, and top it off with the whopping rotor blades and the high-pitched whine of the screaming Huey engines. Suddenly the sounds fill your head and are coming from just about everywhere you look.

I didn't appreciate it at the time, but that eagle flight training was prophetic. Virtually every time I found myself involved in some sort of airborne assault, it was a genuine "FUBAR" experience. That's Army talk for "fucked up beyond all recognition".

We learned how to rappel down steep slopes and straight down from elevated towers. The latter was training for unloading helicopters that couldn't land because of uneven or marshy terrain. Once again, actual events in Vietnam later proved the rappelling unnecessary. In combat, the chopper crews simply got as low as they safely could, and then just booted your butt out the door.

One night out on a rifle range, the instructors introduced us to the starlight scope. It was pretty high-tech for 1969, and amplified the low light from stars enough to make out shapes and movement even on the darkest nights. The scope's screen generated an eerie green light, and moving people stood out as slightly brighter blobs of light. You could tell you were looking at a figure with two legs, but it was impossible to make any more detailed identification. So it wasn't possible to distinguish good guys from bad guys—you only knew that *somebody* was out there. There were relatively few starlight scopes in those days, and that one occasion was the only time we trained with them. In Vietnam, I had only infrequent access to a scope, but often wished I had one.

We spent a weeklong bivouac in a swamp, probably the closest thing to real jungle that the Army had to offer. We played games in the muck with aggressors, nervously avoided the cottonmouths in the countless streams we crossed, marveled at moonshine stills we found hidden back in the marsh, and took turns being "in command" of a squad. The individual command stints were graded according to candidate performance, but the exercise was structured in such a way that it encouraged avoidance of the aggressor forces. Grading of candidates rewarded rote actions and discouraged inventiveness and creativity. With lots of cookie-cutter future leaders to assess, the cadre could only give each candidate about a half hour of squad leader time. So they really had little to evaluate, and couldn't make very accurate assessments of our command competency. Of course all of us felt extraordinarily confident and well prepared after passing our leadership tests.

Sure we did.

Because the NCO school was intended to be a serious and intense experience, the training was sufficiently difficult that not everyone could master the course. Some candidates found the classroom work beyond their capabilities (or their interest), and flunked enough of the tests to get themselves washed out of the course. A few others were daunted by physical performance standards that were tougher than those we had to achieve in infantry AIT. And a few candidates who originally signed up for NCOCS hadn't intended to go through the complete school—they just wanted a little more time stateside. Every week, a few more bunks were empty as candidates quit or were washed out by the instructors. Most of the washouts found themselves immediately headed to Vietnam. That was sufficient incentive for the rest of us to apply ourselves even harder.

Fort Benning was known for a few eye-popping demonstrations of military equipment and exercises, sometimes staged for visiting VIP's and even a few foreign dignitaries. Candidates at NCO school and OCS often got to attend these as well, and they were memorable. One was an aerial demonstration involving F-4 Phantom jets firing missiles and cannon, followed by a mach speed run directly over our heads. The jet appeared low on the horizon rushing toward us, and there wasn't any sound. It flashed over our heads, ghostly silent, and then the sonic boom hit. Whoomp! Heck of a show!

There was another time we hunched down in covered bunkers and watched through periscopes as 105 mm howitzer artillery rounds exploded just a few dozen yards away so we could learn to appreciate the awesome destructive power of artillery. When I didn't blink, I could actually see the blur of a streaking shell just as it smacked into the ground and exploded. And boy, those shells sure did blow—a ground-shaking "kerrump" that left your ears ringing, a bright flash in a gray cloud of smoke and dirt, viciously throwing off heavy chunks of ragged shrapnel in all directions.

That session also included instruction on calling up artillery fire missions, how to adjust fire on a target, and how and when to use the various types of artillery rounds: high explosive, white phosphorous, and smoke. The smoke rounds were sometimes used to mark a target before the whole battery of guns was cleared to "fire for effect", which meant letting fly with a barrage of rounds. Smoke was also a navigational tool. If you got lost, you could call smoke over a topographically recognizable point on the map, and wait to see where it showed up in the sky. It was suggested that we try not to put the round anywhere we thought our location might really be. Shrewd advice.

The scene at Fort Benning most indelibly etched in my memory was a display by "Puff, The Magic Dragon", from the Peter, Paul and Mary song. (Word was that the singers were more than a little unhappy with that label on a machine of war.) Puffs were ancient, lumbering C-47s that had been adapted for extended patrolling and fire support for ground forces. These old prop planes carried considerable firepower. They were each equipped with three miniguns, which were six-barrel

Gatling guns capable of firing up to 6,000 rounds per minute. Comparing a conventional 30-caliber machine gun to a minigun was no contest—kind of like comparing a roller skate to a Corvette. The minigun was truly a fearsome weapon. One of the instructors liked to say that it could put a round into every square inch of a football field without much difficulty.

My NCO school company was on a night exercise, and one of these Puff airplanes was working on a practice range a few miles away. When the miniguns opened up in the dark, they didn't sound remotely like guns. The sound was more a deep buzzing, or a low-pitched ripping noise. But the sight was even more chilling than the sound. It looked like someone was pouring red iridescent Kool-Aid out of the C-47, a long stream faintly resembling water out of a garden hose, slowly bending and streaming to the ground far below.

From our vantage point, the red Kool-Aid really did look like an unbroken torrent. The iridescence came from the red glow of tracer bullets in the ammo belts, which were typically placed every four bullets. That meant there were three unseen bullets between each of the points of light that made up the thread that looked unbroken to us. It was mind-boggling to think how much lead was hitting the ground beneath the Puff. I developed a healthy respect for miniguns that night. It struck me that, with such awesome firepower at the Army's disposal, it was impossible that North Vietnam could even begin to compete with American military might.

In fact, miniguns did have a fearsome effect on the bad guys. The Vietnamese people were rather superstitious, and captured Viet Cong documents indicated they took the "Dragon" nickname literally. Some Cong units had orders not to shoot at the dragon, because weapons would only aggravate the monster.

NCO school plodded on, week after week of classes and cadre, ranges and radios, bullets and bayonets. Some of the subjects were intensive, while others were scratch and sniff. But we were told that our training included at least some introduction to virtually everything we might encounter in

Vietnam. What little free time we had at night was spent doing homework, or writing home to families and girlfriends. Weekend passes were rare, as weekends often included more training. Soldiering was definitely not your eight to five job.

After three months of this, we finally made it to graduation day. The occasion even featured a graduation ceremony. Steady attrition of washed out candidates had thinned our ranks by a couple dozen, but there were still more than a hundred of us almost-sergeants to parade around in dress greens behind flags and guidons from the Fort Benning Infantry School.

As ceremonies in the Army go, it really wasn't bad. There was a military band playing Sousa marches, followed by a short film on the history of the Fort Benning infantry program. There was a Commanding General to read a speech about how important we were to the war effort in Vietnam, and to tell us about the fine traditions of Fort Benning that we must make every effort to uphold. After he sat down, we were subjected to a mind-numbing succession of speakers that I swear included everyone at the post except maybe the MP gate guards. Finally, we all had to march across the stage, toss off a snappy salute, and receive our graduation certificate.

I remember feeling a little abandoned at the graduation ceremony. A few parents, wives and girlfriends who lived close enough to come sat in the audience. But there were otherwise no interested witnesses to the less than historic event of our graduation. It was quite a change from the happy gathering that had marked my college graduation only a year before.

Graduation signified the completion of the first phase of Non-Commissioned Officer Candidate School, and brought a probationary promotion for most graduates to sergeant E-5, usually called "buck sergeant". The three or four candidates who scored at the top of the class were promoted to staff sergeant E-6. We were permitted to sew the appropriate insignia on our uniforms, but the promotions were contingent on successfully passing the second phase of training. For the E-5s, that second phase was assignment as cadre to an infantry AIT training company for one cycle, usually back to Fort Polk, and satisfying the instructors there that they could be effective NCOs.

The E-6s, myself included, were assigned to a new NCOCS training company right there at Fort Benning to repeat the three-month course as "tactical NCOs", helpers for the permanent party training staff. And the good instructors on those training staffs were more than familiar with the fact that us tactical NCOs had all too recently been nothing more than lowly candidates, so in their minds we were only pretenders to the rank. The stripes on our sleeves demanded a little better treatment from the instructors than the trainees got, but we never completely felt we were legitimate NCOs. The plus side, if any existed, was that we didn't have to take any crap from the trainees.

Because the newly minted E-6s had a couple days off before new NCO school classes began, I made the mistake of showing up at my new duty company in civvies since technically I was on a pass. After reporting in and stowing my duffel in the barracks building I was to be responsible for, I roamed over to the mess hall to grab a bite. I was barely in the door before a lifer E-6 mess sergeant braced me. "Who the fuck are you and what the fuck are you doing in my mess hall out of uniform?" "Hey Sarge", I said genially. "Sorry, I'm one of the new tach NCOs just arrived from the last class." Theoretically, I had the same rank as the obnoxious jerk, and it was OK for assigned staff to be in civilian clothes when no class was in session. But I was every bit as intimidated as a brand-new candidate (which is what he most likely had thought I was). Even with my explanation, he had no more use for me than a raw recruit. He let me stay in *his* mess hall for a meal, but that experience set the stage for the next three months. Tactical NCOs were destined to live a lonely life, accepted by neither the trainees nor the permanent party.

Classes began three days later with the arrival of a company of anxious new trainees, fresh from infantry AIT. In no time, I found myself plunged back into the now-familiar routine of the NCO school curriculum, this time as a trainer (sort of) rather than a candidate.

The trainees dubbed me Sergeant Starch, based on the

appearance that came from breaking starch every day. Breaking starch was putting on a freshly laundered and starched fatigue uniform, which always came back from the base laundry stiff as a piece of plywood. Fatigue trousers were starched so heavily that the insides of the pant legs stuck together and made a ripping noise as you pushed your legs into them. Since fatigue trouser legs were rather roomy, about half the material inevitably remained stuck together and jutted out behind each leg like trailing wings, or fins on an old Cadillac. Sounds pretty dumb now, but then it was an appearance that defined looking sharp.

Of course the candidates broke starch every day, too. But their fresh look didn't last very long as we put them through all the exercises and sweaty training. Me, I usually stayed fresh and starchy all day. I actually didn't mind the "Sergeant Starch" label. It beat the heck out of the disparaging stuff I heard from the permanent party.

If there was anything I had somehow missed going through NCO school training as a candidate, I sure couldn't imagine what I might not know after hearing it all over again as a tach NCO. The three-month class went by, and finally the whole deal was done. I had been in the Army for about eleven months and was officially a staff sergeant E-6. I had been shaped and molded into a highly trained, intensely motivated soldier and keenly skilled leader of military men. A lean, mean fighting machine.

Yeah, right.

I had orders for Vietnam, Nixon and the bickering Paris peace talk delegates hadn't ended the war—hadn't even slowed it down—and I had run plumb out of delaying tactics. Time to get my ticket punched; beautiful Southeast Asia was beckoning to me. Civilian life was a distant memory.

I had to outprocess from Fort Benning, meaning I had to go around to various places on the base and certify I wasn't stealing any equipment and didn't have any overdue library books. Had to pay a visit to the battalion infirmary for another round of shots and a beginning supply of quinine pills, to get me ready for the jungle. Because it was just one guy, the docs used needles instead of the pressure guns they used for mass inoculations. I had the pleasure of six different shots to get me all caught up, and spent the next two days sick as a dog. My arms were too sore to break starch, and the first day I barfed everything I ate.

My orders included 24 days of leave time before I was to report at Fort Dix, New Jersey for transfer overseas. I went home and got married. Her name was Linda, and she was cute as a button. She was a tiny thing, maybe 100 pounds dripping wet. Gypsy-dark and less than five feet tall, she was the physical opposite of me (as I'm on the tall side and fair-haired—sort of a California beach bum without the good looks). She liked to have fun, was mischievous as hell, and had a smile that lit up my life.

We had known each other less than a year and a half, most of which I had spent training to become a slayer of Viet Cong. So the decision to tie the knot was, in retrospect, probably unwise. Our relationship owed much to the postal service, and to one very nice weekend when I had been given a pass and she had joined me in a motel outside Fort Benning. We only left our room for food.

My pal Bobby had married his college sweetheart while I was in NCO school, so Linda and I settled into the apartment I had shared with him before being drafted. It was well located and close to some of Linda's friends. I wanted to know she would have people to help her while I was away, and it was nice to be familiar with the place she would be living.

At the time, our marriage felt right. Despite the cloud hanging over the two of us because of my imminent departure, my leave was a happy time. Even though the marriage wasn't destined to last, I don't look back and second-guess myself. As it turned out, those few happy days gave me some memories to carry around during the coming year—memories of a girl I would often think about, and ache to be with again. That the memories were idealized and would prove to be more wonderful than the girl herself really didn't matter. They helped me get through the next year.

Chapter Four

It is a very long way from New Jersey to Vietnam. It took the best part of 24 hours aboard a chartered 707 jetliner, including brief stops at Anchorage and Kyoto for fuel, to fly to Cam Rahn Bay. No seats were wasted; there was a GI in every one of them. Time passed at a crawl, the slow pace magnified by a sun that stretched out the day, stubbornly refusing to set as the plane chased it westward.

I was lucky enough to get a window seat. Although I was blocked into a corner, the seat provided a certain amount of quiet and privacy. The specialist 4th class next to me in the middle seat thankfully wasn't much more talkative than I felt like being. A few of the usual poker games were scattered around the cabin, but I noticed that many of the troops aboard spent most of the long trip quietly keeping to themselves. When I wasn't dozing fitfully, I was thinking about where I was going and what I had to leave behind me.

It wasn't at all a cheerful trip.

The sun finally inched its way below the horizon while we were somewhere over the Pacific. It was after midnight, local time, when we began our descent into the airbase at Cam Rahn. While still well away from the coast, the pilot turned off every light on the plane, all the exterior running lights and interior cabin lights. The announcement from the flight deck indicated that was standard procedure for aircraft approaching a war zone. Somehow, it really hammered home the reality of what was happening—this was not a safe place to be, and airplanes were targets.

As the plane touched down an officer got on the intercom

and provided instructions on how we were to de-plane. Among other things, he mentioned that there would be a line of bunkers to our right, and we were to jump in the bunkers in the event of incoming fire. We might have been trained soldiers, but there wasn't one of us on that plane who had ever heard bunker procedures discussed before on a jetliner. Not a comforting thought.

The welcome speech succeeded in heightening our anxiety, but no incoming fire greeted us as we climbed down the stairs to the tarmac. Instead, I was enveloped in a humid blanket of hot night air filled with exotic scents, and not terribly pleasant. The still, moist air obstinately hoarded the smells from the day— smoke, spicy food odors, the stink of fish sauce, and a cloying sweet smell like decaying flowers. Mingled with these was the stench of garbage rotting in the streets, and a hint of stale urine. Even the heavy haze of jet exhaust didn't mask the unusual bouquet of odors hanging in the hot, almost motionless, air. I idly wondered if other countries smelled as bad to foreign visitors as Vietnam did, and decided that my first impression was not a very positive one.

The balance of the night was spent on more of the Army's endless paperwork. "Welcome to Vietnam. Who's your next of kin? Where do you want your pay sent? Who should be notified in the event of your death? Are you familiar with the Army's life insurance policy?" By first light, I found myself on board a C-130 cargo plane lumbering north toward Chu Lai and the 23rd Infantry Division, the "American" Division.

The American was the largest infantry division operating in Vietnam, consisting of three rifle brigades and a squadron of armored cavalry. It was something of a patchwork unit, as two of the rifle brigades had at one time been independent elements and the third was "borrowed" from another division. Originally born in the steamy jungles and mountains of New Caledonia during World War II, the American had been deactivated after the big one and then brought back to life for the Vietnam War. In April of 1967, the formerly independent 196th Light Infantry Brigade and what had been the 3rd Brigade of the 25th Infantry

Division were both assigned to Task Force Oregon, marking the first time in the war that Army troops were deployed in I Corps (which was the northernmost of the numbered U.S. military sectors in Vietnam).

Task Force Oregon initially moved into the Quang Ngai and Quang Tien provinces of southern I Corps to ease the pressure on Marines operating near the Demilitarized Zone between North and South Vietnam. In September of 1967, the previously independent 198th Light Infantry Brigade was added to the task force and the three brigades were designated as the reactivated 23rd Division, or Americal. The Americal had only a four year existence in Vietnam, as it was disbanded again in late 1971 during the gradual decline in American troop strength from the high of 543,000 which was reached in 1969 — just about the time good ol' Hobie arrived at the party.

Because the Americal was a conglomeration and had not enjoyed a continuous existence, it had little of the tradition and history felt by soldiers assigned to more storied units. It didn't have the same feel as, say, the Big Red One or the 101st Airborne. In fact, when the Americal's southern cross insignia replaced the shoulder patches of the two previously independent rifle brigades, soldiers from the 196th and 198th took the somewhat unorthodox step of moving their brigade shoulder patches to the front pockets of their fatigue jackets so they could continue feeling loyal to their former brigade insignia.

The Americal's home base, Chu Lai, was a town on the coast of the South China Sea. Chu Lai was less a real Vietnamese town and more an Army presence, and I noted years later that it disappeared from most Vietnam maps after Hanoi won the war. Chu Lai was in Quang Tien province, one of the five Vietnamese provinces in I Corps. Spread out to the west from the seacoast was the Americal Division's area of operations (called an "AO"), and each of the three rifle brigades had responsibility for a part of the division AO. The topography of the Americal's AO ranged from marshy coastal lowlands to triple-canopy jungle, much of it broken by hills.

A large part of the division AO was designated as a free-fire zone, meaning we weren't technically required to obtain clearance to fire on suspected enemy targets. The rural civilian population, largely dirt-poor peasants, had been forcibly relocated months earlier, so patrolling GIs could reasonably presume any Vietnamese they came upon were bad guys. Although it was helpful to the longevity of American soldiers not to have to wait for someone to shoot at you first, it wasn't very healthy to be Vietnamese in a free-fire zone. As you might imagine, the attitude of "shoot with impunity" fostered by a free-fire designation cost more than a few Vietnamese civilians their lives. Long emphasis on maximizing body counts as a measure of success in the war had cultivated a GI point of view that any dead Vietnamese was pretty much automatically a Viet Cong.

The Americal AO encompassed most of three provinces. South of Quang Tien province, which included Chu Lai, was Quang Ngai province. North was Quang Nam province and the Vietnamese city of Hoi An. Further north and beyond our area of operations was the province of Thua Thien with the well-known and often embattled historic city of Hue, and the Quang Tri province which was right on the DMZ. The marines headquartered in Da Nang were responsible for the latter two, the northernmost provinces in I Corps.

The infamous village of My Lai was in the Americal's AO. In later years I would sometimes answer a question of where had I been in Vietnam by saying, not proudly, it was about 30 miles and a couple years from My Lai and Rusty Calley—who had been a lieutenant in the 3rd Brigade of the Americal when his platoon had carried out that grisly civilian massacre.

My first look at Chu Lai gave me a sense of contradictions. Its location on the South China Sea was filled with potential (under different circumstances) to be developed into an incredibly beautiful resort destination. The ocean nudged into a naturally sheltered harbor, with cliffs rising sharply on both sides and a spacious sandy beach right in the middle. Sloping slowly uphill from the harbor and the beach, the base sprawled for miles in a jarring, untidy patchwork of military buildings, roads, and junkyards—all grimly trying to deface the gentle seaside beauty of the place. Adjacent to the Americal post was an airbase, dispatching and servicing both Army and Air Force equipment. Helicopters of many varieties, jet fighters and strike aircraft, and cargo planes full of men and supplies came and went all day and night.

Instead of pleasure boats in the harbor and parasailing tourists hanging in the sky, there were Navy warships in the harbor and mean-looking Cobra helicopter gunships bristling with miniguns and missiles sweeping up and down the coast to discourage unwanted visitors.

To the south and west rose a line of mountains. The Viet Cong frequented the southern peaks, and found any number of places to set up portable rocket launchers within range of Chu Lai. This area was dubbed "Rocket Pocket" and was the source of periodic bombardments of the base. These attacks were most often the nuisance variety—a little damage, a few casualties, and life went on. Sometimes, it could get heavy, but the VC didn't have long to hang around and fire their stuff because artillery batteries on the base would start flinging everything from 105 howitzers to eight inch guns back at them within minutes of incoming rockets. And, Cobra gunships could get up there in a hurry with their load of miniguns.

A few miles outside of the Chu Lai compound was a Vietnamese village named Tam Ky. Over the years, Tam Ky alternated between being a Viet Cong stronghold and a village fairly sympathetic to U.S. troops. Allegiance to one side or the other all depended on the politics of the current village chief. Tam Ky had once been the site of a Tet offensive battle, and was *never* considered safe for GIs by themselves or at night.

But Tam Ky and Chu Lai co-existed in a nervous and mutually dependent relationship. For many village residents, the Army was a source of revenue. Hundreds of Tam Ky villagers came into the installation every day as laborers, cleaning ladies (for the brass), and waitresses in the officer and NCO clubs. A lot of the girls worked at the world's oldest profession, too.

Unofficially, of course. And the Army needed those scut workers to do jobs that left soldiers free to do soldier work.

At any given time, a significant proportion of the Vietnamese workers were covert Viet Cong, trying to learn whatever they could about activities at the base. There was no effective way to screen them out, and the Army valued the cheap labor more than absolute security.

In one telling incident about a month after I passed through Chu Lai, the rocket pocket erupted in a fairly heavy night attack. A half dozen rounds dropped around the base, one damaging a Phantom on a runway. Artillery batteries at the base returned fire, and the following morning a Ranger platoon was airlifted into the area suspected of being the point of origin of the attack. They found a Viet Cong killed by the artillery, and somebody recognized him as a barber who worked on the base. A little unnerving to think that guy had worked with a razor on soldiers' heads every day.

So I found myself in Chu Lai within perhaps 14 hours of arriving in Vietnam. I was trucked from the airbase to a replacement center—sort of a supply warehouse that deals in people. Various field units put in their requests for warm bodies, and the replacement center allocated newly arriving GIs to the requesting units based on MOS and (supposedly) the urgency of the request. I spent a few days there while more paperwork was pushed around.

I met another staff sergeant E-6, a lifer supply sergeant, at the replacement center. We had a few beers together at a ramshackle NCO club that was located nearby right on the beach. He had just arrived for his second tour in Vietnam, but wasn't terribly anxious about it since he was essentially a non-combatant. I was happy for his companionship, as most of my "peer" E-6s wouldn't give an instant NCO like me the time of day. In fact, one career NCO I met in the replacement center took one look at me and sneered, "How long have *you* been in the Army, two weeks?"

Over beers, my new friend the supply sergeant taught me a few useful expressions in Vietnamese. All I had previously picked up from my training was a short booklet of phonetic Vietnamese. I had tried the phonetic book earlier in the day on a Vietnamese girl. That only got me a puzzled look.

My drinking buddy told me that "Dung lai" meant "Halt". That seemed like a good thing to know, even if I couldn't say "Or I'll shoot". "Di-di meant "beat it", and "Di-di mau" added considerable emphasis, on the order of "Get the hell out of here". Hello was "Chau", and sounded just like the Italian "Ciao". "Sin loi" was a verbal shrug of the shoulders, sort of a Vietnamese "Tough shit". "Dinkidau" was nutso or crazy. There were a few other expressions he taught me, but most were guaranteed to piss off anyone who understood them. Like "Duma", which supposedly meant "Fuck your mother". Such is the average American's grasp of a foreign language.

We walked in the dark down the beach from the NCO club back to the replacement center, listening to the surf breaking on the sand. I noticed guard towers facing outward every few hundred meters. Even the South China Sea was a potential source for attack. It brought me back to the reality of where I was, after an evening out drinking in a joint that could have passed for a comfortably well-worn neighborhood bar at home. It was a sobering sight.

Each of the Americal combat battalions out in the field had rear area headquarters, called "trains areas", at the base in Chu Lai. The trains areas were staffed by REMFs, which was the not-so-affectionate name used by combat troops to describe those in the rear who had cushy, non-combatant jobs. "REMF" was the acronym for "rear echelon mother-fucker". These were the headquarters staff, clerks, supply staff, motor pool, administrative people, and anyone else lucky enough not to be slogging through the jungle with a gun.

A lot of the REMFs wore sharp-looking camouflage fatigues, which were colored with random uneven patches of greens and browns to make the wearer blend into foliage. Uniforms like that would give combat soldiers a real stealth advantage in the jungle. Strangely, regular infantry units in the field rarely saw camouflage fatigues. I later learned that the fine folks in the rear had access to a lot of good stuff, and had first choice of supplies on their way to the front. It was one of the many ironies of military life; the supply chain that existed to provide for the needs of combat troops could be mighty picked over by the time it reached those troops.

While I was at the replacement center, I was issued jungle fatigues and jungle boots. Although jungle fatigues were the same standard olive drab color as stateside fatigues, they were made of a much lighter material. The fatigue trousers were baggy, with large thigh pockets in addition to the usual compliment of pockets. More storage room for ammo magazines and grenades, I guessed. The boots were a combination of leather and canvas, much lighter than the spit-shined pair I had worn jogging up and down Agony and Misery back at Fort Knox.

In an attempt to make it harder for enemy soldiers to distinguish officers and NCOs from other GIs, the bright yellow chevrons of NCOs and the shiny collar insignia of officers were replaced by black designations of rank. We certainly wouldn't want the guys in charge to be prime targets for enemy snipers. In the case of officers, the change to black meant you couldn't tell the difference between a 1st and 2nd lieutenant, or a major and a lieutenant colonel—not that anyone cared, except maybe 1st lieutenants and lieutenant colonels.

After a few days of waiting at the replacement center and sucking beers at the NCO club at night, I finally received orders assigning me to one of the battalions of the 196th Light Infantry Brigade. I was picked up by a clerk with a jeep, and delivered to the trains area for my new unit. I was introduced to a few of the REMFs, including the mess sergeant and motor pool sergeant. Then I spent an hour or so talking with the battalion sergeant major, a career NCO named Wilkes. His rank was actually sergeant first class E-7, so he was an acting sergeant major. Wilkes was a good guy for a lifer, and didn't act at all derogatory about my shake 'n bake NCO inexperience. Although the captain who was commanding officer of the Headquarters Company was nominally head honcho of the facility, everyone in the trains area knew that Wilkes was really the man, the Top Kick.

Wilkes explained that "Headquarters Company" was the term for the rear area units for each battalion. They were responsible for all the support needed by the battalion's rifle companies in the field. The other parts of a light infantry battalion, the combat units, were typically designated A, B, C and D companies, referred to as Alpha, Bravo, Charlie and Delta. Combat battalions also frequently had a reconnaissance platoon, dubbed Echo Recon.

The sergeant major was probably the first E-7 I had met since entering the Army who didn't bleed and pee olive drab. He was a tall, rangy Texan with 29 years in the Army and plans for retirement at the end of his tour in Vietnam. I later got to know him fairly well, but our time together at that first meeting was cut short as I was summoned to the helicopter pad and soon found myself aboard a chopper headed for LZ Professional and my new duty assignment.

Dotted throughout each brigade's AO were battalion firebases, called LZs (for "landing zone"). They had names like LZ Bayonet, LZ Hawk Hill, and LZ West. They often weren't much more than small hills, and most could accommodate only one or two rifle companies and some attached artillery. Firebases typically had reasonably permanent defensive positions dug in and reinforced with sand bags, sometimes with wood or corrugated metal roofing. Because of frequent rain and fairly crowded living conditions, most LZs were unappealing places — muddy, smelly, dilapidated, and often vulnerable to ground attack.

The battalion to which I had been assigned was located at a firebase named LZ Professional. Soldiers in the battalion, the 1st Battalion of the 46th Infantry, called themselves "The Professionals". The site had been chosen earlier in the war because it overlooked an old Viet Cong trail, the Burlington Trail, which reportedly went all the way to Laos. The original mission of LZ Professional and the 1st of the 46th Infantry Battalion had been to interdict enemy movement on the Burlington Trail and deny its use to the bad guys. There had even been a fairly significant ground operation named Burlington

Trail from April to November of 1968 in which the 198th
Infantry Brigade had fought for dominance in the area. It had
been during that operation that most of the civilian population
was moved elsewhere and the area designated a free-fire zone.

LZ Professional was comparatively small for a firebase,
and the four rifle companies in the battalion cycled on and
off the LZ so that one company always manned it while three
others were patrolling around the AO. The routine was one
week at the LZ, usually performing maintenance duty as well
as security, and then three weeks out in the bush. There was
also the reconnaissance platoon, Echo Recon, but they came
and went independently—setting up ambushes for unwary
Cong and conducting long-range patrols. They apparently had
some pull with the REMFs back in Chu Lai, because they got
camouflage fatigues.

I can clearly recall that first ride on a "slick" out to LZ
Professional. Slicks were standard Hueys with no armament
other than door guns, which were M-60 machine guns mounted
on each side. Unlike choppers stateside, the ones in Vietnam
generally didn't have any doors. So every time the helicopter
banked, especially on that first ride, you just knew you were
going to slide out and fall. And a lot of chopper jockeys had a
little cowboy in them, standing the machine on its nose for fast
acceleration and pulling tight turns that had me staring out the
open door straight down at the ground. I got a white-knuckled
grip on the seat frame, and didn't let go. You couldn't have pried
me off.

Helicopters were transportation workhorses in Vietnam.
They could go almost anywhere, they were comparatively fast,
and they could serve as platforms for a variety of lethal weaponry.
Choppers delivered supplies, the mail, and even Agent Orange.
They could carry fresh troops into battle, and haul the broken
ones back out again. Distances that required days to travel on
the ground could be crossed in minutes aboard a Huey.

A considerable variety of helicopters were deployed in
Vietnam, ranging from tiny LOH observation choppers used
for aerial intelligence and ferrying senior officers, to the ever-

present UH-1 Huey, to double-rotor CH-47 Chinooks that carried whole platoons, to the intimidating Cobra gunships, to huge skycranes capable of lifting considerable weight. I once saw a skycrane dangling a busted up Phantom jet fighter that it had retrieved from somewhere in the jungle, taking it back to Chu Lai for repair or salvage.

Choppers were also incredibly noisy. When the temperature and the humidity were just right, which was often, you could hear the distinctive "whop, whop, whop" of an approaching helicopter miles away—long before ever seeing it. Stealth was not their long suit.

It was 25 or 30 miles from Chu Lai to LZ Professional. We flew high, because there undoubtedly were Viet Cong somewhere down in the jungle below hoping for a clean shot at a helicopter foolish enough to fly within range.

I was struck by the view of the land below us. It was overwhelmingly green, more shades of green than I had ever seen. Intense hues of emerald and jade dominated the expanse beneath the Huey, so bright and saturated they shimmered. Miles of dense puffy trees were punctuated by rays of sunlight glinting off streams and rice paddies. It was rolling country, interrupted by an occasional line of hills flowing into yet another valley. All this was back-dropped by a sky so blue that it looked like a view through a photographer's polarizing filter. The landscape was spectacular, and from high in the air Vietnam was a picture of quiet, pastoral beauty.

It was hard to imagine that a war was going on down there.

The strange peacefulness of the lush scenery passing below was lulling, and I wasn't conscious of time. But the end of the flight quickly jerked me back from my daydreams. Landing at LZ Professional gave me a brief overhead view of the firebase, and it wasn't pretty. The helicopter descended quickly and flared to gently set down on a cleared pad about halfway down the hill.

LZ Professional was unlike anything I had ever seen before, and there was a hint of surreal to it. The place really was a dump—at best a hill, but more a lump of greasy mud, surrounded by miles of coiled razor-edged concertina wire to foil assaults by the bad guys. It held a few semi-permanent structures that provided housing and an office for the battalion commander, various staff officers, ammunition storage, communications, and a rickety kitchen. Sandbagged bunkers dug deep into the mud around the perimeter of the hilltop housed four to six GIs each.

The firebase was a bustle of activity and noise. I stood there looking around, trying not to appear too wide-eyed. A 105 mm howitzer artillery battery at the very topmost point of the hill was booming out a fire mission to some unseen place in the jungle, the thumping of the big guns actually vibrating the ground where I stood. The battalion's recon platoon was just coming back up the hillside with an unhappy looking Vietnamese, possibly a prisoner? He was dressed in black, and his clothes really looked like pajamas. (I had heard references for years to Viet Cong and their black pajamas.) I noticed his sandals; they appeared to be made out of an old truck tire. I learned afterward those were called "Ho Chi Minh racing sandals".

A wobbly stripped-down truck—it might once have been a jeep before its rear end was modified for cargo—was slowly picking its way down the hill to the chopper pad, slipping precariously through ruts of mud on the pathway. It was going for the pile of supplies that came with me on the Huey.

And then there were the smells, even more pronounced than I had noticed on arrival in Cam Rahn. The hot air was saturated with moisture and odors, and felt like a damp, sour blanket across my face. The smell of the jungle itself was sort of woodsy, but with an edge of decay. There was the odor of damp and mildew that comes when everything is always wet. There was an earthy smell like on a freshly plowed farm field. And there was the smell of burning shit.

Jungles don't have any plumbing. With the output of between 120 and 150 men on the LZ at any given time, just about the only way to handle human waste was to make it disappear—

into the air. Couldn't simply dig holes; they would fill up too fast and get unbearably aromatic, too. And you didn't want to build privies down the hill and away from the occupied areas. That would make answering nature's call awfully hazardous, as the bad guys would be tempted to sneak up and booby trap them. So standard operating procedure on firebases was to burn the stuff.

Under the four-hole latrine were 55-gallon drums, cut in half. Once or twice a day, a couple of luckless privates would get shit duty. This entailed pulling the half drums out from under the latrine and mixing kerosene or fuel oil in with the waste. The mixture was burned, producing a thick, foul black smoke. The poor guys on shit duty had to stay there stirring it occasionally with a paddle to make sure it completely burned away. A truly memorable job.

The Huey stayed on the pad, engine running, for the five minutes it took to unload it, while I absorbed the sights and sounds around me. Then it revved up, leaned forward and lifted off, and I was stuck in what felt like a madhouse.

Still, the event of a new arrival was reasonably well choreographed. First to the headquarters bunker—"Staff Sergeant Steve Jennings reporting for duty, Sir!"—for a specific unit assignment. Then to a supply bunker to get equipped. I drew a rucksack, web pistol belt, C-rations, canteens, a poncho liner (a lightweight quilted blanket that did a fair job of providing warmth on cool nights), an M-16, 20-odd magazines for it, and lots of ammunition.

There is something you need to understand about the significance of drawing "lots of ammunition". Under most circumstances, particularly stateside, the Army flat out didn't trust its troops to have live ammo in their possession. For one thing, it was dangerous to have every Tom, Dick and Harry walking around carrying real bullets. Ammunition was something tightly controlled, and only issued in measured quantities to soldiers on a firing range. In the states, if you were caught with even a single unauthorized round, it meant disciplinary action. So it was more than a little sobering to be allowed to help myself to boxes and boxes of live munitions. It drove home that Toto definitely wasn't in Kansas any more.

When you were new to a particular M-16 it was important to "zero" it, which meant adjusting the sight for accuracy. You picked a target about 100 yards away, made trial shots, and adjusted left or right, up or down until you reliably hit the target. So I went about halfway down the hill to a dump area below the chopper pad that doubled as a range for zeroing weapons. I was uncomfortably aware of some rather large rats scurrying around in the debris, looking for an easy meal.

The M-16 I was issued had been banged and bumped around the block for a few years, and the best I could do was adjust it to hit six inches to the left at 100 yards. So I learned Kentucky windage early on, and always remembered to target a little right every time I fired my rifle at any kind of distance. While I was there at the dump practicing, I even shot a rat.

M-16 magazines in those days were designed to hold 20 rounds, but most GIs loaded 18 or 19 because a full load of 20 put too much pressure on the spring mechanism, which increased the risk that the gun might jam. Early M-16s reportedly had an unfortunate tendency to jam, so extra caution with the magazines was wise. If an M-16 jammed, it always occurred at precisely the moment you most needed a gun that would shoot reliably, say in a firefight.

A jammed weapon was especially likely when magazines stayed full and unused for weeks at a time, as they often did. The frequent rain and oppressive humidity made things worse. Let a full magazine sit around long enough, it would rust into a solid block. When GIs cleaned their weapons, they also sometimes stripped the bullets out of their magazines and oiled them before reloading—a little preventative maintenance.

I managed to get my hands on some tracer rounds, and it seemed like a good idea to put a couple at the bottom of each magazine I loaded. That way, the last few rounds fired off would be an alert that the magazine would soon be empty. Although I hadn't experienced a firefight, I guessed that I probably wouldn't be carefully counting my bullets. (Let's see, was that bullet I just fired number 15 or number 16?) I thought it might be useful to have some warning of an impending empty gun.

A couple of loose rounds went in my pocket, just in case. I don't know that I ever decided what "just in case" really meant. Was it so I had at least a few extra rounds to fight with if I somehow ran out of magazines? Or were those rounds there so I wouldn't have to worry about being taken prisoner and hauled off to a place worse than the aggressor camp at the Escape and Evasion course in infantry AIT? I don't think I ever gave myself an honest answer, and maybe I didn't really know. It just felt like something I should do.

You have to understand that nobody was guiding me along in this process. There was no helpful mentor explaining what gear to take, or how many magazines or canteens to carry. New guys were pretty much on their own to outfit themselves for the jungle and combat.

M-16 ammunition came from the manufacturer packaged in cardboard sleeves of twenty rounds. Those sleeves were tucked inside cloth pockets sown in a row on a long strap. Once the ammunition was loaded into magazines, the full magazines could be slipped back into those cloth pockets and the whole arrangement could be draped over a shoulder and worn like a bandoleer. Each of the straps had seven pockets, and the makeshift bandoleer was a functional way to keep ammo readily accessible across your chest.

I whipped up two bandoleers to carry, a bandoleer and some extra magazines for my rucksack and my pockets, and one to go in the M-16. Without any guidance on how much ordinance to carry or how often I might be able to get more, I struck a compromise between my intensely felt urge to have enough ammo to fight the entire rest of the war, and the practical limitation of what I could physically carry.

Canteens were critical and, as trite as it may sound, water was life. But canteens were frequently in short supply on LZ Professional, especially the two-quart size. I managed to scrounge up six plastic one-quart canteens, all that the supply bunker had on hand right then. That sounds like a lot of water, and it sure was a lot of weight, but there would be times I was glad to have it. There was only room for one canteen on my web belt, so the others hung from D-rings hooked to my rucksack. It was an untidy assembly, but it worked.

Add in a few hand grenades, some smoke grenades (to mark location for an incoming helicopter or for an air strike), a pressure bandage for those sucking chest wounds they kept telling us about in basic training, a new supply of quinine to keep from getting malaria, a jungle knife strapped to my leg, bug repellant, a duplicate set of dog tags (GIs were told to lace the extra set into their boots—it helped to identify the dead when only pieces were left), and I had been transformed into an impressively well-equipped government issue fighting man.

Now I was ready, or at least looked like I was. I felt like I was stuck in some bad dream. It was unreal, and astonishing. Who was I kidding? What the hell was I doing here, and why in the world would anyone in his right mind think I was anything remotely like a combat soldier? Except for being a little cleaner, I looked like everyone else on the firebase. But I felt like an unready intruder, like I didn't belong.

My battalion had a policy of temporarily attaching new NCOs and officers to a company other than the one to which they were ultimately assigned, in order to give the new leaders a few days to adapt. It helped a little; the new guy learned a few things and avoided looking like a complete idiot in front of troops he would have to command. Instead, he looked like a complete idiot in front of people who had to put up with an "FNG" (fucking new guy) for a while, and didn't much like it.

There was a common understanding among soldiers in Vietnam that FNGs were to be avoided and ignored. It was a primary reason why I had found myself selecting and packing my gear without any direction. The idea of a one-year tour of duty was a new concept for the military. An unintended and probably unexpected byproduct was the continuing polarity between GIs who had been in country for a while and had experienced some combat, and virgin FNGs who had been hanging around street corners and chasing girls back in "The World" only days before.

The new guys were considered a liability, susceptible to mistakes that could be fatal to themselves and others. More seasoned troops ostracized the newcomers, both because they wanted to minimize the risk of getting greased due to a screw-up by an FNG, and because there wasn't much point in getting to know a guy with such a short life expectancy. It didn't take long for FNGs to feel the isolation. I got the picture loud and clear by the end of that first day.

I think it might even have been worse for instant NCOs. Not only was I an FNG, I was a "pretend sergeant" presuming to command lower ranking people who had been in Vietnam awhile and who knew the score. Not surprisingly, the reaction of some seasoned GIs to a newly arrived shake and bake NCO bordered on contempt.

The battalion Executive Officer, a surly major with a barrel body, one thick eyebrow that ran completely across his forehead, and an ever-present cigar (guys in the battalion said the cigar made him look like Lassie taking a dump), had instructed me to come to his bunker for a "visit". He liked to spend a few minutes with newly arriving replacement troops — "getting to know my people". He asked me a few questions about my background, and appeared to be thoroughly disinterested in my answers. He affirmed what I had already observed, that FNGs should expect a probationary cold shoulder from just about everyone else. And he told me to keep my nose clean and stay away from drugs.

The XO informed me that my eventual assignment would be to the battalion's Bravo Company. I was to spend the night on the firebase, then temporarily join Delta Company on patrol the following day for a week or so of familiarization. A resupply chopper was going out to Delta Company the next day, and I would be on it.

I spent the afternoon looking around the LZ. It was about as dreary a place as I could have ever imagined. There wasn't a single living plant or blade of grass anywhere on the hill inside the concertina wire perimeter. The bunkers all had oozing mud walls and floors, and the trail used by the shaky little jeep/truck to haul supplies up the hill and trash down it was a greasy maze of overlapping ruts. The mess building was a small corrugated metal kitchen used for preparing hot meals (a coveted reprieve from C-rations), and was so unkempt it would have sent any self-respecting stateside health inspector running for cover. It was some indication of the taste-numbing blandness of C-rations that GIs voraciously ate all the stuff prepared in that kitchen.

At the highest point on the hill, just above the battalion CO's bunker, were the 105mm artillery batteries and the 81mm mortars. The guns and mortars could be quickly positioned to aim at any point in the battalion AO that was within their range. Some of the "gun bunnies" prided themselves on a speedy response to a fire mission request. Others, I was to learn, approached their jobs like bureaucrats—I'll get to it right after my coffee break.

I felt very much the outsider as I idled about the small firebase. I watched other GIs, some busy on various work details, others just sitting around, and a few sleeping. Any that I approached passed me by with unseeing stares, or perhaps a grunted response to a "How're you doing?" Not a lot of small talk on this hill.

As I passed by the latrine, I watched the two privates on shit duty nonchalantly leaning on their stirring paddles, apparently unaffected by the choking smoke rising out of the drums. I shook my head in amazement. What an incredible place this was; I wondered how long it took to develop such practiced indifference.

LZ Professional had one quad-50 gun mount positioned to overlook the Burlington Trail. Someone mentioned that it was going to be test-fired. I was curious, so as I walked around exploring the firebase, I made a point to wander over and see it.

A quad-50 was a Rube Goldberg contraption consisting of four separate, but jointly mounted, 50-caliber machine guns. One operator could fire all four simultaneously from a single trigger mechanism. I had never seen a quad-50, but recalled from training the intimidating sight of a single 50-caliber gun spitting out its huge bullets. I think quad-50s were most likely anti-aircraft batteries converted to ground use, and this one was intended to rule over the Burlington Trail.

It took a long time for the Spec 4 who was manning it to get all four ammo belts threaded. It apparently wasn't a quick response weapon. I had a humorous thought that the quad-50 would be more useful for battles that were scheduled in advance. (How does your Tuesday afternoon look? Got an opening for a firefight? What time's good for you?)

At last it was ready, and he started firing into the valley below. For about ten seconds it was an impressive show—very loud, tracers drifting downrange, the sight of debris being viciously kicked up where the heavy bullets were thudding into trees and the ground a half mile away. Then the guns began to jam.

The poor guy tried for the next fifteen minutes to get all four guns operating at once, but they kept jamming. Every time one would jam, he had to stop firing to clear the offending gun. I found myself wondering whether this mount was considered a key element of base defense against a ground assault, and hoped it wasn't. So much for the devastating power of a quad-50.

Late in the day after grabbing some hot chow, I went looking for a place to spend the night. There was a bunker on the LZ that was intended for transient personnel, troops who were just passing through and not part of whatever company was on the firebase at the time. That bunker was a little larger than most and actually had a few benches stuck in the walls, but other temporary residents had already laid claim to the benches. So I spread my poncho liner on the dirt floor of the bunker and prepared to spend my first night in a war zone.

Once the sun went down, it was totally dark in the bunker; you literally could not see your hand in front of your face. It wasn't easy to sleep. For a while I stayed awake thinking about Linda, and where I was and the year ahead of me, and wishing I was just about anywhere else. Then the rats came. I heard them first, scuttling in the dark. Something brushed my face, and I almost went through the top of the bunker.

I spent the balance of the night sitting up with my back against one of the bunker's walls, convinced that the relatives of the rat I shot earlier in the day were determined to pay me back. I didn't sleep much, between the rats and the periodic noisy fire missions from the battery of 105s on the hilltop.

My year in Vietnam had really begun.

Chapter Five

The next morning, a little groggy from lack of sleep, I hitched a ride on the slick going out to resupply Delta Company, my temporary unit. I felt a little like the condemned man taking his final walk as I climbed into the chopper. Once the Huey was airborne, the crew chief leaned over to me and said it was okay to lock and load. Up until that point, I didn't have a magazine in my M-16; it was customary to clear your weapon while on the firebase.

There was something about slapping home a magazine of live ammunition and chambering a round. It was the first time in my Army experience that I had loaded live ammo anywhere other than a firing range. This was no training exercise or trip to a range. It was real, and it was disquieting.

The day was already hot, and I was sweat-drenched. We headed west, and the wind through the open doors was cooling. More remarkable multi-hued lush green vistas flashed below us, with an occasional stream or hill breaking up the beautiful monotony. This time the chopper flew a lot lower, and the distance wasn't as great as my ride had been on the previous day. The door gunners were nervously alert, scanning the ground for any sign of a threat.

Despite the early heat, the sky had clouded over and was threatening rain, unlike the day before when the sun had put a sparkle on the streams we saw. The cloudiness made everything look more subdued, but no less green. The monsoon season was coming, and the sun would soon be giving way to clouds and rain every day.

Seen up closer than on my first flight, the jungle appeared

almost unbroken, a thickly woven blanket of textured green. I found myself thinking what it was going to be like, living and getting around down there. It looked impenetrable.

After about five minutes of straight-line flying, the jungle suddenly opened up below us and the pilot dropped toward a clearing. Soldiers were moving about below, making room for the Huey to land. When we touched down, it was quickly apparent that some sort of action had just taken place. Delta Company was set up in a defensive perimeter around the cleared area in which sat a couple of hootches—Vietnamese grass shacks. Two young Vietnamese males in the ubiquitous black pajamas and conical hats sat in the center of the clearing, their hands tied behind their backs with pieces of hemp rope. Some of the Delta Company troops were agitated and gesturing angrily at the Vietnamese.

There had been a brief firefight, but nobody was hit. The two Vietnamese may or may not have had anything to do with it. They claimed to be innocent bystanders, to the extent anyone could understand what they were saying. They kept repeating, "No VC, no VC". As was so often the case, I later came to understand, a combat unit in this AO could find itself suddenly involved in a fight without ever seeing the bad guys or getting a clean shot back at them. That proved to be one of the most frustrating, and frightening, aspects of being out on patrol.

Evidently destined for interrogation by ARVN authorities, the two Vietnamese were loaded on the chopper that had brought me while the crew chief kicked off a few bags of mail and supplies. The rotor had barely slowed the entire time it was on the ground, and in moments both the whine of the engine and the pitch of the whopping blades changed as the big rotor grabbed for air to lift it back into the sky. The pilot on this bird had no interest in hanging around to see if there were more bad guys in the trees.

So there I stood in the jungle, without even the thin sanctuary of a mud-crusted firebase. Only a few days before I had been on leave at home with Linda. I had been partying, driving fast cars, eating fast food, watching movies, listening to records, drinking beer, sleeping in a real bed with clean white sheets and a beautiful warm girl by my side—just *days* ago! Now I was a reluctant warrior in a strange and forbidding distant place, wondering whether I would ever live to leave it. No transition, no adjustment from a familiar life to an alien one. All that was comfortable and ordinary was gone. Someone had waved a cruel magic wand and turned my whole world on its head. I felt very inadequate—an imposter in the midst of legitimate soldiers—and very, very alone.

That lonely, empty feeling weighed on me more heavily than my rucksack. My feet were frozen in place and my legs didn't want to move. Delta Company troops passed me by without stopping or noticing. To them, I wasn't even there. I had a profound sense of being ensnared in some bizarre dream. I could think of very few things I wouldn't have gladly given at that moment to be anywhere else.

Yet a part of me knew there was really nothing I could do but shrug off those unsettling thoughts and go find someone in charge. As much as I felt immobilized, the fears were still not as powerful as the terrifying prospect of coming off like a pussy in front of all these strangers, these seasoned veteran fighters who all looked so much more soldierly than I felt. And there really was no alternative, nowhere to run and hide. The chopper was gone; I was on my own. All of the rehearsals of the past year were over and the curtain had gone up for real. Can't run to mommy for comfort and protection. Time to be a big boy now.

There were to be more moments like that—helplessness, fear, inadequacy all threatening to overcome self-control. People have continued to ask me over the years, "How did guys do it, especially in Vietnam when the folks at home had pretty much turned their backs on the war effort? How did you manage to find the will to keep on going?" The answer has nothing to do with heroics. There simply was no option. You just sucked it up and did it, because you just plain didn't have any choice.

The next ten days were a prologue to jungle life in Vietnam. I had a single interaction with the Delta Company Commander when I reported to him, and he passed me off to one of his platoon leaders. I was a wide-eyed FNG, and followed them around like a curious puppy while they completed the balance of their patrol cycle and rotated back to the firebase.

I watched and learned. In any profession, the real thing is always a little unlike training programs. The Army was no exception. Local radio procedure was considerably different from NCOCS, and was important for me to know. I learned various operations practices like setting up a secure night laager and patrolling techniques developed for jungle warfare. I learned how to properly pack a rucksack and balance the heavy load of equipment, food and water, and ammunition.

I was introduced to shackle code radio transmissions, a procedure intended to communicate a unit's position in code to avoid giving it away to eavesdropping VC or NVA, and was mildly puzzled that neither AIT or NCO school had included a single mention of shackle codes. Since they were a regular, sometimes hourly, part of our lives anywhere in the combat AO, it was a peculiar omission from training.

Although I had a brand new set of jungle fatigues, the basic field uniform proved to be something less. Because of the heat and humidity, most GIs wore their fatigue trousers and an olive drab tee shirt. Nothing more. No fatigue shirt, and no undershorts. Skipping the underwear was mildly surprising and a bit weird at first, but heat rashes, crotch rot and other forms of jungle crud were a constant problem from moist chafing. So a minimalist approach to underwear helped prevent these unappealing byproducts of jungle life. The final element to our uniforms was an OD towel draped around our necks as padding for rucksack straps and to wipe the ever-present sweat from our eyes.

There was another E-6 instant NCO in Delta Company. Mike Keene was a squad leader in the platoon to which I had been temporarily attached, and I purposely tried to spend some time with him. Maybe because we both had been to school at Benning, we hit it off. He was a lot more tolerant of my FNG status than most of the others in the company, a kindness that made me very grateful.

Mike and I talked a few times at night after the day's patrol was over and we were settled into a night laager. He gave me some tips to keep from making a jackass out of myself, and shared his own experiences as a new arrival a couple of months earlier. It was a little reassuring to know that others had felt the same apprehensions and sense of inadequacy that plagued me. We were kindred spirits in many ways, both recent college graduates, both married shortly before going to Vietnam, bound by similar memories of the NCO school. He had graduated first in his NCOCS class.

Mike was from Kansas, and his new wife's name was Laura. They had met at Kansas State. He was a tall good-looking red-haired kid, with an easy smile and an affable nature. Mike was likeable, and his squad clearly respected him. I found I genuinely liked him, too.

He told me about the monotony of slogging around in the bush, and common mistakes made by FNGs. He also told me to take nothing for granted, including the competency of most of the officers in the battalion chain of command. Mike was particularly contemptuous of the staff officers, the S-1 and S-2 and so forth. They were for the most part majors and captains who didn't actually have a command; instead they performed administrative functions like operations, intelligence, and personnel for the battalion commander or his executive officer on the LZ.

Mike related the most recent example he had seen of a screw-up by a staff officer. Just the week before, Delta Company had been on a patrol when, without any warning, artillery shells began dropping dangerously close. Since the bad guys didn't have any artillery in our AO, it didn't take a mental giant to figure out Mike's company was being shelled by their own batteries. By the time a frantic company commander could get through to LZ Professional to stop the barrage, a GI had been seriously wounded.

Most guys in Delta Company believed a staff officer had failed to check the most recent update of unit locations before giving the OK to an artillery fire mission. I made a mental note to be extra careful with our artillery.

My "post-graduate" education from Mike and his squad covered a lot. Sometimes the whole company traveled together, other times we split into platoons and patrolled different areas. In the evenings we set up defensive positions, and Mike took me around to check each one. He and the platoon leader or platoon sergeant walked the perimeter both before and after dark, making sure positions were well placed and claymores properly armed. Other American units had learned the hard way that the VC sometimes crawled up close to night laagers and turned the claymores around, aiming them back at the perimeter. Then, when an attack started, the defending GIs would trigger them, blowing a deadly wall of steel pellets right into their own ranks. It was pretty important to set out the claymores in a way that the defensive position could keep track of them.

Sleeping on watch was a big problem, for everybody. You never got enough sleep, guys were always tired. Days were filled with physical exertion, humping around in the boonies with heavy loads in energy-sapping heat, and sleep at night was painfully interrupted by a rotating watch. Our fatigue was worsened by a constant wearying tension from the understanding that we were out in "Indian country", and always potentially vulnerable to an attack.

Because of that fatigue, standing watch could be tough. You sat by yourself in the dark for a couple hours, listening to night sounds and the heavy breathing of the other men in your defensive position. Drowsiness nibbled at you and your eyelids felt an irresistible weight pulling them closed. Unless the laager was in a relatively open area, jungle canopy erased starlight and made the darkness so complete that your only effective sense was hearing. And, of course, it was the responsibility of squad leaders—the job I expected to get—to make certain their men stayed alert on watch. Mike had heard of an instance when a GI in another company had fallen asleep on watch, and Viet Cong had crept in and slit his throat.

Hearing stories like that gave me the willies, and a heightened incentive to stay awake. For weeks after Mike told me the story, whenever I took my turn on watch I kept imagining shadowy figures creeping toward my position, evil bloodthirsty Cong with huge knives clenched in their teeth eager to slice the soft flesh of sleepy young Americans.

As we grew to know each other, Mike confided in me that he had actually been a little gung ho during his training, a real soldier's soldier, and had put considerable effort into achieving the distinction of first in his NCOCS class. By contrast, I hadn't been all that motivated to get any particular class ranking. Whatever interest I'd had in finishing high enough to graduate as an E-6 was driven by the added pay, and maybe some satisfaction from finishing toward the front of the race. Like me, Mike had been drafted. Unlike me, he had gone in feeling he had a real obligation to answer the call and to defend his country from the spread of communism. He had been told there was a legitimate reason for us to be in Vietnam, and he accepted it.

But, Mike told me that the months he had spent on the ground had eroded his gung ho attitude. He had developed doubts about the war, and the way he perceived the U.S. was fighting it. In particular, Mike couldn't understand the apparent absence of objectives, or why the chain of command always kept line companies in the dark about the flow of the war. He said he was growing weary of endlessly patrolling the same territory, looking for VC or NVA, and simply moving on. It seemed pointless to him; just walk around in the jungle until you find someone to fight, then head somewhere else and do it all over again. Why fight someone for a piece of land, then turn around and give it back? We sure weren't making South Vietnam any more secure for the civilians, or for that matter, ourselves.

Intelligence, at least at the platoon level, was practically non-existent. It was rare to know much about a mission in advance, or to get any information on enemy units suspected to be in our AO. You were expected to trudge along, find bad guys, and kill them. The job of the military was to break things. Those in command evidently didn't feel it was important for the grunts on the ground to know anything more than that. A lot of the officers were elitists, projecting an attitude that the rest of us were in some lower and considerably more ignorant class.

Mike said that the VC really controlled the pace of the war. The time and place of combat was almost never our call. It was instead dictated by whether the enemy decided that conditions were favorable for a fight. He told me that contact was often brief, the Cong hitting quickly and by surprise, then fading away before any significant firepower could be brought to bear. As often as not, you never even saw the bad guys. GIs found that incredibly frustrating, almost like fighting with ghosts.

Somewhere along the way Mike mentioned that a lot of GIs got messed up by booby traps, usually made from grenades, antipersonnel mines, and salvaged dud bombs or artillery shells. The VC were accomplished scavengers and could turn almost any explosive device into a booby trap, left behind on a trail or in an abandoned hootch, or even hidden on a body to eventually kill or main some luckless GI. That was infuriating. You couldn't even shoot back.

Mike was clearly disillusioned, as he had come over full of belief and was becoming convinced that his allegiance might have been misplaced. After getting a firsthand look at the war, he was increasingly sure the whole thing was a pointless, but deadly, exercise in futility.

Hearing him talk, it all sounded pretty pointless to me, too.

About a week had gone by after I joined Delta Company. The captain had stopped our column for a mid-day break in a heavily wooded area. It was a murderously hot day, and the effort of moving through the thick brush with heavy loads had taken its toll on our collective stamina. A few GIs were flirting with heat exhaustion. I felt pretty wiped out, but was thankful I didn't have any signs of heat exhaustion.

We were spread out, sprawled on the ground and leaning back on rucksacks. Most guys were relaxed, if hot and uncomfortable. Some were sucking on canteens, and most appeared unconcerned. There hadn't been any enemy contact since the day I joined them. No real perimeter had been set up where we took the break, as we had simply halted the line of march. I had no idea if this was good or bad. I knew so little that I rarely thought to challenge what I saw around me. Besides, all I wanted to do at the moment was nurse a canteen of tepid water and chew salt tablets. And it was inconceivable that anyone in their right mind would want to engage a hundred plus well-armed men. Especially on such a mercilessly hot day.

Mike Keene's platoon was first in the company column, and his was the point squad. For whatever reason, possibly to scout a bit in the direction we would soon resume, Mike and a couple of his guys walked a few hundred yards away from the balance of the company. Most of us didn't even see this happening; the jungle was too thick.

The sudden sound of one shot. Then silence, as heads jerked up and people dived to the ground. Then the staccato racket of four or five automatic weapons opening up, the distinctive popping noise of M-16s. No idea what the hell is going on. Confusion. People running. Heart jumping out of my chest. More gunfire. Can't tell where the sound is coming from. How many guns? Where? Good guy guns, or bad guy guns?

Can someone please tell me what the hell is happening? Does anybody know what we're supposed to do?

Fear is a funny thing. You can be confronted with a danger that is real and perceptible—it can be seen, identified and reacted to. In a strange way it's a bit comforting to have an idea what you're dealing with. Then there is the unseen and the unknown. The woods could have been full of crack NVA regular troops for all I knew. The uncertainty made it all the more frightening.

Some of my infantry training had emphasized getting as low as possible when under fire, but to stick your weapon up and return fire, even when there is no apparent target. It's called putting out suppressing fire, discouraging an enemy from making an approach. But there was nothing to be seen, nothing to shoot at. I couldn't even figure out where to put out suppressing fire. How the hell can you shoot back? I was in the middle of a bunch of guys just like me, and any shooting I might have done would be more likely to hit good guys than bad guys. It was the first time I experienced the chilling feeling that I might really die, and I couldn't even fight back.

After less than a minute (that felt a whole lot longer), it was quiet again. Heads cautiously peaked up and GIs looked at each other with quizzical expressions. A short time later, four men came back into the company position carrying Mike's body on a poncho liner. His eyes were open. He actually looked alert, like he wanted to say something but couldn't make the words come. I had a ridiculous urge to tell him to get up, but he wasn't there any more.

I had never seen a dead human being before outside of a funeral home, and most of them had been old. This was different. Mike was young, and would never get the chance to live his life. However briefly, I had *known* him; he had meant something to me. And now he was gone.

There had been one lone Viet Cong with some antique single shot carbine probably left over from the French Indochina War. He fired his one shot, and Mike was the unlucky target. All of the subsequent gunfire that had changed an entire infantry company into ground cover had been the recovery of the other stunned grunts Mike had taken with him—they put their M-16s on rock 'n roll and let fly into the bush. Never saw a thing, didn't hit a thing. The VC just melted away, leaving Mike dead on the ground. Another swift firefight with an elusive foe who came and went like smoke, just as Mike had described to me. One less American for the Cong to have to fight another day.

It could have just as easily been me. There were so many ways Mike and I were alike, and I could almost picture myself limp in his place as they carried him past me. Just the night before we had smoked and talked quietly for well over an hour. I felt again like I was caught in a bad dream.

The somber procession passed right by me. Mike's face was pale. There wasn't much blood on his shirt; he was dead before he hit the ground so his heart hadn't continued futilely trying to pump through the new and unwelcome opening I could see in his chest.

I had looked at my first Vietnam War casualty. Everything around me drifted strangely out of focus and was moving in slow motion. It all seemed very, very wrong to me. What could possibly be the reason, the justification, for this? Where was the validation for a life cut short, for expectations unrealized? What glorious mission had his death accomplished? What stirring story of the noble fallen warrior should we tell his lonely young widow? And how about the mother who nursed him, raised him and loved him? Will she be comforted by how well he served his country in our glorious battle against the northern half of some meaningless backward country that nobody in the U.S. gave a shit about any more?

I knew then what my one, single objective would be while I was in Vietnam. Survival. I had found purpose. Nothing else mattered. Not the politics of Nixon and Ho Chi Minh, not the ambitions of opportunistic battalion commanders hoping to get promoted by piling up body counts. Not the strident hawkish pronouncements of Bob McNamara, one of the leftover "best and brightest" who was the misguided chief architect of the war (and who admitted years later that it had been a mistake). Not the miserable waffling of leaders in Washington who couldn't decide if we should be in the war or get out, or the peace negotiators in Paris who couldn't even decide on the shape of the stupid conference table. Not the corruption-riddled government of South Vietnam, or the inept and cowardly ARVN Army. Nothing mattered but avoiding the fate of this staff sergeant with the red hair and the boyish face being carried to a clearing to await the dust-off chopper and the body bag.

Red was the color of his blood flowing thin,
Pallid white was the color of his lifeless skin,
Blue was the color of the morning sky,
He saw looking up from the ground where he died.
It was the last thing ever seen by him.
Kyrie eleison.
The Association

Chapter Six

The balance of my apprenticeship was uneventful, and my temporary assignment came to an end just as Delta Company was due to cycle back on the firebase. Even in ten short days, I felt changed somehow. It would be a stretch to say I'd been under fire—that bullets had been directed at me personally— but I had seen the disturbing consequences of soldiering and was more convinced than ever that I wasn't cut out for war, and certainly not a war that was rapidly becoming pointless. I felt as though something inside of me had been deeply affected by Mike's death. Maybe I was still an FNG, but I wasn't the same guy I'd been when I arrived.

I hadn't even seen the enemy yet, but anger was starting to replace indifference. Back in the states, I had thought it silly to be singing cadences about wanting to go to Vietnam and kill a Viet Cong. But one of those anonymous Asian communist pajama-wearing runts had already snatched away a new friend, and somehow I knew I could kill him for that. During training, I often wondered if I could really kill someone, actually look at another human being and squeeze the trigger. Now, I had a strong sense that I was indeed capable of taking a life. In fact, I knew I would have grimly relished the opportunity to blast away at the SOB who nailed Mike.

I was thinking about Mike, and missing his companionship, as we walked the last half mile to the firebase alongside the Burlington Trail. (You didn't walk *on* the trail, any trail, unless you wanted to try out the latest in VC booby traps.) LZ Professional looked a lot different from the bottom of the hill than it had when I came and left by helicopter. It was still ugly, but it looked a little more formidable as we stared up at its concertina wire and fortified bunkers with interlocked fire zones. That was good; maybe Charlie saw it the same way.

"Charlie" was the Viet Cong. The label came from "Victor Charlie", which was phonetic radio talk for "VC". It was one of the nicer labels—most of the time they were "gooks" or "dinks" or "slopes". I was learning fast. When I thought about Mike, my newly acquired vocabulary of pejoratives started coming more easily to me.

With my temporary company going on the LZ, it was time for the company already up there to rotate off and head into the bush for three weeks. The company coming off to begin its patrol was Bravo Company, my permanent assignment. So guess who didn't get to spend any down time on the firebase.

Missing a rotation on the LZ also meant no change in clothes, which I hadn't taken off since the day I left Chu Lai. (In the jungle, getting ready for bed didn't mean putting on your pajamas. You might risk taking off your boots on rare occasions, but you slept in your clothes.) I didn't look at all like Sergeant Starch any more. My fatigue trousers were caked with mud all the way up to my crotch and my shirt was sweat-stained with patches of white from the dried salt. Three weeks later, when I finally made it back to Professional, the seams in my fatigue trousers were actually rotting away. Talk about couture al fresco. Funny thing, though, you sort of get used to having the same clothes on all the time. I certainly wasn't offending anybody; they all smelled and looked as bad as I did. At least I no longer looked like an FNG. I still didn't feel very soldierly, and I definitely didn't feel like a take-charge NCO, but I looked like I fit in.

I gave my thanks to the folks in Delta Company who had accommodated me for a while, and met my new company commander as he came down the hill. He was a captain, somewhere around thirty, with eight or nine years in the Army. The meeting was a little awkward; I had never reported for a duty assignment to a company on the march before, and I'm not real sure he had been expecting me right at that moment. I walked alongside him for a time, answering his questions about me, my background, my training and so forth.

The captain assigned me to his 2nd platoon, twenty-something grunts headed by a young second lieutenant named Tom Warren. His was the trailing platoon in the company, so I stood waiting at the side of the moving column like an idiot while the rest of the company passed by. "Hey Sarge, waiting for a streetcar?" "What ya know, Sarge? You lost?"

By the time 2nd platoon made it down the hill to where I was waiting, the CO had alerted Lieutenant Warren by radio to be looking for me. I reported in to him, and learned with considerable surprise what my new job was to be.

There were only two other NCOs in 2nd platoon; both were E-5 shake and bakes. That made me the ranking NCO and consequently the platoon sergeant, right from day one. It was more than a little daunting. Not only was I an FNG but I was the goddamn platoon sergeant, the number two guy in the whole freaking platoon! Oh shit, I don't need this, I'm not ready for this! There are other people's lives at stake here!

But Lieutenant Warren was an okay guy, and he acted like it was no big deal for a one-year wonder to be elevated so quickly to such responsibility. Maybe it was no big deal, but I sure didn't feel terribly confident. The lieutenant assured me he would show me the ropes, and told me to fall in with the moving platoon.

That was my beginning with Bravo Company. The next three weeks were filled with more watching and learning. Not surprisingly, the guys in my new platoon were slow to accept me and I was fortunately smart enough not to push it. I tried to stay attentive, and somehow avoided doing or saying anything really stupid. It was obvious I was being sized up by the troops, and I sure didn't blame them. It felt just as crazy to me as it must have to them—a make-believe NCO, a shake and bake, a college boy with a whopping 12 months in the Army, acting as their platoon sergeant. I knew I had a lot to learn, and that the experienced soldiers I was supposed to lead were the best source of that knowledge. If I had any advantage at all, it was

the added training from NCO school. Although much of that
training proved to be inappropriate to a guerilla war, the extra
months of schooling gave me an edge over most of the other
troops, who had received infantry AIT at most. There were
actually a few things I knew that they didn't, and that helped
earn me some credibility.

In truth, we were a platoon of kids, not a professional
soldier in the bunch. Not one of us, including the lieutenant
who wasn't all that long out of OCS, had much more than two
years in the Army. Most of the guys actually had less than a
year, the newest ones as little as six months. This intrepid little
group was out there in real-life killing fields, playing soldier.
It wasn't that we were dumb or incapable people, and all of
us had received reasonably adequate training, as far as it went.
But training classes don't make infantry soldiers. And the best
leaders of infantry soldiers are people who have done it before.
None of us qualified. So we learned as many GIs did in Vietnam
at that point in the war—the OJT way.

Like I said, in the early days of the Vietnam War the
Army didn't have to field platoons of teenagers with leaders
who weren't much older. Combat infantry companies in the
middle 1960s had a much more conventional distribution of
experienced officers and NCOs. But the continually escalating
need for warm bodies as the war effort increased to more than a
half million men under arms had stretched the military beyond
its capacity to get and train people. I found myself part of a
platoon that could just as easily have been a bunch of guys in a
class at some junior college.

When President Kennedy and later Johnson presided over
the war's earliest years, whole divisions that had trained together
were sent to the war intact. As time went by and members of
those original units were rotated home, either as casualties or at
the conclusion of their one-year tour, the troops who replaced
them were much less experienced and were predominantly
draftees. Although career officers and NCOs were required to
serve more than one tour of duty over the decade-long course of
the war, many were promoted beyond the reach of combat and

others were clever enough to garner rear area assignments in relative safety. That meant the combat burden fell increasingly on green troops as the conflict wore on, ironically eroding U.S. military effectiveness at a time when the greatest numbers of soldiers were committed to Vietnam.

There is nothing quite so unmotivated as an unprepared military called upon to fight an unwanted war.

Lieutenant Warren was true to his word about helping me out. He spent a lot of time with me during the first few weeks, teaching me stuff they never mentioned in all my stateside training. He was discreet too, meaning that he didn't act like he was conducting remedial training of the class dummy, or do it in front of an audience of cynical grunts.

Sometimes we patrolled in full company strength, other times we split up into three platoons to cover more ground and check out a greater number of targets reported by scouting helicopters. It was a quiet time; no contact with the enemy, no guns fired.

When the company split into platoons, Lieutenant Warren kept me at the front with him so I could observe and listen. Because the terrain was usually difficult, we normally moved in single file. In such a column, it was customary for the platoon sergeant to be toward the rear and the platoon leader to be close to the front. Since I was new, however, he figured I could learn faster if I spent time up front with him. He was right, and I learned quickly.

There was a lot to know about radio procedure. I had figured out shackle coding while hanging around with Delta Company, but now there were platoon sergeant responsibilities to master. Each platoon had two PRC-25s, one for the platoon leader and one for the platoon sergeant. We each had an "RTO", a radio/telephone operator, to carry them. Lieutenant Warren was "One Six" and I was "One Niner". The numbers signified platoon leader and platoon sergeant, respectively. The prefix to these numbers specified that we were 2nd platoon in Bravo Company, and was changed every few days to confuse Charlie, or at least to keep him from getting on our frequencies and pretending to be an American unit. So I was India One Niner to his India One Six, or Bronco One Niner to his Bronco One Six, and so forth.

Radio traffic was fairly constant, consisting of various units transmitting their locations in shackle and updates between field units and LZ Professional. Location reports were required at least hourly, to minimize the chance of artillery or air strikes occurring near friendly forces. During periods of no enemy contact, there would sometimes be quiet lulls. But if anyone thought Charlie was around, the airwaves got busy.

The lieutenant told me about various approaches to deploying troops in the jungle. Ironically, the single file patrol column most often used because of terrain constraints was probably the absolute worst way to field your men. Any frontal contact caught the column with relatively few soldiers in position to return fire, and was more vulnerable to multiple casualties. The bad guys could shoot face on, like plinking at a row of dominos. Enfilade fire, I think it was called.

But the jungle simply made most any other approach impractical. Hacking our way through thick foliage was slow enough in single file; it would have been a crawl with a multi-column front.

Days went by, and I found myself settling into a routine. Although I had been wound up like a cheap watch after the ambush that cost Mike his life, a couple weeks without contact took the edge off. That was a common problem in Vietnam—prolonged boredom and relaxed vigilance followed by a few minutes of unexpected battle and sheer terror. The fight would end, we'd pick up the pieces, and everyone would be extremely cautious for a few days or weeks. But it was hard to stay hyper-alert when nothing was happening. I suspect that more than a few guys bought the farm in Vietnam because of inattention bred by days of numbing monotony.

We had been traveling south, and were several miles from LZ Professional. Although it varied in thickness from place to place, most of the time we were in jungle. It was unlike anything I had ever seen before. We were surrounded by strange trees and plants, and animals most of us had never seen. There were bushes with leaves the size of umbrellas. You could sit under them in the rain and stay mostly dry. There was thick-bladed elephant grass that sometimes grew taller than a man, with serrated razor edges constantly nicking at passing flesh. Most of the trees, complete with an occasional chattering monkey and lots of exotic birds, were different from anything back home. They grew tall, cresting in a thickly tangled mat far above the ground. In places, the canopy looked impenetrable, the treetops woven together to completely shut out the sky.

There were vines hanging from the trees, sometimes so thoroughly snarled you could only pass through with the aid of a machete. They grabbed at moving GIs, slowing and tripping and frustrating. Vines would snatch at equipment, and could rip off a canteen or a smoke canister or even a hand grenade that was too tentatively attached to the rucksack or web belt of an unwary soldier. At times the vegetation was so thick you had to stay close to the man in front of you to avoiding breaking the column and getting lost. Staying close, despite the necessity, was not wise. In the words of a Fort Benning instructor, "One grenade can get you all".

When vines didn't trip and tangle, the elephant grass would cut us as its razor edges slid over the sweaty arms and faces of passing troops. It normally didn't cut too deep, but there were always fresh bleeding cuts, burning from the sweat.

We chopped our way through unending vines, only to find ourselves in rigidly thick stands of bamboo. Even taller than the elephant grass, the bamboo would sometimes grow into a wall so solid that two or three GIs would have to move up and hack at it with machetes. A half hour on point, cutting through bamboo shoots with a machete, left a man arm-weary and barely able to lift his rifle.

It rained a lot. During the monsoon season it rained every day—often all day long. Most of the time the rain was steady and gentle, just a constant unvarying water torture. It made staccato noises on the giant leaves, dripped off the vines, sloshed in our boots. It drizzled down the edges of our steel pots and ran with the sweat off our bodies. It dampened and discolored our cigarettes and turned them into mush that wouldn't light. It ruined the occasional pad of writing paper for letters back home. It soaked our poncho liners, adding to the weight of our loads when we rolled them up in the mornings and stuffed them soggy into our rucksacks. And it rusted weapons, ammo, grenades, radios, D-rings, watches, cigarette lighters and everything else that was metal.

In some parts of the battalion AO, there were rolling hills that sloped into lush valleys. The valleys were laced with streams and intermittent swampy rice paddies. Once in awhile a hillside stream would tumble over a drop-off into a gentle waterfall. Because the jungle gave way, reluctantly, to the streams, they were tempting avenues that avoided the vines and thick undergrowth. The problem was that Charlie knew that, too. A favorite VC tactic was to set up an ambush along a streambed and pick off the first few guys in a column that was careless or impatient enough to walk a stream. And streams, like trails, were often booby-trapped.

The streams and waterfalls and rice paddies were sources of water to keep our canteens full. But the water was generally unsafe for drinking without first treating it. We purified the water with Halizone, a chemical that had replaced the old iodine tablets GIs used in earlier wars. Even though we were in a low population area, enough people and assorted critters used waterways as toilets to make them suspect for drinking. You wouldn't know that from looking at the water. Except for the sludgy rice paddies, the water we found in flowing streams was clear, fresh and cool. It was awfully tempting to drink it without doctoring it up with bitter tasting Halizone.

The water really was vital. Although we got a lot of rain, the climate was always oppressively hot and humid. On many days, the temperature topped out well above 100 degrees and the wet air took on an almost solid form, clogging the lungs. If we were patrolling in an area that was relatively open, the sun beat on us like a furnace, cooking our heads inside the steel pots. On such days, energy was sucked right out of us. It took a tremendous effort just to keep plodding along, left right left. On more than one occasion I remember thinking, "Please God, don't let Charlie be around here anywhere. I don't have the strength to fight." Or I'd beg Him not to let me be the first guy to get weak-kneed and keel over from the weight of the load and the merciless sun.

Where the jungle was thickest, the baking sun wasn't able to penetrate the dense canopy and it was unnaturally dark. Usually, no breeze entered either, and the air was still and stagnant. Those thick areas were unpleasant, both because they squeezed sweat out of a man as fast as he could drink water and because they were downright eerie—a prehistoric world where people didn't belong.

Intensifying the effect of pounding heat, we carried heavy loads. Rucksacks, weapons, and other gear averaged 40 to 80 pounds, depending on the type of weapon each GI carried and on how long it had been since the last resupply. On top of our own gear, each of us typically strapped on a hundred rounds or so of belted 7.62mm ammunition for the M-60 machine guns. The guys who carried the "pigs", the M-60s, couldn't begin to haul all the ammo they needed in addition to the heavy machine guns.

Humping a load like that through the steamy jungle and up and down hills was hard work, and we sweat constantly. It wasn't unusual to go through several quarts of water every day. On the rare occasions when our clothing dried out, it was stained white with salt from our sweat. So we ate salt tablets like candy and drank a lot of water. Even when I didn't feel like eating, which was fairly often, I wanted a drink of water.

Even eating sometimes required water, because much of our food supply was LRRPs, freeze-dried mush that had to be reconstituted to eat. "Lurps" were named for the long-range reconnaissance patrol teams that first began using the freeze-dried stuff on long, covert missions into enemy controlled areas. Resupply choppers brought whatever was available, and LRRPs alternated with C-rations on a fairly regular basis. Because they had no water content, LRRPs were lighter than C-rations. So many of us preferred to carry LRRPs and hoped we always had enough water in our canteens to be able to eat them. None of the "entrees" were all that appetizing, but the Halizone tablets made the chow bitter anyhow.

Wandering through the sight-shortening green snarl, finding water was more often an auditory exercise than a visual one. The bubbling murmur of nearby water could be heard from a surprising distance, long before breaking through the tangled foliage to actually see it. We were always alert for the sound.

When the jungle was thick, hills could be treacherous because of mud and unpredictable footing. You could be pushing your way through the undergrowth and suddenly see the guy in front of you fall out of sight as he stepped off an unseen abrupt drop-off. At such times, not many eyes and ears concentrated on whether Charlie was around. It was one foot in front of the other, and hope you got through in one piece.

As we slogged through low ground we would sometimes come upon rice paddies. There were old paddies, out of use and shabby, more swamp than tended field. And there were a few that were being actively cultivated. We rarely saw anyone actually working on the paddies—any people around quickly faded away into the jungle at the sound of approaching GIs. But we never forgot that we were in a free-fire zone, and that any Vietnamese out toiling in the muck were more likely than not to be farmers by day, killer Cong by night.

Sometimes we found ourselves walking beside the remnants of stone walls and crumbled old buildings, often so hidden in the thick growth that you wouldn't notice until you tripped over them. There had been plantations in Vietnam when the French occupied the country. I couldn't help wondering what the history of such ruins might have been, what sort of people might have once called the crumbling walls home. Did French families live there? What had their lives been like, what had they grown, and what happened to end it all? The jungle had apparently given way for a time to rubber trees and some other tended crops, but had quickly reclaimed the untended land when the plantations were abandoned.

The long days of worming our way through the jungle fostered a mental numbness. It was easy to be distracted, and the jungle was strangely fascinating. At times it was hard not to imagine you were simply out for a hike in a dense forest, surrounded by soothing vistas that were both unfamiliar and, in some ways, striking. At other times the surroundings were ominous and we felt the uneasy paranoia that bad guys lurked behind every tree.

When heat and weariness wore us down, troop movement slowed to a trudging crawl. Each man hoped that the enemy wasn't near, and that he wouldn't embarrass himself by dropping out. The air became thick and unpleasant, like breathing through an old, unwashed quilt. I was grudgingly grateful to the sadistic instructors back in the states for the hours of PT that had sufficiently conditioned me to endure all this. "Agony" and "Misery" back at Fort Knox were cupcakes.

Regular combat units advancing through the jungle were anything but stealthy. Although much has been written about the ability of small teams of Green Berets, Rangers, and LRRPs to move around undetected and perform covert missions, regular old grunts like us made a lot of racket. The idea of catching our enemy by surprise was laughable most of the time, particularly when we traveled in full company strength.

There was the collective sound of combat boots hitting the ground with more attention to balance than furtiveness. Stumbling was the trade-off sometimes made necessary by focusing more on scanning for bad guys and less on watching where we put our feet. There was the noise made by gear hanging from D-rings on rucksacks banging around, and the sound of M-16 barrels clanking against bandoleers. There was the painful thump of a slip and fall on muddy, uneven ground, generally followed by an angry curse. A LAW tube strapped to a rucksack might bump against a tree, or the whip antenna on a radio might tangle in a mat of vines. Voices murmured, even when strict silence was ordered. A steel pot could thud against a low-hanging branch. If the brush was thick, there was the metronome thwack of machetes chopping through the vines and grass and bamboo.

I sometimes had an image of Viet Cong, laughing so hard they were rolling on the ground, listening to the anvil chorus of a passing Army column, cracking up at the pathetic noise discipline of GIs in the jungle. Even when we really worked at it, silent movement of anything much larger than a squad was almost impossible.

One time some jackass in my platoon tripped and discharged a round. Hey Charlie, here we are! If you haven't already heard us thrashing around in the jungle, here's a nice loud gunshot to attract your attention. It really honked me off when that happened. In addition to signaling our presence, the bonehead private could have easily shot the guy in front of him. M-16s had safeties, just like any other gun, and the dumbest GI knew to keep his weapon on safe. Plus it usually wasn't necessary to carry a chambered round, because the spring-loaded T-bar grip on the M-16 bolt allowed for rapid chambering from the magazine. Sadly, a lot of very average GIs went to Vietnam, and many of them had slept through much of their infantry training. I sure was no super-soldier, but I continually marveled that more guys weren't killed by blunders like that.

Most of the time there was a certain dull routine to being on patrol. In fact, monotony was sometimes a worse enemy than Charles. Wake up at dawn or before, maybe eat something, pack up the rucksack, move out, stumble around all day, find a place for a night laager, maybe eat something, set out the claymores, go to sleep (until your turn for watch). Then start all over again.

Diversion might come from contact with the bad guys, or from orders to sit and stay put for a while (which usually happened right before an eagle flight), or from a resupply chopper. The latter meant food, ammunition, cigarettes, occasionally a special treat like a few cans of warm beer, and mail. God, how we lived for the mail.

Mail was something you never got enough of. It didn't matter if there was a letter for you on every resupply; it wasn't enough. Guys with big families were the luckiest. They could always count on some relative feeling concerned, or guilty, and dashing off a letter "to cousin Tommy in the Nam".

For me it was letters from Linda—sometimes two or three depending on how long it had been since the last chopper. My folks wrote, too, and my sister and brother who were still in college. Even my sweet old grandmother wrote to me, usually reminiscing about stuff like how much she used to love hearing me sing the theme from the Davy Crocket movie when I was just a toddler, or how she used to walk me down to the neighborhood store with its wood slat floor and help me fish around in the ice chest for a Nehi orange soda. It didn't matter what people wrote in their letters. It was contact with folks back in The World who really gave a damn about whether we survived this ordeal. Only twice in my whole tour did a resupply bird come in without mail for me, and both times left me feeling unreasonably depressed and abandoned.

For most guys, the letters from wives and girlfriends were always the best. Sometimes the letters had been scented with perfume, delightfully evocative girl-smells guaranteed to make us lonely and horny grunts feel the ache of separation, the longing for missed softness and warmth and gentle touches from loved ones far away. Those letters were read over and over, each word savored, each pledge of love reminding us how much we missed holding and loving the special people in our lives.

The letters were filled with unimportant, insignificant stuff—the day-to-day mundane things that people write in their letters. It was all wonderful to us; the handwriting, the stories of classes at school and crazy Aunt Meg and the new car and the rotten weather and the big party and the new neighbors who moved in across the street.

Sometimes, Linda wrote about her loneliness, and how hard our separation was on her. Once in awhile she wrote how she missed my touch and recalled how we liked to make love when we first awoke in the morning, sleep-warm and gentle. Letters like that were bittersweet. They were marvelous to receive and they brought back memories of her that were far beyond the capacity of my unaided imagination. But the letters also left me depressed because they were a reminder that I couldn't be with her and wouldn't come home to her for a long, long time.

Resupply, including the mailbags, took place every three to six days. The frequency depended on the accessibility of our location to helicopters, and on the demands for air support elsewhere in the AO. It depended on how badly we needed stuff, like if a firefight might have dangerously depleted our ammo. Getting ready for a supply chopper could be a tricky business. First there was the minor matter of finding a clearing of sufficient size to land a Huey. And it was normally prudent to look around the chosen area some, just in case Chuck might have an idea about bagging himself a low-flying chopper.

Once the area was deemed secure and the resupply bird was approaching, a smoke canister of red or yellow smoke was popped to let the pilot know where we were, especially if the canopy was thick. The landings could be interesting, as we often had to make do with limited space. I had to give a lot of credit to the warrant officers who flew those helicopters. They were remarkable guys, and many of them could do amazing things with their machines.

I well recall the first time I experienced a resupply in a tight spot. I remember, because it was yet another lesson in how differently things were done in Vietnam than what I had learned in the states. We had secured a mucky clearing that was hardly larger than the rotor span of a Huey. As it made an approach and began to flare over the trees at the edge of the clearing, I did what any well-trained NCOCS graduate had been taught to do—I stepped into the clearing to provide the pilot with hand signals to center him in the LZ (landing zone) and help him touch down.

Dumb move.

These guys had learned to rely on themselves—period. To the pilot, I must have been as annoying as a bug splat on a windshield. So he landed as if I wasn't even there. Meaning it quickly became clear that his forward momentum would put him, umm, right about where I was standing with my flapping arms and candy-assed NCO school hand signals. I back-peddled, lost my footing, and sat right down in the muck as this huge

Huey drifted overhead, the rotor downblast kicking up spray and mud all over me.

He got down, I got up, and everything was cool. I felt like a fucking idiot, and I never again used my terrific Fort Benning hand signals. New motto—if he can fly it without my help, he can damn sure land it without my help. The only good thing about the whole episode was the letter from Linda in his mailbag.

Chapter Seven

Doc was nuts. Medics were universally called "Doc", and 2nd platoon's medic was one of the first guys I got to know. I have no idea what a psychiatrist would have said about Doc, but something was badly broken inside him. He made it all the way through his tour of duty unscathed, but Vietnam got to Doc in a place somewhere deep within him that he didn't show to anyone. When he finally went home he was physically alive, but really screwed up.

Doc was a 19-year-old specialist 5th class (Spec 5), short, but stocky and very strong. He had a look that most guys could never read. You couldn't tell when he was feeling good, or when he might get in your face at the slightest provocation. I've always envied people who say they can read a person's mood through their eyes, but about all I can manage is to pick up on mood indicators like body language and facial expressions. With Doc, most people never had a clue, and there weren't any mood indicators. He was genuinely inscrutable.

He had been in Vietnam between three and four months when I arrived in 2nd platoon. Doc was Regular Army, meaning he had volunteered, which was how he had become a medic instead of meat for the infantry. I never knew whether he had anticipated coming to Vietnam when he enlisted—he might have thought he could arrange to stay stateside. But he was wild enough that maybe he wanted to see the war.

Doc's best friend was a Private First Class everybody called "TC". If I ever heard the name that went with the initials, I've long since forgotten it. I can't recall hearing him called anything else. He was short, too, but thin and wiry. He looked like a strong breeze could push him over, but the look was deceptive. TC was as tough as Doc, and they watched each other's back. I thought that the two of them together, in a bad mood, could probably empty out most bars.

When I first met Doc, he was already carrying the Chicom AK-47 automatic rifle that was his trademark. Medics are customarily viewed as non-combatants, responsible for the health of their units and not fighting, and the only weapon most of them carried was the venerable 45-caliber pistol. I learned that he had taken the AK-47 off a dead VC—one he had personally killed the month before—and decided to keep it.

Lt. Warren told me the story. The platoon was walking near the top of a ridgeline, looking for signs of several VC spotted earlier by a "loach" (LOH, for light observation helicopter). It was overcast, with a steady rain and humidity in the air so thick you could almost squeeze it like a sponge. Purely by coincidence Doc had been the fifth man in the single file column, behind the point man, his backup, the lieutenant, and the lieutenant's RTO.

The jungle was practically a wall, and the point man was spending as much time cutting his way through it as he was watching for the bad guys. They walked right into an ambush, and were hopelessly into the killing zone before the Cong opened up. Both the point man and his backup were hit and everyone else was trying very hard to melt into the ground, each guy hoping somebody else would stick their head up and return fire.

Doc, I was told, emptied his 45 at the VC, then grabbed the wounded point man's M-16 and charged the VC position, blasting away and bellowing like some berserk bull. Probably scared the shit out of Charlie, because they ran. Doc killed one of them. Dropped the little SOB before he could disappear into the brush, and claimed the VC's AK-47 for himself. He carried that AK-47 for the rest of his tour, and took it home as a war trophy.

That bizarre episode later earned Doc a Silver Star. At that time in Vietnam, a lot of medals had been cheapened because they were often indiscriminately handed out for fairly trivial events (how about a Purple Heart for a cut from a C-ration can?). But I never saw a cheap or indiscriminately awarded Silver Star. Even in Vietnam, they meant a lot and you could be confident that a Silver Star recipient had done something very special.

After his one-man assault, Doc changed. He developed a suicidal fondness for walking point. Absolutely nobody wanted to walk point, not even TC, so it was normally a rotational assignment. Doc just didn't care, and I'd guess he wound up as point man—his choice—probably half the time we were out as a solo platoon or found ourselves as lead element in a company operation. Fate must have smiled on him; he never got shot, or walked into a booby trap, or got any of the other interesting surprises that Charlie liked to give infantry point men.

Any time we were in a firefight and killed or captured VC or NVA, everyone knew to strip them of any AK-47 ammo they had and give it to Doc. AK-47s used a 30-caliber round, but its shape was incompatible with the NATO rounds we used in the pigs, the M-60 machine guns. The communist rounds had fatter shell casings than the NATO rounds, even though the bullet was the same size. So Doc couldn't simply poach some ammo from the machine gunners, and was dependent on what we could scrounge from the bad guys. We managed to keep him supplied, though, and he never ran out of ammunition.

Doc always threatened that he was going to take a knife to any VC we captured. He wasn't terribly interested in persuading them to give up military secrets, he just thought it would be fun to do a little whittling on them. I never knew if it was talk or if he would really do it, because the lieutenant and I usually watched him closely if we had any Vietnamese nearby. I think he liked to sound like a badass, and he often mentioned cutting some gook's ear off, or even his pecker. He was quick with a Zippo, too. If hootches needed burning, he was right there with his lighter to help out. It wasn't lost on me that My Lai was fairly near our area of operations, and that Rusty Calley had been in the same division as we were. There had been enough atrocities in Vietnam, on both sides, and I sure didn't need any more on my watch.

Doc was really a puzzle to me, and I could never understand the way his head worked. Although Vietnam was a truly dehumanizing experience, I had no stomach for slicing on VC, even after I grew to truly hate them. And I couldn't relate to those who thought it might somehow be a kick to try it. I guess if a man lives and acts like an animal long enough, the distinction between man and animal gets blurry. There is a lot of cruelty in war.

For all his peculiarities and anger, Doc was a good medic. If you bothered him with something like blisters, he wouldn't give you the time of day. But if you were wounded, he'd crawl through an open field and murderous fire to get to you and give medical aid.

Looking only at his assault of the ambushing VC and his willingness to walk point, it might have been easy to mistake Doc for some kind of hero. I don't think he was. Rather, I think he had seen too much at too young an age. He had become cynical and world-weary, and he just didn't care any more. So the perennial point man and tough guy medic was really more an empty shell than a John Wayne.

Medics typically spent six months in the bush assigned to a combat unit, then spent their last six months in some rear area capacity—maybe in a hospital, or as a medic in a battalion trains area. Doc eventually wound up working in our battalion Headquarters Company in Chu Lai, and I later watched him become an alcoholic during the last months of his tour. He sat in the NCO club every single night and often put away a fifth of vodka. He was a genuine mushbrain by the time he went home.

One of the two sergeant E-5s in 2nd platoon was nicknamed "Chief" because his nose and cheeks were angular and prominent, and made him look a little like an American Indian. He wasn't Indian, but the name stuck. He didn't talk much, even seemed a little aloof. He didn't act like he was better than anyone, but was kind of distant, living in a different world.

He was about as animated as a rock. Back on the LZ, there

were times I'd see him sit for hours without so much as moving. I suppose he was just pensive, but nobody ever asked him what he was thinking about. Although I can't say we were buddies, I liked him. Chief was reliable and frequently was a help to me in keeping the platoon functioning properly. He was peculiar, but then again we all were in one way or another.

My RTO—radio/telephone operator—was a sandy-haired little guy named Kenny Whitman. He was maybe 5'8", and couldn't have weighed more than 125 pounds. How ironic that the smallest GI in the platoon was carrying one of the heavy PRC-25s.

The relationship between an NCO or officer and his RTO was often a close one, and I got to know Kenny fairly well while we were together. He was 19, and had been drafted right after high school. He'd been in Vietnam seven months, and was already counting the days to the end of his tour. He was single, but talked like he knew every girl in his hometown of Deerfield, Illinois. It was a source of pride to me that a lot of guys for whom I was responsible made it through Vietnam unharmed, and I was particularly happy when Kenny ended his tour and went home intact.

We had two M-60 machine guns in 2nd platoon. The guys who carried them, Costellano and Patterson, were both pretty big boys, which was good. The guns were heavy, and long humps through the jungle in our AO carrying one of them could wear you out in a hurry. Costellano, in particular, was ideally suited to be a machine gunner. He was well over 6'2" and had to push 230. I can still picture walking behind him, the M-60 lying across his shoulders, one hand loosely draped on the stock and the other over the barrel. It wasn't a carrying position that made for quick response to an ambush, but it was a damn sight more sensible than trying to haul it around at port arms, like the actors do in those war movies.

There were eight black guys out of 30 total GIs in my platoon. 1969 was an unusual time in the relations between races. Big city riots were still fresh in a lot of minds, the black power movement was growing, the Civil Rights movement attracted media coverage of protests, and the idiots of the white lunatic fringe thought that Martin Luther King had been a communist and had deserved to be assassinated.

The Army, even in a war zone, wasn't immune from the racial strains that existed then, and there had been scattered occurrences of fights between whites and blacks. There had even been a few cases of fragging, which was when someone blew up another GI with a hand grenade. (The term "fragging" came from "fragmentation grenade", the technical term for a hand grenade.)

Racial unease often led to whites and blacks purposely staying separate, even in the jungle. Since everyone was, to some degree, dependent on one another, there generally was no overt animosity. Necessity, as they say, makes for strange bedfellows. But there was tension and mistrust just beneath the surface of this apparent normalcy.

I grew up around Detroit, had gone to school with brothers, and had several black friends in college. It seemed to me that a conscientious platoon sergeant should make an effort to know and work with everyone in the platoon equally. Maybe I was still carrying around some of that idealism that inspires student types to want to make the world a better place.

So I spent some time with my platoon's black soldiers. It was a little awkward at first. I'd find them off by themselves and I'd just sit down and talk with them. A lot of times I was doing most of the talking, as they weren't exceptionally responsive. A few were good singers, and liked to sing Motown songs. Well hey, I grew up with Motown—I knew those tunes. And sometimes we'd just talk about life back in The World. To their credit, they put up with my efforts.

Demitrius, "Dee" we called him, was a spec 4 from Georgia and for whatever reason was a little more tolerant of an annoying, but well-intentioned, white instant NCO than were some of the other blacks. He was a savvy soldier, and I made him the third squad leader along with Chief and Buzz Gallagher, the two E-5s. Some platoons were made up of three squads, others had four. It was simply a matter of how many warm bodies we could field at any particular time. Most of the time we were understaffed, so 2nd platoon normally had three squads.

Dee and I got to be friends, and that went a long way to making me OK with the other blacks. Some of the other white guys started noticing what I hoped was a subtle shifting of attitudes, and in time the platoon became more and more color-blind. I don't know how important all this was for platoon harmony, but I like to think it made a difference. It just seemed like such a simple, obvious thing to me. How the hell can you survive a war with Charlie when you can't get along with, or rely on, your own comrades?

Chapter Eight

You tend to get accustomed to the way things are. People want to look for patterns, and get comfortable with the familiar, however unpleasant it may be. I had never really thought about something happening to my platoon that would change the fragile status quo into which we had settled. I was getting reasonably established as platoon sergeant, despite a few early missteps like my episode helping the resupply chopper to land. After an initial few weeks, the rest of the guys in 2nd platoon were beginning to accept me. I had apparently graduated from FNG status at some point, and some GIs actually talked to me from time to time. It never occurred to me that I was only one step away from being a platoon leader. Lieutenant Warren had that job, and he was doing it just fine as far as I was concerned. I certainly had no interest in it.

Bravo Company was working the northernmost part of the 196th Light Infantry Brigade's AO, assigned to carry out a generic search and destroy mission. When the brass didn't have a more specific operation, missions were always called "search and destroy". The term was even a cliché on network news. I'd heard it dozens of times from Walter Cronkite before I even got drafted.

The company had split into its individual platoons to cover more territory in a faster time. Early on the first day of our platoon sweep, 2nd platoon had come upon a single hootch in a small clearing in the jungle. The body of a young Vietnamese man was on the ground not far from the hootch. It was impossible to tell how long he had been dead, or even what had killed him. The corpse was bloated from the gasses of heat-accelerated decomposition, and the distended skin was so translucent that a close look revealed the worms at work underneath.

While one fire team went inside the hootch to search it, the rest of the platoon milled around outside, our eyes often drifting back to the dead Vietnamese. It was hard to shake off a morbid fascination with that grotesquely misshapen body. A few GIs even pulled out Instamatic cameras and took pictures.

At another time, in another place, I have no doubt the sight of that swollen body being slowly consumed by the jungle would have left me nauseated. Somehow, though, the certainties that had once formed the core of my world weren't so rock-solid any more. They had started to shift around, sliding in directions that were altering my sense of reality. This gruesome sight that should have disgusted me did little more than arouse curiosity. The corpse didn't even seem quite human. It looked more like a plump wax dummy.

There was nothing showing on the body to suggest cause of death. We didn't get too close and we didn't try to roll him over, primarily because it was common knowledge that VC sometimes booby-trapped corpses, friend or foe. And besides, nobody wanted a close sniff of the odor rising from the deteriorating remains. Was he a VC, or just some miserable peasant who stubbornly refused to leave his ancestors' land? Were there others nearby? Was he killed by Americans, the ARVN, or VC? Did anybody care?

I didn't.

I realized I was thinking of him as just another dead gook. The word, and the disdain it signified, came too easily. A piece of me, deep down inside, sounded a faint warning note. I wasn't at all sure how well I still knew myself, or whether I liked very much what I was becoming.

Moments after the fire team went into the hootch, one of them shouted that they had found another body. I ducked inside, and almost backed out again because of the smell. There is simply no stench like death, especially when its handiwork is left to simmer in the jungle heat, in the close confines of a dink hootch. It hadn't been too bad around the ballooned corpse outside, particularly since I had kept my distance and stayed upwind. But in the small hootch, the reek was overwhelming.

I stayed, trying not to gag, long enough to determine that the body was another young Vietnamese male. This one had a much more apparent cause of death. The entire back half of his skull was blown off. The gray and white and red stuff inside had congealed on the hard-packed dirt floor where he lay. "Congealed"—there's a repulsive word. It aptly summed up the scene. I left.

We completed a search for weapons or documents, but there was nothing to be found in either the clearing or the hootch that would answer questions on the allegiance or demise of the two dead Vietnamese. Since they met the two conditions of a primary objective of the war—body counts—we radioed our find back to the company commander who forwarded the news to battalion where the body count tally of each unit was recorded on a large board in the operations bunker. The two conditions? Body counts had to be Vietnamese, and they had to be dead.

In time we moved on, leaving the jungle to complete its work on the corpses. Burying the bodies of your enemies was stuff of other wars in nobler times. In Vietnam, we left them to rot.

The time we had spent at the hootch put us behind schedule for linking up with the rest of the company, roughly three klicks (kilometers) to the southwest. The captain wanted to assemble all three platoons before nightfall in order to set up a company-sized night laager, and it wasn't at all clear we were going to get there before dark. But hurrying to make up time was generally impossible in the jungle. The speed of troop movement was directly correlated to the thickness of the jungle, and not much could change that. Besides, the faster you tried to go, the riskier travel became.

After a half hour of particularly slow going, chopping and groping our way through the tangle, we came to a shallow stream flowing in the general direction of our planned rendezvous.

Although the jungle grew right up to the edge of the water, the foliage resentfully gave way to the stream. The moving water opened a narrow corridor where vines didn't snarl and elephant grass didn't slice across exposed skin on faces and arms.

We had covered less than half a klick since leaving the hootch. Although I was at the rear, I could hear the murmuring water and could tell that the lieutenant was weighing whether to use the stream as a path for a while. On the one hand, walking a riverbed was a welcome relief from the frustrating and unyielding jungle, and made for comparatively fast travel. On the other hand, it was a risk. If any bad guys were around, they were certain to hear and figure out what we were doing. If they could get out in front of us, it would be a simple matter to set up an ambush or a booby trap and wait for the GIs to blunder into it.

For Lieutenant Warren, on this day, practicality won out over prudence. Our column moved into the stream and for a time we all enjoyed an improved pace and relief from the thick vegetation. In deference to caution, the spread between men was increased to 25 feet, making it more difficult for Charles to give us multiple casualties, but the spacing stretched the platoon out over a distance equivalent to two and a half football fields.

A half hour went by, then an hour. We were making good time, and we relaxed a little. From my position third from the rear of the column, I couldn't see what happened. But I heard it plainly.

The sound of an automatic weapon startled us, almost certainly a VC machine gun because it didn't make the familiar popping noise of an M-16 or the telltale metallic chinking sound of ammo belts churning through an M-60 machine gun. After a few seconds, I heard a single M-16 returning fire. The weak response was undoubtedly because our increased spread between men left relatively few people positioned close enough to shoot back.

Kenny, my RTO, was frantically trying to raise the front of the platoon on his radio, but not getting any answer. And ahead of me as far as I could see to a point where the stream made a curve out of sight were GIs down in the water making an effort to become part of the streambed.

The gunfire couldn't have lasted more than 30 seconds, and was followed by an creepy stillness. I had absolutely no idea what to do. I hunkered there in the shallow water behind a pitifully small rock considering my options. It was obvious that nobody in front of me was in any hurry to jump up and either confirm the fight was over or participate in it. They were quite content to stay in the stream and keep their heads down. With no answer to Kenny's radio calls, there was no way to know what condition the front of the platoon might be in. Unless somebody went up there.

So I went. I didn't really think about it. By rights, I should have sent someone else. If the platoon leader was down—and his RTO's failure to respond to Kenny was ominous—I technically had no business unnecessarily exposing the next in command. Me. But I hadn't learned to think that way. What I was thinking instead was that I had no right to ask anyone else to do something I wouldn't be willing to do myself.

And for me it was really a question of needing to do something. Couldn't just indefinitely lie there in the stream watching twigs float by, and couldn't really make any decisions about what to do next without knowing the status at the front of the platoon. I didn't feel comfortable about starting a flanking action, because others at the front might have moved laterally into the bush and a flanking effort by the back of the platoon could result in us shooting at each other.

It was a long walk to the front of the platoon, and I was the only one standing. My M-16 was on automatic and I had a round chambered. I kept expecting the walls of the jungle on both sides of the stream to erupt in fire, all targeted neatly on my sorry young ass. As I worked my way up the line of grunts in the water, I got a lot of upward looks that clearly questioned my sanity.

Considering how vulnerable the platoon had been in the open stream, the damage I found when I reached the front of the column was not nearly as bad as I had feared. Rydell, the point man (not Doc on this day) had a flesh wound in his thigh. The bullet had furrowed its way across the front of his leg, gouging out about an inch of flesh. The lieutenant's RTO had damaged his radio when he dove for cover, explaining why Kenny and I couldn't make contact right after the firefight. Finally, Lieutenant Warren had taken a round in the heel of his right boot.

The rest of the point squad had set up defensively on the right side of the stream, facing in the direction from which the shots had come. No sign of bad guys, and it was quiet. Lieutenant Warren had his boot off, and was massaging his leg. The bullet had barely grooved the skin of his heel, but the impact of the high velocity round had traumatized his entire leg, leaving it numb and useless. When I saw him down, I hurried over and asked him how he was. I called him "Tom", and I think it was the only time I ever addressed him by other than "Sir" or "Lieutenant Warren" or "El-tee". Somehow, all that rank crap doesn't mean so much when a guy is shot.

He was shaking his head, amazed a bullet that had inflicted a relatively minor wound could have so completely incapacitated his leg. "Goddamn it, Jennings. The fucking thing felt like a baseball bat hit me. I thought my foot was blown off! I can't feel shit in my leg."

Doc had crawled up and was tearing open a pressure bandage to put on Rydell's thigh. The lieutenant's RTO was hiding behind a rock, fussing with his radio, trying to get it to work. The balance of the front squad was on high alert, but staying low. None of them were terribly interested in adding to Doc's patient load.

The ambush had come from a branch in the stream, a stagnant channel that took a perpendicular heading to the right from the main streambed and abruptly ended about a hundred yards away where the jungle closed back in on it. I knew we had to take a look, to make sure that Chuck had departed, so I gestured to Ortiz, the point man's backup. He put on a great show of reluctance, but got up and joined me as I started wading down the channel. We sloshed through the muck ever so slowly, scanning the tangle of growth that came right up to the water on both sides and in front of us, peering intently into the shadowy mass for any sign of movement.

The round went right by my ear. It made a cracking sound, like a dry stick breaking.

I don't know that I can describe what I felt. The bullet was meant for me. It was supposed to have smacked into my head, an event that would have left me seriously dead. This war was suddenly very personal. Someone had fired a weapon at me, not at some other guy, but *me*!

I felt fear. Honest to God, gut-clamping, take-a-leak-down-your-leg fear. But I felt something else as well. I was angry. There is nothing quite so rage-inducing as the realization that another person is trying to inflict major harm to you. As irrational as the thought might have been, I was stupidly astonished that somebody was shooting at me and I hadn't even done anything to him. What the fuck are you shooting at me for, you little slant-eyed cocksucker! You don't even know me!

All those thoughts rushed through my head in the half second or so it took to plunge forward on my face in the murky water. All the way down I was pumping out bullets on automatic fire. I didn't even feel my finger clamped on the trigger. I was dimly aware of Ortiz next to me, cranking out rounds, too. I went through a magazine in nothing flat, slapped home a full one, and started squeezing off aimed bursts toward the vine-choked bank at the end of the channel, from where I believed the shot at my head had come.

I could hear Lt. Warren barking angrily at Buzz Gallagher and the lead squad. Thankfully, some of those other grunts in the front were getting off their butts and joining Ortiz and me in returning fire. We formed a ragged skirmish line in the channel, and laid down a heavy wall of fire toward the ambush point. Patterson was grinding a long belt of ammo through his pig, and the wall of vegetation at the channel's end was shredding into salad as the bullets ripped into it. After a minute of deafening gunfire, it didn't appear that anybody was shooting back at us and I called out to cease fire.

We gingerly approached the end of the channel, climbed the bank out of the slimy water, and found...nothing. Some shell casings were on the ground, but nothing else. Not even a hint of blood to let us know we had hit anyone. The ambushers faded back into the jungle like phantoms, leaving us angry and frustrated, and pumped full of adrenaline. Come back and fight, you chickenshit gook!

I was no longer a virgin. I had just qualified for a CIB, the Combat Infantryman's Badge. That's the blue and silver medal that looks like a rifle with a wreath around it. The CIB is awarded to troops in a combat zone who come under hostile fire, and was the most obvious symbol that its wearer had been to Vietnam. At that moment, I wasn't at all sure I wanted one very much.

Once we were reasonably confident the area was secure and the bad guys were done sniping at us for a while, I had Kenny call for a dust-off. Neither of the casualties was in any condition to continue on with the platoon, and Rydell the point man was going to need stitches to close up the groove in his leg.

Unfortunately, the jungle was so thick that there wasn't any hope of finding a clearing anywhere close to land a helicopter. When we heard the dust-off approaching, I popped smoke in the stream to give the pilot an idea where, under the thick canopy, we were located. It always surprised me to see how much colored smoke poured out of those canisters—they made a heck of a cloud.

Once the medevac pilot spotted the tendrils of red smoke drifting up through the canopy over the narrow slit that was our stream, he hovered above us and lowered a jungle extractor—a long cable with a canvas seat dangling from it.

One at a time, and achingly slowly, the two wounded men were pulled up to the hovering dust-off. My admiration for these chopper guys went up another notch. Nothing made a better target than a helicopter hanging motionless just above the trees. If Charlie hadn't disappeared after chewing on us he could have knocked down a Huey with very little effort. The whole operation dragged along in slow motion.

Once the medevac finally finished loading our damaged goods, it tipped forward for momentum and climbed out for the trip back to LZ Professional. It suddenly dawned on me, as we picked up our scattered gear and prepared to move out again, that I was now acting platoon leader. Trust me, I had no surging feelings of power or accomplishment. I really didn't want the job.

It was yet again a situation that didn't offer any choice. We were out there in the jungle, I was the ranking guy, and there was no resource from which a new lieutenant was going to magically appear. So I started doing the things it seemed I should be doing. I got on Kenny's radio to call the company commander with a sitrep on the ambush and change of command of his 2nd platoon. It was also time to be getting the hell out of the stream. There were only a few hours of daylight left and not enough time to link up with the rest of the company, so the captain ordered me to take the platoon south and find a suitable night laager at dusk.

After an hour or so, the jungle began to thin out and I could see we were walking through a low area between two parallel ridgelines. It wasn't really a valley, but the terrain made it feel like one. Ahead of us, the bottomland was grassy, more open than the dense jungle behind us. Sometimes grassy bottomland was an indication of nearby rice paddies.

Purely on a whim, I decided to change our course 90 degrees and take the column up to the ridgeline on our left. We might get a better look around, see whether there were paddies and/or people nearby, and possibly spot some high ground to spend the night. At worst, it might keep us from slogging through wet lowlands.

We were halfway up the side of the ridge when 105 artillery rounds started slamming into the grassy field toward which we had been walking only minutes before. We hit the ground and watched in astonishment as four, five, six HE (high explosive) rounds smashed into the ground between two and three hundred yards away, throwing chunks of dirt and grass and shrapnel into the air with deafening explosions. The ripping "karrump" sound of the detonating shells left our ears ringing.

I remembered Mike Keene's story about friendly fire. My sentiment at that moment was about equally divided between blowing a gasket and shitting a brick. That was American artillery, and it was landing exactly where my platoon would have been! How in hell was this happening? We hadn't called for any artillery; I wasn't even *thinking* about artillery! If we hadn't changed course, we would have been hamburger.

The sheer scale of wartime operations and the risk of accidentally exposing U.S. forces to our own fire demanded incredible attention to the position and movement of constantly shifting military assets. It was vital to keep close track of every unit, particularly those on the ground in combat AOs. Each commander of a ground unit had to report at regular intervals his unit's location, coded in shackle to keep Charlie from figuring out where we were. We used a date-sensitive codebook, which was fairly straightforward as long as you knew the correct date. And knowing the date was rarely a problem in Vietnam, where GIs marked off every completed day of their tours. The RTO would raise battalion headquarters on his PRC-25, find the right page in the shackle book, and announce his intent with "I shackle" followed by phonetically pronounced numbers and letters. It sounded like meaningless mumbo-jumbo, something like "I shackle whiskey zulu sierra seven niner niner echo." Similarly, any call for helicopter support was shackled to avoid tipping our hand and giving the VC a target.

Kenny and I had been dutifully sending in our coded locations since Lt. Warren got hauled up in the medevac. Anyone looking at our reported line of march couldn't have missed that we were dangerously close to the impact point of that ill-thought fire mission. When the 105s finally quit falling and we cautiously lifted our heads again, I took the handset to the radio and began indelicately telling the firebase what I thought about our little barrage. I was most definitely violating radio discipline, but at that moment I didn't give a rat's ass who heard me. I wanted someone to know that American artillery had narrowly missed waxing us, and that our last reported position made it unthinkable for rounds to be landing there. "And what dimwitted needledick OK'd the goddamn fire mission anyway?"

I didn't get a satisfactory answer, just an admonishment about radio procedure. Battalion HQ speculated that the shells might have been intended for another impact point and dropped short or long. Not terribly comforting. But I was mildly thankful that we wouldn't be back on LZ Professional for a while. I had visions of some of the guys in the platoon stopping by the 105 batteries to express how much they appreciated the close artillery support.

Incredibly, that wasn't to be the end of our turn as targets for the gun bunnies. We continued along the ridgeline to the south for another half hour, until it widened into an ideal high point to spend the night. It was the first time I was completely responsible for the night laager, so I meticulously (I was probably a pain in the butt to the other guys) set out six perimeter locations and a center command location. It normally was a routine activity, but what the heck, it was my first time. Usually the lieutenant did it.

The claymores were set out, we ate some C-rations, smoked a last butt, spread out poncho liners, and settled in for the night. It had been a long day, and we were even more worn out than usual.

Watch was rotated among the guys at each position, so that someone would be awake at all times. Most guys liked first watch; it was a lot easier than being awakened in the middle of the night. I didn't mind last watch, although many didn't care for it. On last watch, as the night began to give way to the morning, Charlie sometimes used the confusing first light for assaults on sleep-groggy GIs.

Long before the sun makes its appearance, the night starts fading from black to steadily lighter shades of gray. Shadows play in the almost-night, and straining eyes feed fertile imaginations with vaguely threatening images. For a brief time just before the sun approaches the horizon, the night takes on a glow and the jungle landscape borders on surreal.

In some ways I enjoyed those early moments of the day. The

first tentative rays of sun sometimes painted the countryside in pastels. If our night laager had enough elevation to not be closed in by jungle, I was often treated to really spectacular sunrises. That was reason enough to stand last watch, and I probably had the last one as often as anyone.

I thought it must have been 4:00 or so and time for my watch when I felt myself being shaken awake. But it wasn't 4:00, it was midnight. Kenny was waking me, incredulous that I hadn't been jarred out of sleep by an artillery round that had just landed maybe 200 yards outside of our perimeter and that had the rest of my platoon awake and buzzing. I was so tired, I hadn't even heard it.

Twice in one day! As disoriented as I was, it took awhile to sink in that we had once again been entirely too close to the impact point of friendly fire. My guys were grumbling about which side was the more dangerous enemy. Still, I wasn't inspired sufficiently to repeat my radio apoplexy of the artillery episode earlier in the day—I couldn't even manage a little fury. So I told Kenny to call it in and I went back to sleep. I just couldn't stay very intense about anything for very long out there, even our own people shooting at us.

I never did hear a reasonable explanation for the half dozen rounds we narrowly avoided in the afternoon, but we were told that the shell outside our night laager resulted from a short round aimed toward another, more distant, fire mission. A short round was a shell that wasn't prepared with the correct powder charge, making it drop short of its intended target. I knew that it happened from time to time, but knowing it didn't make any of us feel a whole lot happier.

Mike was right. You really were on your own out here.

Chapter Nine

One of the defining realities of the Vietnam War—perhaps of most wars—was the unabashed and often transparent ambition of field commanders. Career officers, many stuck in the same rank for some time, saw an opportunity to earn promotions by pandering to the senior staff's eagerness for body counts and narrowly (but imaginatively) defined "victories". I don't mean to suggest this was universally true, but there were more than a few lieutenant colonel battalion commanders eager to win their birds—promotion to full colonel. Advancement much beyond lieutenant colonel was difficult for Army officers during peacetime, so the war offered a unique chance for career enhancement. A tour in Vietnam could get an otherwise stagnant career moving again. As you might imagine, some commanders cared a whole lot more about that next promotion than they did about their troops.

It was usually apparent to us field grunts when the brass up at brigade headquarters was planning some kind of major operation. In addition to the scoop in a very effective rumor mill, we could see signs of the more opportunistic battalion commanders pushing hard to maximize headcounts of combat-ready troops. The theory was that brigade would "award" a difficult operation to the battalion that could field the most GIs. Anyone with a working trigger finger back in the trains area was at risk. Orders went out to round up the sick, lame and lazy and get them assigned out to a rifle company. It was as though the various commanders were competing to show the highest state of combat readiness, so that brigade honchos would recognize their military leadership skill with the plum assignment.

There was a place in the 196th Brigade's AO about 23 miles west from Tam Ky called Hau Duc. We called it Dragon Valley. Every so often, some brilliant strategist at brigade, or even clear up at Americal headquarters, would decide that we needed to conduct an operation in Dragon Valley. And then some lucky battalion commander would get the call.

The place had no evident tactical value, to us anyway, and wasn't generally known as a VC stronghold or a staging area for NVA. But bad guys were sometimes spotted there, and by fate or coincidence, it was always our luck to find some eager to take us on. And almost every time one of our units went there, we got our butts kicked. I had the pleasure of visiting Dragon Valley twice, and they were both memorable trips.

When the battalion brass planned the operation that led to my first incursion to this fabled valley, the three rifle companies not on LZ Professional were scattered widely through the AO. The best way to quickly get separated units together in a distant place at the same time (hopefully allowing minimal reaction time for the enemy) was a helicopter insertion—an eagle flight.

My platoon was in a company-sized night laager the night before the eagle flight. Lieutenant Warren was back with a new pair of boots to go with his mended foot and Purple Heart. He had also been unexpectedly promoted to 1st lieutenant. I had a wry thought that getting shot might not be all that harmful to a career. Shortly after dusk, he was called to a briefing with the company commander. When he returned, he sat down with me and the squad leaders—Chief, Buzz, and Dee. About all we knew was that three companies were being airlifted into Dragon Valley the next morning, one company at a time, using some twenty slicks with Cobra air support. It wasn't known whether we could expect a hot LZ; reconnaissance had been inconclusive. If there were any specific objectives the brass had in mind, they were on a need-to-know basis for us. And we evidently didn't need to know. We were simply to go in and patrol—the ever-popular "search and destroy" mission.

I thought about the mock eagle flight training back at Fort Benning, and wondered if the coming day's adventure would be more orderly. I told myself it had to be—this was real combat and lives were now at stake. No margin for inept execution and chaos; this would have to be a skillful military operation.

Silly me. In years since those glorious days in the wonderful Republic of South Vietnam, I've learned more about how air assaults are actually supposed to be conducted. Usually some effort was made in the days preceding an eagle flight to obtain intelligence about the area to be assaulted. Overflights might be made looking for signs of enemy forces and likely resistance points—topographical features that would afford good fields of fire on the LZ (landing zone). Insertion planning would anticipate neutralizing those points, and each unit in the air assault would have an assigned sector to secure around the LZ. And each unit commander would have a mission objective, or at least a compass direction to head toward once the LZ was secured.

That kind of useful detail had somehow been overlooked in the air assault training we received at Fort Benning. Ignorance is bliss.

The combat units that regularly flew around in helicopters, like air cavalry and aero-rifle platoons, did indeed receive comprehensive training on how to conduct airborne attacks. It was evidently thought, however, that such subtle details would be lost on us common leg infantry soldiers who only rarely climbed aboard a Huey. The only piece of helpful information I recall getting as we prepared for the next day's insertion was to watch for green tracers around the LZ. The ammunition used by the bad guys in their automatic weapons mostly came from Communist China. Unlike the red tracers in our ammo, the tracers in Chicom bullets glowed green. It was one way to determine if the LZ was hot.

We moved out of the company night laager at first light to a flat, open area scouted the previous afternoon. The terrain was low and grassy, almost marsh, and the jungle opened up nicely for Hueys to land. We spread out, little knots of restless GIs waiting for the helicopters.

The sound came first, followed quickly by the dots of

approaching slicks. As they closed with us, the sky looked to be full of them and the rotor noise overwhelmed all but the loudest shouting. I had never seen that many helicopters flying together—it was a remarkable sight. As they drifted down for a brief touch on the ground, the small bunches of five or six guys waiting in the grass jumped on each one and grabbed for handholds. The big rotors bit into the air, the Hueys leaned forward, and we were off and flying toward Dragon Valley.

I had no idea how long or short a trip it would be. Some of my guys were looking out the open door, watching the ground flash by below and the other slicks flying close by on either side. A few of them were watching me, maybe with the curious notion that I had some idea of what was going to happen. I assumed that when we arrived at our destination the Huey crew would give us some indication of whether the LZ was hot. And I also assumed that somebody would tell us where the hell we were going when we hit the ground.

Have you ever heard the expression, "Assumption is the mother of all fuck-ups"?

We had been flying less than ten minutes when I saw a pair of Cobra gunships ahead of us, strafing treelines on both sides of a grassy clearing very similar to the one where our trip began. The Cobra was truly a mean machine—even the look of it was intimidating. It was a narrow helicopter, barely wide enough for the pilot's shoulders, and its shape vaguely resembled a shark. It carried a two-man crew. The turret gunner sat in the front seat and the pilot sat in the back seat, responsible for the rack munitions as well as flying the bird. These Cobras were equipped with miniguns and M-5 kits, which were sort of automatic repeating versions of M-79 grenade launchers. With the rotor racket and turbine whine of the slicks, I couldn't hear firing from the Cobras. But it was clear they were blasting the heck out of both treelines.

It was also clear we were to be set down in the wet, grassy clearing. I leaned forward to yell into the ear of the warrant officer copilot and asked if the LZ was hot. He shrugged his shoulders. I thought, thanks for nothing. Then the two door gunners opened up with their M-60 machine guns in a back and forth strafing pattern, slicing at the jungle's edge. The gunfire was barely audible over the helicopter noise, but the live fire was more than a little unnerving. I watched the tracers float down toward the trees, arching slightly downward as they lost velocity. Then the slicks dropped to roughly four feet off the ground and flared, the crew chief hollered at us to get the hell off, and we jumped out.

And there we stood, right in the middle of this painfully open marshy field, looking around at other small groups of GIs who were similarly standing there looking around for some hint of what to do next. If it weren't so scary, it would have been comical. "Please Mr. Custer, I don't wanna go!"

The din was incredible. There were the straining chopper turbines and crackling door guns of the departing Hueys, the angry buzzing of the Cobras' miniguns and the "phoomp, phoomp, phoomp—boom, boom, boom" of the grenades being spit out of the M-5 kits. The sound of gunfire was everywhere, and it was absolutely impossible to sort out where it all was coming from. There might have been a regiment of NVA regulars in the trees shooting at us, or just as likely not even one single bad guy. We had no way of knowing, and the fear was all the greater for the uncertainty.

I stood rooted in one spot for what seemed like an eternity, painfully exposed, not sure which way to go and unable to spot Lieutenant Warren or the company CO. In reality it was probably less than five seconds before I told myself "screw this" and lit out for the nearest cover. When I moved, the guys in my load and the two chopper loads nearest to me moved as well, like they had been waiting to see someone act like he knew what he was doing. There we were, 16 guys slogging as fast as the muck would allow toward the closest line of trees at the edge of the clearing. I guess the others figured sergeants were supposed to know what to do. (What a silly concept!) We opened up with our M-16s as we ran, despite not seeing any opposition. Putting out suppressing fire supposedly encourages the bad guys to keep their heads down, which presumably makes it more difficult for them to shoot back at us. And I was powerfully motivated to do <u>anything</u> that would keep people from shooting at me.

It took forever to get to the trees, even running as hard as we could. We flopped down behind the first available cover. Not yet ready to believe the jungle was empty of VC and still not sure where the company was heading, I preferred prone over upright a whole lot. Kenny was yelling in the radio handset, asking whether anybody had an interest in letting us know what the hell we were supposed to be doing. Grunts on either side of me were shooting into the jungle. The noise around us was still deafening, and the chaos was tangible.

Suddenly a Cobra flashed overhead, it's minigun ripping. Now there is one characteristic of miniguns that I neglected to describe in all the weapons info I mentioned before. Just as they put out an almost unbelievable amount of lead, they spit out an equal amount of brass—the empty shell casings. So this sleek killing machine was roaring directly over us, the chainsaw noise from the minigun earsplitting, and the brass was falling straight down. On us.

The buzz was ringing in my ears as I felt the dozens of hits on my back and legs from the hot brass. I absolutely knew I was shot. It was a certainty. In seconds, there would be pain. With as many hits as I had felt, I was sure I was a dead man.

I lived with those thoughts for maybe two or three seconds before my brain started working again, sorting out the sensory data and recognizing that I had only been strafed by falling brass and not by bullets. But the experience was as terrifying as anything I ever went through. The line between perception and reality is thin; the mind believes what it thinks is real. I was convinced, however briefly, that I was going to die.

Then the Cobra was gone, slashing the trees with grenades and minigun bullets as it moved away. I was not dead, just covered with spent brass. I felt really foolish, but a quick look around gave the sense that others had experienced a similarly disconcerting moment. Anyway, there was still the little matter of an assault going on...of something, or someone, who might be somewhere. We crawled further out of the marsh and into the comparatively sheltered trees. And found nothing.

In time the confusion subsided, the noise abated, and the other waves of the eagle flight arrived with the other two companies. If it had been a hot LZ, and I'm not sure anyone truly knew, Charlie had long since departed. My guys were all intact, and there was no radio chatter about casualties, so it was a fair bet the LZ had been cold (not counting all the rounds burned off by the good guys). All of our firepower was basically for insurance, which wasn't such a bad thing when you thought about it.

You wouldn't have believed it was a routine, uncontested eagle flight by the way we felt. We had fought a battle, even without an enemy. As Doc remarked, "I feel like I've been rode hard and put away wet". A little knowledge from the poobahs about what we were doing would have gone a long way to minimize the unnecessary wear and tear on our emotions.

The scrambled and separated pieces of the three companies milled around and eventually linked up at various points around the LZ. By the time all of this was completed and companies were reunited, it was well into the afternoon. Then the three companies set off in different directions with orders to conduct search and destroy patrols at various coordinates in Dragon Valley. Bravo Company headed northwest, deeper into the valley, looking for a night defensive position as dusk approached.

I never much cared for company-sized operations, except for the added security that came from a greater number of warm bodies. Most company commanders adopted the same single-file troop movement used for platoon and squad patrols. This could easily involve spreading a hundred plus men over an area as much as a kilometer. If the front of the column got into a jam, the rear of the column was ill positioned to be much help. And the disarray that accompanied first contact in most firefights kept the commanders busy figuring out how and where to return fire, meaning they typically didn't get on their radios right away to let the trailing platoons know what was happening. So the folks in the rear got down real low and tried to imagine what might be occurring up front.

And sure enough, the next morning we packed up the claymores, rolled up the poncho liners, and headed out in a single-file column. Second platoon was last in the column of the company's three platoons. As platoon sergeant, I was at the rear of my platoon, which made me the third guy from the last in the whole freaking strung-out line.

I wouldn't call our route a trail exactly, but it was enough of a pathway to suggest that others had used it. Just like with streams and rivers, using established corridors was something of a trade-off; improved speed of travel versus increased vulnerability.

During the early years of the war, GIs and ARVN (South Vietnamese) troops had used trails with impunity. Sometimes, American units found themselves on the same trails used by VC, on rare occasions at the same time. Later in the war it was considered crazy for anyone to use a trail. They were obvious sites for ambushes, and they were all too often booby trapped with tripwires connected to explosives, or buried land mines, or holes dug in the ground with sharpened bamboo punji stakes set in the bottom and camouflaged by mats of leaves and sticks.

Our company commander was a bright guy, and understood the risks of walking established trails. It seemed to me that he was intentionally tweaking Charlie's nose, asking for contact.

Sometime around mid-morning it hit the fan. There was an explosion, like a grenade, followed by several rifles and at least one machine gun. The bad guys had set up an ambush and lobbed an M-79 grenade into our column. Yes, the VC had U.S. grenade launchers, taken off dead GIs. I learned later that the round had grazed and bounced off the shoulder of the third man in the column and detonated right behind him—full into the chest of the fourth man. The shrapnel spray had found two others close enough to take hits, including a minor wound for the platoon leader, but the man who had taken the brunt of the blast was hurting real bad.

It was incredibly frustrating to be close, hearing but not seeing. Those of us at the rear followed the play of events by the sounds, as nobody was making sense on the radio. We could hear M-16s returning fire, and then an M-60 was moved up and began firing. That slowed the rate of fire from the bad guys, and at last the radio traffic began to sound like the people at the front were getting organized.

The ground to our right at the rear of the column sloped uphill to a ridge, and I was a little nervous that we could be exposed to perpendicular fire from the ridgeline. I set the trailing squad of 2nd platoon in a defensive position, keeping watch up the hill for any movement.

Just as I finished, Lt. Warren got a call from the CO to have a squad from 2nd platoon try to flank the enemy position. From the sounds of the firefight, we had a rough idea that the bad guys were to the front and left of the lead platoon, so Lt. Warren radioed back to me at the rear to take our middle squad into the bush on the left. Strangely, it wasn't a scary prospect, being asked to sneak up on an enemy position. By then we had learned how bad our casualties were, and maybe we were hoping to catch Charlie unawares and do a little payback. As we moved into the jungle, it was vaguely reminiscent of creeping through the woods back at Fort Polk. Once more, I felt like the whole scene was steeped in unreality.

Nine of us crept through the dense tangle for about ten minutes, slanting away from our stalled column toward the periodic bursts of automatic weapons fire we could hear in front of us. A regular gun battle was raging ahead and to our right. The lead platoon finally had both their pigs up front and strafing the area where they had taken fire, and the machine guns helped dampen the rate of fire from the ambushing gooks. Still, Charlie was doing a decent job of popping caps right back at them. Every time the VC squeezed off a burst, my group instinctively dove for the ground even though it was probable that they hadn't yet detected us and weren't directing fire at us.

We never got all the way to the bad guys. After we had maneuvered a few hundred meters, my RTO got a call for me advising we were to return to the column. Didn't say why, but I was an obedient soldier and so back we went. Typical Army. Go here. No, go there instead. No, let's just have you stand in line and wait awhile.

It turned out that the reason for the captain's change of tactics was his unexpected success in getting air cover. There was a CAS—close air support—flight nearby (I never did see the jets because the jungle canopy was too thick), and they were closing on our ambushers. With the big stuff en route, I surely didn't have any quarrel with breaking off the flanking effort and getting my people out of bomb range.

We barely made it back to the column when we heard the Phantoms coming in. When the air is hot and humid, as it invariably was in Vietnam, the noise from a screaming jet engine sounds a lot like heavy canvas being ripped. It's a frightful sound and carries for miles, rolling on the wet air like grotesquely twisted thunder. And, I learned then that the ground really does shake when high explosive bombs hit close by. I recall thinking I was glad we had air superiority in Vietnam. I would not have enjoyed it at all if those things were falling on me.

The pair of Phantoms made three passes in all; two with what were probably 500-pound bombs and one with napalm. The lead platoon put smoke out in front of their position, and gave distance and bearing to the enemy element. The bombs were ferocious—we could hear shrapnel whistling and trees cracking from the explosions. But, oh the napalm. The guys at the front actually cheered when the napalm blew. Toasted Charlie.

After the jets left, Bravo Company still had to determine if there were any hostiles hanging around and still alive. Incoming fire had stopped when the first bombs went off, but that didn't necessarily mean it was all over. There was the added little problem of getting our wounded out and back to a hospital. By this time the captain's RTO had a dust-off on the way, and it showed up with a Cobra in support. It wasn't at all clear whether the bad guys were gone. What was left of the lead squad was gingerly probing toward the bombs' impact point, but they were moving very slowly. So the dust-off was understandably cautious, too.

The point squad was uneasily dodging between the shallow bunkers the VC had used to ambush us. The GIs would edge in toward a hole and get close enough to toss a frag, then dash up quickly to check for any gooks that might still be moving. Concurrently, the middle platoon of the column had located a small clearing off to their right and marked it with smoke for the approaching medevac helicopter.

The man who had taken the M-79 grenade was a mess, out cold and in shock, his chest dotted with tiny bloodless holes where the shrapnel had penetrated. Other less serious wounded were waiting near him for the chopper, all wide-eyed as they watched their unconscious buddy. The RTO was agitated; he knew how bad the M-79 casualty was hurt and was practically begging the dust-off to land.

Reluctantly, the medevac started a landing pass toward the clearing. At the last moment, something spooked the pilot and he broke off the landing, slamming his cyclic forward to stand the Huey on its nose for forward velocity. The RTO was beside himself, yelling into his handset for the chopper to land. There didn't appear to be any incoming fire, but it was hard to tell with all the racket from the rotors and the periodic grenade explosions from the guys at the VC bunkers.

Kenny and I were listening to this drama unfold on our own radio, a few hundred yards away. Suddenly, a new voice came on the radio, calm and deep, with a southern drawl. "This is Blue Ghost." It was the Cobra, talking to the medevac pilot. "Looks to me like the LZ is okay, and there's a kid down there dyin'. You had a couple tries at it, now I want to see you put it down...or I'll have to help you down."

I'm not kidding. That's what the Cobra jockey said. And the dust-off went in so hard and fast it bounced on its skids. The wounded were loaded on board, the Huey powered up for a take-off, and then both choppers were gone.

Bravo Company stayed around the ambush site patrolling for dead or hiding VC for the next hour. The people scouting out front found the bodies of three gooks who had probably been caught in the open when the napalm hit. They were badly burned by the jelly and almost unrecognizable as formerly human. One of them was facedown, his uniform and most of the flesh on his back and legs burned away. His leg bones were visible. It was a little unsettling to note the remains of a uniform, because VC didn't have uniforms.

A little further back were a series of hastily dug shallow bunkers from which the ambush had initially come. There were two bodies in one of the bunkers, and a single body in another. The rest were empty, likely an indication that the other bad guys got away. All three of the bodies in the bunkers had been killed either by our fire or the explosions from the CAS bombs. They wore the uniforms of NVA regulars, not the black pajamas of Viet Cong farmer-fighters. That was very sobering. Most contacts in the battalion AO had lately been with VC. Running into a North Vietnamese Army unit could mean that a larger force was in the area, undoubtedly better trained and equipped than most rag-tag Cong outfits.

And we had only been in Dragon Valley one day.

Chapter Ten

Night was coming. We needed to find a reasonably secure place to set up a company-sized night defensive position. With the discovery that NVA forces were in our vicinity, most of us were a tad uneasy and everyone was being a lot more vigilant.

Because Dragon Valley truly was a valley, with distant high ridges on both sides, there was quite a bit of high ground from which to choose. One hill looked especially promising to Bravo Company's nervous cadre. It was fairly uniform, with a rounded top sufficiently large to accommodate 100 or so men without forcing us to bunch up too closely. The top was smooth enough to provide sweeping killing zones for the claymores, and it was easy to set up interlocking fire from adjacent defensive positions. And it was about the highest point around, meaning it was a little less vulnerable to mortar or RPG attacks from a higher hill.

It had been a long day and grunts on watch found it more difficult than usual to stay awake and alert. I had done a shift around midnight and had returned to a deep sleep when I felt someone kicking me back to consciousness. I shook my head to clear the cobwebs, and suddenly realized that the whole company was quietly stirring (okay, as quiet as a company can be). Seems that two perimeter positions had reported to the headquarters position that they heard something further down the hill, so the CO had ordered a "Mad Minute".

I've read a lot about Vietnam over the years and don't recall ever seeing a reference to a Mad Minute, so let me tell you about it. Basically, everyone in the company opens up in unison with everything they have. The idea was that if Charlie was stupid enough or unlucky enough to have his ass hanging out while sneaking up the hill, we might surprise him with some very serious hurt. Or, the intimidation of that much firepower might scare the crap out of anyone even thinking about beginning a climb up our little redoubt, and could possibly persuade them that a hill assault would be better postponed for another day.

The signal to start the Mad Minute was to be an M-79 firing a white phosphorous grenade. The "floop" of the round leaving the barrel was all we needed to hear—didn't even wait for the blinding white flash of the willie peter explosion—and all hell broke loose.

The firepower of an American rifle company really was an impressive thing to see. M-16s raked the slopes with automatic fire. M-60 machine guns flung evil-looking red tracer streaks all around the hillside. Hand grenades went arching down the hill, blasting away big chunks of earth along with everybody's night vision. M-79s pumped out their explosive missiles, which tore up the approaches all the way to the bottom. Some moron even fired off a LAW, undoubtedly because he was tired of humping it through the jungle and this was a convenient way to lighten his load.

And then it was over.

The quiet following such ear-pounding din was unnatural. Couldn't hear a thing, except some ringing in my ears and commanders yelling "Cease fire!" at the diehards who wanted to crank off another few rounds. No night sounds, no insects, no return fire from an imaginary horde—nothing. The night felt close, like the inside of a tomb.

Whether or not there had been enemy soldiers down there, the effect of a Mad Minute was a rush. People were pumped up and convinced that *somebody* was there. Needless to say, it's not prudent to go snooping down the hill for a look-see while it's still the middle of the night. Not many of us slept for the balance of the night. Guys on watch shifts had lots of company.

In the morning a squad patrolled around the base of the hill. They actually found a body, and it was wearing an NVA uniform. He had been practically cut in half by a traversing machine gun. Just one gook, and no other indication of how large or small an enemy force there might have been, or whether the violent spewing of so much ammo from our night laager had dissuaded a bunch of them from paying us a visit in the dark. I'll always believe it made the difference. It sure made a difference to at least one NVA soldier.

It was the morning of our second full day in Dragon Valley. The captain decided to split Bravo Company into platoons to make our sweep cover a wider area. All three platoons were to head generally northwest, but we would be operating with roughly a klick of separation between each platoon. Since a kilometer is just over six tenths of a mile, we would be far enough apart that we wouldn't be likely to shoot each other, but close enough to help out if needed.

Second platoon moved out of the night laager. Lieutenant Warren was third from the front behind the point man and his backup, and I had the rear. We were the element furthest to the right, and consequently responsible not only for the terrain ahead but also the right flank of the dispersed company. The captain and the three platoon leaders spent much of their time during the day on the radio to make sure position updates were current and that we didn't run into each other, setting off an all-American firefight. Or get any unwanted artillery party favors dumped our way from good old gun bunnies on some distant firebase.

The day was hot, and draining, and uneventful. We plodded at a crawl down the valley, our pace slowed both by the undergrowth and the residual caution sparked by the events of the day and night before. There was really no effort at silence. Charlie knew we were here, and we knew that he knew.

Hours went by. We were on edge expecting at any moment to run into another ambush. Sweat was pouring off us in the stifling heat, and our uniforms were soaked. At midday we broke for chow, the column moving off to both sides of our line of travel to produce a temporary elliptical perimeter. The break was a welcome relief, but most of us were too wrung out by the relentless heat to eat anything. I nursed on a canteen and smoked a butt.

After a half hour or so, Lieutenant Warren passed the word to saddle up and we groggily lurched back into a patrol column. The feeling of anticipation was almost palpable; it was as though everyone in the platoon knew with certainty that Chuck was up ahead waiting for us. And, like dumb sheep, we kept shuffling toward our fate.

Sure enough, it finally came about an hour after our break. Doc was walking point, and I heard the sound of an AK-47 open up. (There is a marked difference between the report of an AK and anything else we carried.) The reports I heard were Doc, getting in the first punch. The bad guys had set up an ambush all right, but our foxy medic had spotted something in a tree before they could spring it on us.

Lieutenant Warren had purposely kept one of the pigs well forward, and in seconds Costellano's machine gun had joined Doc in pouring out a withering wall of lead. Looking back, I think the M-60 might have been the most important infantry weapon of the war. It certainly had a penchant for taking the enthusiasm out of anyone downrange from it. A pig weighed in at 24 pounds, which is why the big guys in an outfit always wound up as machine gunners. It put out fire at a devastating 550 rounds per minute, and had an effective range of 800 meters. It was best used in bursts of seven to ten rounds—long periods of sustained fire overheated the barrel—and the characteristic sound it made was well known to both friend and foe. One soldier with an M-60 machine gun who knew what he was doing was the equal of any rifle squad, and then some.

It really kicked ass.

Costellano and most other machine gunners carried their pigs at port arms when contact seemed likely, with a belt of 50 to 100 rounds loaded and ready. The gooks never had a chance to get their ambush cranked up. Seconds after the first gunshots, Kenny got a call from the front of the column directing me to wheel the back of the platoon left and forward to increase the firepower we were putting on line. By the time we were in position, though, it was almost over. A few desultory rounds continued to come from a stand of bamboo in front of us, so

Chief told his grenadier to drop a couple of M-79 rounds into the bamboo. Two HE explosions, a few stalks of knocked-down bamboo, and the incoming fire was silenced.

I made a quick check; nobody hurt. We took our time moving up to check the ambush site. The afternoon shadows were starting to lengthen by the time we had cleared the area and called in the four dead NVA we found. One of them was still in the bamboo, and had been ripped up pretty good by the M-79 grenade. Then I spotted a blood trail heading south, away from us, and we cautiously set out after the wounded bad guy.

For once, luck was with us. We found the last NVA soldier sprawled on his stomach only a hundred yards or so away. He was gone. Out of gas. Call in another body count. We were certainly doing our part for the war effort today, making our moms proud.

Because the captain wanted to keep his company split into platoons for at least another day, our next task was to put some distance between us and the dead NVA and then find a platoon-sized night laager. Daylight was fading, and we weren't keen on looking for a defensive position in the dark. That's when the radio lit up.

Since all the company radios were on the same frequency, my RTO and I heard the rather distressed call for assistance from 1st platoon. They were furthest on the left, perhaps two kilometers away. They had literally stumbled into a firefight with what they thought were five NVA regulars. Killed one, wounded and captured one, and the rest faded into the jungle. One GI was wounded, but not too seriously. That was good— the chances of a dust-off were growing less and less likely with the waning daylight.

What was causing the alarm, though, was the place all this happened. First platoon had discovered what looked to be an NVA training facility. Amazingly, our guys had surprised the five North Vietnamese when the column came out of the jungle into a cleared area occupied by two reasonably permanent oversize hootches. The clearing was well concealed, hard to spot from the air and not terribly obvious to any but the most attentive patrols passing near it. First platoon had found underground tunnels (which they hadn't yet explored), and enough supplies to establish that the place had regular use.

And then there was the Chicom 51-caliber machine gun they found.

When I heard that, I honestly felt the hair on my neck stand up. A 51-caliber machine gun was major weaponry to the NVA. Made in China (hence the term "Chicom"), it was a lot like our 50-caliber gun, and the gooks loved to use it to knock down helicopters. The thing was, that silly little caliber of difference between our 50 and the Chicom 51 translated into a tremendous difference in the length and weight of the rounds. This was a BIG machine gun, and the NVA was not going to take its loss very lightly.

That was why the 1st platoon was scared. They were worried that the bad guys who got away would come back with some of their pals and stage a counter-attack to get the gun back. So they wanted the other two platoons to join them and keep them company overnight in Charlie's pleasant little campground. And the captain, who was traveling with 3rd platoon (the middle element, roughly a klick closer to the anxious 1st platoon) agreed with their assessment. That meant it wasn't going to be an optional appearance for us.

By then it was practically dark. In the jungle, under the thick canopy, "dark" can be an absolute. It was a black, overpowering curtain that settled over you, gradually stealing your eyes until sight was gone altogether. If you have ever been in an underground place like Mammoth Cave when they turn the lights out, you know the kind of dark I'm talking about.

In order to reunite the three platoons, we had to do a night walk. Few things were hated by leg soldiers more than moving at night. Yeah, yeah, war movies always show GIs sneaking around at night, surprising bad guys as they suddenly appear out of the gloom with knives clenched in their teeth. It wasn't like that. Charlie owned the night. We, on the other hand, were blind men, groping our way through the thick foliage and the hated, clutching vines, each man holding for dear life to the rucksack of the GI in front of him. Although a few of the elite outfits—LRRPs and Rangers for example—were pretty good at night travel (and often had starlight scopes to aid them), regular rifle companies were notoriously inept. This was a real-life Escape and Evasion course, without the benefit of a Louisiana moonlit sky.

There was a very real risk that we might get a break in the column, which would hopelessly separate the platoon in the dark. We clung to each other, and walked full on into trees we couldn't see an inch in front of our faces. Vines knocked steel pots off heads, and wrapped painfully and unseen around necks. I felt thorns rake across my cheek, and the warm wetness of blood trickling down my face.

Because we were walking through rolling, uneven terrain, people were blindly stepping off drop-offs and sliding down muddy embankments. I had my hand on the back of the man in front of me, when he suddenly wasn't there anymore. He was somewhere below, sliding on his ass in the dark, loudly growling and cursing. I took another tentative step and went right down behind him, as did the guy behind me and the one after him, on and on, piling up at the bottom of the slope in an unhappy tangle of legs and guns and rucksacks.

My eyes were wide open, but they registered absolutely nothing. That night I gained an appreciation for the challenges blind people face every day of their lives. We were groping our way across some of the most inhospitable landscape on the planet, and we couldn't see shit.

The fate of the whole platoon was up to Lieutenant Warren. He was guiding our course through the snarled growth, following the faintly luminescent dial of his compass. He held the compass in one hand and hung on to the point man with the other, steering him to stay on course. It wasn't a good time to be on point—he was the first to kiss many of the trees in our path. The rest of us were simply along for the walk, wishing we were in the modestly more comfortable surroundings of a night laager.

It took us more than three hours to move the two

kilometers to the NVA training camp. Incredibly, we were successful in linking up at the site. The 3rd platoon, closer to the camp than we had been, had already arrived and the captain had set up a headquarters. The last few hundred meters of our approach were guided by radio from the site. They could hear us coming as we blindly busted and thrashed through the jungle, so we got course corrections as we fumbled about for our cohorts' location. As soon as we got there we were directed into positions to fill out the defensive perimeter, where we set out our claymores and prepared for an NVA attack that everyone hoped would not come.

It didn't come.

I think I may have slept about an hour during the night. The time stretched on forever, morning refusing to make an appearance to break the grip of total darkness. Night sounds were amplified, and the most harmless rustle of wind through leaves drew a quick response of turning heads and straining eyes, of rifle muzzles shifting toward the sound. GIs sat in defensive positions with their hands tightly wrapped around claymore firing mechanisms. Nobody smoked, which was unusual for an Army unit, even at night.

At last a dim light began filtering through the canopy, ending the longest night anyone could remember. The faint pre-dawn glow revealed a chilling outcome of our ill-advised night maneuvers. The perimeter, hastily set out in the dark, was appalling. There were huge gaps in some places and other positions that were practically right on top of each other. The position next to me actually had a claymore aimed at us, rather than outward. If there had been an attack and the claymore fired, all four of us in my position would have been toast.

As soon as it was light enough to move around, the CO sent two squads out to patrol the area around our perimeter. Poorly placed defensive positions were readjusted, in case Charles was still around and looking to get his 51-caliber gun back. Nobody had eaten since the middle of the previous day, so we took turns chowing down on some C-rations. I opened a can of cardboard crackers and plastic cheese. As I was picking a cracker out of the can, I glanced at my hands. They were so covered in filth and dried blood from the night walk I barely recognized them as my own. I kept eating anyway.

There were still the little details of 1st platoon's wounded man—who was stabilized but still needed evacuation—and the captured North Vietnamese. A chopper finally made it to our location, picking up both of them along with the NVA machine gun. The Huey didn't take any ground fire, which was a good sign that the bad guys hadn't stayed in the neighborhood to vent their displeasure over the appropriated weapon. It was just possible that the tactic had worked, that the presence of an entire company instead of the single platoon had dissuaded the remaining NVA from paying a call on us.

The underground tunnels that 1st platoon had found still needed to be explored and/or blown away. Discovering tunnels was not as frequent an occurrence in our AO as it was in some parts of Vietnam, like over at Cu Chi for instance. Consequently, we never really had any troops with tunnel rat training, which was an in-country school where short, thin, crazy guys were taught how to worm their way into tunnels with a flashlight and a 45 pistol. It was a claustrophobic experience that most guys flat out declined to do. "Shit no, I'm not going in there. What are you going to do if I refuse, send me to Vietnam?" Still, 3rd platoon had a couple of fearless little suckers who were willing to crawl into the gooks' holes.

Tunnel complexes were typically storage facilities, or underground compounds for enemy elements to hide, train troops, use as hospitals, and even command and control facilities. There were some places in Vietnam where the tunnels went on for miles, branching into complex interconnected underground cities invisible to patrolling helicopters and to ground units passing directly over them. The tunnels in our little NVA training site turned out to be mostly for storage, with large caches of food (mostly rice) and ammunition, including a substantial stock of ammo for the 51-caliber machine gun we had taken. Fortunately, they weren't occupied by any NVA.

Once our wannabe tunnel rats had determined the nature

and extent of the tunnel network, the captain ordered them destroyed. Cries of "Fire in the hole" echoed around the NVA camp as GIs tossed hand grenades into the various openings. In the largest underground room, we wired up charges of C-4 and then blew them with claymore detonators after withdrawing a respectable distance away. The thump of the explosion was muted, but the ground shook from the sympathetic detonation of Chuckie's ammo hoard.

We finished off by putting Zippos to the hootches. The company stood back and watched as the buildings burned to the ground. Although the jungle pressed in close to the burning hootches, moisture in the heavy vegetation prevented anything but some minor scorching of the surrounding leaves. In three weeks it would be difficult to recognize the clearing as recently inhabited.

Once the destruction of the base was complete Bravo Company packed up and shuffled back into the jungle, leaving the smoldering ruins and collapsed tunnels behind. It was time to continue our fine search and destroy operation, to wander deeper into Dragon Valley in search of Charlie.

That Chicom machine gun later wound up decorating the battalion trains area back in Chu Lai as a war trophy. It was still there, wearing a fresh coat of shiny black paint and a plaque that proudly proclaimed the heroic battle that led to its capture, when I went home at the end of my tour of duty.

The balance of the week in Dragon Valley was quiet, for us at least. One of the other two companies that participated in the operation never had a single contact. Unfortunately, the battalion's Delta Company got beat up and bloodied pretty badly, with six dead and eight wounded GIs. They got routed, and just about had their butts run out of the valley. Looking back, it seems like a high price for one captured machine gun.

We gotta get out of this place,
If it's the last thing we ever do.
Eric Burdon and The Animals

Chapter Eleven

The jungle that dominated most parts of our battalion area of operations was filled with lots of strange critters, many that hadn't previously been experienced by visitors from the far side of the world. Although a few guys in my platoon had grown up on farms and had at least some familiarity with wildlife, most of us were either from concrete and asphalt cities, or suburban sprawls where the closest thing to jungle was an unkempt lawn.

There were lots of snakes with us out there in the bush. With the possible exception of the cobras and kraits, which we (thankfully) rarely saw, nobody had any idea which ones were poisonous. Not that anyone wanted to have much to do with snakes, either way. Point men were often as leery of something wiggling in the grass as they were of booby traps and ambushes.

One variety, a thin green snake between one and two feet long, was especially common. Grunts called them bamboo snakes. I never heard any other name. Grass green, they blended with just about anything in the jungle and were difficult to spot until you were practically standing on them. We suspected they were poisonous—it's probably prudent to think poison when you consider *any* exotic snake in a strange jungle—although we never did find out for sure. Kenny once tried to find out. He took a leak at the side of a trail one time and found himself peeing right on top of one. When he realized the grass was stirring, he stopped pissing in mid-stream and backpedaled faster than I'd ever seen him move before.

Monkeys sometimes announced their presence from the tops of the tallest trees, but you rarely saw them. They had no interest in coming down to check out noisy GIs passing by. And of course there were dozens of colorful birds, although most were so unused to having people around that they quieted at the sound of an approaching patrol. Yet another clue for Charlie that the Army was in his neighborhood; the birds suddenly stop making their usual racket.

Probably the most unusual animal I saw there was a tiny deer-like thing, no larger than a small puppy. We called them mouse deer. One time we came across one so frightened of us that it just froze and didn't run away. I reached out to touch it, and I could feel it shaking. Somebody wondered out loud if it might make a tasty variation from C-rations. Doc wanted to slit its throat. Making light of the badass jungle hunter, I managed to convince him to leave it alone and we moved on. I knew that I was getting more and more unaffected by death and killing as the days went by, and was feeling a little disturbed by the deadening of my capacity to be shocked. Still, the idea of indiscriminately offing a scared and helpless little critter saddened me. I thought about my reaction to Doc's eager suggestion as the column moved on and realized I was feeling less compunction about blowing away VC than slicing up a mouse deer. Had killing people become easier to justify than a tiny animal that was too stupid to run from danger? Go figure.

There were all manner of odd insects—strange filmy-winged wasps (to which I gave a wide berth), eight-inch long centipedes with a reportedly poisonous bite, and an extensive assortment of beetles and bugs. Even insects that were familiar to us, like ants, packed a surprise for the unwary GI. At least one variety of Vietnamese ants came equipped with a stinger, and was grouchy besides.

I first discovered the fire ants (at least that's what the grunts called them) when I sat down with my back propped up against a tree trunk on a break from patrol. In seconds, my ass was stinging and I was jumping around and brushing off dozens of ants that were stinging me right through my fatigue trousers. The pain wasn't agonizing, but it sure hurt enough to make me a lot more attentive when I set my butt on the ground for the remainder of my tour.

Then there were the leeches.

They were disgusting little slug-like blobs, and they were everywhere. I'm personally convinced that leeches were the most abundant form of wildlife in all of Vietnam.

There were two types—ground leeches and water leeches. The water kind was green and the larger of the two, usually about six to eight inches long. They were most often found in rice paddies and marshy areas, and I count it as a small blessing that I never had a water leech bite into me. A water leech was no laughing matter; very hard to get it off, and it left a dime-sized welt that stubbornly bled for a long time.

Ground leeches were brown and a lot smaller, maybe three inches long, but they really were everywhere there was vegetation. If you were in the jungle, you had to deal with ground leeches—no option. Instead of blousing our fatigue trousers like they did stateside, we kept our pant legs stuffed down into our jungle boots to keep the slimy buggers from crawling up a leg. As an added precaution, we soaked the canvas at the top of our boots with bug juice, an Army-issue insect repellent that didn't keep many insects away but did a hell of a job on leeches. They hated it. One drop on a leech and the little worm writhed like it was on fire.

At night, you either took steps before bedding down to discourage leeches from sleeping with you, or you could count on waking up with company. Since there was no place to sleep except on the ground, it was important to tuck a poncho liner tightly around your entire body, head and face included. Even with precautions, waking up in the morning was frequently accompanied by the discovery that a few leeches had been persistent enough to find their way into your poncho liner. They'd be rolling around in the cloth, bloated and content after a meal at your expense. Disgusted, GIs would stomp on the stuffed leeches, popping them like water balloons and leaving a bright red stain on the ground.

Hammocks were great for getting out of the reach of ground leeches, except for the more enterprising ones that dropped on you from tree branches. But there weren't many guys who had hammocks, or who wanted the extra weight to carry. The VC sometimes had some nifty lightweight mesh hammocks. The problem was they were so short that only Kenny could use the ones we procured from VC casualties. Kenny took great delight in pointing out the advantages of being short, while the rest of us picked leeches out of our poncho liners.

A few grunts got folks at home to send them hammocks, but most of the ones from the states were too heavy to hump around. One poor guy's well-meaning mother sent a canvas hammock that must have weighed ten or fifteen pounds. She had dyed it OD in her laundry tub, mindful of the need to camouflage the white canvas, but never considering the weight she was adding to her son's load. The homemade hammock came in on a resupply chopper, all neatly tied up in brown wrapping paper. When junior opened mom's package and realized what it was, he hefted it and knew at once that he couldn't afford the extra weight. He sadly left it behind in the night laager, probably to be scavenged and turned into packs or pouches by inventive VC.

Leeches were hard to remove. Once they got hooked on tight, they wouldn't let go. Trying to pull them off risked tearing them and leaving a piece attached. I knew of three ways to make a leech let go (four, if you want to count waiting for it to drink its fill and fall off). First was bug juice. Every GI carried a small squeeze bottle of the stuff tucked in the elastic band that held a camouflage cover on his steel pot. That was the traditional spot to carry it because it provided quick access. The trouble with bug juice, though, was that you had to make sure it didn't get in your eyes or on other sensitive body parts—then you found out why leeches squirmed so when you zapped them with it.

The second method was to sprinkle salt on the leech. Yes, we had salt—in little paper packs that came in C-ration boxes, something like you get in fast food restaurants. But leeches were indiscriminate callers and didn't restrict themselves to mealtime visits, so salt was often an impractical solution unless you were willing to shuck off your rucksack and go rummaging around inside it to find a box of Cs. The third method was to touch the leech with a burning cigarette. Sort of self-explanatory—I'd let go too if someone stuck me with a lit butt.

The damn things were on the ground and in the trees. They would drop from the foliage on unsuspecting GIs passing below, latching on a neck or crawling down an open collar to find the soft skin between shoulder blades. With the weight from heavy rucksacks numbing our backs and shoulders, we often didn't even feel them crawling on us. They moved like inchworms, stretching out, then bringing their back end close to their front end with their middles hiked up in the air. I've still got scars from bites that became infected, and I still shiver when I think of them sliding around on me.

The thickest I ever saw them came one evening at dusk. We had stopped for the night, and I was looking for a flat spot to spread out my poncho liner. As I looked down, I saw dozens of the slimy things inching their way toward me. They completely encircled me, and all were targeted directly at me as though they had some kind of homing radar. It was weird, like iron filings turning toward a magnet on a smooth table.

I cut off a tree branch and swept a six-foot area reasonably clean of them. Then I took my trusty bug juice and sprayed a perimeter big enough to lie down within. Sort of a moat. I used the whole bottle, but the alternative would have been ugly. I shuddered to think of awakening in a soggy poncho liner in the company of all those leeches laden with my blood. Fortunately it didn't rain that night and the bug juice stayed potent enough to keep most of the little vampires away. Only a couple of them found a way through my moat. They enjoyed a filling last meal, and in the morning were quickly dispatched to leech heaven.

A week or two after Hau Duc, we were on a sweep looking for VC and had stopped for a mid-day break on a wooded ridgeline. The company's three platoons were widely separated on the ridgeline, to avoid making too tempting a target for Charlie (you don't want to bunch up a lot of people—it improves the unit-cost effectiveness of hand grenades and the like for the bad guys). Rucksacks and bandoleers came off. Some guys ate a cold meal, some wrote notes. I started to write a letter home.

I heard some murmuring. Someone posted at a perimeter position had seen movement below the ridgeline where no friendlies were supposed to be. It was on my platoon's side of the company, so I grabbed my M-16 and signaled to Dee and his squad to come with me. We moved away from the platoon position down the ridgeline looking for VC or whatever had caused the motion that had been seen. A little over a hundred men were behind us not even an eighth of a mile away, yet I can't begin to tell you how alone we felt on that ridge as we headed further away from the main force. I thought about how Mike got shot. The situation had been remarkably similar to what we were doing.

We moved as silently as possible, hoping not to alert anyone to our approach. The hill was slippery, and huge leaves impeded our view for more than a few dozen yards in any direction. Our attention was split between watching for signs of Charlie, and watching where we placed our feet.

As we worked our way down the hillside, I suddenly felt a twinge in my crotch. It felt like I had accidentally caught my pecker while pulling up my zipper. Except that couldn't be my problem, because jungle fatigue trousers had a button fly, not a zipper. What a peculiar irony. Someone might be out there in the jungle waiting to kill me, and I was standing there distracted by a very private, but very compelling, discomfort in my pants.

It got worse—I mean it really HURT! It was not something to be ignored, and I was finding it increasingly difficult to concentrate on tracking the elusive Chuck in the woods with this wholly unwelcome sensation competing for my attention. Trying to keep my eyes on the jungle beneath the ridgeline, I stuck my hand in my pocket and rearranged my package. No help; it still hurt, a lot.

I had no choice. I unbuttoned my fly and out came my crank, with an ugly brown leech attached and blissfully sucking away. If there was any erotic symbolism in that image, it was entirely lost on me. I was nervous and being unwillingly sidetracked from one unknown threat by a much more immediate and painful one.

Remember what I said about bug juice on sensitive body parts? Well, I can't think of anything much more sensitive. So much for bug juice and remedy number one. I hadn't thought to pack a lunch when we lit out after whatever was still down the hill from us, so I was fresh out of salt and remedy number two. And so, there I stood with my johnson hanging out, weapon in one hand, lighting a cigarette with the other to zap my leech. The other guys just stared; they couldn't believe it. I think somebody snorted. Talk about tight patrol discipline. "Smoke 'em if you got 'em." Here's your choice, soldier. It's about your dick; you can either have it blown off or chewed off.

There was a certain black humor in all of this. I was reminded of the line from Leon Uris' *Battle Cry*. "This is my rifle, this is my gun. This is for fighting, this is for fun."

Oh, by the way, we never did find any VC. After my little smoke break, which persuaded my stowaway to take his appetite elsewhere, we continued down the ridge and found some recent tracks, but that was all. If someone had been there, he probably left to avoid giving himself away guffawing at the crazy GI who was flying a leech on his flagpole and lighting up a Marlboro. Today I have to admit that it's a funny story. Right then, I didn't think there was one damn thing even remotely funny about it.

I told Dee and his squad if anyone dared to breath a word about it I'd find a way to get even. Of course the whole company knew within the hour, which is about how long it took me to stop bleeding. Even Doc made it a point to come by and observe, "I sure hope you aren't looking for a medic. I'm fresh out of teeny tiny pressure bandages."

Har, har. Fuck you, Doc.

Chapter Twelve

It was time for Bravo Company to cycle back to LZ Professional.
It would be something like my fifth time there, counting first
arrival. We had been out in the bush for about three weeks
and were in line for the comparative comfort of a firebase. Hot
meals, a shower, a change of uniform, and a perimeter modestly
more secure than those we improvised on our overnight stops
in the jungle were among the luxuries awaiting us.

I had been in Vietnam about four months. Incredibly, LZ
Professional looked mighty good to me as we covered the last
quarter mile to the base of the hill near the Burlington Trail.
I couldn't help a wry smile as I thought about how negatively
the filth and primitive conditions had affronted my then tender
sensibilities when I first saw it.

Luxury, or at least comfort, is a relative thing. If you're
well off it doesn't take much deprivation to make you feel
uncomfortable. You get used to the trappings of ease and
contentment. But if all you have is what you're carrying on your
back, your bed at night is a piece of wet ground covered by a
soggy and malodorous poncho liner, unappealing food comes
out of a plastic bag or a can, and people are trying to shoot you,
then even a pile of mud and sandbags like LZ Professional can
seem almost pleasant. Almost.

Since firebases had no plumbing or source of water,
helicopters had to regularly bring in fresh water along with all
the other supplies. Water was transported in enormous rubber
balloons, called blivets, which were suspended beneath twin-
rotor CH-47 Chinook helicopters. GIs called the Chinooks
"shit-hooks". They were the trucks of the air, always coming

in with a heavy load dangling underneath on a winch line and hook.

Water blivets had no rigid structure. They were just thick-walled rubber balls, and very heavy when filled with water. Imbedded in the blivets were standard faucet fixtures so they could be hooked up to a hose. If you put a blivet high enough on the hill, gravity would provide a workable approximation of running water.

A couple of blivets were located near the mess kitchen, as a general water source for the firebase. Another blivet usually fed the single shower on the hill, which was a crude arrangement of two by fours supporting a tin can with holes punched in the bottom. That was fed by a short pipe from a jettisoned wing tank off an F-4 Phantom, also supported on a rickety frame of two by fours. The wing tank was kept full by the blivet a little further up the hill. Sometimes if we got lucky, the sun would heat the water in the wing tank enough to make for a warm shower.

The blivets and that one shower were popular places when a company came off patrol. Guys were eager to pour out canteens full of river water and muddy rice paddy water tasting of Halizone, and fill them with fresh, if rubber-flavored, water from the blivets. Lines of GIs newly returned to the hill would form at the shower while waiting a turn to wash off the accumulated crud of three weeks in the jungle before putting on clean fatigues from the supply bunker.

The LZ offered modestly better medical facilities than Doc's rucksack. Minor wounds, cuts from elephant grass, and leech bites sometimes took forever to heal because of the constant moisture and chafing. Open sores occasionally developed cellulitis, dying and discolored flesh immediately around the edges of the sore. On the firebase we could get ointments and dry bandages, and every so often bottles of tetracycline for ongoing self-treatment. If the weather was dry, we could lie in the sun and let the warm rays dry out oozing sores.

When I had first arrived in country, I'd had plantars warts

on both my feet. I took my boots off to check the condition of my waterlogged, fish-belly white feet and noticed that the warts were gone. I suspected I owed my cure to the silt from streams and rice paddies. Jungle boots had small screen-covered openings on the sides just above the sole to allow water to run out of the boot. It was a good feature, because we often got water in our boots and the holes fostered quick drainage. After crossing some type of water, we walked along for a while with water squirting out the sides of our boots. The problem was the screen; it wasn't fine enough to keep out silt, which would accumulate in our socks. When the socks dried, the effect was a little like fine sandpaper. It was likely that I had, over time, simply ground the warts away in my sandpaper socks.

I guess that was at least one good outcome from life in sunny Southeast Asia—no more plantars warts. Always a silver lining.

A few days on the firebase gave us a chance to replace rotting fatigues and worn out jungle boots with new ones. It was a time to get a haircut, often just a hack job given by a buddy. We could get a little soap and shave off the stubble of days on patrol, sometimes even two or three week beards. Out in the jungle, nobody minded a sloppy disheveled look. In fact, a lot of grunts thought a grimy unshaved face gave them a badass look—kind of a game face for our unending match with Charlie. Back on the LZ, though, we had to live up to a higher standard of military protocol. Mustaches were okay, scruffy beards had to go.

Rotation on the firebase was a time for resupply and to relax a little. Ammunition that had been expended or had begun to rust could be replaced. Hand grenades, claymores, LAWs, smoke canisters, quinine tablets, Halizone, fresh batteries for the radios, LRRPs and C-rations were all available in normally large quantities. Letters that hadn't yet made it out to the jungle on resupply birds were waiting for us. And we could actually sleep, longer than the three or four hours we commonly got in the bush.

There were mess kits full of gray-looking food from the

mess shack, but we wolfed it down. It was hot, and it was a nice change from mostly tasteless C-rations and LRRPs. I had lost a lot of weight, down from 175 when I arrived in country to about 155. Out in the bush there were lots of times we just didn't feel hungry. After humping through the shit all day, we were often too tired or sapped by the heat to have much of an appetite. So time on the hill was an opportunity to eat a little better.

If our timing was really good, we might even have the luck to be on the LZ when a load of warm beer came in. Quite a treat, warm beer. By the time it got to a combat zone, the beer had been subjected to treatment never imagined by the good folks at Miller and Budweiser. The cases had sat in the holds of ships and in the broiling sun on pallets in harbors, had bounced around in deuce and a half trucks and slung beneath helicopters, and had generally been abused in ways beer shouldn't endure. It was nothing like the six-pack you just bought down at your corner store. It was invariably skunky. When opened the cans gushed foam, so you sucked and slurped fast to keep it from spilling. It was awful, and we loved every drop of it.

There wasn't much in the way of "entertainment" up on LZ Professional and, aside from the ever-present list of details—scut work to keep idle hands busy—not a lot to do. There was the loathsome shit duty, stirring the burning sludge in the crusted drums. Some guys would get KP in the raggedy-assed shack that passed for a mess kitchen. If they were lucky, they might even filch some chow to take back to their bunkers. There were digging and construction details, largely maintenance efforts to buttress against the constant erosion of our mudhill. Occasionally, a daytime patrol would be sent out to check the area immediately around the firebase, to make sure the concertina wire was in good condition and to see whether there were any signs of probing by the VC. And once in a while the brass sent a squad out at night to set an ambush on the Burlington Trail in case Charlie was dumb enough to walk on it.

We played poker, and listened to the MACV station on transistor radios. We read the *Stars and Stripes* and the *Southern Cross*, Army newspapers. The latter was published by and for the Americal Division, and took its name from the Americal insignia—four stars on a field of blue, representing the Southern Cross, under which constellation the Americal had originally been born during World War II. As you might imagine, both the Armed Forces Radio and the newspapers fed a rather biased diet of news to us, reinforcing the glorious purpose that had brought us here to end the spread of communism and telling us how we were winning the war and kicking Charlie's ass. We knew it was a crock of crap, and they knew it too, but at least it gave us something to do.

You wouldn't find in either newspaper much discussion of the protests against the war that were becoming increasingly common back in The World, or a lot of discussion about all the efforts to wind down the war. We knew what was going on from accounts we read in the occasional real newspaper someone would get in a package from home, or from stories related by FNGs newly arrived in Vietnam. We knew, too, that Nixon was starting to decrease troop counts in anticipation of the ARVN taking over complete responsibility for the war.

Surprisingly, the growing awareness that the war really was at least beginning to wind down had a negative effect on morale, for several reasons. First, a diminishing war and deactivation of some combat units didn't mean that any of us would get an early out. The Army simply slowed the pace of new troops coming in, and reassigned soldiers from units being shut down to other battalions where they finished out their tours. Second, it was pretty depressing to be fighting in a war that everybody wanted to see ended, because GIs were still getting wounded and killed—losses that were all the more difficult to understand or accept when everyone from the president on down had announced their intent to be done with it.

And finally, everyone knew that once the U.S. forces were gone and the Army of the Republic of Vietnam was running the war, it would only be a matter of time before Uncle Ho and his rocking NVA would be marching through the streets of Saigon. I don't think you could find a U.S. soldier in all of Vietnam at that point in the war who believed the ARVN could or would stand on its own once the United States had discontinued active military support.

In other words, we all knew that the whole disgraceful thing had been for nothing. All those thousands of dead GIs, all the disrupted lives, the staggering costs in monetary and human terms, the discord back home—it all meant nothing. Years and years of horrors in this godforsaken piece of shit of a country hadn't accomplished a thing. Nada. Zilch. The culmination of our involvement in Vietnam was obvious and certain, and it was discernible a long time before it actually arrived. And that's a little rough on the morale of men who were still being asked to bear arms and die for the "cause".

Army newspapers, particularly the ones published by the divisions themselves, were the ultimate in self-promotion. Various combat operations throughout the country were covered in glowing detail by these rags. Even the most FUBAR screwed up effort came off sounding masterful in the *Southern Cross*. The biggest highlight of the American's paper was a weekly unit-by-unit accounting of enemy body counts.

The body counts were such a joke. Headlines in the paper trumpeted announcements like "Weekly Recap—Division Soldiers Tally 114 Enemy", or "Air, Arty, Infantry Combine To Get 53".

"*Last week saw dozens of the enemy fall to the guns of the American.*"

(No kidding, the newspapers really said overwrought stuff like, "fall to the guns of the American".)

"*In Operation Frederich Hill, the 'Polar Bears' of 4th Battalion, 31st Infantry received 13 Hoi Chanh, of which six brought their families. Elsewhere in Operation Iron Mountain the 'Jungle Warriors' of the 3rd Infantry Brigade accounted for 31 enemy killed. The lightest action occurred in Operation Geneva Park as the 'Brave and Bold' of the 198th Infantry Brigade tallied eight enemy killed.*

Early in the week, Charlie Company of the 4th Battalion killed two VC while on a sweep northwest of Tam Ky. Recon platoon later in the week killed four VC in separate incidents also northwest of Tam Ky. The 2nd Battalion 1st Infantry operating west of Tam Ky found several enemy caches during the week. Company A found 14 cases of 51-caliber ammo and 40 batteries early in the week.

Towards the end of the week, the Recon platoon of the 2nd Battalion 1st Infantry located a cache which yielded 900 rounds of 30-caliber machine gun ammo, 100 rounds of 51-caliber machine gun ammo, and 200 7.62mm rounds. In the same area, Company D came across a trench line which contained 1,000 AK-47 rounds and 4 Chicom grenades.

Soldiers of the 3rd Battalion 21st Infantry killed 18 in brief encounters throughout the week. The Recon platoon tallied three dead VC when they fired on the enemy 11 miles west of Tam Ky.

The 'Professionals' of the 1st Battalion 46th Infantry killed five enemy soldiers in the thick triple canopy jungle southwest of Tam Ky.

In another action northwest of Quang Ngai, Delta Company, 1st Battalion 52nd Infantry, while maneuvering in mountainous terrain, found one NVA body. The kill was attributed to enemy contact the company experienced the previous day. Found near the body were one AK-47, three fully loaded AK ammunition clips, two Chicom grenades, one pair of field glasses and other miscellaneous items".

And so on, and so on, in numbingly repetitive detail. Recounting those vitally important body counts from the week's skirmishes filled up several pages of the paper. No event, however minor, was omitted. It must have been important to the reporters who published the paper that every unit in the division get some kind of mention.

"Such and such rifle company observed a Viet Cong in a black uniform running along a trail. They engaged him with small arms fire to kill him."

Which loosely translated into, "A unit of GIs, highly motivated by the unremitting emphasis on body counts, saw a gook in black pajamas who was stupid enough to be running on a trail in the open, and they greased his ass."

What was most amazing about the newspaper accounts was that they were so incredibly dispassionate, so detached. It was like reading the box scores, or the weather report, or an article about the grand opening of some bowling alley/convenience store in Bumfuck, Iowa. Gore, mayhem and bodies rotting in the jungle were the stuff of division journalism, all aiming to convince the paper's readers (us) that the war was being decisively waged against that evil communist enemy. We were very confident and quite pleased that, because of our virtuous efforts, the bad guys wouldn't be making an amphibious assault on New York any time soon. And everything in the paper was reported with the emotion and intensity of an IRS manual.

I wondered about the "miscellaneous items" found near NVA body whose kill was "attributed to enemy contact the previous day". Let's see, could the miscellaneous items have included a photograph of a wife and smiling baby up north somewhere?

As I idly paged through the most recent edition of the paper, I was struck by my own competing reactions to the clinical analysis of the week's action. On the one hand, I felt a sense of approval, even satisfaction. Mow those little bastards down. Some of them have probably taken shots at my guys and me. Every one of the kills reported in the *Southern Cross* was one fewer bad guy for me to worry about.

But the articles also troubled me. Was this the whole point of a half million men under arms and uncounted tons of equipment and munitions moved here from the other side of the world? To generate body counts that could be gloriously reported by gloating Army newspapers? For a war nobody believed in?

I had a difficult time balancing how I felt, or should feel, about such prideful announcements of the "kills". Part of me wanted not to care. Those were dead dinks; why should I give a damn? But part of me felt depressed over what was happening—to me, to the people around me, to the folks who could write such trash, and to this poor, backward country. How many completely apolitical Vietnamese peasants, uncaring about either North or South Vietnam, or about American good intentions to win their hearts and minds, were blown away every week and tallied into the body count—that remarkable measure which had come to be worshipped with a religious fervor by the brass and the politicians and the network anchor men?

It was a moral dilemma I had neither the stomach nor the will to confront. I crumpled up the newspaper and turned to cleaning my M-16. When I got done with the stripping, cleaning and oiling, I still didn't want to think about it. I took a nap instead.

Because we and our gear were almost always wet from rain, sweat or river crossings, weapons needed to be cleaned and oiled conscientiously. We did the best we could on patrol, but field-stripping an M-16 in the pouring rain wasn't the most effective way of ensuring a working gun. So time on the firebase, even if the bunkers were mud pits, was still an improved opportunity to make sure barrels were clean and firing mechanisms were rust-free and oiled. I think I cleaned my rifle once a day when we were up on Professional.

Once in a while, the company on the LZ got a visit from Doughnut Dollies. These were Red Cross workers, almost all of them young women, who were flown into the firebases of forward units to hand out coffee and doughnuts, or maybe serve up stuff in a chow line, or just hang out and talk with the GIs. They weren't allowed out on the ground in the bush, but firebases were certainly combat zones and you had to admire the gals' willingness to put themselves in harm's way in order to give us grunts a little diversion. Sure, we were there, but we didn't have a choice about it.

Tough to know what motivated the Doughnut Dollies. Maybe a sense of adventure, or even a genuine interest in "our boys over there". But getting a visit from them was a nice distraction from the more mundane facets of our soldiering lives, and it was awfully good to see the fresh, round-eyed faces of real American girls after so long. So good, in fact, that crude unwashed grunts were downright courteous and respectful when the Doughnut Dollies came around—an honor not always accorded to the Asian bar girls back in division base camps.

Thanksgiving arrived while we were up on the hill. The event was marked by the best meal I can ever remember our grungy little firebase mess shack putting out. Turkey rolls, pre-mix stuffing, powdered potatoes, and a couple other less identifiable artificial concoctions. It was great, and we ate like pigs. We even got a can of warm beer.

I took a heaping tin plate back to my bunker and sat up on the piled sandbags, eating my turkey and staring down into the valley below. I told myself I had a lot to be thankful for—a supportive, concerned family, a beautiful wife, a college degree and a promising future. Heck, I should feel grateful just for still being alive. But my magnanimous self-persuasion could only take me so far, and was soon replaced with a serving of self-pity. I thought about the people in my life back home who were celebrating their Thanksgiving without me. I wanted to be there with them, not sitting on top of a muddy pile of sandbags overlooking a sun-baked jungle valley and eating an imitation turkey dinner.

On the last night Bravo Company was to spend on LZ Professional before heading back on extended patrol, a squad from our 3rd platoon got picked to set up a night ambush about a klick or so to the west of the firebase, just off the Burlington Trail. Participating in a night ambush wasn't usually too difficult. You went out at dusk to set it up, laying out claymores and setting up a small position near any spot likely to be traveled by the bad guys. Ninety-nine percent of the time absolutely nothing happened and it wasn't a heck of a lot different than any other night in the jungle. Rotate watch, fight not to fall asleep on your watch, listen to the sounds of the night and try to pick out the noises that don't belong.

Even a regular Army unit could pull off an effective night ambush, because it didn't require any movement once it was set. So noise discipline wasn't a problem (as long as the guys didn't start jawing), and in the pitch dark an ambushing squad was almost impossible to detect.

About halfway through the night, the rest of us on the LZ awoke to distant automatic weapons fire and the recognizable sounds of detonating claymore mines. The firefight lasted three minutes or so, then the heavy stillness of the night settled back on us.

Kenny was with me in my bunker. We were listening to the radio, hoping that nobody got hurt. Probably some gooks using the Burlington for fast night movement and the 3rd platoon's squad dropped the hammer on them but good.

The reality turned out to be much more unsettling. The word went around later that the S-2 intelligence officer (there's an oxymoron for you) who ordered the night ambush and the S-3 operations officer who was monitoring the movement of the battalion's recon platoon hadn't bothered to talk to each other. The recon guys were on their way back to LZ Professional from an operation further to the west. And they walked right into the night ambush.

Recon people were second only to Rangers and Green Berets in their ability to move at night. Unfortunately, in a rare lapse in judgment, they took the easy route and walked the trail. Since neither unit was aware of the other, both the 3rd platoon's ambush squad and Recon believed they were in a scuffle with Chuck. In Army parlance, it was an all-American firefight.

Two dead and three wounded went down before anyone figured out what the hell was happening. One recon soldier took a claymore almost straight on. The blast took off one leg and tore most of the rest of him to ribbons. He was dead before he hit the ground.

There was even a proper name for this insanity. Incidents like the botched ambush and my earlier flirtation with our artillery were called "friendly fire". Has a nice official ring to it. "Sorry Mrs. Jones. We regret to inform you that your son Johnny was killed by friendly fire while on patrol defending the grateful, freedom-loving people of the Republic of Vietnam." The Army's own estimate was that some five to ten percent of all casualties were from friendly fire. But I don't believe anybody really knows how many of Vietnam's dead and wounded were the result of all-American firefights, or misdirected bombs, or artillery accidentally dropped on good guys. But the episodes I knew of personally were starting to add up. The Army was sometimes the Viet Cong's best ally.

Things like that weighed heavily on us. It bred an emptiness that ate away at us, brought on by such completely unnecessary death and destruction. There was sadness for the guys who got wasted (what an amazingly apt word that was—"wasted") and empathy for their buddies in the platoon. There was a sort of guilty relief that it happened to someone else, not us. It was especially easy to feel that relief if we were fortunate enough not to have known the casualties too well, and the recon platoon normally didn't have much to do with the regular leg troops. Finally, there was a helpless rage at the stupidity and ineptitude that allowed the lives of GIs to be so meaninglessly and so casually discarded. It was a booster dose of the bitter medicine I had tasted when Mike Keene died.

Life in a war zone doesn't leave much time to dwell on these things; you have to continue trudging. The thoughts never quite leave, but the Army tries to keep everyone busy enough so there isn't much opportunity to ponder too deeply. And the pace of time passing was never altered by the loss of a few more lives, justified or otherwise. So, the following morning Bravo Company went through another methodical change of units on the firebase, loading up our rucksacks and unceremoniously turning the sloppy bunkers and rusting concertina wire over to another bunch of crusted and bleary-eyed grunts climbing up the hill.

While we were on the LZ, Lieutenant Warren received orders for his R&R (Rest and Recuperation, a one-week vacation from the war) and had flown out for a week in Australia. That made him extremely happy, and made me something less than ecstatic. His departure meant I was unhappily back in charge of 2nd platoon as acting platoon leader.

The company CO included me in a platoon leader meeting, and advised that we had orders to go "search and destroy". We were to visit several points north of the firebase where "enemy activity" had been observed. Those "observations" of enemy activity were sometimes a stretch. Passing helicopters might see something suspicious, or out of place, and report to battalion that Charlie might be in the neighborhood. As often as not the sightings were meaningless. Bravo Company's current orders resulted from an overflight by a "loach" (LOH, or light observation helicopter—a small, round, two-man plastic bubble with a rotor on top and a skinny stick of a tail). Each platoon was to investigate an unusual sighting by the loach. My orders involved a water buffalo spotted roughly four klicks northwest of LZ Professional. Water buffalo generally meant there were Vietnamese nearby, but they were as likely to be peasants stubbornly refusing to leave the land as they were to be VC.

We thought it kind of silly to be chasing down water buffalo sightings, but the other platoons had equally uninspired assignments so we at least didn't feel we got the short stick. As usual, we were hunting ghosts, the battalion brass hoping to maneuver units into chance encounters with Charles.

The captain elected to put himself with 3rd platoon, as a brand new platoon leader had just arrived to replace the previous lieutenant who had completed his tour of duty and left for The World. That was somewhat flattering to me, as the captain might have decided to travel with my platoon in the absence of Lieutenant Warren. I guess he figured I could handle a water buffalo. Or maybe he was betting that SSG Jennings, even with only a few months in country, had more field experience than a brand new second lieutenant FNG in 3rd platoon. Tough decision for the captain—which "leader" was least likely to screw up.

Somewhere during the course of the patrol, the company was going to be linking up with an ARVN unit working in our area of operations. "ARVN" was the Army of the Republic of Vietnam. These were the people we were supposedly fighting for, providing training and equipment so they could one day completely take over their war against North Vietnam. Unfortunately, most ARVN troops at that point in the war were a joke, unmotivated and largely incompetent, and GIs didn't much care to work with them.

A friend of mine told me years later that ARVN troops weren't always such inept losers, which was a generous characterization of the view most of us had for them. My friend did two tours in Vietnam, one in the early days when the U.S.

role was still mostly that of advisor, and another at the very end of the war. The ARVN troops he knew and served with during his first tour were capable counterinsurgency fighters, needing only American equipment and air support to effectively match up with the VC and NVA. The U.S. Army helped to change that, in part by arrogantly pushing the ARVN aside and showing them how a _real_ Army does its thing. Not surprisingly, the ARVN grew content to let us do the fighting, and they became more and more dependent and corrupt as the years went by and the U.S. deployment increased.

By the time it was my turn to join the party in 1969, ARVN soldiers were not particularly inspiring examples of fighting men. They frequently went out of their way to avoid contact with the bad guys, and were slower than a REMF supply clerk to commit resources to an operation. When we looked at them, we saw a bunch of chickenshits who were content to let us fight their war for them. There was zero respect for them, or anything they did.

The other components of South Vietnam's military, the Regional Forces and Popular Forces (the RF/PF forces were known as "rough-puffs") were militia units and typically not well equipped or well organized. However, the rough-puffs, as raggedy and untrained as they were, usually put a little more effort into fighting the war than did most of the ARVN it was my misfortune to know.

It was about 9:00 in the morning when Bravo Company moved off the LZ, rucksacks packed with a new supply of LRRPs and C-rations, clean socks, fresh ordinance, and dry poncho liners. Magazines had been refilled with ammo, and we were all just thrilled ever so much to be getting back on patrol. When donkeys fly.

I had my orders. We were off to hunt that most ferocious of big game, the water buffalo. I felt like Elmer Fudd. "Be vewwy, vewwy quiet."

The 1st platoon was heading in the same general direction as 2nd platoon, so we flanked each other for the time it took us to get to the coordinates where my water buffalo had been seen. The two platoons were several hundred meters apart in the bush—far enough to be well out of sight, but close enough to provide quick support if needed.

My amazing mission proved to be over before it had hardly begun. About mid-afternoon, the 1st platoon came upon a water buffalo—apparently my water buffalo—near a deserted hootch by a narrow stream. They must have thought it would be a kick to bring it down, so one of their M-60 gunners opened up and put about 100 rounds into it.

At first, when the machine gun started firing, we thought the other platoon had been ambushed. Most of my guys automatically dropped to the ground, even though the gunfire was obviously not close by. But Kenny quickly got the word on his radio what the shooting was about and that the water buffalo hunt was over, so we closed with 1st platoon to check out the area.

The dead water buffalo lay on its side at the edge of the stream. Whoever owned it would be mighty pissed; a water buffalo to a Vietnamese was like a tractor to an American farmer. I wasn't sure what the point of killing it had been, but was hard pressed to care very much. The 1st platoon leader evidently didn't try much to stop his guys from shooting it. He was an officer, so who was I to question their actions.

Both platoons scouted the area, and found nothing informative or even remotely military. Still, after dropping the water buffalo I wasn't eager to hang around to see who might happen by. I raised the captain on the radio. He said I was to head west for the balance of the day and then find a good night laager. So that's what we did, and spent the night uneventfully on a small hill at least two klicks from the well-ventilated water buffalo.

The next morning, in no hurry to rush off to find new things to kill, I decided we would begin our day leisurely. That was one of the few perks when I was acting platoon leader; I had a lot of freedom to exercise my entrepreneurial side. I had Kenny periodically send in location messages with coordinates near the hill we were on, as if we were scouting around the base of the hill in search of some Cong mystery. I had to use locations that were reasonably close to the night laager, to avoid the possibility of someone thinking we had moved on and deciding for whatever reason to drop artillery in the area.

Meanwhile, we sat in relative safety and goofed off the whole morning. Lazy? Perhaps, but I prefer to think of it as unmotivated. Or even better, taking a well deserved couple hours off. Like I said, the circumstances of a war from which our country was clearly disengaging had created an attitude that was, at best, unenthusiastic about becoming an unnecessary casualty. If the world's leaders wanted the war to be over, why on earth should grunts like us question their wisdom? So I was just doing my part to help it slow down a little.

I sat on the ground, back to a tree, rifle leaning casually against my ankle where I could grab it quickly if needed, and tried to write a letter home. My mind was drifting, idly toying with images of stuff back in The World that I missed. Beyond the obvious, like Linda, family and friends, I found there were lots of little things I wanted to see and hear and touch again. Obscure stuff, little details of life that I had taken for granted were missing from the austere environment of a Vietnamese jungle. I sat for a long time thinking of one image after another, surprising myself with recollections of things that I had never really appreciated or thought of as terribly meaningful.

I thought about the clean, cool feel of fresh cotton sheets when you first slip into bed on a winter night. I recalled the flavor of a lake trout, caught, cleaned, cooked and eaten all within minutes. I remembered picking apples in an orchard, relishing the crisp juicy sweetness of autumn's best fruit right off the tree.

There was a memory of the enticing feel of smooth asphalt under the tires of a good car, a convertible with the top down, wind in your hair, telephone poles rushing by too fast. There was the pristine, unmarked look of a countryside blanketed by a fresh snowfall on a brisk winter morning. And the woods in autumn, filled with reds and yellows and oranges of falling leaves.

I remembered baseball games, and shopping malls, and big screen movies and rock concerts, walks on the beach holding hands, slobbering kisses from an enthusiastic dog, chipping in for a birdie on the 18th hole, roaring down the road on my motorcycle, playing breathy Stan Getz ballads on my saxophone, not very well.

I recalled the hamburgers and fries and milkshakes at the local drive-in restaurants, and cruising Woodward Avenue just north of Detroit with my high school buddies, looking for chicks or somebody to drag race. I thought about the big juicy steaks cooked on the charcoal grill in my family's back yard, and cold beer buried in ice in a cooler. I found old memories of ice cream cones on hot summer nights, Christmas cookies made in cozy warm kitchens, the crackling of birch logs in the fireplace, and the house-filling aroma of a Thanksgiving turkey in the oven.

I thought of my overprotective, but genuinely caring mother, and wondered what she might be feeling about her son far away in an unimaginable place doing unthinkable things. Her idea of the war was naively narrow, largely gleaned from the evening news and the opinions expressed by her friends at church. She somehow remained unaware of how unpopular the war had become, and didn't grasp the futility of an abandoned cause. She felt proud that I was serving my country in a time of need, and I didn't have the heart to tell her in my letters what it was really like.

I reflected on the girls I had known in my life, and how much that softer side of humanity was missed in this primitive place where brutish men were trying to kill each other. I thought about the little feminine looks and gestures, the tilt of a head, the seemingly careless toss of long hair, the soft down on a girl-smooth neck, the crystalline bell-like laughter from a delighted female, the provocative look of silky fabric draped and flowing over soft curves. Linda had a way of raising her arms to run her hands through her hair, a uniquely feminine gesture that, with apparent innocence, had the added effect of lifting her breasts in a perky, come-hither sort of manner. A lot of women do it, acting innocently unaware of the effect it has on guys. It was such a little thing, and I missed it so much.

I remembered the feel of Linda's hand in mine, of long walks in the woods, of quiet moments alone together. I thought about watching her quietly sleeping, curled tightly against me, knees drawn up, lips barely parted and begging to be kissed. And I remembered the soft, eager feel of her body and her hands as we made love.

I was driving myself nuts. I got up and walked around the night laager, shaking off the memories and trying to drive the longing out of my head. Better to try not to think so much; it only made it hurt that much more. I couldn't begin to express how completely I had grown to detest Vietnam—this shabby, primitive country with all its discomforts, the people we were fighting, and even the people for whom we were supposedly fighting and who didn't really give a shit one way or another. I could only focus on all that had been taken from me, and that I had been brought to a place I didn't want to be, doing unpleasant things for no discernible purpose.

By the time I told the guys to saddle up and get ready to move out, it was almost noon. One morning's idleness didn't strike me as all that appallingly derelict, and nobody in the platoon was complaining. Most significant, the morning was free of casualties. Still, we couldn't continue slacking off without arousing suspicion. So eventually we had to leave our little hilltop and venture off to seek adventure and fortune. Chief was his usual profound self: "Might as well go. Can't dance, too wet to plow, too windy to haul rocks." Whatever.

My objective, frankly, had been avoidance. I didn't want to hunt for Charlie any more than he wanted to be hunted. Most often, nobody died when you weren't fighting. That was a good thing. Despite my best efforts at prevention and a morning of idleness, though, it turned out to be a bad day in Black Rock.

We had been underway about an hour, moving in the usual single file column. We weren't particularly quiet, kind of normal GI travel. I didn't mind. It wouldn't have bothered me if anyone heard us, as long as they went the other direction. I wondered how many other unit leaders currently wandering around in the steamy Vietnam jungle were similarly unmotivated.

The terrain we passed through alternated between dense undergrowth and rolling hills, many of which opened into occasional exposed grassy areas. The grassy landscape was nice—it was good to get out of the triple canopy jungle for a while and enjoy easier going.

Doc was walking point, TC his backup man, and I was third as acting platoon leader. We walked up a gently sloping hill toward a natural berm, an earthen outcropping that ran perpendicularly to our right and blocked our line of sight up the right side of the hill. Our line of march took us to the edge of the berm and around it. I had closed up a little on Doc and TC, leaving Kenny several paces behind me, because I wanted to get a look around the corner of the berm. The three of us at the front of the column reached and rounded the berm's front edge, and found ourselves in a flat clearing.

Face to face with six Vietnamese sitting on their heels and eating rice out of little bowls.

They were at most 35 feet away from us. They were young men, some looking like not much more than children. We stared at each other, Americans and Vietnamese both equally astonished at the surprise encounter. How they missed hearing my platoon noisily clanking up the hillside was beyond me, but they were evidently as shocked as we were.

In the very brief seconds we stood there I had the thought that they might just be peasants and that my biggest problem was going to be keeping Doc from whittling on them. After so many contacts with an unseen, shadow opponent, how could these boys sitting so carelessly out in the open be bad guys? It was then that the one closest to us suddenly rolled to his left and came up with an AK-47 that had been out of sight behind a basket.

He was small, like most Vietnamese, and his move for the gun was incredibly quick. So fast and fluid was his roll that he was on his knees bringing the AK muzzle up toward us before my own reactions started to catch up. We had been holding our weapons to loosely cover the group, but absent any signs of hostility we weren't actually aiming and hadn't clicked off our safeties. Even in a free fire zone, civilized people didn't gun down apparently unarmed kids. My hands went on autopilot and flipped the safety to semi-automatic while beginning the arc that would line up the gook for a shot. It was no good; his fast jump put him ahead and I knew he had us.

The VC kid was quick. But Doc was just a hair quicker with his own AK-47, and snapped off three rounds. One of them went through the VC's throat, tumbling him backwards in a spray of red before he got off a single shot.

There had been no Army training on gunfights in the mold of old western movies, where combatants stand in a street and sling lead at each other from the hip until only one side is still standing. But that's exactly what we did.

The swift move of the first VC had brought the other frozen Vietnamese to life, all lunging and scrambling in different directions and coming up with weapons in their hands. I knew that the sound of Doc's AK-47 shots would additionally have put the remainder of my platoon, still behind the turn of the berm, instinctively on their bellies.

Which meant that Doc, TC and I were the only GIs on the wrong side of the berm, and would likely be on our own while the rest of the platoon crawled for cover and considered their next move.

The M-16 is best used as a shoulder weapon, taking advantage of the stabilizing effect of a sturdy pistol grip, face on the stock, sighting a target down the barrel. Practice on training ranges didn't really encourage other styles. Hip-shooting just didn't seem appropriately "military".

But shooting from the hip was the only choice we had. The brief moment it would take to lift the rifle to my shoulder was precious time wasted. This was coming down to a duel of reactions—who had the fastest ones and could put out more rounds first. TC and I moved in unison, joining Doc in spraying bullets at the scattering VC. A thought scurried through my mind about how recoil made a rifle barrel rise, and I tried to hold it down as I pumped off rounds as fast as I could pull the trigger.

I guess you could call it a form of suppressing fire. We were damn sure trying to suppress any chance for the VC to shoot back.

It became a ballet in slow motion. A round went by my face; it surprised me how clearly I heard it. Someone's bullet—no idea whose, maybe mine, maybe not—hit another VC in his chest, the force throwing him backward and leaving an ugly dark wet bloom on his black pajamas. He floated improbably through the air, then crumpled in an awkward and lifeless pile.

My finger kept squeezing, a back and forth metronome beat on the trigger. I was conscious of tracer rounds coming out of my M-16, vaguely remembering that I had intentionally loaded a few tracers at the bottom of my magazines to let me know when they were almost empty. One VC had lost his will to stand and fight, and was running toward the far end of the berm while ineffectively pointing his rifle back at us and popping off rounds. I finally put my M-16 up to my shoulder, sighted, fired, and saw a piece of his skull come off. As I squeezed the trigger, he was looking at me and swinging his AK toward me. I could see his face clearly, and it was contorted by fear. Thinking back, I wonder what he might have seen on my face as I fired the bullet that killed him.

I pulled the trigger again and realized the bolt was retracted and locked. That had been the last round in the magazine, and my M-16 was waiting patiently for a new magazine. The most lethal weapon in the world is little more than a paperweight without ammo. I fumbled in the bandoleer across my chest for a fresh load, and saw TC put a burst into the last remaining gook. It blew through his chest and erupted out his back in a fist-sized exit wound. The VC actually stood there for a moment staring back at us before collapsing. He looked incredulous, not believing he was all but dead. Then he dropped, a wet lump on the grass.

It was over. This unlikely and macabre dance of destruction had taken less than ten seconds. After months of chasing

Charlie all around our AO, of suffering hit and run ambushes, of feeling the frustration that came from never seeing your adversary, of watching friends get shot by shadows we couldn't catch, the three of us were staring in disbelief at what had just happened.

Adrenaline surged, hearts pumped crazily, lungs worked much too fast. A heady exhilaration to be alive, a primal feeling of supremacy in mortal combat. Victors against superior forces. A classic *mano a mano* contest, a tribute to testosterone. On this day, we were the better men. We claim victory, they claim death.

There was also the shakiness in my knees at the realization of how close this had been. The dizzying speed of our firefight hadn't permitted any time to think, or be scared. Afterwards, there was plenty of time to be scared. I struggled to keep myself from sitting down, keeping my legs stiff. Unseemly to exhibit cracks in the armor—not at all what John Wayne would do.

A few faces cautiously appeared at the front end of the berm as the GIs who had been just behind us in the column peeked around the corner. Incredibly, the three of us had not been hit, not even a scratch. We stood there, surrounded by broken bodies, shell casings and blood, numbly surveying the mayhem. I looked at the VC I had shot. His brains were leaking out on the ground. I turned away.

And I found myself again cursed by ambivalence. How enviable to be like Doc—he felt nothing but hate and disdain for these people; killing wasn't difficult. He quite possibly had enjoyed it. I didn't feel terribly warm and loving toward them— especially right at that moment—but I wasn't sure that I hated them. Maybe I did hate them—shit, they tried to kill us! And yet, however different our cultures and our loyalties, these were still people. Hell, they were just kids!

Six young lives had been snuffed out, and I had been part of it. I had shot down another human being. It might not have been the first time. After all, I had popped enough caps and sent plenty of ammo downrange since arriving in this funhouse. But up until now, I was just discharging my weapon in the general direction of where bad guys might be. This time I had looked into the faces of people I was killing. There had been no doubt about the outcome of shooting my rifle. I had etched on my memory an image of blood and brains and gore that I knew would never go away.

I wanted to think of them as "just gooks". Part of me was already doing just that. I knew it would be easier to inflict death, and live with the knowledge of having done so, if I could view the bad guys with contempt. And that feeling was beginning to come more easily to me. Ominously, I felt a part of me, deep down inside, that was whispering rationalizations and dismissing gook-killing as necessary and insignificant, even a little satisfying—a release of frustration and rage at all the wrong things this war symbolized.

I felt sadness, not guilt. There had been no choice. Corny as such expressions are, it had been a case of kill or be killed. And there was definitely no feeling of heroism. Like I've said, I think heroism requires choice, and there simply hadn't been any choice for us. What I felt instead was a weary resignation, an emptying sense that the world had just lurched in a new and not very pleasant direction, and me with it.

Chapter Thirteen

It was becoming a week for FNG officers. In addition to the new second lieutenant in 3rd platoon who the captain was babysitting, the battalion had sent another fresh-faced lieutenant to Bravo Company for his orientation assignment before getting permanently assigned to another company. Since the captain already had his hands full training the 3rd platoon's new guy and 1st platoon had run into some problems out to the west and didn't need a tag-along brown bar, I found myself getting charged with showing the ropes to the company's temporary FNG lieutenant. I wasn't thrilled.

Brand new 2nd lieutenants had a deserved reputation for not being able to find their ass with both hands, even if you gave them a map. The captain allowed that the situation would be a little awkward for me, since the new lieutenant obviously outranked me, but he still wanted me to look after him and keep him from hurting himself or the platoon. "Just keep him alive, Jennings, and see if you can teach him anything."

I <u>definitely</u> wasn't thrilled. "Yes suh, Mr. Boss."

It had been two days since our toe-to-toe shootout with the VC kids when a resupply chopper brought in our newly graduated OCS product, 2nd Lieutenant Marshall Courtney. He was skinny, dark-haired, and wore glasses with lenses like the bottoms of Coke bottles. I wanted to like him, to cut him the same slack that my temporary company had cut me a lifetime ago. But he was a total nerd—you almost expected to see a pocket protector on his fatigues—and I had the uneasy feeling that he was going to be a loose cannon, a risk to himself and to my platoon.

We started out well enough. I was appropriately deferential to his rank: "Yes Sir." "No Sir." "Your call, Sir." I tried to veil my manipulations sufficiently to let him direct the show, but with my script. Since he was smart enough to know he was on unfamiliar ground, it seemed to work. For a while.

I stayed up front with him in the platoon leader's spot when we patrolled, rather than go back to the rear of the column. Chief had been sort of filling in for me in the platoon sergeant's spot at the rear anyway, and I kept him there. His squad didn't mind at all, because having Chief in the rear meant they were always drag squad and none of them had to walk point.

I showed Lieutenant Courtney how a point man worked as we moved through the bush, and how the backup man had to be even more vigilant than the point man when we had to chop our way through thick foliage. I gave the lieutenant clues to watch for on patrol, like how to spot booby traps before they nailed you, and how to recognize VC signs. I told him about the different topography around the battalion AO, and the various contacts we had made with VC and NVA during the last few months. I tried to convey the frustration he would soon experience because of the infuriatingly elusive phantom enemy we faced.

At night after the defensive positions were in place, I sat with him and talked about being a grunt in Vietnam. As I covered different subjects with him, I was struck by how much I had absorbed myself since my first days in country. So much in this strange place was so new and unfamiliar, even to a graduate of the intense training at Officer Candidate School. He was a little overwhelmed at how much he didn't know. Heck, he even needed help learning how to fix dinner.

Our usual fare, C-rations and LRRPs, could be made a lot more tasty with a few simple additives such as Tabasco sauce and onion salt coaxed from accommodating relatives back home. The two absolutely worst C-rations, a watery concoction of ham and lima beans and another mixture of ham and eggs that had the consistency of dog food, could actually be gagged down if they were sufficiently doctored.

Most guys used C-4, the plastic explosive that we carried for blowing up tunnels and bunkers, to make a cooking fire. A little piece of C-4 pinched off the block like a hunk of clay could be ignited to produce a low blue flame—not terribly noticeable at night, but very hot. It wouldn't explode, so they said, without a detonator, making it a reasonably safe and very popular fuel. Mixing components from both C-rations and LRRPs—a can of Cs, a bag of freeze-dried something, a tin of plastic cheese melted over the top—in a canteen cup held over a C-4 fire was the essence of GI creative cooking. Julia Childs probably wouldn't have been interested in our recipes, but the results were a definite improvement over eating the stuff as it came. Meals were topped off with C-ration canned fruit or pound cake for desert, a pack of four ancient cigarettes (the tobacco often fell right out) and a few sheets of toilet paper. The Army just thought of everything we might need.

I went over battalion maps with the new lieutenant, re-familiarizing him with topographical designations he probably hadn't seen since OCS. We talked radio procedure, and the process and reliability of artillery and air support. I told him about my own platoon's close calls with fire support from LZ Professional, and the usual lag in receiving CAS or helicopter gunship assistance. "In other words, you don't want to get yourself in a jam with no way out, because you can't always count on getting timely support from anywhere."

Lieutenant Courtney learned fast, maybe too fast. Within a couple days I could sense he was starting to have thoughts like, "Is this all there is to it?" It was becoming apparent that he was itching to run a platoon. So I wasn't surprised after three days with us when he suggested during an evening conversation that I could return to my platoon sergeant role the next day.

It was about time for us to join with the ARVN platoon that was working in our AO. Bravo Company's captain was still with 3rd platoon, and radioed instructions to link with him and the ARVN on the following day. I thought it was interesting that he used both the one six and the one niner call signs, meaning he was intentionally sending his orders both to the

FNG lieutenant and to me. In the morning, we broke our night laager in a steady drizzle under a gray sky and headed toward the rendezvous, Lt. Courtney taking charge.

When I was acting platoon leader, I was meticulous about keeping track of our position—all the more so after taking unwanted artillery fire. It was the platoon leader's responsibility to know where we were at all times, and to keep battalion headquarters informed as well. At the column's rear, however, it was a lot more difficult to know our location and line of march. Changes in direction at the front of the column affected us in the rear many minutes later. In time, you decide not to bother trying to follow the map and put away your compass. It requires a certain trust that the map-reader up front knows what he's doing. In the case of my new, temporary el-tee, that was a powerful leap of faith.

It was something of a surprise when the platoon stopped around mid-day, and Kenny told me the lieutenant had radioed back that he wanted me to join him at the front. I worked my way up the column, where Lieutenant Courtney took me aside and confided that he wasn't exactly sure where we were. Mind you, he didn't actually use the word "lost", but that was sort of the gist of it.

I was annoyed, but tried not to show it—especially in front of the other guys, all of whom were tired and wet and in no mood to be lost in the bush at the hands of Lieutenant Dweeb. Being lost wasn't as bad as it sounds, because we knew where we had been only hours before and you just don't travel huge distances quickly on foot in the jungle. Finding ourselves was simply a matter of getting good coordinates for our present position.

Surrounding us were a number of small hills, all around 100 to 300 meters high. The vegetation was thick, but fortunately not the sight-shortening triple canopy. We actually had lines of sight to most of the higher hilltops from our low vantage point. Placing our position on the map would only require identifying one or two of the hills by their topographical features and taking a bearing to our location.

Lieutenant Courtney and I had gone through comparable training at Fort Benning on many subjects, he in OCS and me in NCOCS. We both thought of calling in an artillery airburst smoke round to mark one of the hills with known coordinates, providing us with a visual clue to determine our own location. However, he hadn't thought it all the way through and wanted to mark the hill closest to where we estimated we were standing.

At first blush, that may seem to make sense. Get the smoke where you have the greatest likelihood of seeing it. Unfortunately, Charlie could have similar ideas. "Dinkidau GI sending out invitation to party." And I was more than a little apprehensive at the notion of letting the gun bunnies fire anything, even a smoke round, at coordinates we thought were close to us.

Reason prevailed, and I convinced the lieutenant to call for an aerial smoke burst above the hill that our topographical map showed to be the highest among those near us, but not too close.

Smoke is a low priority fire mission, so a half hour passed before we got word that a round was on its way. Luckily, I guessed right about the hill where it would likely appear, and I was looking right at it when the white puff popped in the sky. Knowing that one location with certainty allowed us to calculate our own coordinates, and we were soon back on our way.

Buzz Gallagher gave me a knowing look as I worked my way back to the rear of the column. "Lieutenant Dickhead lose his compass?" I decided I would keep my map handy after that, even at the rear.

We moved on, shuffling through the mud and the crud in an unending drizzle, muzzles pointed down to keep out the rain. I pulled a soggy cigarette out of the spare bandage pouch on my web belt where I usually kept an open pack. It was stained almost completely brown from the dampness that had leaked through the pouch, and the filter had split open. I tore off the filter and stuck the wet cigarette in my mouth. It took a while to light, but I finally got a drag. It tasted like shit. Then the rain dripping off the front of my helmet splashed on the lit ash, and it didn't matter anyway.

About an hour after the lieutenant's little compass exercise, Kenny got another call from the platoon leader's RTO at the front. Courtney thought he saw VC on our right flank and was letting me know to pass the word at the rear of the platoon that he was about to have one of our machine guns open up. Almost panicked, I grabbed the radio handset and—perhaps a bit forcefully—reminded the good lieutenant that we were meeting American and ARVN platoons, and that their last reported positions would put them on our right.

Once again I slogged up to the front of the halted column. In a small concession to good sense, the lieutenant had decided to wait for me before grinding away with the M-60. Sure enough, he had accurately spotted that there were people moving roughly 500 meters away on our right flank. It looked like they were dressed in black—easy to think we were looking at gooks in black pajamas—but I had learned a long time before that wet jungle fatigues seen from a distance in the flat light of an overcast day appeared to be black, not OD. ARVN troops also wore OD uniforms, and theirs were even more deceptively black when they were wet.

Although the new lieutenant wouldn't have known about the wet uniform color illusion, he did have a rather prominent responsibility to understand that decisions involving machine guns are pretty final. You can't say, "Oops, didn't mean it." I was getting the distinct picture that my FNG platoon leader was an unusually FUBAR honcho, even for a brand new brown bar. Lieutenant Warren couldn't get back from his R&R fast enough to suit me.

As we cautiously closed the distance with the figures on our right, we soon realized they were indeed the ARVN we were supposed to meet. It would not have been a good move at all to crank up that machine gun. Even though I had no use for ARVN, it's just not very good manners to grease a platoon of your allies. The lieutenant would have been in deep doo-doo, and probably wouldn't have stayed a lieutenant for much longer.

The two units managed to get close enough together to establish that we were all good guys before anyone accidentally dropped a hammer. Hooking up with the ARVN proved to be a real giggle. There were about 25 of them in all, under the command of an earnest young officer who was about four feet tall (heck, they were *all* about four feet tall). The Vietnamese were wearing sharp looking OD uniforms designed a lot like ours, and were equipped with brand new American gear. Their M-16s looked so new they might still have had cosmoline on them. I thought of the warped sight on my own sorry M-16, and here were these useless gooks with brand new guns that they probably had never fired. Go figure. Nothing too good for our comrades in arms.

They were lightly loaded. Astonishingly so. The ARVN soldier who carried the PRC-25 wasn't carrying anything else, just his radio. No food, not even a weapon. Traveling light is one thing, but you had to be fucking crazy to walk around in Indian country without a gun. I looked at little Kenny with his radio, a rucksack, his M-16, and a strap of machine gun ammo for Patterson's pig. The two RTOs were almost the same size, but Kenny and his gear actually looked like a soldier.

Either the ARVN knew how to live off the land like the VC did—and they looked entirely too tidy to believe that—or their view of an infantry mission was a lot more cushy than ours.

Nobody in 2nd platoon knew how to speak Vietnamese, and the ARVN officer had only a handful of English words. He liberally inserted those few words into animated singsong bursts of Vietnamese, while we all stood around scratching our heads. As I had been learning more and more about Lieutenant Courtney, I wasn't too surprised when he hauled out a copy of the handbook on phonetic Vietnamese and started talking to the ARVN officer.

He tried; I'll give him credit for that. It was comical. The two officers babbled at each other for 20 minutes, neither accomplishing much more in the way of communication than swapping cigarettes. Most of the guys wandered off, bored. I saw Doc, leaning against a tree, sleeping. Some of the other GIs were politely listening to the ARVN chatter, but most were making a serious effort to ignore our South Vietnamese pals. Then, thankfully, the 3rd platoon and the captain arrived, taking charge of the proceedings.

Fortunately, the CO knew a little Vietnamese. Even better, the 3rd platoon had a Kit Carson scout and he knew enough English to be a passable translator. Kit Carson scouts were Vietnamese civilians who worked with American infantry units. Not every company had one, and some were better than others. Most of them were Hoi Chanhs, former VC who had surrendered under the Chieu Hoi (open arms) program and switched their allegiance to our side. They got paid, which was more than they normally got from the VC, and the treatment they received from Americans was a whole lot better than what they had experienced from their former VC brothers. Since the recruiting program employed by VC wasn't subtle—a typical approach was for a group of VC to walk into a peasant village and inform all the young males that they could either join up or die—it wasn't surprising that a few of the "draftees" became willing turncoats.

Still, it was tough to completely trust somebody who might have been shooting at you a few months before. Their abilities varied considerably, but the better Kit Carsons improved a unit's effectiveness at tracking and locating the bad guys, or avoiding ambushes and booby traps. A few of them had brought fairly detailed information with them on VC operations in our AO.

Translating for the captain, the 3rd platoon's Kit Carson soon bridged our communication gap with the ARVN officer and we all got on the same mission page. The captain, earning my undying gratitude, decided to keep the ARVN platoon with him and the Kit Carson. That was fine with everybody in my platoon, except maybe Lieutenant Jeepers who must have thought it would be really neat to go patrolling with our new Vietnamese buddies. I could already see grumbling in the 3rd platoon, as those grunts realized the lightly loaded ARVN would soon be mooching their C-rations and ammo.

It was late enough to call it a day, so the three platoons set up a company night laager before heading off in different directions the next day. It was a pretty sad defensive position — the ARVN didn't bother carrying claymores — so we improvised and spread out the ones we had. I wasn't going to miss these ARVN guys at all.

In the morning we recovered our claymores and prepared to head out on our own. It was still raining, and impossible to get or stay dry. When it rained for days on end we got chilly, even in a warm place like Vietnam. It was hard to stay warm at night, even wrapped up in a poncho liner, and the only other piece of clothing some of us had available to put on was a fatigue jacket (that's a shirt, to you civilians). Of course it was always as soaked as everything else. But another layer, even wet, was better than nothing.

All the stuff in our rucksacks was wet; nothing was immune from the constant rain. The only dry exceptions to the perpetual sogginess were the treasured items we wrapped up in long sleeves of plastic we scavenged from resupply — letters we'd gotten from home, writing paper for letters to send back, extra packs of cigarettes, pictures of wives and girlfriends and family. I had a six-foot piece of plastic sleeve, and I wound it around and around the few things I needed to keep absolutely dry. It worked, even when under water while crossing a river.

Socks were always wet from slogging through streams and rice paddies, and the constant rain just ensured they would never dry out. We changed them anyway, usually at night before rolling up in our poncho liners. Wash the crud and the silt from rice paddies out of them, or at least let them hang inside out in the rain. Put on another dirty pair, still imbedded with yesterday's crud.

Infantry needs its feet, and you learned to treat you own as well as circumstances allowed. At night, on the rare occasion we felt the area was sufficiently secure, we sometimes took our boots off when we turned in. A little fresh air helped to fight off immersion foot. Most of the time, though, the boots stayed on 24 hours a day, and usually wet.

After a bite for breakfast and a last quick meeting with the captain, 2nd platoon packed up its gear and bid farewell to the crack ARVN boys. The CO had given me orders to check out another dubious VC sighting to our northeast. So our intrepid little band of soggy soldiers humped along in a rag-tag column through the jungle, thinking dry thoughts and wishing we were just about anywhere else.

Lieutenant Courtney was being very managerial, seemingly unfazed by the incessant rain. He was a man on a mission. The novelty of where he was and what he was doing hadn't worn off for him quite yet, maybe because he hadn't seen people's insides strewn on the ground or burned flesh peeling off a shrieking human. It wouldn't take long before he'd get a chance, I knew. And then it would be interesting to see how much enthusiasm he still had for this fiesta.

As it soon turned out, if it hadn't been for his RTO he would have been a man in a body bag.

About two hours out of the night laager, we walked into a clearing and an ambush. Grunts scattered, leaping for cover and melting into the ground. Now, I always thought that hitting the dirt when you're under fire was an instinctive act. I swear I cannot recall a single instructor in any of my Army training classes ever saying, "Okay, listen up, girls. If you ever come under enemy fire, the first thing you want to do is get your sweet little asses down on the ground so's you make it a little tougher for Charlie to shoot you." Nope, I think they all just naturally assumed we could handle that bit of combat discretion on our own. Speaking for myself, I never had any trouble figuring it out.

It was no surprise, then, that the whole platoon made a quick trip into the mud when the VC carbines started cracking. Everybody except Lieutenant Dork, who just froze and stood there, looking incredibly pathetic. We could have pinned a target on him.

Now, it's true that not one of us was in any mood for an ambush. We all had been doing fine, thank you very much, merely being miserable in the chilly drizzle, and wallowing around in the mud dodging bullets was heaping indignity on top of discomfort. But this lieutenant was trying very hard to be dead. It was as though he didn't really understand what was happening.

A few GIs in the lead squad were trying to help the point man and his backup by putting out suppressing fire while the two of them crawled backward out of the clearing. As ambushes go, this one was pretty weak—only a few carbines popping away at us and no automatic weapons. But our frozen lieutenant stood in the clearing and stared vacantly while bullets zipped by him in both directions.

The platoon leader's RTO, whose name was Mills, suddenly came flying across the clearing and smashed into the lieutenant with a cross body block that would have made Gordie Howe proud. The hit knocked Courtney's legs out from under him and he went ass over teakettle. They went down hard, but intact, the lieutenant confused and disoriented by the gunfire and his collision with the ground. He probably never realized that he owed his life to the RTO's quick move. Later, Mills told me he actually got a perverse pleasure out of smashing into Courtney. "It isn't often you get to cold-cock an officer and get thanked rather than court-marshaled."

In what had become a standard, futile scenario, we returned fire to an unseen adversary and accomplished nothing more fruitful than lightening our loads of ammunition. The VC just melted away. As much as I never wanted to repeat the OK Corral shootout of a few days earlier, it had been a refreshing change to actually see the bad guys lined up in front of us and know that something useful had been achieved by all the bullets we tossed out there.

Lieutenant Courtney composed himself, probably relieved that his lapse had taken place in front of a temporary platoon assignment instead of his permanent command, and we moved on. We still had to check out the "VC sighting". The humbled lieutenant suggested I stay up front with him for a while. Faced with a choice between doing a job I hadn't wanted in the first place or letting Lieutenant Newbie do it, I thought staying at the front might be the preferred alternative. Chief went back to the rear.

We shambled along, still wet and miserable in the drizzle, but a little more on edge after walking into the ambush. Now we knew that Chuck was in the neighborhood, and he knew that we were, too. I let Courtney handle the map, but I occasionally peeked over his shoulder and I made sure the RTO looked up the shackle codes for our location transmissions. It was so wet, the RTO had to keep a piece of plastic over the radio handset so it wouldn't short out.

As we moved northeast, the jungle gave way more and more to rolling hills and lowland grassy expanses. It was once probably good farmland, and I thought it was more than a little likely that we would find some peasants still working the soil.

It was afternoon when we found the bunker and the rice cache. The point man practically walked into the bunker. He stopped so short his backup almost walked into him. The column came over the top of a squatty hill, and right there on the far slope was a Vietnamese boy no more than five years old, sitting on his heels the way all gooks did and playing with a stick in the dirt. Just beyond him was an opening in the ground, a hole leading to a bunker dug in the hillside.

Sure, it was a free fire zone. But I like to think most GIs wouldn't simply grease a little kid. Damned if I knew what he was doing out there, but there he was.

He saw us. He didn't run away, or even make a noise. He just stared at us. When the point man beckoned to him, the kid stood up and started walking toward us. I suddenly thought about a training chapter I had read somewhere about VC using children to get grenades close to unsuspecting GIs. I wished the point man hadn't beckoned to him, but it was already too late to do anything about it and I didn't want to call out for fear it would alert anybody who might be in the bunker.

The kid reached our point man, who must have read the same chapter. He patted the kid down and, satisfied he wasn't carrying, turned back to the hole in the ground. Lieutenant Courtney took charge of the kid and I focused my attention on the bunker. Nobody in <u>this</u> platoon was going to crawl into that hole without some idea of what might be down there, that much was certain. But we couldn't just leave it.

The point man's backup, an FNG named Brady, had a LAW strapped to his rucksack. I tapped it and gestured at the opening to the bunker. He understood. Brady edged to the right a little, to get a straight shot. We hollered some Vietnamese stuff like "Di di mau" to let anyone who was underground know he had company. The lieutenant dragged out his stupid phonetic Vietnamese booklet again and shouted something unintelligible that was supposed to mean, "Come out with your hands up." The kid looked at him like he was weird, which of course he was.

We waited. Nobody came out of the hole. Brady fired the LAW.

Jesus, all hell broke loose. It was a perfect shot; I could actually see the rocket go through the opening. The loud report of the round in the tube was followed a split second later by the muffled explosion of the charge inside the bunker. Some chickens that had been scratching in the mud nearby went freaking nuts, leaping in the air in a tornado of feathers and squawking.

And a pig came bolting up through the hole where the LAW had gone in, squealing and grunting and throwing an absolute hissy fit. I think my mouth was hanging open. I wasn't sure which was more strange—that a pig came out of the hole, or that the pig would have survived the LAW and was even alive to come out of the hole. He should have been pork chops. The pig snorted and squeaked and disappeared around the side of the hill. For all I know he's still running.

Smoke was curling out of the bunker's opening. The lieutenant repeated his "Surrender" message. Normally, that would have been kind of unnecessary after a LAW explosion, but the pig's survival gave us some pause about how much damage the shape charge had done inside the hole. Brady crawled close enough to pitch a grenade into the bunker, making another loud whumping boom and setting the damn chickens off again.

We surrounded the bunker, and waited. Nothing happened. After ten minutes or so, emboldened by the absence of noise or activity at the hole, Kenny volunteered to take a look. He was the smallest guy in the platoon, and nobody wanted to contest him for the privilege of peeking in the bunker.

So Kenny cautiously crawled into the opening with a flashlight and a 45 pistol, just like a real tunnel rat. After a minute or two, he called out that the bunker opened up into a single underground room, a storage facility of sorts. At the back he found a couple of sleeping pallets, and a rice cache of about 500 pounds. The cache pretty much guaranteed we had stumbled on a VC hangout of some sort, but it didn't explain the unaccompanied kid.

I scavenged some C-4 from around the platoon and jury-rigged a charge with a claymore detonator. Kenny slithered back down the hole and set the charge in the rice cache. When everyone was clear, I blew the charge. It didn't collapse the bunker, but it turned the rice into inedible dust.

Lieutenant Courtney and I didn't think we should leave the kid. It just didn't seem right to leave a child alone in the bush, especially after some major damage to the bunker that could have been his home for all we knew (not to mention scaring his chickens and driving off his pig). So, when we finally moved out we took him with us.

In reality, he probably wasn't alone out there. His relatives could easily have been part of the ambush that almost ended Courtney's storied military career, and the kid might have been simply holding down the home front until they returned. But Americans, even us evil baby-killers, had a natural reluctance to abandon a kid in the wilderness.

Orders came over the radio for us to head back to the firebase, now about two days travel to our south. The lieutenant apparently didn't mind babysitting duty, and it kept both of them out of my hair. So it didn't bother me that he was off doing patty-cake while I was back to running 2nd platoon.

All the little guy had was a ragged tee shirt and a thin pair of shorts. Walking barefoot evidently didn't concern him, and he didn't have any trouble keeping up with us. He never uttered a sound, but once in a while the lieutenant got him to smile (probably those dumb phonetic Vietnamese phrases). He ate our food, even hungrily, and I gathered from his familiarity with C-rations and P-38 can openers that Army food wasn't completely new to him.

Passing through a rice paddy on the second day he was with us, the kid came up with a big green water leech on his leg. The leech was huge, at least seven inches long, and hung down from his thigh to well below his knee. It must have hurt, but the kid didn't wince or let out a peep. Chief squirted bug juice on the leech to get rid of it and Doc patched up the bleeding wound (something I doubt he would have done for any of the guys). So Doc, the consummate dink-hater, was warming up to our tiny traveling companion. Somehow, because of his tender age and uncomplaining, friendly demeanor, the kid didn't seem like "just another gook', even to cynical guys like Doc.

The last night in a laager before temporarily returning to LZ Professional to drop off our "prisoner", I gave the kid a piece of paper and a pencil to play with. I will never forget what he drew. It was a picture, in the same stick figure art drawn by five-year-old kids everywhere, of a little boy standing beside a hootch. In the sky above the standing boy was a sun, and also a crudely drawn helicopter with tiny pencil dots underneath it—like stuff falling to the ground. The dots were bullets. Strafing bullets falling to the ground where the little stick figure boy was standing.

Not your typical drawing from a little kid.

The funny thing was, the kid acted natural about it. Like the picture he had made for me was a common, expected part of a five-year-old's life. No big deal, just another helicopter gunship coming down the street, just like the ice cream trucks in American suburbia.

I thought about the refrigerator art that hangs in countless American homes. Happy pictures of smiling faces, normal scenes of ordinary people doing everyday things. Crayon sketches of houses and dogs and trees and bright yellow suns with rays around them. Pictures of kid stuff and kids' worlds displayed by proud moms and dads and grandparents on kitchen cabinets and refrigerator doors.

And here was this earnest-faced pint-sized Vietnamese kid, raised under God knows what circumstances and likely having seen things unthinkable to the parents of kiddie artists back home, drawing a picture of the mayhem we had brought to his country. I remembered the night at Fort Benning when the airborne Puff the Magic Dragon was shooting miniguns on a practice range. I wouldn't want to be on the ground underneath something like that, and the kid's picture seemed to say that he had experienced the real thing.

I didn't know who I was any more. I wanted to be a tough guy. Tough guys had the best chance of surviving and going home. Tough guys were unaffected by emotion and moral dilemmas—they just followed orders and killed anything that wasn't a good guy. They were immune to the chaos and gore and the little tragedies that war brought to the lives of innocent bystanders. Real tough guys most certainly wouldn't give a shit about some little gook kid and his troubling picture.

My experiences since arriving in Vietnam were hardening me, moving me closer to that tough guy I thought I needed to be. But it was like there were two of me, and one of us still believed something was very wrong with the kid's picture. The badass part of me wanted to shrug it off, but the idealistic part of me wanted to cry out in protest. I felt torn, not sure any longer of the absolute certainty of right and wrong. And I was aware that an emptiness, a hollow spot, had been growing in me for some time.

I thought about what the war was doing to these people. The hollowness inside me spread a little more. I felt very sad.

...And do you have a picture of the pain?
Phil Ochs

Chapter Fourteen

Every grunt looked forward to stand-down with the anticipation of a child waiting for Christmas morning. Bravo Company was due, everyone knew it, and we were pumped for it.

Stand-down was a time when a company got recalled to the Americal Division base at Chu Lai for three days away from the war. There was a special compound that was reserved for the use of companies on stand-down, and combat units rotated through it one after another. The compound had barracks buildings, a mess hall, and perpetually full coolers of beer. It was a time to simply check out, a time to drink and sleep on real bunks and drink and eat and drink and get a haircut and drink and get fresh clothes and drink and...you get the picture. Stand-down didn't happen very often, only once or twice in a tour for guys in the 196th. But a stand-down was second only to an R&R on the list of good times.

I got 2nd platoon back to LZ Professional okay, dropped off the kid and the FNG lieutenant, and picked up Lieutenant Warren back from his R&R. He had a pussy-whipped smile on his face after a week in Australia, and we were mighty glad to have him back. The lieutenant was full of stories about drinking and partying and expensive whores, a week of eating and boozing and screwing. Because he was single, he had picked Australia over Hawaii—which was where all the married guys went on R&R to meet their wives. He had blown a wad of dough, but his grin didn't come off for two or three days.

On his third day of R&R he met some Aussie gal, not a hooker, and she spent the remainder of his week with him. He swore he had fallen in love and would be going back to see her after his tour was up, but the rest of us knew he probably would never see her again. Anyway, his batteries were charged and he was just about broke.

And he wasn't particularly thrilled to be back. He was a commissioned officer, but he wasn't a lifer and didn't share the zeal for our dirty little war that so many of the asshole field grade officers spouted. In fact, although he tried not to show it, I could tell he was feeling pinched by some of the same conflicts I had been feeling.

Mixed in with his undoubtedly exaggerated stories of drinking and partying, Lieutenant Warren told us about a disturbing conversation he'd had with some Australian officers he met at a club. The Aussies were convinced that the U.S. had already given up on the war, and were simply marking time while slowly downsizing troop strength. At the same time, they had been hearing rumors of a troop build-up along the Cambodian border. Finally, and difficult to believe, they told the lieutenant that they had heard persistent rumors that secret U.S. bombing was going on in Cambodia, despite the end of Operation Rolling Thunder in late 1968 and American assurances that the bombing had stopped.

Lieutenant Warren said to me, "It's like we can't decide whether to shit or get off the pot. And if the Australians are right about secret bombing in Cambodia, there'll be hell to pay back in The World when the McCarthy people find out."

It took a while for the secret bombing came to light, but the Aussies turned out to be right and there was indeed hell to pay.

During out brief stay on the hill to exchange lieutenants and turn in our shrimp-sized Cong, Kenny Whitman got his orders to go home. He had been marking off his days on a calendar and was down to two weeks. For some reason he got a drop, which meant an early out from his tour. It also meant he didn't have to go back to the bush again, which was always a relief to a short-timer. Nothing was worse than getting nailed when you only had a few days left. The orders had him flying back to the States out of Cam Rahn Bay in three days. He was happier than a pig in mud, and I was glad for him, too.

That was the nature of the Vietnam War. People were always coming and going, the faces of the people in our unit constantly changing. Sooner or later there would be some FNG to replace Kenny. I was already thinking about who I was going to tap in the interim to temporarily hump Kenny's radio.

The shifting roster of names and faces was a bit strange, and you never completely got used to it. There had been guys in the platoon I never even knew, because their tours ended shortly after mine began. A few others rotated out not long after I got to know them. Most astonishing, I was actually getting to be one of the more experienced grunts in the platoon, even with half my tour to go. I thought that was really bizarre—new guys were probably looking at me the same way I looked at Mike Keene and the Delta Company GIs a terribly long time ago. I could remember how scared and inadequate I felt when I first arrived. Heck, there were times I still felt pretty inadequate, and I could never completely shake the image of 2nd platoon as a bunch of kids out playing soldier, not one of us a serious professional.

I shook Kenny's hand and put him on a chopper to Chu Lai. He had been a good RTO and a better friend. He promised to write, which of course he never did (a lot of guys leaving Vietnam found they didn't want to sustain any connections to an experience they wanted to put behind them), and he gave me his parents' address in Illinois. I felt a little lonely as the Huey revved up and leaned into the air. At least I had the satisfaction that he was going home in one piece. To the extent that I had felt in many ways responsible for him, maybe because he was my RTO in addition to being one of my charges in the platoon, I enjoyed a sense of accomplishment that he was alive and intact.

I watched the helicopter shrink in the distance, then turned and walked back down to the bunkers where the platoon had temporarily borrowed space and got my gear together. Our stay on the hill had only been one day, but at least it was one day that we didn't have to spend in the jungle.

By mid-morning we had climbed down the hill and were

headed west, moving parallel with and north of the Burlington Trail. I had no idea what our orders were. I assumed Lieutenant Warren had some idea of where we were going, but he was acting kind of drifty. His head was still floating around back in Australia and he was dreaming about his new sweetie with an amusing regularity. And it really didn't matter what the orders were—the mission would always be some variation of "hunt for Charlie".

Several days passed, my sense of time dulled by unmotivated trudging through the bush all day followed by an exhausted collapse into another night in a defensive position. It was hot, like always, and the rainy season was showing signs of ending. We had no contact, not even any signs of VC mischief.

Bravo Company was about a week away from a return to LZ Professional when the good news came. Stand-down orders arrived instructing us to break off the operation and find an open area for a flight of slicks to pick up the company on the following day. By late afternoon we had located a suitable place and set up a perimeter. I don't think an entire NVA regiment could have pushed us away from that prospective LZ, that doorway to a stand-down. We were like a mean dog with a bone; don't even think about trying to take those coolers of beer away from us.

The night was filled with boasts of how much beer could be consumed in one stand-down, and with the anticipated relief at the thought of three relatively war-free days back in the rear with the REMFs. If any Viet Cong had been around, they would surely have passed us up because the whole company was wide-awake.

As if on cue, the morning broke clear and bright and dry, buoying spirits that were already sky-high. What had been only yesterday a company of surly, cynical, misanthropic grunts was now a bunch of young bucksnorts eager to get to a party. A mighty thirst was quickly building.

The transportation announced itself long before any Hueys could be seen on the horizon, and the company spread into scattered groups for an eagle flight. This was one air operation where I wouldn't have to worry about disorganization, or about bad guys waiting for us at the other end. No hot LZ this trip, just cold beer.

We were in the air for maybe 15 minutes on the trip to Chu Lai. Because it was a sunny day, it was a lot like my first trip out to Professional many months and a lifetime ago. Strange that the bucolic beauty that struck me so on the first trip now seemed routine, even faintly ominous. From the distance of an airborne view, landscapes always appear so pristine and don't reveal the imperfections we can see up close. Now that I had been down there, crawling around in the muck and vines and elephant grass, picking off leeches and playing cops and robbers with Charlie, the scenery from above wasn't quite as spectacular and beautiful.

The pick-up and flight were thankfully uneventful—nobody wants to get in a fight on the way to a party—and we were soon at the Chu Lai airport. A quick trip on deuce and a half trucks to the stand-down compound, then let the good times roll.

Wisely, guns and other munitions were taken from us and locked away. It wouldn't be terribly fitting to have some GI get shit-faced and pop a cap on someone he decided he didn't like very much. Even in war, guns and booze make dangerous companions. As soon as the ordinance was under lock and key, the coolers were open for business.

I waited for the initial stampede to subside a little. After all, I was supposedly a ranking NCO and probably had a responsibility to preserve at least a little decorum. Once the mob thinned out a bit, I went over to the coolers and grabbed a can of the coldest beer I'd held since leaving Detroit. I noticed with considerable satisfaction that the coolers were still well stocked, even after the surge of my thirsty throng.

Nursing the first brew, I wandered around the compound's area. The stand-down facilities were located within sight of the South China Sea, and I found a makeshift picnic table with a nice view of the beach. I sat down in the sun—it somehow didn't feel quite as wilting by the ocean as it did in the jungle—

and watched the waves marching up to the shore, breaking into bubbling foam that chased running birds up and down the sloping beach. It was soothing, and reminded me of the great beaches on the Gulf coast of Florida.

Why couldn't I be there instead?

After a while, the squad leaders—Chief and Buzz Gallagher and Dee—came over and joined me. Buzz handed me a fresh beer. Dee had a deck of cards, so we started playing poker. Pretty soon, the game grew and the table was packed with players and onlookers. Somebody had gotten a bottle of Chivas from the PX, and it worked its way around the table. More beers, more hands, more hits on the bottle of scotch, and before long I was both mellow and missing about half the cash I'd had at the beginning of the game. I didn't even care. I went off and found a bunk in one of the barracks, and had the first unbroken sleep for six straight hours I'd had in months. No watch, no ambushes, no outgoing or incoming artillery, no bad guys, no firefights, no leeches crawling in my poncho liner. Just unconcerned sleep, helped along by a few too many beers.

The Chu Lai dump was located a half mile down the beach from the stand-down compound. An Army division base camp was actually a small city, and it generated a fair amount of refuse. The dump contained not only trash and scrap, it also was home to cast-off supplies and equipment from supply rooms not authorized to have the stuff. Military regulations encouraged wastefulness. If a unit didn't use material it was budgeted to receive, it would lose the allocation. Better to keep the allocation and throw excess equipment away. Or, a creative supply sergeant might get his hands on something that wasn't authorized for his unit, and have to pitch it if he was facing an inspection. It was certainly preferable to send stuff to the dump than get in trouble for having unauthorized equipment.

As a consequence of this profligate supply mentality, it was said you could find just about any equipment you might ever imagine in the Chu Lai dump. Some supply sergeants swore that if you had the knowledge and the tools you could build a helicopter from discarded parts and fly it out of the dump.

Might not even need the tools; you could find them in the dump, too. And the discarded ordinance in the dump could probably arm your chopper. A truly fine example of your tax dollars at work.

Anyway, it was the dump that served as my alarm clock the next morning. There was always a fire burning in one part of the dump or another, and one hot spot evidently found a cast off bomb or some other fairly substantial explosive. Jesus, talk about a bad way to wake up, especially after a night of sucking on beer cans. It was close enough to actually feel the explosion as well as hear it. Coming out of booze-induced sleep in an unfamiliar place to the sound of a large explosion was mighty disorienting, to say the least. I was on the floor grabbing fruitlessly for a weapon before my eyes were completely open.

A few hung-over faces peered out of barracks doors trying to figure out if the place was under attack. There was a battalion trains area right next to the stand-down compound, and the REMFs over there were acting nonchalant. That was a clue both that we weren't under attack, and that stuff in the dump exploded with some regularity. Seeing those courageous Remington rangers (typists) and motor pool patriots reassured us twitty nervous leg combat troops that we weren't getting VC rocket fire and that all was well. Okay, we're up, so let's go have a beer.

Stand-down provided an opportunity to do some shopping at a PX, and there was one conveniently located right across from the compound. Most stuff in a wartime PX was really a bargain, a whole lot cheaper than even stateside PXs. Booze and cigarettes were a fraction of their stateside cost, and you could get cameras, watches and stereo gear so inexpensively that they were almost mandatory purchases. If you wanted, the PX staff could have some merchandise shipped directly to your home. I bought an entire new stereo component system sight unseen, and had it shipped to Linda. I had been building and trading up sound systems since I bought my first tape recorder with savings from a paper route, and the new PX sound system was going to be the nicest one I had ever owned. I hoped I'd make it home to actually hear it.

Recalling (a little dimly, I admit) how good the Chivas had tasted the night before right from the bottle, I bought a couple more for myself and the squad leaders. I even picked up a six-pack of Aussie beer for our lovesick lieutenant. I wrapped up my shopping trip with a waterproof Seiko watch and a Ronson butane cigarette lighter. I had a CIB engraved on one side of the lighter and the burning rope unit insignia of the 196th Brigade engraved on the other.

A trip to the rear for stand-down also meant access to real (okay, sort of real) barbers, who could usually improve on the clip jobs that GIs gave each other back on the firebase. Most of the barbers were local Vietnamese from Tam Ky. We knew that some of them were Viet Cong, but their objective was to gain intelligence about activities in Chu Lai, not to kill unsuspecting grunts in their barber chairs.

Most of us were pretty shaggy, and long hair was simply an inconvenience in the heat and muck of the jungle. Besides, long hair gave bugs another place to hide. So I went and got a nice short buzz cut from some young Vietnamese guy who kept telling me "You numba one, Sarge" while he was giving me "numba one haircka—make you look good, girls all want fucky, fucky". Yeah, yeah, I always found that a new haircut got me laid. Just cut the goddamn hair.

When he finished cutting, he started massaging my scalp. It felt good. Then he put his hands just above my ears and began rolling my head around on my neck. Not knowing what was coming, I went with the flow. Suddenly he turned my head sharply, making my neck bones pop like you might crack the knuckle of a finger. That didn't feel too good, and ended my haircut. I later learned that Vietnamese thought neck manipulation was an essential part of getting a haircut and routinely shared the spine-cracking custom with their GI customers. Most guys had it happen just once, and ended all their future gook haircuts before the barber got to the part where he tried to twist your head off your shoulders.

You could get a lot of other things besides cheap booze, cigarettes, and stereo gear in a division base camp. The Army tried to play it down, but drugs were pretty much everywhere in Vietnam and a lot of GIs spent their tours looking for Mary Jane and Lucy in the sky with diamonds. Grass was plentiful, and stronger stuff was easy to come by, too. Huge, pre-rolled marijuana cigarettes called Chu Lai 101s were openly sold all over the base, despite the Army's strong anti-drug policy. You didn't want to flagrantly smoke them in front of officers or most senior NCOs, but usage was widespread and was tacitly condoned by non-lifers, as long as it was reasonably discreet. The attitude toward drugs became less and less tolerant as you got closer to combat areas, because most guys didn't want a stoned out grass-head watching his back in a defensive position. But there were places in the rear you might have mistaken for a Cheech and Chong movie.

Some of the Chu Lai 101s were reportedly laced with a bit of heroin, for an extra kick. The story went that enterprising VC were hoping to erode the effectiveness ground troops by getting marijuana smokers hooked on something stronger. I never knew if that was true, or just a good story planted by the Army to dissuade curious grunts from giving the stuff a try. But GIs puffing on cigar-sized joints were a fairly common sight, probably even more so during stand-down.

So, in our little party compound there were guys smoking dope in addition to guzzling prodigious quantities of brew. Whatever your poison, just about everybody in the company was feeling no pain. I'd smoked marijuana in college, but I was just apprehensive enough about the possible squirt of heroin in the local grass that I decided I didn't need to take the chance.

The Chu Lai airbase was home to both Army and Air Force flyboys. It was the center of operations for the helicopters that worked the Americal AO, and also for the Phantoms that provided close air support. Even in our continuous inebriation, we were aware of the constant comings and goings of aircraft. Sometimes we sat on the beach and watched the fighters flying in and out, sucking on beers and feeling just fine.

On the final day of stand-down we were treated to some unplanned entertainment by the Air Force. Most of us were half in the bag, some playing cards, some writing letters home, a few sleeping. No one paid much attention as a lone Phantom took off over the harbor, then banked to head inland. A few of us did notice, however, when the jet turned again and began flying east, back toward the water. It was a curious direction for a mission, unless he was hunting sampans and sharks. The war was the other way.

Which is why I happened to be looking at it, puzzled, when the parachute appeared.

Being a lowly ground-bound grunt, I was not terribly well acquainted with the more glamorous profession of driving jet strike aircraft. Plus I was watching all this through a blurry Budweiser and Chivas haze, so it's possible that my comprehension was just a little diminished. Still, I was clever enough to suspect that a parachute was probably not part of the normal take-off checklist. In fact, I thought it might be entirely possible that parachuting pilots were not normal for any part of flying jets.

So I said, "Aha" and was sure I was on to something when a siren started wailing at the airport. I took another swallow of beer—it was tough to get too excited about something that seemed so unreal—and watched the jet just keep flying while the parachute slowly floated down toward the harbor. Nothing appeared to be wrong with the airplane. It was doing fine without anyone on board. I guessed that the pilot's exit had been prompted by a warning gauge of some sort, telling him the plane might disagreeably blow up or something.

Then the jet began a gently banking turn and looked for the first time like it was losing altitude. We stood and watched, a company of gassed grunts holding beer cans and looking goofy, as the Phantom made a gradual 180-degree turn. Which left it heading right smack at the Americal base.

The pilot and his plane made it to the ground at almost the same moment. The pilot came down in the South China Sea, and his jet almost made it back to the airstrip. The jet skimmed into the hillside above the harbor, empty but still under power. It managed to slam right into the middle of Chu Lai, in a sliding, burning, shrieking crumple of metal. It took out two supply sheds, but incredibly no barracks or other buildings with people in them. Some of us noted, with a certain disrespectful glee, that the Americal Division's commanding general's compound wasn't too far beyond where the twisted wreck finally came to a stop. That would have been very unbecoming. Imagine the evening news reporting the demise of a division commander at the hands of an empty Air Force jet.

It was close enough to see and hear the whole show, but not close enough to pose any danger—to us anyhow. So we hoisted our beer cans in a toast, and expressed our appreciation to the Air Force's flying demonstration with a round of applause. Humor is where you find it.

That night, our last night of stand-down, was the fight. I found out later that it was started by eight or ten REMFs from outside the stand-down compound. They came in looking for free beer, and got mouthy when they were asked to leave. Some pushing and shoving turned into fists, and the brawl was on.

I walked out of a barracks door right into the middle of it. The evening had been rainy, and I was wearing an old rain jacket I'd found hanging in the barracks. A little tipsy, I didn't stop to think that the rain jacket covered up the sergeant stripes on my sleeves. So I'm wading into the scuffle like an NCO in charge, pulling people off other people and yelling orders to break it up, and nobody in the boxing lineup knows or cares whether I'm a dirtbag private or General Fucking Westmoreland.

Something banged hard against the side of my head, and I went down—out like a light.

I wasn't unconscious very long, but when I came to the fight was over and the combatants gone. My head hurt, from whatever had hit me and from all the beer. Worst hurt was my dignity, such as it had become. With all the Charlies in Vietnam who wanted to see bad things happen to me, it was hard to face the fact that some GIs wanted a piece of me, too. If those REMFs had such a need to fight, it seemed to me that they could use some time in the jungle fighting a real enemy. I wouldn't have minded letting any of them take my place; I just didn't need to fight someone that much.

Chief wandered by while I was still rubbing my head and sat down beside me. He told me that Bravo Company's senior medic had been whacked on the head with a hammer by one of our visitors and had been taken to the base hospital with a concussion. Apparently stand-down wasn't the safe place I had thought.

I went back to the coolers for more beer. A lot more beer.

Chapter Fifteen

Ever notice how you look forward to something, then once it's over you feel like it never happened? That's what stand-down felt like after, oh, maybe two days back in the bush. A distant memory; even the hangovers were long gone.

Back to the business of war. We had countless rice paddies to cross, klicks of jungle to cut through, hootches to burn, leeches to pick off, and people to kill. Let's go search and destroy.

The end of stand-down, as you might imagine, was just a little blurry. We recovered our gear and were flown by Chinooks out to the valley overlooked by LZ Professional. There wasn't sufficient room on the hill for a flight of shit-hooks, so the choppers dumped us in the valley and we humped back up the hill.

I had a new RTO to replace Kenny, an FNG named John Fournelle. I'd asked the squad leaders if anyone else in the platoon wanted to volunteer to hump a prick 25, and nobody cared for the load. So the most recent new guy got elected. Poor sap actually thought it was a bit of an honor to carry Sarge's radio, so I guess you could say we had a win-win situation.

John and another new arrival, Fred Becker, had joined the platoon as we were boarding the Chinooks leaving stand-down. Both of them were private E-2s, fresh from Tigerland at Fort Polk. They had each been given a 30-day leave after their infantry AIT, and then a plane ride to The Nam. John was kind of an average guy, not really remarkable in appearance or personality, but certainly genial enough. He was shy, and obviously intimidated at joining a "veteran" infantry platoon. He had just turned 19, another kid in a platoon of boy soldiers.

Bravo Company didn't get to stay on the firebase. We had one day to sweat the beer out of our systems and load up on food, ammo and water. Then it was back to the boonies. We didn't mind leaving Professional all that much, because the hill was way too crowded with two separate rifle companies occupying it.

Our orders took us southwest, and the company split into platoons working parallel, with two or three klicks of separation. We had settled back into the usual monotonous routine, playing hide and seek with Charles. I think we had been back out something like five days when I was hit.

It was another dismal day, overcast and rainy, but still oppressively hot. Second platoon was patrolling on the far right of the company spread, noisily wandering around doing soldier stuff. Lieutenant Warren must have been as miserable as the rest of us — he'd gotten a little lazy and was leading the column down what had not long before been a jungle trail.

Undergrowth in the bush grew so thick and fast that it was usually impossible to guess how much time had passed since a trail was last used. This one was so grown over it was sometimes tough to tell it really was a trail. I suppose the apparent lack of use made us feel we could walk it in comparative safety, like it had probably been a while since Chuck was in town.

I was in my usual place toward the back of the column. I could hear a machete way up front, opening the trail in places where the clutching vines and elephant grass had completely reclaimed it.

It seems incredibly unlikely that twenty-some grunts could have walked by the tripwire before any of us saw or hit it, but that's what happened. The wire had been there for some time and was well camouflaged by new growth. Murphy, the guy in front of me, must have snagged it and set off the booby trap. It was a grenade tied low on a tree at the side of the path.

The explosion startled the hell out of us, and it got Murphy pretty bad. Both of his legs were ripped up, and he had shrapnel in his buttocks as well. By comparison I was lucky. I took three pieces of shrapnel in my right thigh, and went down feeling like a white-hot ice pick was being driven into my leg. My ears were ringing from the explosion, so I could barely hear John Fournelle hollering "Medic!"

God, it hurt! Doc came scrambling back from the middle of the column, oblivious to the potential of gooks waiting in the tangled jungle on both sides of the trail. He rightly went to the more serious casualty first, trying to stop the bleeding from Murphy's shredded legs. Charlie was smart; a grenade might not always be powerful enough to kill us unless we happened to be right on top of it, but mounting the booby trap low ensured that legs would be chopped up. Infantry pukes without legs don't have much value.

I had a pressure bandage out and pressed to the hole in my leg that appeared to be leaking the most. The leg was starting to feel numb. I tried to stand, but it wouldn't hold me. I looked around at the thick vegetation and wondered if we were going to get incoming fire, and decided that the booby trap must have been an old one. I found myself disassociating from my surroundings, and wasn't terribly motivated at that particular moment to care much one way or another about Charlie and the unpleasant possibility of guns going off. A feeling of disbelief had settled over me. It couldn't really be happening. Sure, people got hurt on a battlefield, but that wasn't supposed to happen to me! It was the same feeling an invulnerable 16-year-old has when he wraps his father's car around a tree.

Doc turned to me. He slit open the leg of my fatigue trousers and shook some anti-bacterial powder on the holes in my thigh. He tied down the pressure bandage, and gave me some crap about being lucky to get such a pussy wound. The shrapnel hadn't hit any veins or tendons, just muscle. I knew he was right, but at the moment I didn't feel all that lucky. I wasn't a stranger to blood by any means, but I had managed to live my whole life up to that point without any foreign objects being forcibly introduced into my body. There was something very unnerving in the realization that someone tried to kill me with jagged little pieces of hot shrapnel, and could have succeeded. And it really hurt.

Lieutenant Warren came back to check on us after calling for a dust-off, and was setting out fire teams on both flanks in case any bad guys came around to check out the noise from their nasty little surprise. When Doc advised him my wound was on the light side, he told me not to spend too much time goofing off in the hospital. No malingering in this platoon. Sympathy didn't seem to be his long suit.

There was no option for either Murphy or me to remain with the platoon. I couldn't walk, and needed to have the shrapnel removed. Murphy obviously had to have some surgery to repair his shattered legs. The medevac was en route, and Chief's squad was looking around for a clearing. I was about to experience one of those special moments in Vietnam, a ride on an air ambulance.

The dust-off arrived with a noisy pounding of rotors, touched down long enough for the two of us to be loaded, and was heading for the 91st Evacuation Hospital in Chu Lai before it dawned on me that this meant time away from the boondocks. Every day a GI spent out of the jungle—whether R&R, stand-down, time in a hospital, whatever—was time when the odds of dying were significantly reduced. They were like free days deducted from your tour of duty. I wasn't exactly elated, I hurt too much. But it did improve my outlook on having some unwanted holes in my leg.

The 91st Evac was a bustling place. Medevacs were coming and going fairly frequently, and blood-spattered grunts in various stages of distress and consciousness arrived with disturbing regularity. Murphy was quickly dispatched to surgery. I was sent off to a blood ward to be patched up.

There were two types of wards, in the vernacular of infantry troops. Blood wards were for wounded guys, and shit wards were for all the other maladies that could get us. A lot of non-trauma infirmities, like amoebic dysentery, resulted in the unpleasant byproduct of unrelenting diarrhea, which is why they were called "shit wards".

The staff tried to keep patients on blood wards separated between the really serious wounds and those that were more negligible. Many of the guys who got sent to wards with severe wounds didn't make it, and sheet-covered gurneys and body bags were a common sight in those areas.

Medical types scurried around on wooden walkways between tents and Quonset huts that housed the sick and wounded. The officers on staff were mostly young; many were recent medical school graduates fulfilling their military obligations. A lot of them had the vacant look that comes from presiding over an endless stream of gore, of young bodies bent, broken and split open like over-ripe peaches. The enlisted personnel were generally nurses, both men and women, and had the same look.

I had seen a similar look on GIs in the field. Grunts who had the "thousand yard look" appeared to be staring at something a long way away, even when they looked right at you. It came from seeing too many things that civilized people shouldn't have to look at. I wondered if I ever looked that way.

I found myself swept up in the hustle and was soon picked clean of shrapnel, bandaged, and bathed. They scrubbed the jungle crud off me with sponges, then put me in a bed with real sheets in a ward of guys with minor wounds. My leg still hurt, but not as much as it did back in the bush. Someone had given me a shot before painfully digging around in my thigh, and I was getting groggy.

In total, it took about two hours from the time the booby trap detonated to the point where I found myself patched and comfy in a bed in the rear. Not at all like past wars, when wounded soldiers might remain where they fell for days, losing blood and developing infections. It was something to be grateful for. I slept.

There were 32 guys on the ward, mostly lower ranking enlisted men along with a few NCOs and one Chief Warrant Officer. Rank was kind of meaningless to most people in a hospital, except for a few anal-retentive senior doctors. And it certainly wasn't an important consideration to patients who spent all their time with their butts hanging out of those silly hospital pajamas.

Most of the wounds on my ward were not life threatening. One guy had lost an arm, and there were a couple others who might not walk again. A few unsmiling doctors made daily rounds to check on the progress of their charges and to occasionally order a change in medication. They didn't talk much, particularly to the patients, and many of them were kind of unfriendly. I suspected that duty in an evac hospital had a tendency to wear people down, and that some of the docs might have reached the saturation point that made patients simply a burden to be tolerated.

The nurses, on the other hand, were really good people. They rotated shifts in the ward, and there was always at least one person on duty at a desk by the door of the long Quonset hut, even at night. One young medic, a spec 4 named Rocky, had regular duty during the day and was a hit with the guys on the ward. He was always in a good mood, and showed genuine concern for his hut full of damaged troops. He took a lot of good-natured ribbing over his name, getting labeled "Rocky the flying squirrel." As soon as he came on the ward, someone would yell, "Hey Squirrel, where's your bedpan?"

I stayed at the 91st Evac for eight days while my leg healed. It wasn't a vacation, but it sure beat the field. Our ward had a supply of paperback books donated by some charity back in the states, and I read a book or two every day. Seems like a lot of reading, but there wasn't much else to do during the day except lay there. Besides, it had been a few months since I'd read much of anything other than the journalistic masturbation that passed for newspapers in the Army. After a few days, I could get up and move around. So I was allowed to go to the hospital's mess hall for some pretty good chow (all Army doctors were officers, and they liked to eat well).

There was a lot of empty time in a hospital. More time to think than I was used to having out in the bush. That wasn't good. If I didn't distract myself with a book or a card game, I found my thoughts drifting to home and to Linda. I missed her so much, and I still had a very long time to go.

When I couldn't stand the idleness any more, I'd drag

myself out of bed and go limping around the hospital compound. My leg hurt when I walked, but the exercise was good for it and I could tell the wounds were healing up okay.

Within a few days I got to know the hospital grounds fairly well. I could even move around well enough to get to the occasional movies that were shown in the mess hall after sunset. We rarely knew what was going to be shown, but it didn't make much difference to people who were greedy for almost any taste of life back in The World. I only saw two flicks while I was there, and the second one turned out to be *The Green Berets* with John Wayne.

I have to tell you, I wouldn't have minded a movie on just about any other subject than Vietnam and I considered leaving when the picture started. But I stayed and watched. There were 35 or 40 guys in the room, hooting and booing at the unrealistic Hollywood send-up of a war we were living firsthand. It was such bullshit, it could have been produced by the Army's propaganda department. It was so bad it was actually kind of funny, and by the end of the movie we were laughing uproariously. Like I said, humor is where you find it.

From time to time, the 91st Evac got visitors. There was a high sympathy factor for guys in the hospital, and lots of folks wanted to be seen as supportive. Some of our visitors were motivated by a genuine concern and compassion for us. As you might imagine in a place where people were dying, there were a lot of clergy stopping by to say hello and ask if there was anything they could do for us. Sometimes we got visits from REMF staff officers out of brigade or division headquarters. Although a few of them were nice guys, it felt like many of them were just going through the motions, not really giving a rat's ass about the wards full of busted up kids.

One time, Nguyen Cao Ky came through the hospital to express his gratitude to the fine American soldiers who were making all those sacrifices for his country. He was at the time South Vietnam's vice president, elected in 1967 along with President Nguyen Van Thieu in a supposedly free election that the U.S. had been pushing for. Ky had been South Vietnam's premier for a time before the elections, and before that a general in the RVN air force where he had been something of an icon as a flyboy. In 1965 while he was premier, he had been quoted as saying Adolf Hitler was one of his heroes. Jesus, we sure knew how to pick our allies.

Again I was filled with my own peculiar brand of Steve Jennings ambivalence. On the one hand, I was touched at the gesture by a presumably busy and important man. But my cynical side, which I noted had been getting a lot more dominant lately, saw it as a cheap insincere manipulation by an opportunistic government official, especially when I observed the photographer tagging along behind him. Ky moved along quickly, shaking hands and saying "Hi, howaya" a lot.

Ky had a reputation for flamboyance, and he played his role to the hilt. He was wearing a bright purple scarf tied around his neck and puffing out from his uniform shirt. He had on a pair of expensive designer sunglasses, even in the relative dark of the ward. And he sported a revolver with what looked to be a pearl handle. I think he was trying for a movie star look, but it was tough for us to be impressed by a short, skinny gook who was trying much too hard to be cool.

The visit wasn't a complete loss, though. Ky had brought along an absolute fox, a young Vietnamese woman (wife? mistress? secretary?) in a sarong dress slit clear up to her crotch. Everyone in the ward was ogling her, and all heads turned like spectators at a tennis match whenever she leaned over a bed to greet another GI. She knew damn well the effect she was having, and wiggled her cute little butt for her appreciative audience. All in all, there were worse visits.

It was close to Christmas, and packages of good stuff were coming to ward residents from concerned relatives and generous strangers almost every day. Cookies, candy, popcorn, canned food, and the ubiquitous fruitcakes (yep, people even sent fruitcakes to Vietnam, no joke intended).

It's a real challenge to bring a feeling of Christmas to a subtropical climate like Vietnam, but the staff at the 91st Evac really gave it a try. Short, scrawny trees with homemade ornaments began appearing around the hospital as orderlies and nurses worked to generate a holiday spirit. Cut-outs of snowflakes, candy canes, and stuffed Santas shared space with medical instruments and transfusion bottles. Rocky put a tree by his desk in the ward, and took to whistling Christmas carols. I gave the staff a lot of credit for the effort; they tried so hard to generate Christmas cheer. Strangely enough, though, I found it all kind of depressing. It was in some ways an unwanted reminder of the parts of my life that had been taken away, and which I wanted more than anything to have back.

In a real stroke of luck, Bob Hope's touring show performed in Chu Lai while I was at the hospital. Although only a small percentage of combat troops in the field ever got to see those shows, hospital patients got priority to attend. The balance of the crowd was mostly made up of Chu Lai REMFs. So there I sat in the second row of a hurriedly constructed open-air pavilion, watching the ageless and tireless performer and his gaggle of beautiful babes. There were probably 100 of us from the hospital, all dressed in those dippy pajamas and robes. I found myself near Murphy, who was sitting in a wheelchair, and I was relieved to find out he was okay.

The Golddiggers, a television dancing troupe of drop-dead gorgeous gals, were part of the show and set off an impossibly loud and lusty cheer from the hordes of horny GIs in the sprawling crowd when they wiggled and bounced onto the stage in their miniskirts and go-go boots. Bob also trotted out Miss World, Austria's Eva Rueber-Staier, for us to drool over. She was tall and willowy, with long silky blonde hair, and she flowed across the stage like warm honey. A testosterone-saturated throng of hundreds caressed her with their eyes, while she traded one-liners with the comedian.

At the end of the show, Hope led the audience in a sing-along of some Christmas carols. There were more than a few hard-case grunts in the crowd with teary eyes, thinking of Christmases past and loved ones a half world away from Chu Lai. Parts of my life I once took for granted in a different lifetime suddenly seemed precious, and an empty ache welled up in me. It was all the more intense because there was absolutely nothing I could do to get back to those things any time soon.

It was Christmas, and I wanted to be home.

Chapter Sixteen

By the time I got back to 2nd platoon, Bravo Company had completed a cycle up on LZ Professional and was off again on a new assignment. I caught up with the platoon via a resupply chopper, somewhere to the north of the firebase. My leg was pretty much healed, and I had clean fatigues and fresh gear. Murphy had been sent home—his wounds were bad enough to end his war—so I was the only one hitching a ride back to the boonies, along with the mail bags, C-rations and ammo boxes.

Nobody cheered to have me back. It wasn't like being on some high school football team, and grunts rarely showed anything approximating emotion. I was just another warm body arriving, although at least I wasn't an FNG. Everyone knew I wasn't any more thrilled to be there than they were. So there wasn't much point to making a big deal out of me returning. A few guys asked about Murphy, and a couple said they were glad I was okay. After an hour, it hardly seemed I'd ever been gone.

I slipped back into the routine as though I had been a grunt in the field my whole life. Within a day or two my clean, rear-area look had faded and I soon fit right in with my jungle-worn companions. It didn't take very long to once again get crusted in mud, sweat salt, and dried blood from elephant grass and bug bites. My momentary return to pajama-clad Sergeant Starch quickly faded into a distant memory, more aptly replaced by Sergeant Scuz.

For the next two weeks Bravo Company worked the area east of the firebase. We criss-crossed the AO, patrolling a sector between five and fifteen klicks from Professional. Our mission was—you guessed it—search and destroy.

It was quiet. The bad guys must have been busy elsewhere, or taking their own version of a stand-down. Our wanderings took us into an area we had previously patrolled at one time or another, and I was mildly surprised to realize that it was somewhat familiar to me. For a city kid who hadn't spent a lot of his life roaming through woods, I was pleased to be developing some ability to distinguish one piece of jungle from another and find my way around without getting lost. My map was an important safety net, but you didn't want your nose so completely rooted in a map that you didn't notice Chuck waiting for you in the weeds.

As the company headed further east, we worked our way into some sectors I knew we hadn't previously visited. In one of the places that was new to me, I saw craters from the big bombs that high-flying B-52s had dropped. It was impossible to tell what the bombers had been after; the craters were strung out over an area with unremarkable terrain features and without any clues as to what enemy facilities might have made the area a target. It could have been a spot where troop movement had been seen, or possibly the location of a long-departed camp. It was just more jungle, but now with man-made acne scars. Maybe the bombs had been for interdiction. Somebody thought that bad guys might be sneaking some munitions through the area, so they dumped a few tons of bombs on them to discourage more permanent housekeeping.

The craters were huge inverted cones, most more than 40 feet across at the top. All of the surrounding jungle near each crater had been ripped away, big trees splintered and broken like so many pencils. New growth was only beginning to take back the wounded ground. The centers of the craters were ten to fifteen feet deep, frequently holding pools of water at the narrow bottoms. I couldn't conceive of explosions that would blow away tons of earth and leave holes like these. The impact of a 105 artillery shell or a mortar round barely dented the ground in comparison to the craters left by the B-52 bombs.

Even more beyond comprehension was how it must have been for any unlucky gooks caught beneath those falling apocalyptic meat-grinders. The bombs had obviously blasted the piss out of acres of jungle, and anyone close by would have been lucky to get out alive. The shrapnel and shock waves must have produced a staggering killing radius.

The terrain was pockmarked by a line of craters for a half mile. Our column picked its way over the broken ground and around the moonscape holes, frequently altering the line of march to avoid yet another crater. One guy slipped on the loose mud at the edge of one hole and slid, cursing, down the side into the rank pool at the bottom. The sides of the crater were slick, and sloped enough that he needed a hand to get back out.

A little further to the east we came upon a scene out of a science-fiction movie. A hilly area, possibly a klick across, was totally stripped of foliage. Trees stood starkly, their empty branches as barren as a north woods in winter. No vines, no elephant grass, no ground cover—just denuded trees, many dead and leaning precariously.

It was curious, so different from the terrain we customarily found ourselves patrolling that it was unsettling. We walked through the distressed area, fascinated by the improbable destruction to that one odd piece of jungle. It was soon apparent that we were considerably more vulnerable walking through there, without the familiar choking cover of jungle to keep us hidden.

At the time, I had no idea what could possibly have brought such strange devastation to that stretch of jungle. I thought of the bomb craters we had seen earlier, but the complete destruction of all living green stuff was beyond the capability of even the huge bombs from B-52s.

Back then, none of us had ever heard of Agent Orange. The U.S. realized it would be easier to locate and bomb Charlie if scouting helicopters could see him moving around, and the jungle cover was an inconvenient obstacle to catching him in the open. So various aircraft were charged with dumping a defoliating chemical on areas thought to be prime places for Charlie to be hiding. It was years later that the unhealthy after-effects of chemical spraying started catching public attention as more and more Vietnam veterans complained of unexplained illnesses. So we ignorantly went on with our hunt for Mr. Charles, wondering about that strange patch of bare jungle, and unaware that we were tramping through a toxic waste dump. I suppose it was better not to know. We had enough to worry about already.

On the fifth day after I had rejoined the platoon, we came to a long open valley running north and south, and bordered on each side by fairly straight ridgelines made up of rows of hills. We had climbed the closest hill as we approached from the west, and the valley opened up before us as we crested the broad and relatively clear hilltop. We overlooked the southernmost end of the valley, and could see it stretching out for miles to the north.

Our line of march wouldn't take us down into the valley we overlooked, as we were directed to continue to the southeast from that point. That was fine with us, because there had been some reported VC activity down there. Some other lucky company had drawn that particular short straw and was approaching the valley floor, unseen to us, from several klicks away at the north end.

It was midday and Bravo Company was expecting a resupply. Even better, the anticipated chopper would be bringing a hot meal (we didn't often get hot chow out in the boonies, so it was a treat when we did). The hill we had topped was an inviting place to temporarily set up for a meal, and had a good spot for the slick to land.

We settled in for what would be a few hours, securing a moderately defensible position on the hilltop. Since there hadn't been any contact for a while, the edge was off and the guys were relaxed. The day was dry and sunny, hot as always, and we waited expectantly for a decent meal while kicking back and taking it easy. The view from our high perch looking down into the valley really was spectacular, a scene like you might find in the foothills of the Smoky Mountains.

The resupply bird came and left, and we ate hot chow and opened sweet-smelling pink envelopes containing homey news, love and longing from wives and girlfriends back in The World. It was a good day.

A few of us idly noticed the very distant thump of big guns firing. It was hard to place the direction, and the deep thuds didn't sound like 105s. That meant it probably wasn't coming from Professional, since a 105 battery was all the battalion had available on the firebase. The sound was so far away that those of us who even heard it weren't paying a lot of attention. The low thumps had to be much too far away to affect us. The noise of war—explosions, big guns pounding out fire missions—was a fairly constant part of life in the field, and didn't attract attention unless it was close to wherever we happened to be at the time.

I'm not exactly sure why it is so, but it seems to be a part of the human condition to constantly relearn the same lessons. Our fateful lesson was that you don't want to judge what might be according to your narrow experience of what is.

There was a battery of eight-inch guns in the northern part of the 196th Brigade AO, on another battalion firebase well away from most of the sectors worked by the 1st of the 46th, the Professionals. None of us had ever seen them, in fact, nobody could recall a fire mission close enough to be aware of them coming in. You need to understand something about eight inch guns. They are just what the name suggests—they shoot an artillery round that is eight inches across. Not eight inches long, mind you, but eight inches in diameter across the bottom of the round.

Meaning they were really big mothers.

And the big shells were landing in that pretty valley below us, a distance that looked to be approximately a half mile from our cozy little hilltop. The incoming rounds made a low whooshing noise, ominously conveying a warning both of their size and of their imminent arrival. Bright, ripping explosions were starting to appear on the valley floor, leaving neat round puffs of smoke hanging in the trees.

Because of the distance from us, the explosions weren't terribly alarming and didn't appear to pose any threat to us.

Nobody was diving for cover; artillery blasts we knew about couldn't affect anything as far away as we were.

Then I heard a new sound. Sort of like a boomerang, it was the noise made by something large and unusually shaped flying through the air. Think of something about the size of a toaster. "Shoop, shoop, shoop, shoop." Somehow, instinctively, I knew it was a large chunk of shrapnel. Inbound to our hilltop.

Nobody moved. There wasn't anywhere to go, no foxholes to jump in, relatively few trees to hide behind. Besides, from the time we first heard it to the time it came down was maybe three seconds. So we sat there, helplessly, and listened for what felt like a lifetime to an unseen chuck of metal fly toward us and smash into the hillside less than 100 feet from one of the company positions. The last instant before it hit, the piece sounded like an inbound Volkswagen and I could feel the thump as it plowed into the ground.

Since none of us had witnessed incoming artillery of this size before, we had no idea that big chunks of shrapnel could sometimes remain intact and fly fairly long distances from the point of impact. I didn't think I wanted to be a spectator to exploding eight-inchers again anytime soon.

The company saddled up and got the hell out of there before any more bowling balls flew our way. It was astonishing how many different ways there were to get yourself killed in Vietnam. I had enough trouble watching out for Charlie; it was a royal pain in the butt to have to duck our stuff, too.

The following day, we got orders to split into platoons and begin a sweep to the north, in the general direction of Hau Duc (you remember Dragon Valley?). Some activity had been noticed in the area by loach choppers, and we were the unit close enough to check it out. I thought about the fun we had on our last trip to that playground.

The farther north we went, the thicker the jungle became and the slower we moved. It was raining again, making the ground slick and slowing our column all the more. And since most guys knew we were walking in the general direction of Dragon Valley, the pace was probably slowed additionally by a basic lack of enthusiasm.

For two days we slogged and cut and inched our way through the unyielding green wall, progressing at most only two or three klicks a day. Apparently, our slow progress was making someone at brigade headquarters impatient. The reports of enemy activity were getting cold and less valuable as time went by. Old intelligence is sometimes more useless than no intelligence, particularly when it concerned a foe who moved around so quickly and effortlessly. It was clearly important enough that HQ wanted someone on the ground up there like right now.

So it was decided that we would send one platoon ahead by air to patrol the suspect area, avoiding the further delay that chopping our way to it on the ground would have caused. Normally, the insertion of a single platoon would have been a job for the battalion's echo recon platoon, but they were tied up in something way out to the western edge of the AO. So guess which platoon got the short straw?

The word came down early in the day that 2nd platoon was going on an air insertion, and we spent the next several hours searching for a clearing big enough for Hueys to land. It might have taken us days to find a suitable opening in that thick stuff, or to chop one out by hand. But a passing resupply helicopter spotted a likely place and passed the word to battalion, who forwarded it to us. By noon, five slicks with a Huey gunship escort had picked up my platoon for a ride north.

I couldn't help but think about the last eagle flight. It didn't thrill me much to be doing it again. I had been quite content, thank you very much, to be walking around with lots of companions in an area where nobody was doing any shooting. I really couldn't muster much passion for a visit to Mr. Charles' neighborhood, and I don't think any of the other guys had much gusto either. But we were good soldiers and did what we were told.

The target LZ was to be a reasonably clear hill roughly two klicks south of Dragon Valley. A LOH had scouted for a platoon-sized insertion landing zone, and found a big enough area that had the added advantage of a little elevation. The loach hadn't taken any fire, and the pilot hadn't seen any sign of bad guys on the ground, so there was a hopeful expectation that the LZ would be cold.

The five Hueys with troops flew in a line, while the gunship stood off to the right. The first two choppers in the line arrived at the LZ, flaring and tentatively squatting down to hover just above the ground to drop off their loads. The hillside was too uneven to land, so the pilots just tried to get close. There still wasn't any evidence of a threat, and the Huey door gunners were holding their own fire.

The lead Huey had Buzz Gallagher and half his squad aboard. Just as it settled and hovered, at the point where a helicopter is most vulnerable, it suddenly started taking automatic weapons fire from a tree line to the left. I saw a PFC named Lindahl get hit and spun to the ground as he jumped off the hovering slick and tried to dash for cover. The other grunts in the slick were scrambling to get off.

As it fought to hold its position just above the ground, the helicopter abruptly clipped a tree with its tail rotor. It started a brief spin, then thumped down hard, still taking withering fire from the left. It was obviously no longer able to fly.

All of this happened so fast that the first bird was damaged and down before any effective return fire started. The situation wasn't exactly out of control, but the advantage was clearly Charlie's. The left-door machine guns on the remaining slicks opened up on the bad guys, and the gunship was maneuvering to get a line of fire. It took all of ten seconds for the other choppers and Lieutenant Warren to decide to abort the insertion. The three Hueys that hadn't started a final approach veered off, while the second Huey and the gunship tried to get Gallagher's squad and the crew from the downed first bird. Radios crackled with frantic traffic as Lieutenant Warren and the pilots tried to bring some order to the confusion.

I watched from the open door on the fifth slick, along with one fire team from Dee's squad. We hung about fifty feet over the LZ, pumping out as much suppressing fire into the trees as we could. On the ground it was chaos. The GIs from the first chopper were trying to find cover and were back-pedaling toward the second Huey, which was still hovering off to the right and behind the disabled slick. Two members of the crew from the downed helicopter were helping Lindahl, and I could see Gallagher's people returning fire.

The Huey gunship, which was only carrying its crew and consequently had room for most of the stranded squad, was dropping in to pick up anyone who couldn't fit on the already loaded second Huey. Machine guns blazed from its sides, and missiles roared from its racks into the trees where the heaviest fire came from.

The other three slicks in the air were trying to help. All six door gunners and many of the grunts on board who could get close enough to a door to stick their rifles out were blasting away at the hillside around our ill-fated LZ. I was already into my fourth magazine, shooting over the head of the crewman on the door-mounted M-60 machine gun.

I watched as two of Gallagher's men, along with one of the two warrant officers and one of the door gunners from the crashed chopper made it intact to the second Huey and dived in. The addition of four passengers to the load made for more weight than the helicopter was supposed to carry, and the rotor was straining to get it back into the air.

The pilot had touched down right at the edge of the flattest part of the hilltop and was facing the downslope. He wound up the RPMs as high as the engine could manage, and in desperation pushed the cyclic forward while pulling the max on his collective. The Huey sort of hopped a couple times, leaned forward like it was going to roll over on its nose, dragged along on the front of its skids for a few feet and then plunged down the side of the hill just barely off the ground. The forward speed helped improve its lift enough that, incredibly, it was finally flying and gaining altitude. Without the hill, it might never have lifted off.

Meanwhile, the more lightly loaded gunship had touched down and was trying to retrieve the rest of Gallagher's squad. Two guys were on either side of Lindahl, supporting him and half dragging him to the gunship. They practically threw him on board, and then they and the rest of the crew from the banged up chopper lunged in after him. Just as quickly the gunship was up and retreating from the continuing enemy fire. I quickly scanned the LZ and didn't see any other GIs, just muzzle flashes signaling that the bad guys were still shooting at us from the tree line.

This entire aborted insertion took less than two minutes. And then the four remaining slicks were heading back to the original pickup point and the rest of Bravo Company to figure out what to do next. The gunship made a side trip to LZ Professional to drop off Lindahl at the battalion aid station, then came back to drop off the remainder of Gallagher's squad at the pickup point.

By the time the various choppers had dropped us off and left, another hour had passed. So it was late afternoon before anyone realized that Buzz hadn't been on any of the birds coming back from our failed mission. He wasn't with the company, and a radio check confirmed he hadn't been dropped off with the casualty at the firebase. He had to be stuck back at the hot LZ.

I had never really considered what it might be like to be abandoned out in the jungle, nobody around except people who want to kill you. It was a frightening enough prospect to be alone in the jungle, even without gooks all over the place. Sure, it was something that does happen in a war, particularly to fliers who have the misfortune of drawing equipment that isn't working too well, or pilots who get too close to bad guys with respectable aim. But for draftee ground grunts who were used to having lots of folks around to keep them company in the boondocks, the idea of being stuck out there all alone was a little terrifying.

The captain lit up his radio, trying to get some choppers back to the LZ for Buzz. It wasn't going to happen; everything that could fly was tied up somewhere else, even the Hueys we had just ridden. He was really hot. "All the freaking equipment we have in this goddamn armpit country and I can't get one crummy helicopter?!" Despite our having confirmed the intelligence at brigade HQ of enemy activity at Hau Duc, there was nothing available to help us out. Artillery and air strikes didn't seem real smart, since Buzz would also be on the receiving end. It was frustrating—somebody needed help and we couldn't do anything.

Lieutenant Warren and I just stared at each other, both of us wondering if we could or should have done something different to prevent stranding one of our guys. There really wasn't; the troops from the downed ship went to two different helicopters and nobody was spending a lot of time counting noses right at that moment. That didn't stop me or the lieutenant from second-guessing, since we both viewed ourselves as responsible for everyone in the platoon. I felt like hell, and wanted to do something to get him back. Nobody was in the mood to sit around and wait.

The earliest we could get air support to carry us back to the aborted LZ would be first thing the next morning. Even a night-walk wasn't a viable option, because the distance was at least a two-day effort on the ground. Hard as it was to face, we really didn't have a choice.

The captain had to calm down his company. A lot of guys wanted to head right out to look for Buzz, and had to be persuaded that we wouldn't be able to get there any faster, even with a night-walk. It was a bad bet to risk the company, since Buzz was in all likelihood dead or captured. I'm not sure which outcome seemed worse.

So our dispirited warrior band, once again chased from the mouth of Dragon Valley, settled in for a night of thinking about Buzz and what his chances might be. It was an unusually cheerless night.

The next morning we got word that five Hueys, enough for a platoon, would be coming to try the insertion again. Since Buzz was our guy, 2nd platoon was chosen to return. Happily, an aero-rifle platoon from another battalion (ARPs were a lot like air cavalry, more accustomed than us to riding around in choppers and pulling air assaults) was coming along for support.

Most of the time, aero-rifle platoons had their own dedicated choppers, so we didn't have to scrounge up a ride for them.

We had a couple hours to kill while waiting for the helicopters. The night laager had been selected for its proximity to the clearing we had used for the previous day's flight, and was consequently on fairly low ground. To the southeast, a line of hills marched off into the distance. Coming off the closest of those hills was a narrow, winding stream that passed near our laager. At the very base of the hill, the stream hit a drop-off and briefly formed a miniature waterfall. The water was cool and clear, and the waterfall tempted a few guys to improvise a shower under it.

The stream was so clear that several of us filled canteens. We were low on water, and had run out of Halizone, but the clear water looked to be a better bet than some of the muck we had slogged through further back in the valley. But as good as the untreated water tasted, it would later prove to be a mistake.

While we waited for our ride, I overheard some discussion with the firebase about prepping our destination with artillery to discourage Charles from repeating his reception performance. Fortunately, since there was no way to determine if Buzz was still near the LZ, or even alive, the idea of prepping the hill was quickly ruled out.

It was late morning when the birds finally arrived to pick us up, and we were soon on our way back. As we lifted above the tree canopy, I could see the other flight of ARP Hueys off in the distance to our right. The ride to our hilltop LZ was short, but the approach was slow and methodical because of the previous day's debacle. Without any preliminary artillery, the pilots on our slicks were ready to balk at the slightest indication of incoming fire.

The aero-rifle platoon came in on our right, settling down on the far side of the LZ and hustling to set up positions in whatever cover they could find. Our Hueys landed two at a time in line on the left side, near the wrecked chopper, and we squirted out the doors like passengers from a rush-hour subway.

The LZ appeared to be cold—nobody was firing and there

weren't any muzzle flashes coming from the trees down the side. But, as usual, the noise of the massed helicopters made it impossible to hear gunfire, and we had a nervous few moments. Second platoon hustled into a ragged perimeter on the left side of the LZ and we flopped on our bellies, ready to return fire if necessary.

As each chopper disgorged its edgy load, it quickly stood on its nose and beat it out of there. An ARP gunship and one slick stayed nearby, out of range, just in case we needed help or a dust-off. We kept low and alert as the din from our herd of air elephants receded. When the racket had quieted enough so they could be heard, the squad leaders did a quick check of their people to be sure everyone was present and intact.

And that's when we heard Buzz hollering at us.

Since most of us feared he would be dead, it was a little eerie to hear his voice coming up the hillside. He even sounded kind of pissed—certainly a positive sign. "Hey assholes, it's about fucking time." Ah, yes, same old irrepressible Buzz, clearly unchanged by his night alone in the bush.

We scrambled down the side of the hill and found him under a pile of brush and branches. He had been thrown from the busted Huey when it clipped its tail rotor and had hit his head, knocking himself out. Unconscious, he had rolled part way down the hill. As he tumbled, he caught his right ankle in some rocks and broke his leg. Everyone in the remaining Hueys had been focused on the far side of the LZ and had never seen his plunge.

Buzz said that when he regained consciousness, "There were gooks everywhere." He could hear them chattering away as they scavenged through the downed chopper and stripped out its ammo, medical kit, door guns, and anything else that wasn't bolted down.

His slide down the hill had left him next to a fallen tree. When he realized how close the bad guys were and that his leg was useless, he pulled himself up tight to the trunk, dragging his leg, and pressed into it hoping he would either be missed or thought dead if he was spotted.

Buzz was sure he would be found, but the bad guys were

too excited about the helicopter and didn't spend much time looking around the hill. In time, they left and he set about cutting some brush with his jungle knife to more thoroughly cover and camouflage himself. It was the worst, Buzz said, when no helicopters came back and then the sun went down. "I didn't know if you dicks figured I was dead, or y'all were just too stupid to notice I wasn't there." We, of course, assured him it was easy to not notice him even when he was around.

"The gooks came back to the chopper once during the night. I stayed real quiet. One of 'em came over near where I was hiding and took a leak, but he didn't get close enough to spot me. I heard 'em talking, but couldn't see if they were regulars or VC that shot us up."

A lot of sarcastic cracks masked the relief we felt at finding Buzz alive and reasonably intact. Aside from his leg, he wasn't too bad off. He had lost most of his gear in his slide down the hill, so he hadn't had any food or water in about 20 hours.

Lieutenant Warren told Buzz he should get his ass back to work after goofing off all night. "But since you aren't much good to anyone without a gun, we're gonna put your malingering ass on a chopper and send you back to get resupplied. As soon as you get a set of crutches, I'll expect to see you back here." What a sympathetic guy, that el-tee.

We called in the slick that had been standing off the LZ, put Buzz aboard and packed him off to the hospital in Chu Lai. The aero-rifle boys were directed to mount up and head south. We got orders to go north. Toward Dragon Valley.

The other two platoons of Bravo Company were to be airlifted to a point about a klick north of 2nd platoon, where we would link up and go hunting for the bad guys who bushwhacked our insertion. I had a real uneasy feeling about going up there, especially after the botched operation and Buzz's solo overnighter. Whoever had been our skirmish partner seemed a little better organized than most of the VC we came across, and I couldn't help recalling the NVA unit we met on our last trip to Hau Duc.

Little did I know.

Chapter Seventeen

And the night comes again to the circle-studded sky.
The stars settle slowly, in loneliness they lie.
'Til the universe explodes as a falling star is raised,
Planets are paralyzed, mountains are amazed.
But they all glow brighter from the brilliance of the blaze.
With the speed of insanity, they die.
Phil Ochs

The early light was a deep amber, and dark figures cut from black velvet roamed about silhouetted against the dawn sky. The low murmur of a slowly stirring Army company mingled with quiet morning sounds. Burning C-4 dimly glowed blue under canteen cups of C-ration powdered coffee and cocoa.

The company night laager was roughly a klick from the southern end of Dragon Valley. We had set it up early, before dusk, the day before. The captain wanted some extra time to meet with his three platoon leaders and work out some kind of plan before we began our little jaunt into the dragon's mouth.

Night was struggling to become day, and it would soon be time to saddle up. I was leaning back on my rucksack, propped up against a tree, watching the company come alive. Like many around me, I was fussing with my gear. Field-strip the M-16 one more time, making sure the firing mechanism was covered with oil and rust-free. Eject the magazine and manually strip out the bullets one by one, wipe them with some C-ration bumwad, lightly oil them, then individually snap them back into the magazine.

I watched Chuck Patterson, who carried one of 2nd platoon's two pigs, wiping down the long belts of 7.62mm ammo he carried draped over his shoulders. TC was sharpening his knife. Ortiz was sharpening a machete. Doc spent some time checking his Chicom ammo, then turned to repacking his medical gear. Dee was helping one of his new guys, an FNG who inherited an M-79 from the soldier he replaced. Dee was showing him how to set up the big rounds in a bandoleer so he could get at them quickly. Even Lt. Warren was rechecking his gear, stripping and oiling his M-16.

On most any morning, some guys would be cleaning or arranging gear. There was always something that needed attention, needed cleaning. But this morning it looked like a barracks detail in basic training preparing for an inspection. It looked like everybody in the company was busily cleaning and repacking and rearranging their stuff. There was none of the usual morning banter. Instead there was a low-level current of gloomy apprehension about the day and the destination.

The whole area south of Hau Duc, including Dragon Valley, had been dubbed by someone over at the 198th Brigade as a no-man's land. It was probably as much from superstition as from reality, but people died there, out of proportion to almost any other place in the whole damn AO. It didn't help to know that Charlie was definitely nearby.

Lieutenant Warren and I had talked with the 2nd platoon squad leaders about our orders. One of Buzz Gallagher's team leaders, a spec 4 named Dickinson, was pitch hitting for Buzz while the hospital tried to fix his leg. Dickinson was a good guy. He had eight months in country and was still alive.

The company was to sweep in platoons, but nothing smaller. Evidently battalion HQ agreed that the odds were good of NVA regulars being in the neighborhood, and didn't want anything as small as a squad running into an NVA force, whatever size it might be.

The valley was wide; it would require three spread-out platoons to adequately sweep through it. That also meant the surrounding high ground might be tempting for the bad guys—a neat platform for dropping crap on us in the valley.

For that reason, the brass decided to bring back the aero-rifle guys. This time there were two platoons, to be set down by their air cav choppers on the ridgelines on both sides of the valley. They would be distant enough that we wouldn't be able to help each other, but it was reassuring to know that the high ground wasn't being defaulted to a possible opponent. We could concentrate on the valley floor, and on any surprises that might be waiting for us there.

Since the captain and the platoon leaders all thought there was a good chance of contact, they decided to move each platoon in three parallel squad columns instead of the usual single column. Although movement is slower and a lot more difficult, a wide front would enable us to generate meaningful return fire from multiple points. It was significantly preferable to the limited firepower coming from the first two or three guys at the front of a single column.

With a warning from the captain to maintain visual contact, the three platoons shuffled slowly out of the night laager, each platoon then dividing into three squads spaced 30 to 50 meters apart. Just under 100 men, in nine separate columns, fanned out across the lowland bush at the outskirts of the valley.

How can I find a way to describe what it was like to be setting off into a place that felt like death. There was a bizarre unreality to the scene—this just didn't connect to anything in the life experiences that had formed me and the beliefs I carried around with me. What on earth was the point of tweaking Charlie's nose? Nobody in the whole damned world claimed to want any part of this war any more. The sentiment was universal—it was time for Vietnam to go away. The diplomats had been yammering in Paris for the best part of a year, and yet here we were, almost certainly walking into a battle, feeling very much in the middle of a war that ought to be over.

I really needed somebody to tell me what was wrong with this picture. No, strike that. I knew what was wrong with it; I needed somebody to tell me why it made any sense to do what we were doing.

I felt like I didn't know myself any more, like I was an observer of a completely alien happening, watching myself and the other guys from a different place. It had been almost two years since I had been on a college campus. I hardly remembered that person. It had been a lifetime ago.

John Fournelle, my new RTO, broke into my wandering thoughts to tell me he heard on the radio that the ARP platoons had landed on the high ground about the time we broke the night laager, and were paralleling our course along both ridgelines. I took some comfort knowing that the flanks were covered.

Second platoon was the middle of the three platoons. Lieutenant Warren and I took spots in the two outside squads, so one of us was on each side of the platoon. Doc, who as the medic wasn't part of any particular squad, was walking point for Dickinson in Buzz Gallagher's squad. That was Doc's way—he didn't ask, or volunteer. He just stepped out in front of everybody and started doing it. Dickinson was relieved he didn't have to tap someone for the duty. He was finding that this squad leader crap was not much fun when you had to put your friends in harm's way.

The bush was thick, but not as bad as the triple canopy at the far end of the valley. Machetes were whacking away at the more tangled spots, their telltale metallic dings and clunks resonating out ahead of us, a dissonant chorus singing "Here we come".

The day was growing warm, hot even, but it wasn't raining. We were as wet from sweat as if it had been raining, in part from the exertion and in part from the growing certainty that something would soon happen. Something unpleasant. An hour went by, then two, then three. The company trudged along, nine columns snaking deeper into Indian country.

And then the valley blew up like the freaking Fourth of July.

The first thing I heard was the distinctive "thocka thocka thocka" sound made by Chicom automatic weapons. And I heard it coming from several different directions. Lots of directions. I went down so fast that my rucksack gave me a body blow between my shoulders as it caught up with me, momentarily knocking the air out of my lungs.

I heard M-16s returning fire, so I gingerly raised my head and started crawling forward to get in position to help. It was risky for people like me who were further back in the columns to start shooting—too many good guys between us and the bad guys.

I got to a point where I could see Doc. He wasn't shooting, he was bending over TC. There was a hole in TC's chest, just below his ribcage. Doc was visibly frantic, working desperately to keep TC's insides where they belonged with a pressure bandage.

Predictably, pandemonium reigned. The incoming bullets were like angry bees snapping at the jungle vegetation. Big bees. Some GIs were trying to disappear into the ground. Our return fire was still really feeble. I yelled back to bring up a pig; we desperately needed machine gun firepower to help quell the wall of incoming metal. I turned and crawled beyond Doc to a downed tree where I could get a line of fire at the bad guys.

And then the mortars and the RPGs started.

That's when I knew our asses were really hanging out. It was rare to run into a VC unit in our AO that was equipped with any kind of heavy guns. The North Vietnamese Army, on the other hand, frequently had Soviet-made and Chicom stuff that could put a hurt even on armored units. We were undoubtedly facing an NVA outfit of some sort. A large and very well equipped sort.

The mortar most frequently used by the NVA was an 82mm piece, capable of hurling a six and a half pound shell 3,000 meters. The choice of 82 millimeters was no coincidence; it was designed to be one millimeter larger than the U.S. 81mm mortar so the gooks could use captured American mortar rounds in their own tubes.

The other widely used NVA grief-dealer was the Soviet RPG-7. Something like a recoilless rifle, the RPG (for "rocket propelled grenade") sent a round up to 500 meters that could penetrate 320mm of armor. RPGs were cheap to produce, and just might have been the Soviet Union's most widely exported weapon after AK-47s. They look like long sticks with vaguely football-shaped lumps on the business end. If you've ever seen pictures of fighters in Afghanistan, you've seen RPGs.

My steel pot was no match for an RPG.

Most of us had never been on the target side of this kind of heavy stuff. It was not fun. The explosions were deafening, the ground shook. Huge chunks of trees and dirt and shrapnel filled the air. The middle of a tree nearby unlucky enough to take a direct hit from a fire-trailing RPG round practically vaporized as I looked at it. Nothing left but toothpicks. I heard somebody off to my right screaming in an unnatural voice two octaves beyond human capability.

I've read that soldiers who are subjected to pounding artillery can sometimes just flat check out. Some of them sit down and cry, or slip into some catatonic state, sort of mentally pulling the covers over their heads to keep the monsters away. Armies on both sides in World War II reported people snapping under the pressure of intense shelling.

I'm sure what we got paled by comparison to the daylong artillery barrages of the big war, but it scared the bejesus out of us. And it was murderously effective, inflicting heavy casualties. I had never experienced anything like it before, and I never want to again. It's amazing, and it says something about their resolve, that the awful and endless bashings we gave to North Vietnam via B-52 strikes alone weren't enough to make them give up the war.

The jungle had been turned into a giant Cuisinart, shredding vegetation and people effortlessly. Round after round smashed into the company, casually knocking aside trees and pulverizing the grunts trying desperately to hide behind them. It was clear we had to pull back and get the heck out of the kill zone. The NVA mortars were firing for effect, rounds going down the tubes as fast as hands could get out of the way of the launching shell. The North Vietnamese had set their patterns well ahead of time to waste anyone unfortunate enough to walk through this particular piece of jungle.

My ears were ringing; I couldn't hear a thing. Squad leaders were gesturing wildly at their men, smacking them on their heads to get their attention. Nobody on the ground wanted to look up or stand up, even to run. It was just too scary, and more than a little unhealthy.

The explosions were going off at a rate of more than one per second. It was almost suicide to raise your head in an attempt to return fire. If you did manage to squeeze off a few rounds, the NVA machine guns immediately marked you and traversed to pour a withering burst back at you. The jungle was filled with a cyclone from hell.

I was looking in that direction when a round hit about 50 meters to my left. Brady was there, within a few feet of the impact, running toward the rear. He came apart like a gruesome rag doll ripped open by a petulant child. I didn't even bother calling out to Doc. There was nothing to put back together again. Brady was dead before the first hunk of him hit the ground.

My mind refused to believe what I had just seen. I kept staring stupidly at the wet mess on the ground that used to be Brady. This couldn't be happening, just a bad dream. Everything around me was suddenly moving at an unnaturally slow speed. Colors were extraordinarily intense—the greens of the jungle, the miniature suns of the exploding mortars, and the bright red mist of exploding people.

Another soldier, who had been with Brady just before he jumped up and started running, had also seen Brady get shredded. He was paralyzed with terror, and I could see that he was crying. He just sat there, tears running down his face, helpless and disconnected from the storm around him. I thought about working my way over to him, but then Chief was suddenly there at his side, slapping him across the face and trying to break through his shock.

The radios were screaming with orders to pull back. Pitifully ineffective return fire was coming from along our extended front. Smoke and dust choked me. The smoke was starting to get so thick from the relentless barrage that it actually helped hide our retreat. The mortars kept coming, pounding and killing, but at least we were getting a smokescreen to shield us from the NVA small arms fire.

I crawled off to my right, and found myself next to Doc again, still struggling with a limp TC. We got on either side of him, looked at each other, and somehow found the guts to stand up. I kept wincing, my body fully expecting to get smacked by the stuff angrily zipping by us.

Doc and I headed back the way the column had come as fast as we could go, groping through the smoky haze and listening to chunks of shrapnel thudding into the trees around us, loping and stumbling and half-dragging TC. He was pale, almost white, and the front of his tee shirt was drenched in a thick wetness. The blood looked black on his OD shirt. He was in bad shape.

By the time our survivors made it out of the mortars' reach, the captain had a fire mission called in to the 105s on LZ Professional and had made a separate request for air support. The artillery was prompt this time, and within minutes the incoming shells were dealing some of the same shit back to Charlie that we just came through. I could hear the rounds streaking in from the firebase and blasting loudly into the trees just beyond the point of our forward progress. Those gun bunnies were back on my good list again.

The aero-rifle platoon way over and out of sight on our left was in a firefight up on the ridgeline. It was likely that some of the NVA mortar tubes were up there, and the cav guys would hopefully divert their attention for a while. The other ARP on the right ridgeline was pouring machine gun rounds and M-79 grenades down into the general area on the valley floor where most of the incoming fire had originated, adding to the howitzer shells that were now slamming into the jungle. Any little bit helped.

The company was badly disorganized, and reeling from the attack. Seven wounded, including TC, were on the ground getting aid from the company's three medics. I knew Brady was dead, and other reports sounded like two or three more had been killed in 3rd platoon. All of the bodies were still back there, most in more than one piece. We were dazed, and a lot of guys still had distorted looks on their faces that can only come from sheer terror. This was big-time butt-kicking, and it was far from over.

We knew that the bad guys were capable of determining whether or not the battle would continue. If they thought they could do added damage and that the odds favored them, we would be fighting for some time. However, they could just as easily evaporate into the jungle if they wanted this round to be over. The one thing that might keep them hanging around for a time was the intense barrage of artillery—it's not smart to expose yourself when the stuff is hitting the fan.

The old man was nearby, talking on his radio. Jets were inbound, with two Cobras coming in behind them. The 105 fire mission was being terminated to clear the air space above the target.

I heard the jets before I saw them. They screamed in from behind us, right over our heads, and dropped their loads just as they passed above us. Five-hundred pound bombs and napalm went arching into the NVA positions. Although the jungle was too thick for us to see where they were hitting, we could follow their impacts by the orange fireballs above the treetops and the ground-shaking thumps of the HE blasts.

After our dose of it, I felt a grim satisfaction that we were giving it back—in spades. I now had an appreciation for how it felt to be bombarded, but I was so pissed off and shaken by what had happened that all I could sense was the gratification that Charlie was getting his turn.

I thought about Brady, blown to pieces right in front of me. Fuck you, Charlie.

I was becoming Doc. I didn't care, and I felt very empty. I wanted to hurt the gooks, wanted to spray a magazine of bullets into somebody and watch the holes appear in his body while he danced for me. I was filled with rage, and wanted nothing more than to lash out at something. I had really learned to hate.

The jets quickly expended their ordinance, and were soon gone. The Cobras weren't far behind, though, and almost seamlessly took over the assault with miniguns, racks of missiles, and M-5 kits spitting out 40mm grenades into the enemy positions. The once-intimidating angry buzz of the miniguns was music to us. Back and forth they strafed, chewing up the jungle beneath them with lethal shards of metal.

John, my RTO, was still dutifully monitoring the radio, and passed word that the ARPs on the left had overrun an NVA mortar emplacement, killing five. After securing the ridge, they joined their buddies on the far side in firing down at the valley floor.

While all this was going on, Bravo Company was regrouping. The NVA attackers were obviously hunkering down—there was too much stuff landing on them and keeping them from adjusting their mortars back to our retreated location. So we were spending the respite licking our wounds and trying to figure out what to do next.

The seriously wounded, and TC led the list, would need a medevac soon if they were to survive. There was no chance for a dust-off where we were, both because of the terrain and because of the nearby bad guys who would be only too happy to plink a helicopter. And the wounded were too messed up to move very far. Finally, nobody was happy about our dead still left out in the jungle. So it was time to clean up our little mess.

Just as it isn't heroism when you don't have a choice, it also isn't heroism when anger makes you crazy. Those of us still standing in Bravo Company had been pushed beyond some invisible line, and a fury was boiling in us. Citizen-soldiers, unmotivated by a useless war, some of whom normally would spend most of a firefight burrowing into the ground in avoidance, were suddenly pissed off at being knocked around and were making noises about kicking ass and taking names.

Hurt me once, shame on you. Hurt me twice, shame on me.

Even though we were a company of kids, the captain was a seasoned infantry officer and recognized the signs of an opportunity to harness the rage we felt. Plus, he understood that there aren't many people in the human race with the capacity for mayhem possessed by young men between 18 and

25 who feel they have been pushed too far. Perhaps it seems a generalization, but young bucks have peak physical prowess, a potential for savagery, and little of the restraint that age and experience brings to grayer heads. The captain began directing the platoon leaders to set up an assault in roughly the same platoon arrangement we had used coming in. We were going back to finish the job.

The Cobras were ordered to stand off, saving whatever remained of their ammo in case we suddenly needed suppressing fire. The 105 fire mission was resumed; it hardly took a minute from the call until the first round plowed into the NVA positions because none of the gun settings had been changed.

We shed rucksacks and all unnecessary gear, carrying only weapons, ammunition, a few smoke canisters, and all the grenades we had in the company. We were a gnarly looking bunch. Smeared with sweat and mud and blood, eyes full of fury. Bandoleers over bandoleers, long belts of M-60 ammo wrapped around the chests and shoulders of the machine gunners a la Poncho Villa, point men with extra magazines clamped in their teeth for quick replacement. Hand grenades lined up on pistol belts like tools on a macabre handyman's overalls. The captain looked around at us and nodded. "Let's roll."

We moved out, back toward the killing zone. The likelihood of intense mortar fire was now significantly reduced, as the artillery and hovering Cobras would be a strong inducement for Chuck to keep his head down, and at least some of the tubes had been neutralized by the ridgeline ARPs. And the racket of the dropping 105s would mask our approach, unlike a few minutes before.

The trick would be to get close enough to the NVA positions before being detected to reduce or even eliminate the usefulness of their mortars. If we were close enough, Charlie would have to aim his tubes practically straight up in the air, which is as unhealthy for the mortar-loaders as it is for their targets.

We crept and crawled and slithered our way back through the devastated patch of jungle. It was astonishing to see the shattered trees and shredded foliage, the craters in the ground where mortars had struck. I passed near what was left of Brady. I looked away, and had to swallow hard to fight down the rising gorge.

To nobody's surprise, Doc was out in front, a little to my left. I suppose his rightful place was back with the wounded, but there were two other company medics there and not much more anyone could do for the downed GIs. I think Doc wanted to make sure someone paid for his pal.

It was slow going, and a little disconcerting to be moving toward the incoming artillery rounds. We knew they would stop when we got close, but it was still counter-intuitive to be crawling into an artillery barrage. At last Doc hesitated, and I saw the point man on our right flank also stop. Out in front of us was a bunker, maybe 80 meters away. I let my eyes drift to the right, then to the left. There! Another one on the left, with a mortar tube peeking out above the lip. It was feasible that the valley had bunkers like these all the way across, and possibly some deep ones.

While the squad on our right was weighing their options, Doc started inching toward the bunker with the mortar. I motioned to Dee, who had a LAW with him, to come forward. Pointing out the bunker directly in front of us as his target, I told him to wait until Doc was in position at the bunker on the left. Dee nodded, and I turned to cover Doc on his approach.

John Fournelle was a few feet behind me with the radio. I told him to get on the horn and let the lieutenant know what we were doing, and suggest terminating the 105 fire mission because Doc was getting fairly close to the exploding rounds. He was completely focused on the bunker, and was oblivious to the artillery crashing just beyond it.

An eternity passed while Doc covered the distance to the bunker, and I kept expecting a bad guy to peer out of the hole and see the crazy medic with his tail hanging out. Finally he was within ten feet of the bunker's opening, and I saw him reach for a grenade. I signaled to Dee and watched him take aim at the second bunker.

Doc's grenade arched into the left bunker just as Dee squeezed off the LAW. The boom of the rocket bursting out of the LAW tube drowned out the explosion of Doc's grenade, but I clearly saw the bunker erupt. Simultaneously, the LAW round went neatly through the opening in the second bunker, and made a hideous thump as it detonated inside.

Because the LAW is a shape charge designed to release the majority of its energy in a narrow cone straight ahead of its point of detonation, it doesn't always kill in all directions as efficiently as a frag grenade does. A few seconds after Dee's round went off a rattled and bleeding NVA soldier bolted from the right bunker. He didn't make it two steps; I had my M-16 up and sighted, and put out a burst on automatic. It wouldn't have mattered—at least three other M-16s opened up on him at the same time. He did a sickening little shimmy as the bullets struck, and went down hard.

Doc risked a peak into his bunker, and held up two fingers. It was a start, but by my count we had a bunch more to go just to get back to even for what they had done to us. And just getting to even would most assuredly not be anywhere near enough. Gooks were going to die today. Lots of gooks.

We kept moving forward. Way over to the right, I heard another grenade go off and the chatter of M-16s on automatic. Nobody had an interest in firing single shots this day—this was rock 'n roll time.

Suddenly there was a bunker right in front of me, less than 30 feet away. The jungle had been thick before our 105s started ripping things up, and the bunkers were dug in and well camouflaged. If the artillery barrage hadn't rearranged the foliage, I might have crawled right on top of it before seeing it.

I reached back to the side of my web belt for a grenade. Strip off the protective wire clip, pull the pin, let the spring-loaded spoon fly off, and heave that sucker right through the hole. Strike three, you motherfuckers!

And watch it come flying back out of the hole at me.

You know how skin crawls? Well, my scrotum tightened up like wet leather in the sun.

The only thing that saved my ass was that the grenade was pitched a little to the right, and I had approached from the left. I pressed my face into the dirt and listened to the deafening roar of the exploding frag. Something tugged at my pant leg, and I heard something ding against my steel pot. Shrapnel.

Fear gave me a moment of common sense, and I wondered what the hell I was doing there. But then I quickly determined that no body parts seemed missing or damaged, and my anger blazed hotter than before. So much for common sense—it's no contest in a struggle with rage.

GIs are taught to throw hand grenades as soon as the spoon flies. The fuse has an approximately five second delay once activated, but drill instructors urge their charges not to tempt fate by holding a live grenade. Unfortunately, the fuse delay sometimes gave Charlie a chance to grab an incoming frag and throw it back at the good guys.

A rock was on the ground near my face. The proverbial light bulb went off in my head. I grabbed the rock, then unhooked another grenade. Release the wire, pull the pin, let the spoon fly. I threw the rock into the hole and held the hot grenade. "One thousand, two thousand, three thousand." Then the grenade followed the rock through the hole.

The rock came sailing back out just about the time the grenade went in. A split second later it exploded, making a muffled keerump inside the bunker and a shock wave I could feel in the ground beneath me. Gotcha, scumbag! I came very close to giggling. It was not a pretty sight.

I gingerly crept up and glanced inside. The grenade had done its job well. Two more dead NVA.

John had been near enough to catch my trick with the rock. He put the word out on the company net, and got a grateful reply from 1st platoon, also having problems with rejected grenades flying back out of bunkers. Desperate people are inventive. I might have been born at night, but not last night.

And so it went, all afternoon. There proved to be fifteen NVA bunkers spread out in the valley, and we had to approach and take them out one by one. The artillery, jets and Cobras had forced Charlie into the holes long enough for us to get close, so melting away into the jungle to fight another day wasn't an option for a change. The gooks were trapped into fighting us from their emplacements.

A few NVA had been caught in the open when the jets came in. The napalm had turned some of them into crispy critters. I felt no compassion, no disgust at the carnage. It wasn't quite real in any case—a blackened, charred human body doesn't connect with what passes for a sense of reality in most of us. Real or unreal, it didn't matter. I had long since stopped regarding those charred bodies as human. They were something less, and not to be pitied or mourned for the death we brought to them. They were just parts of an enemy war machine, and our job was to break things.

Words like "gook" had become emblematic labels, and I wasn't hearing any voice of conscience admonishing me to reject them, to instead think of these enemy soldiers as other human beings. The transformation of a shy, idealistic college kid into a fiercely driven killing machine was just about complete. The drill instructors who directed their trainees to yell "Kill!" while lunging with bayonets would have been proud of the finished product.

Some of the bunkers were empty, but we had to move on each of them as though they were all occupied. No way to know without looking inside, and nobody was angry enough or stupid enough to take a look without first fragging it. The approach on each bunker was complicated by the bad guys' interlocking zones of fire, where an assault on one bunker could be hampered by shooters in another bunker.

The empty ones were the exception; most of the bunkers were well defended. Charlie saw us coming and fought furiously with automatic weapons and RPGs. I'm sure the NVA in the surviving bunkers had heard grenades exploding and knew what would soon be coming to them. They were intensely motivated to not let it happen and a few more of Bravo Company's best were wasted in the process.

I saw a spec 4 in 1st platoon on our left work his way toward a bunker with a grenade in his hand. He didn't pay close enough attention to a flanking bunker, so he never saw the NVA who dropped him just before he threw the grenade. I don't think it mattered much to the dead GI that the gooks in the other bunker were hamburger less than five minutes later. He twitched a few times on the ground, and then he was gone.

We didn't care how long it took; every bunker was going to be fried. I'm not even sure if the captain could have successfully ordered the company to pull back, we were that caught up in it. In one case, the zones of fire between three bunkers had been set out so well that we couldn't get close enough to the key one in the middle for a frag or a LAW. So Lieutenant Warren got on the horn with the fire control officer on Professional, and slowly walked 105s toward the bunker's location. When he ordered "Fire for effect", a couple rounds actually landed right smack on top of the bunker.

It had been well built, but not strong enough to withstand a direct hit from an artillery shell. We didn't even need to waste a grenade to mop up. The stuff inside didn't much resemble anything like people, but we guessed from pieces of bodies there had been three NVA in the position.

The last bunker was evidently a command post, and the bad guys inside were intelligent enough to surrender. Blood was still boiling in Bravo Company, but fortunately nobody took it upon himself to mow down the four North Vietnamese coming out of the bunker with their hands in the air. Seems kind of silly, doesn't it? Like there are these clear ethical lines dividing the practice of killing into "good killing" and "bad killing". Rules of engagement to guide the ethical army, the moral warrior. It was okay for the NVA to surprise us and blow us to kingdom come. It was kosher for us to grease the NVA in those other bunkers, even the ones that arguably didn't have a prayer against our unshakable passion to burn them out. But as soon as these last gooks decided they didn't want to play any more, it suddenly was verboten to blast them.

Maybe there remained some small slice of humanity in our collective psyche, but I believe that most of the GIs who watched the NVA soldiers come out of that last bunker would have gladly blown them away, surrender or no surrender. I'm not completely sure, because I didn't want to dwell on it for fear of what I might learn about myself. But if I had been alone I might have been tempted to simply drop them where they stood. There was no doubt in my mind that Doc would have done them without a second thought.

Inside the last bunker was a huge cache of food and ammunition, at least a ton of it. Papers and books in Vietnamese were littered around. A few were smoldering, like the gooks had hurriedly tried to get rid of them. We cleaned out the stuff that might have some useful intelligence, and then set a bunch of C-4 charges in the supplies.

Cries of "Fire in the hole!" alerted the rest of the company to take cover from the impending explosions, and then the charges were detonated. Christ, what a bang! The C-4 sympathetically set off the NVA ordinance, including a big stash of mortar rounds, shaking the ground and producing spectacular pyrotechnics all around the command bunker. Rice sprinkled the ground for fifty feet in every direction.

Troops wandered around under the watchful eyes of squad leaders, counting bodies and cautiously inspecting blown bunkers to ensure no bad guys were still alive and hiding in them. Another smaller cache was located and blown. Still another napalm-scorched NVA body was found toward the edge of the bunker defensive line.

I picked up and marveled at a piece of artillery shrapnel. As big as the last knuckle of my thumb, the jagged metal had been impossibly bent and twisted like taffy from an extruder. Even as I rolled it around in my hand, the contorted razor-sharp flanges tugged at my fingers. What a remarkable killing device. People were really quite good at finding ways to rip and tear the fragile flesh of their bodies.

Night was coming, and we needed a good defensive position in case the NVA presence in Dragon Valley was larger than the unit we had fought. Bravo Company pulled back to where the wounded had been left, then continued backtracking and searching for a clearing with adequate clearance for a medevac. It didn't take long to find a suitable place, and dust-offs were called while we set up a perimeter and moved the injured troops. The medevacs were prompt; they had previously been notified that we had a load of busted grunts and had been standing off not far away. TC was still alive, but not by much.

The final tally had been six dead GIs and another nine with wounds ranging from a minor puncture to TC's wide-open chest. Radio chatter indicated the ARPs had one wounded and no dead. I think we counted 38 dead NVA, plus the four live ones from the last bunker. There were no wounded NVA; the hand grenades had done their job well. A Huey picked up the live ones after the dust-offs came and went, taking them to an ARVN compound for interrogation. Better the ARVN than us—the South Vietnamese soldiers had no compunction about torture as an interrogation device. The dead NVA were left in their holes, and wherever else they fell.

I wasn't comforted by our advantage in the body count contest. Six young men, including one in my own platoon, were dead and a bunch more hurt in a meaningless, forgettable event in a war whose time had passed. Hell, the folks at home were being told, and believed, that the war was quieting more every day. Nobody back in The World wanted to pay much attention to Vietnam any longer. The war was widely accepted to have been a costly, painful mistake, and the country was anxious to get on with the forgetting long before the shooting was even over. So what the hell were we doing?

I had always liked things in my life to have a comfortable feeling of order and reason to them. This was insanity.

It took some time for the guys to unwind. Officers and NCOs had to gently prod a few of the more shell-shocked to set up decent defensive positions for the night and get claymores out. It didn't seem likely, but we couldn't take a chance that Charlie might come back for more and find us in a poorly made night laager. If we had been earlier pissed about getting our butts kicked, I imagined that Charlie had reason to be absolutely livid.

That night I lay awake for an hour before finally drifting off, thinking about what had happened during the day. I felt drained, empty, and I was uncomfortably aware that something in me was different. I, and all the guys around me, would never be the same as the folks who had walked into this valley, and I wasn't entirely sure I liked the transformation.

An assault upon the order, the changing of the guard,
Chosen for a challenge that is hopelessly hard.
And the only single sound is the sighing of the stars,
But to the silence of distance they are sworn.
Phil Ochs

Chapter Eighteen

It had been a subtle evolution, but we were a different company.
In prior wars, and even in the early years of Vietnam, entire
battalions of soldiers would enter the conflict together and
become combat veterans together. That quickly changed during
the Vietnam War, in that replacements were constantly drifting
into the mix and changing the complexion of fighting units
as other GIs completed their yearlong tour of duty and went
home.

This unprecedented notion of a combat tour with a time
limit had the effect of producing field units with unbalanced
levels of preparedness and battle experience. The longer the
unit went without a major fight, the more members had
rotated out to be replaced by virgin FNGs. It was typical to
find experienced troops with Combat Infantryman's Badges
signifying they had been under fire serving alongside fresh-
faced newcomers who hadn't yet fired their weapons.

So, when an event like our little bash in Dragon Valley
occurred, there frequently was a discernible change in the
personality of the affected unit. A significant battle was a
shared experience, for old hands and FNGs alike, and always
contributed something to the character of the unit, good or
bad.

It had been a while since Bravo Company had been
bloodied like that, and even guys like me—with a CIB and by
now considered a veteran—had never seen such a fight. We
were a somber group in the Dragon Valley night laager, waiting
for the morning and a likely opportunity to go looking for more
people to shoot at.

In our case, the change was more than the vacant expressions and quiet tension of men who had been through a grinder. There was also a weariness, a slope-shouldered exhaustion like that felt by a marathon runner who had squeezed every ounce of energy into getting across the finish line. I could see it all around me, and I felt it too. We had use fury and hate to overcome terror, and found the intensity in those emotions sufficiently energizing to kick Charlie's butt. The real motivating forces for soldiers in battle are supposed to be purpose and commitment, not rage, but none of us had found much in Vietnam to rally around as a purpose.

The problem, of course, was that purpose and commitment provide endurance, a fuel to keep you going, while fury is only a shot of adrenaline that, once abated, leaves you feeling like a wrung-out rag. Another unfortunate side effect was that our dependency on angry emotions to spur us to battle also shaped our view of the enemy. There was none of the respect for a noble adversary, an opponent who simply has a different political point of view or a claim on a piece of geography that conflicts with our interests, but is otherwise a lot like us. There were no exchanged, respectful salutes between opposing commanders or between dogfighting pilots. Instead, we were incensed at a bunch of gooks and wanted intensely to kill them.

I don't know if there are many good reasons to make war, but the unrestrained release of hate and fury surely are not among them.

We had to get an emergency resupply the next morning. Every single hand grenade and LAW in the entire company had been expended, and machine gun ammo was perilously low. A lot of it had been burned off to cover the approach of GIs trying to get close enough to frag the bunkers. An M-60 can eat a lot of bullets.

The resupply chopper came in just after first light, carrying a heavy load of ordinance. We used the same LZ as the medevacs had used the previous day to haul away the busted up grunts. The thick morning mist swirled around and mixed with the red smoke we popped to guide the pilot, making a curiously unnatural pastel fog in the yellow early light. The scene appropriately reinforced the unreality I was still feeling from the day before.

The chopper lumbered into our clearing, burdened by stacks of ammo boxes and crates of grenades piled high in the Huey's narrow cabin. A few boxes of C-rations, batteries for the prick 25s and a bag of mail finished the load, barely leaving room for the crew. One fire team from each platoon was detailed to break down and distribute the pile left behind by the helicopter, which practically leaped into the sky once its heavy load was dumped.

As a result of the big resupply, we didn't get underway until about 10:00, which was unusually late in the day for us to move out of a night laager. Nobody minded—it was time to sit awhile and write letters home. Not unexpectedly, we were ordered to push further into the valley. It was a reasonable conclusion; I'm sure I would have made the same decision in the battalion commander's place. We were there, Charlie was there, and yesterday's encounter suggested at least the possibility of more enemy forces in the area. Our dilemma, of course, was that none of us had any further stomach for being there, having burned ourselves out in the intensity of the previous day. We would have been a lot happier if the orders had been to head the other direction. Out of the valley.

But that wasn't an option, so we dutifully loaded up our gear and the shiny new ammunition from the morning's resupply, and headed deeper into the valley. Once again, the ARPs were shadowing us on the high ground, providing cover against a flank attack from the ridgelines. All we supposedly had to worry about were surprises in the knotted jungle of the valley floor.

We spent two long days working our way slowly up the valley. It was tedious, not just because of the jungle, but because our progress was intentionally cautious. Third platoon took over the middle, between us and 1st platoon, and had their Kit Carson scouting out in front of them for signs or booby traps. The rest of us moved behind squad point men, carefully examining every tree or snarl of vines or shadow in front and around us.

Such a high level of concentration quickly wears you down, and by the end of the second day we were even more tired than the morning after the firefight. We had carved and chopped our way about two thirds up the valley, and the captain's call to stop for the night was a welcome relief. The Kit Carson had seen a few signs of troop movement and found two booby traps which he disarmed, but otherwise no contact with the bad guys.

It was a weird night laager. Staying on the valley floor meant setting up in virtually unbroken jungle. No defensive position could see the positions on either side, and the thick vegetation limited the range of claymores to a few dozen feet. The lethal steel balls lost their velocity real fast as they plowed through layers of leaves and vines. Finally, a valley night laager was wetter and muddier than a night position on higher ground, and the leeches came out to feed by the hundreds. Nobody cared; we were too tired.

I've often thought back on my time in Vietnam and wondered at the relatively few times we were attacked at night in one or another of those night laagers, and how incredibly fortunate that was. Although many night defensive positions were scrupulously set up, making good use of natural cover and the terrain, there were circumstances where location made a lot of them much less formidable and a few—like our valley floor camp—highly vulnerable. We rarely dug in, as foxholes tended to be sloppy in lower jungle locations, or required an exhausting effort on high ground to trench into the often rocky soil.

And, although it wasn't a regular occurrence, it sometimes happened that a tired GI would nod off during his watch. If Charlie was nearby and tried to probe a position where nobody was awake, he could crawl right in and slit some throats or drop a frag without any risk of getting nailed by the claymores. Minimally, he could get close enough to turn the claymores around, aimed back at the sleepy grunts. A night laager with even one position compromised was sure to take heavy casualties, and maybe even get completely overrun.

Since it was almost impossible for GIs to sneak around during the night, I suppose it might also have been a little difficult or at least unpleasant for Charles to try it. Although the gooks were a heck of a lot better at night activity than us ground-pounders, you still have to think it would take a major gut check for them to go creeping up in the dark on positions only dimly visible in the blackness and with big ugly claymore mines waiting to ventilate them. That may have been one reason for our relative lack of nighttime harassment by the bad guys. Still, it was a commonly held view in our part of the war that the VC owned the night. Maybe if they had known how iffy some of our defensive perimeters were, we might have had more overnight visits than we actually got.

As I lay on the spongy jungle floor, stinking of bug juice to keep the leeches away, I thought back to a time about a month earlier when we hadn't been so lucky, and hoped that our current ill-advised laager wouldn't suffer a similar fate.

It had happened on a platoon patrol, so we were in a comparatively smaller platoon laager. From a topographical standpoint, it was considerably better than the closeness of dense jungle. The perimeter had been set up on a hill, and the vegetation, while thick, still afforded reasonable sightlines and fields of fire.

I had been asleep when the claymore blew. It's likely that the alert PFC on watch who squeezed the trigger had kept us all from being wasted.

He was an hour or so into his shift, a time when the darkness and stillness of the night and your own body's natural instinct to idle down into sleep tended to warp your senses. The night was like a blanket, and soft breezes gently stirred the grass and trees.

At such times, a man on watch felt like he might be the only person alive. It wasn't necessarily scary; in fact it was often a peaceful time, occupied by wandering daydreams of home and family. If it wasn't raining and miserable—conditions that produced a somewhat different state of mind than "peaceful"—the lulling qualities of a night watch brought on an almost dreamlike state and easily wore down a sentry's vigilance.

Some sound in the darkness had dragged him back from

his thoughts of The World. A warning scrape, a snapping twig, the rustle of grass without an accompanying puff of breeze, any unnatural sound might seem out of place in the quiet night and suddenly bring a sharp focus to the drifting attention of a man on watch.

The change is so dramatic it really has to be experienced. One moment you are in a reverie, alone in the middle of the night and trying to mentally replace the unpleasant surroundings with more agreeable memories. Although you are awake and aware, sights and sounds are muffled as if through a fog. Then, in a blink, something so completely grabs at you that all your senses snap to attention and concentration is like an intense white light. It's a rush to total focus.

Another sound! He knows something is out there, close by. A wandering nocturnal critter, perhaps, or maybe Charlie is about to pay a visit. The keen concentration, the uncertainty over what to do, and the fear of doing something wrong brings a quick sweat trickling between his shoulder blades, even on a cool night.

Quietly pick up the squeeze trigger with its wire leading out to the powerful claymore fifty feet away. Listen intently for any clue that someone is approaching the position. Wait with hammering heart, hoping not to detonate prematurely, but desperately wanting to set off the roaring explosion that will wake up his buddies and make him not so alone anymore.

He was a nineteen-year-old kid, in country for no more than a month. And he did good. He held his breath, straining to hear the subtle sounds of stealth. Deceptive smoky figures floated in the tree line. The night was filled with shadows of gray and black, some real and some illusion.

When he could wait no longer and was convinced someone was out front and practically standing on his claymore, he triggered the detonator. The staggering blast and bright flash yanked the rest of us into instant consciousness, and the three other men at his position came out of their sleep with M-16s in their hands.

In seconds the crack of small arms fire rudely overwhelmed

the night quiet, as every position opened up. I was in the next position to the triggered claymore, and could see muzzle flashes and green Chicom tracers in the trees. The flashes betrayed the bad guys' locations and gave us something to shoot back at.

Suddenly there was a muzzle flash close in front of me. I squeezed the detonator for the claymore out in front of our position and pushed my face into the ground as it erupted in a ripping blast. The muzzle flashes stopped. Another claymore went off to my left, followed by a long burst from an M-16. Then it was quiet.

The entire donnybrook was less than three minutes, and was over. No more shooting, no more booming claymores. No more sleep for the rest of the night.

As much as curiosity prodded me to see what might be out there, I had no intention of groping around in the dark. So we spent the rest of the night waiting to see if our visitors would return, and begging they wouldn't. Three of the platoon's six claymores had been exploded. I hoped that Charlie would wait for a rematch until after we were resupplied.

In the morning, we had found three dead VC some fifty feet outside our perimeter. There was a lot of blood, which might have meant we damaged a few more. A claymore does hideous things to a human body; nobody wanted to hang around the VC casualties very long.

That had been the only night attack I had experienced at that point in my jungle warrior career. I shook my head, thinking back on the attack and marveling at our luck. Fortunately, our rather insecure Dragon Valley night laager didn't get a similar visit. That night passed uneventfully, for which we were grateful. The platoon leaders gathered in the morning with the captain to plan the day. Sometimes, platoon sergeants were invited to these little meetings, and Lieutenant Warren took me along to this one.

Our Kit Carson scout recalled there was a little Vietnamese village just to the north of the upper end of Dragon Valley. Technically it shouldn't have been there, and its proximity to the valley suggested its residents were probably VC sympathizers.

But it was rare for an American unit to travel all the way to the north end of the valley (nobody in the 1st of the 46th had been there in recent memory), and the ville had been basically left alone over the years. Once or twice in the past a company out of the 198th had swept it, but those grunts had never found any bad guys or caches, so the ville had never been torched.

The company commander decided we would have a look. If NVA were passing through the valley with any regularity, the situation at the village might have changed. It might have become a more flagrant staging area for the bad guys, or a hiding place for supplies.

When we moved out of the night laager, our pace was still painfully slow due to the thickness of the valley floor jungle. It took us until early afternoon to snake our way through the low foothills at the northern mouth of Dragon Valley out to an area where the triple canopy grudgingly gave way to more open lowland fields and marshes. Our pace picked up in the thinning brush as visibility improved and point men could see more than eight or ten feet in front of them.

It was mid-afternoon when we broke out of the trees and saw the ville. Located near a rice paddy, it was in a cleared area at least a kilometer in size. Because it was so open, our approach definitely would not go unnoticed. In fact, we could already see a lot of activity as Vietnamese scurried around nervously anticipating our arrival. Clearly, news of our presence had preceded us.

There were thirteen hootches spread around the open area, which was a comparatively large number for the rare villes we found in our AO. I could see about 25 people, mostly women and children along with a few very old men. The lack of young men wasn't unusual. Whether they were good guys or bad guys, the males normally hid from American forces. (Says a lot about how well we were winning their hearts and minds, doesn't it?) Chickens and pigs wandered around loose, and a few ancient wooden farm implements leaned idly against hootch walls.

The whole village had a gagging combination of odors hanging over it. The pall of wood cooking fires lingered in the air, there were spicy Vietnamese food smells, and I picked up an earthy scent of mud and grass. There was the unsanitary odor of primitive living conditions. And the Vietnamese people themselves, as impolitic as it is to say so, actually smelled. Really, really bad. Worse than the animals.

One old hag started barking away at us in Vietnamese as we approached. Her mouth had ragged stumps of what had once been teeth, no more than four left. Years of chewing betel nut had done in the rest.

Exhibiting his characteristic (and deeply appreciated) prudence, the captain had 1st and 3rd platoons set up around the ville while Lieutenant Warren took 2nd platoon in for a search. We needed to check every hootch for contraband, look for tunnel openings, poke into the piles of hay, watch for booby traps, and generally determine whether these people were helping or hiding any bad guys.

Most of us had somewhat mixed feelings about the job. As foul a place as it was, it was still somebody's community. I suppose "community" was a stretch, but it was where they lived. This was still long before the 1968 exploits of Rusty Calley had become widely known back in the states, and the grunts in my platoon hadn't yet grown to be so jaded as to think of women and children as legitimate targets. Even Doc kept his knife in its sheath.

Even so, their homes or not, these people were in all likelihood the enemy. The missing men and boys could easily be VC, either hiding and watching us, or off somewhere else trying to kill other GIs. And the weeks and months of this madness we were living through had gradually produced a change in the way many of us viewed the Vietnamese. Like I said before, they seemed just a little less human than us. Thoughts like that came easier when we couldn't understand a word of the gibberish they were blabbering at us, and when their living conditions and body odor were even more disgusting than ours.

I've read that this is a common phenomenon in wars, that soldiers sometimes start seeing their adversaries as less than completely human, or at least significantly different from themselves in the qualities we view as defining what is human. It is a trick of the mind, to make the killing and maiming a bit easier to accept and live with.

We really couldn't afford to be too distracted by thoughts about how human, or inhuman, they were. Civilians, helpless villagers or whatever, these people might be a risk to a bunch of GIs. There wasn't one of us who hadn't heard stories of apparent non-combatants—women or children—getting close to Americans and killing them with a tossed grenade or some other concealed weapon. Our safeties were off and nerves were tight as we made our way into the ville.

Off to my left stood a girl, perhaps 16 or 17 years old. Hard living in these primitive conditions hadn't yet destroyed her youthful good looks, and more than a few pairs of eyes ran up and down her body as we walked past her. She wasn't much younger than my little sister, who was probably sheltered nicely in her dorm room at the University of Michigan right then. I hoped I wouldn't have to discourage any of my guys from hitting on her.

Lieutenant Warren and I directed the squad leaders to have fire teams enter and search each hootch. No groups smaller than three men were to go into the flimsy structures, in order to ensure they could cover each other and search for mischief.

All the while, a strident cacophony of babbling, whining, protesting Vietnamese voices was pelting us unremittingly. The Kit Carson stayed with the captain and the two of them tried to quiet the people down by explaining what was happening, but it was a fruitless effort. The villagers all talked at once in nasal singsong voices, and after awhile even the Kit Carson couldn't sort it out well enough to make him bother responding. The incessant chatter was obviously starting to annoy him, and it wasn't making the rest of us any happier, either.

I personally suspected that the noise was intentional, an unnerving diversion to hinder the search and maybe hasten our departure. I was getting to be a cynical bastard.

I went into one of the hootches being searched by a fire team from Chief's squad. The guys performing the search were doing their job well, methodically picking up and moving the spare furnishings, raising the woven mats on the dirt floor, poking into hidey holes looking for anything inconsistent with a gook village.

A Vietnamese woman stood just outside the open door, watching us suspiciously and with a noticeable flint of animosity in her eyes. I watched her out of the corner of my eye as I idly drifted about the hootch, examining bowls and various cooking implements.

There wasn't much to look at inside the hootch, and an unpleasant stink hung in the air. The smell came partly from smoke blowing in from the cooking fire right outside, and partly from the awful living conditions. Too many unwashed bodies had spent too much time cramped in the one-room hootch, and it had accumulated its occupants' stench just like an old barn. I couldn't help thinking about how these people lived, how different it was from anything I and the rest of the young Americans currently disassembling the village could relate to. I wondered contemptuously if the old woman just squatted in the corner when she had to take a leak.

It was worse than the poverty of run-down clapboard shacks in rural West Virginia or Mississippi slums or the Cabrini Green projects of Chicago. To these villagers, a reeking hootch was a normal life; they knew nothing different or better. There was no comparative lifestyle they could view that would offer a hint to them of how austere their lives were. There was no television to reveal a better standard of living, or the comforts of prosperity and western life from which we had come. This was an ancient and backward culture, a people of the land, way behind in the evolutionary process that had provided other countries with industry and affluence.

The Vietnamese woman at the door noticed me looking at her, and I was surprised to see her expression quickly shift from antagonism to an imploring vulnerability. Since I had stripes and wasn't as systematically hunting through her things as the other GIs inside, she probably concluded that I was a boss man and might be swayed by sympathy for her helplessness.

The funny thing was, I *was* sympathetic. I really didn't like what we were doing, and didn't much like being there. In a way, we were violating these people. But the anger over the Dragon Valley fight was still fresh in all of us, me included. Plus, the squalid way they lived somehow fed the perception that these people deserved only contempt, that they weren't nearly as worthy as the far superior American soldiers who came from a world they couldn't begin to imagine.

I picked up a faded Buddha statue from an indentation in one wall and peered behind it to see if anything might be hidden. The woman at the door positively yelped at me, and I somewhat sheepishly put the statue back. I turned away, and helped the search team finish up by jabbing our jungle knives into the thatch walls, looking for hidden ordinance.

It took only fifteen minutes before the first cache was discovered. Dee found it inside the third hootch, in an underground storage hole hidden under a false mat floor. There were RPGs, 82mm mortar rounds, a few AK-47s, Chicom ammo, and some 51-caliber machine gun ammo. It was big-time stuff and a significant find.

It also meant these people were dirty. It's possible they had been forced to store the munitions. The NVA and particularly the VC sometimes operated that way, taking over villages and conscripting residents and their homes for the communist cause under penalty of death for refusal. But the explanations of why they had the stuff were a lot less important to us than the fact they had it.

The big, impersonal U.S. war machine, us included, had long ago reached the point of indifference about sorting good guys from bad guys. In a war where "they all looked alike" there was no longer any patience for the excuses of intimidation or whatever other reasons that caused otherwise uninvolved villagers to side with the north or the south in political ideology. If a gook was caught with a gun, or somehow helping the VC or NVA, he was a bad gook. Period. Such was the dehumanizing price we paid to fight this war.

It was all that the lieutenant and I could do to keep Doc

from practicing his whittling on the villagers, once that first cache was discovered. There was an almost palpable mood change toward the jabbering villagers after Dee hollered out what he had found. It was clouding up over the little ville like thunderheads over the Texas plains.

I heard a shot, and my head jerked around so fast my steel pot almost gave me whiplash. I saw a young Vietnamese male about 100 yards away, just as he tumbled into the rice paddy. Seems he had just blithely come walking along the paddy dike heading toward the ville, not noticing there were some unusual visitors wandering around. Pretty careless to somehow miss the crowd hanging around; you could say he was a bushel shy of a full load.

He was carrying an AK-47, and that was his death warrant. The two platoons on watch outside the ville were instantly more vigilant. The cloud overhead grew darker.

More than half the hootches had been searched when the next cache was unearthed. It was big, more than a ton of food and ordinance. The Kit Carson was really getting pissed, and the captain didn't look at all happy either. Nobody in the ville knew anything about the hidden supplies, of course. It was like trying to get a straight answer out of a congressman. Nope, not our guns, don't have a clue how they got there, don't know nothing. "No VC, no VC."

Yeah, bullshit you're not VC. "Hey Mamasan, why you got beaucoup bullets, why you got grenades?" The storm cloud was getting positively ominous.

I'm not sure if there was an order, or if the idea just sort of sprung to life, fully formed, all on its own. The ville was coming down.

The two caches were wired with C-4 explosive, using spare detonators from claymores and their long wire leads. Once they were in place, the "Fire in the hole " cry went up and everybody dove for cover. When the Vietnamese saw us ducking, they went absolutely wild, running and yelling in that peculiar singsong of theirs. I don't know if they understood what was coming, but if WE didn't want to be close to the caches, then THEY damn sure didn't want to, either.

When the charges blew, the hootch over the biggest cache just seemed to evaporate. I don't believe there was anything left larger than a piece of straw. The sound of the C-4 charge was so quickly followed by the ground-shaking rumble of the ordinance exploding that it felt like one huge kaboom. Impossibly, the noise from the panicked villagers grew even louder.

Once the dust settled from the two demolished caches, it was Zippo time. Two squads moved systematically from hootch to hootch, setting the dry straw on fire with their lighters. In five minutes, the whole ville was ablaze, shooting off columns of crackling flames and foul black smoke.

I looked at the young girl who had made me think of my sister. She stared back at me. Her eyes were filled with sadness, and they were the eyes of someone far older than she was. There was no hatred there, just an impossibly heavy grief. I couldn't match her stare and turned away, confused at the conflicted feelings I was having.

We moved away from the burning hootches, just in case the search had overlooked any weapons or explosives that the fire might find and burn. And indeed, every so often there was a muted "pow" from one or another of the flaming shacks, probably from small arms ammunition hidden in the thatch walls and cooking off.

The villagers stood by, wailing and babbling, a little less loudly than before. The Kit Carson had given up trying to talk to them and walked away in disgust. He had decided he didn't want anything to do with these ignorant VC-sympathizing peasants.

If you have ever witnessed a house fire, you know how awful the smoke smells. That's partly the byproduct of being inhabited by people. Mattresses and furniture and carpeting all have the residues of human skin that smells terrible when it burns. The blazing ville smelled like that, in spades. There are few things I can think of that smelled worse than the revolting odor carried by that black smoke. Nobody objected when the captain ordered the company to move out. We wanted to be gone from there.

Bravo Company walked away from the destroyed village, past the rice paddy where the dead Vietnamese lay floating on his face, looking back at the smoldering hootches and the crying mamasans. Another heroic day in Vietnam. Another glorious victory in the battle to combat the domino spread of evil communists across the entire face of Southeast Asia.

At the edge of the cleared area, we stopped before heading back into the jungle and looked one last time at what was left of the village. The yakking had largely subsided, the women and children standing in a quiet and disheartened little knot off to one side of the destruction. I felt nothing but a sad emptiness.

Please God, I want to go home. I can't stand it any more.

Chapter Nineteen

The soldiers of Bravo Company, mostly quiet and contemplative, managed to limp out of the Hau Duc area avoiding any further engagement with the NVA force that had been our grisly dance partner. The column turned toward the southeast, and toward somewhat more familiar territory. None of us, even the captain, had any wish for further contact. The blood lust was long gone, our cynicism and hope for avoidance back in control.

It was only a couple of days later that people began to get sick. The first was Bradshaw, a PFC in Chief's squad. He had a screaming case of diarrhea, and was soon as weak as a kitten. He was obviously struggling to keep up with the rest of us, and having trouble with the weight of his rucksack. Other troops in his squad tried to help, taking his belt of M-60 ammo, lightening his load a little.

By the end of the day, Bradshaw wasn't any better and no longer felt like eating. Even worse, four other guys in the company were exhibiting the same symptoms. Unfortunately, I was one of them.

It was really miserable. Every twenty minutes or so, nature called. And she was very insistent: ignore me at your own peril— ready or not, you're going to crap. Within a couple hours, there was nothing left inside me to get rid of, but that didn't matter. Nature's call came anyway.

But most debilitating were the stomach cramps and the gradual sapping of energy. I mean, you can still fight with your pants down, if a bit inelegantly, but it's tough to be a very effective soldier when you hardly have the strength to pick up your gun.

By the evening of the second day with the trots, I was so weak that I almost had to crawl up the little hill where we set up our night laager. About the only thing I could stand to eat was a can of C-ration fruit cocktail, and that ran through me and out the other end in record time. The medics were concerned, and figured the untreated water we drank from the waterfall on the day we rescued Buzz had given some of us dysentery. As clear and delicious as that water had been, it evidently had more bugs in it than our tender GI guts could handle. It figured—just about every place in Vietnam was somebody's toilet.

All I knew was that I couldn't ever remember feeling so sick. I was beyond miserable.

Doc wanted us to go back to LZ Professional where the medics at the battalion aid station could take a look at us. I feebly protested—no self-respecting jungle warrior wanted to be hauled to an infirmary because his butt was leaking—but medics had the authority to order people out of the bush if they felt it was justified, even those who outranked them. A small piece of me felt an obligation to stay with the platoon, but mostly I felt like he said I looked: "Rode hard and put away wet". In the final analysis, I didn't really care where he sent me.

So the next morning, the five of us were picked up by a chopper and flown to Professional. The doc there spent maybe ten minutes with us, and decided we were bad enough that we needed to go to Chu Lai. I wasn't surprised. The aid station on the firebase was better than Doc's rucksack, but not by much. It was really just another bunker, with a little larger collection of medicine than Doc could carry. Four hours later and another helicopter ride on a supply shuttle found me back in the 91st Evac hospital, this time in a "shit ward".

I actually felt worse when I arrived than on my first visit. We all had amoebic dysentery, and it had turned our guts into knots. They gave us Flagel, a medicine that came in big horse-gagging pills that we had to swallow several times a day. They were strong, and sapped me just about as bad as the dysentery, because the stuff was killing critters inside me. I really felt like shit, no joke intended.

Almost a week went by before I started responding to the treatment and began to feel a little better. I spent most of the time on my back, often dozing, because I didn't have much energy for anything else. The docs had us on a special diet, but I usually wasn't very hungry and besides I didn't want to add a lot of intake for my problems at the other end. In time I stabilized a little, and I counted it as progress that I wasn't dashing for the can quite as frequently as when I first arrived.

At the end of my first week I was surprised one morning when Doc walked into the ward, looking for me. "What the hell are you doing here, Doc? How come you aren't out there killing gooks and playing doctor?"

He told me that his orders had just come through for assignment to Battalion Headquarters Company in the trains area in Chu Lai. Most medics only spent half their tours attached to combat units. The balance of their time was spent in a rear area, tending to the sick, lame and lazy who weren't out in the bush.

Doc had previously delayed his rotation to a rear assignment by a couple of months. He had eight months in country, so was only four months away from going home. Even though he wasn't enthusiastic about the petty Army nonsense that came with a rear area job—stuff like saluting, and morning formations, and fussiness about uniforms and appearance, things that weren't part of the more informal setting of a jungle combat unit—Doc had reached a point where he didn't resist the rotation. He really just didn't care about anything, including where the Army chose to put him.

As befit his grumpy character, he wasn't in the least bit solicitous or sympathetic about my wounded digestive tract. He was just looking for a familiar face, not visiting a poor sick buddy in the hospital. No problem, I didn't have much interest in talking about my bathroom habits, anyway.

Actually, the Army itself wasn't terribly sympathetic with GIs who got dysentery. Soldiers who came down with it were considered (I'm not kidding here) to have damaged government property, and that could get you into big trouble. The fact that the property in question happened to be my own personal ass was not important; I had damaged it. Fortunately, the company's shortage of Halizone back at Dragon Valley was a legitimate excuse for drinking untreated water, so the Army folks whose specialty is to monitor that sort of thing decided to let it go in our case.

Doc had learned that TC was still at the 91st Evac. The doctors were trying to get him sufficiently recovered to send him back to the states. I had regained enough strength to get up and walk around, so the two of us set off to find TC.

We wandered around the grounds, the dysentery patient and the burned-out medic, moving from one Quonset hut to the next. It didn't take long to find him. He was on a ward with twenty beds, all occupied by GIs with a wide variety of big-time wounds. The beds were filled with soldiers, kids mostly, who had missing arms, missing legs, heads swathed in bandages, torsos flayed with burns and shrapnel holes. One guy had bandages over virtually his entire body. It was a ward with a high turnover rate.

TC was in the fourth bed on the right. He didn't look anything like when we threw him on the dust-off. He was clean and conscious, leaning back against the elevated top of an adjustable bed. There was an IV hooked up to him, and he even had some color in his face. TC wasn't wearing a shirt, and a white bandage dominated his chest. In the center of the bandage was the discoloration of a wound that continued to seep, stubbornly resisting the docs' efforts to get it to heal.

Remarkably, TC was not only awake, but alert and lucid. He wasn't going to be doing push-ups any time soon, but he was conversational and obviously glad for the company.

Doc and I stood by TC's bed and talked for fifteen minutes or so. He said the doctors told him that his war was over, and he was encouraged at the prospect of an early out. Once he was well enough to travel, he would be sent either to a rehabilitation hospital in Japan where Vietnam casualties convalesced, or all the way back to The World. He was really hoping for a trip home.

While we were talking with him, I happened to glance over to the next bed where a nurse was changing the dressing on a teen-aged kid with a gut wound. I had the bad timing to look over just as the last covering came off the kid's belly. There was an open, gaping wound there, so large I could actually see the wet red and greenish black of his insides moving around. In size, it was like staring into a yawning mouth. I felt like I was falling, and couldn't take my eyes off that impossibly large horror in the kid's stomach. I managed to turn away, but my head was spinning and my vision dimmed. I had to grab the foot of TC's bed to keep from staggering.

I hoped nobody had noticed my reaction, especially the kid with the see-through stomach, or TC who might very well have a similar unimaginable hole in his own body. Not the kind of sick look you want injured people to see.

I thought I had been numbed to all the gore, but I hadn't. Human bodies weren't designed for such mistreatment. Our skin, the shell that holds all that gory stuff inside, is comically thin and poor protection against the toys of war. I wondered how the kid could possibly still be alive.

As it turned out, he basically wasn't alive—just ticking along on borrowed time. I came back to visit TC the next day and the bed beside him was empty.

Doc and I talked with TC as long as we could before the nurses tossed us out. We brought him up to date on Bravo Company since the Dragon Valley fight, and told him with some satisfaction that we had ground up a whole lot of NVA after he was wounded. Sort of a quid pro quo—hurt me, I'm going to hurt you back worse.

Back on my ward, the days dragged by while the Flagel did its thing battling the bugs in my guts. I read the raggedy old paperback books that had been donated by various charitable organizations back home. I discovered author John D. McDonald, and read everything of his I could find. His Travis McGee was my kind of hero, and I developed a lifetime fondness for McDonald's writing while on my back recovering in the hospital.

I wrote lots of letters home, carefully choosing the words I used to describe my stay in the hospital so as not to alarm anyone. It was a lesson I'd learned on my first visit with the shrapnel wounds. Folks at home were prepared to think the worst when you told them you were in a hospital, and I leaned over backwards to downplay my problem. I told everyone not to worry, that I was getting good chow and sleeping in a clean bed—much preferable to duty in the boondocks.

I caught up on newspapers. It was mid-April of 1970, and the war was in a temporary quiet stage. No big battles to report, and body counts were trailing off. I didn't know it at the time, nor did the newspapers, but the lull was due in part to a covert operation of some 30,000 troops being massed at that moment on the Cambodian border in preparation for what would prove to be yet another poor decision by the military masterminds of the war. It was the cross-border incursion that, when discovered by the media, finally opened the floodgates of protests against the war. Until that misjudgment, protests had more often than not been happenings on the college scene and consequently, for many people, easily dismissed as the work of hotheaded and immature students. After the invasion of Cambodia became known, however, a lot of average Joes and Josephines felt betrayed by the government and misled about the status of the war. It led to big-time protest marches, and almost certainly hastened the pace of our withdrawal.

Anyway, the lack of action reported in the Stars and Stripes was encouraging. It was tempting to think that both sides were getting tired of pounding on each other and Charlie might be hunkering down waiting for the Paris talks to agree on sending all the American grunts home.

After ten days I was starting to feel strong enough to get out of the hospital. The docs told me I could go in another few days. That afternoon, one of the 1st of the 46th battalion orderlies (a military version of clerk/typist/secretary/gofer commonly called "Remington Rangers") stopped by to let me know that my orders for an R&R in Hawaii had been approved and would be coming through soon. With luck, I'd be able to go in a week or two.

I was ecstatic. I had been writing to Linda for weeks that I was working on getting a Hawaii R&R, and asking her to let people know at her job that she might need to take time off with short notice. Her letters back sounded excited at the prospect of getting together for a week, even though she knew as well as I did that it would be a very temporary, bittersweet, reunion. As soon as the orderly left, I wrote to her with the good news.

That night I was jerked from sleep sometime after midnight by the sound of running boots pounding down the length of the ward. Other grunts in the beds near me were groggily asking what the hell was going on. Nothing so dramatic had happened before in the hospital and I felt, for the first time, naked without a weapon. It was dark, and nobody seemed to know what was happening. I thought about getting down on the floor. Then I *did* get down on the floor, half under the bed, thinking ironic thoughts about hiding from the monsters in the closet.

The Chu Lai division base had been put on alert. Some perimeter guard station had reported movement outside the compound and near the 91st Evac buildings. The hospital staff people were running around trying to figure out what they were supposed to be doing when potentially threatened with a perimeter breach. Most medical folks weren't terribly soldier-like, and the few of them I saw with guns looked very ill at ease holding a weapon.

A minute or two after the commotion started, I heard small arms fire coming from somewhere outside the hospital compound. Ten minutes later, someone came through the ward and told us everything was secure, we could go back to sleep. Sure we could. I was awake for a long time after that, thinking about my months in the jungle and the temporary reprieve the dysentery had brought. I thought about ambushes, and stray artillery rounds, and forays into Dragon Valley, and killing people. For the first time, I felt a chill at the prospect of going back out there when my hospital stay was over. God knows, I had been afraid plenty of times before, but this was different.

When I first joined a combat unit, I didn't know any better. Even after I was shot, going back to the bush was not such an intimidating thing and I hadn't felt the apprehension that was creeping up on me in my hospital bed.

This time I was plagued by a sense that I might be stretching my luck, and the impending return to slogging through the jungle to trade bullets with Charlie was demoralizing. It wasn't difficult to convince myself that I had been pretty lucky since plunging into the war. The bullet that just missed me after the lieutenant went down, the duel with six young VC by the berm, two trips into the Dragon Valley meat grinder, and those crazy, disorganized eagle flights—all of those had been attention-grabbing opportunities to die. So far, I was reasonably intact, at least physically. Maybe I was pressing my luck. How many times can a man go out there and still come back alive?

Courage was not my strong suit. The idea of people trying to kill me was more frightening now than it had been as an untested FNG. Now I knew what it was really like out there, how easy it was to get wasted. This was not a war worth dying for, and I really had no stomach to go back in harm's way.

There was nobody to talk to about feelings like those. You're not supposed to be a chicken in war. You're supposed to gut it out and keep on trudging toward the guy who is pointing a gun at you. Everybody faced the same risks, the same concerns, the same uncertainties. Nothing special about me, and I knew it was a load I had to carry by myself. And the feelings of apprehension weren't helped by the fact that it was a damned sight more pleasant eating decent food, sleeping in a real bed and taking a hot shower every day than the alternative back in the bush. Let's see, where would I rather be? I finally drifted off to sleep, wishing that my coming R&R was actually my DEROS date to go home.

All told, I was in the hospital about twelve days. I still felt a little weak, but at least my system was getting predictable again and letting me eat normally. I had been dropping over to see TC every couple days, and I went again the day before I was to be discharged from the evac hospital. I figured to say good-bye, because I wouldn't see him again before they sent him home. When I got to his ward, he wasn't there.

I asked the ward nurse if he had been shipped out. He said TC hadn't been so lucky. He died the night before. Just like that.

One day I'm talking to him, and the next day he's simply not there anymore. The memory of Doc and me hauling him, ashen-faced and soaked in blood out of that maelstrom of mortars had dimmed and had been replaced by the image of a healing and smiling TC, propped up in his bed and talking animatedly about getting home to family and friends.

My mind wouldn't accept it. TC had been okay; he had made it back from the edge. He had been snatched away from the battlefield, cleaned and patched and medicated. He got that far, he should be recovering now. Vietnam infantry soldiers knew how much luckier our generation of ground-pounders was than the poor bastards of World War II who didn't have helicopters to speed their wounded to well-equipped evacuation hospitals. Vietnam, for all its unpleasantness, was relatively more civilized when it came to patching up the broken soldiers.

So how could it be that TC hadn't survived to go home? Doc and I got him to a chopper, the chopper brought him to the hospital, and the docs had put him back together. TC made it through the tough part, and I damned sure couldn't understand why he was dead.

The ward nurse was understanding, and knew from my previous visits that TC had been a friend. The nurse's view was that many wounded GIs were really dead when they got hit. The dust-off and all the frantic medical efforts to repair damaged bodies sometimes just prolonged the inevitable. Oh yeah, there were certainly a lot of wounded grunts who survived because of a fast helicopter extraction. But others were hopelessly hurt, and no amount of bandages, medicines and surgery could change their unavoidable destiny. It merely delayed things for a few days. You can clean them up and try to stop the leaks, but a fragile body knows when its time is up.

TC had looked to Doc and me like he was getting better, but his body had been terribly damaged and just couldn't recover from the offending hole in it. The nurse didn't want to be graphic, but I got the picture on how bad TC had been wounded. Another grim reminder that this useless country was an unfriendly and unhealthy place to be.

In a depressed mood that appropriately complimented my weakened physical state, I collected my stuff and finished checking out of the hospital. There wasn't much stuff to collect—my rucksack, weapon and web gear were all back at LZ Professional, which was SOP for medevac patients going from firebases to evac hospitals.

I hitched a ride in the back of a deuce and a half across Chu Lai to the battalion headquarters company. I reported in to Sergeant First Class Wilkes, the acting sergeant major who I had briefly met when I first arrived such a remarkably long and life-altering time ago.

I remembered him being a stand-up guy, and he still was. A no-nonsense type and a little gruff, which was an obligatory demeanor for a 29 year lifer, he still had a twinkle of humor in his eye and had long since abandoned the idea that the Army always knew what was best.

Wilkes asked me how I felt, and if I was ready to go back to my unit. I recalled the unease I'd felt in the hospital at my looming return to the field, but decided to lie to him and said I wanted to get back to work. It just wasn't very soldierly to tell your sergeant major you felt like a wuss and would just as soon skip out on the shooting. No pussies in this Army. "Sure, Top, I'm ready to go kill some more gooks."

He grinned, which told me he was playing with me. I grinned back, figuring the pending R&R orders must have come through. He reached in a drawer, pulled them out and shoved them across his beat-up desk. "You're not scheduled to leave until next Wednesday, but I reckon we can find some work for you around here until then. Unless of course you want to go back to the boondocks for a week?"

"In your ear, Top."

My first stop after the sergeant major's office was a MARS station, a radio broadcast facility that gave GIs access to phone contact with the states. Crude by modern standards of communication that feature wireless satellite phones connecting people all over the world, the (M)ilitary (A)ffiliate (R)adio (S)tation system was basically a network of ham radio operators. These were short wave radio enthusiasts, mostly amateur hobbyists, who maneuvered a trans-global signal as close as possible to the person being called, and then dumped it into the Bell System lines. You could talk for only three minutes, and both parties had to keep saying "Over" to cue the ham operators on which way the transmission was going. It took a little adjusting to the thought that multiple guys with radios in their basements were listening in on soldiers' intimate conversations with their loved ones. But you had to appreciate the ham community's willingness to help out, especially since so many folks back home didn't think much of us "baby killers".

It was the first time I'd had an opportunity to use the MARS system since arriving in Vietnam, and it did feel weird to have such a crowd of people involved in my phone call. But I didn't care. It was unbelievably wonderful to actually talk to Linda. I felt my chest tighten when I heard her voice, barely audible over the squelch as the multiple radios alternated between receive and transmit. I told her to pack her bags, get a plane ticket, and meet me in Hawaii. "Love you, Kitten. See you next week."

The next few days crept by, dragging even worse than the usual slow pace of time passing in Vietnam. I mostly hung around the orderly room, doing odd jobs for Wilkes or running work details of enlisted men in the headquarters company. Typical Army BS, the make-work projects weren't much different from the posts to which I'd been assigned in the states.

A couple of times I had to go over to the battalion motor pool and sign out a jeep in order to deliver a package or some documents to brigade headquarters. That was an okay diversion, and gave me a chance to see more of Chu Lai. The base wasn't much to see, though. Once you got away from the harbor and the scenic half-mile expanse near the ocean, the balance of the base was flat and dreary. Buildings were mostly plywood, sandbags and corrugated metal, and all but the main roads of asphalt were nothing more than hard-packed dirt. During the monsoon season, the roads were thoroughfares of slippery mud.

I reconnoitered the airport, to be certain I knew where to go for my Hawaii trip and, later (dare to think it), my trip home. Most of the air traffic consisted of Phantoms coming and going on sorties to the interior, or C-130s ponderously hauling cargo—munitions, building supplies, food, live GIs, dead GIs. It was all just so much cargo.

On one of my jeep trips, I hit the main base PX for a little shopping trip. I did what any lovesick newlywed twenty-three year old would do in anticipation of a reunion with his girl. I bought perfume and jewelry, and a sexy little nightgown made from Vietnamese silk. Finally, I hit up the battalion finance officer for a little advance, so I'd have a wad of cash for the two of us to play with.

At night I'd go to the NCO club and drink, or play cards and drink, or listen to music and drink. I saw a lot of Doc, especially at the NCO club, although we didn't talk very much. It probably looked kind of strange to a casual onlooker, the two of us sitting at a table together in the bar, not saying anything for long stretches. Both of us were different, and I wasn't sure who had changed the most.

Doc's reputation as a terror in the jungle had carried all the way to the rear, and many of the REMFs gave him a wide berth. I guess I liked him, but it was an ambivalent fondness. He was something of an enigma—loyal, but with the temperament of a thug. I respected him, but still had no stomach for his ideas about how to get information out of gook prisoners. I had never seen him take a knife to a VC, but others swore he had done it. My respect was rooted in admiration for his toughness. There were lines I wouldn't cross that I knew he would, but I had to admit to myself that I was more like him than I was when I first fearfully stepped off the jetliner that brought me over. That was probably a good thing—tough guys were more likely to survive.

My week of odd jobs crawled by, the passing of time painfully slow because I finally had something wonderful to anticipate. I had to periodically remind myself that I was at least better off than humping the bush. I tried to keep busy, tried to avoid looking at clocks. I managed to get a set of summer khakis and low quarter shoes, pinned on my CIB and Purple Heart, and counted the hours.

At last the appointed day arrived. I caught a ride to the airport, took a C-130 shuttle to Cam Rahn, and hopped a plane to Honolulu. It was just about then that my sense of time went to a completely new gear. For so long, my life had been passing at a glacier pace, long days and long nights of fun and frivolity in the jungle. Suddenly, with the arrival of this R&R, my life clock put the accelerator to the floor. The week was a whirlwind, time rushing by in some cruel fast forward. I brought back an assortment of hazy images—of hours on a plane, of places visited, of Linda's face and her smile, of laughter and tears, of endless lovemaking, of long sandy beaches and picnics and warm surf and boat rides, of meals together in restaurants and alone in our hotel room, and of the never-distant awareness that our time in paradise was only temporary and would be quickly snatched from us.

When I arrived in Honolulu along with a planeload of other eager GIs, I was ready to burst from the excitement and anticipation. We deplaned and were put on buses for a short ride to Fort De Russy, where all the wives, girl friends, lovers, moms and dads, and anyone else with a connection to someone in uniform were anxiously waiting. Anxious, both because they missed us as much as we missed them, and because they were all wondering—if only just a little—what to expect.

After all, many in the media were depicting us Vietnam grunts as warped, blood-lusting and withdrawn pathological wrecks, enjoying the war. Heck, many of the incoming replacements in Vietnam told stories about soldiers returning from their tours getting spit on by people in airports. Some of the people waiting for us, having seen the unflattering accounts of wartime activities, undoubtedly worried that their soldier might not be quite the same after months in such a dehumanizing place.

When we arrived at Fort De Russy, the guys on my bus were herded into a large room, already occupied by the waiting civilians. Linda and I saw each other at exactly the same instant, and it was like everybody else in the room disappeared. They just weren't there any more. The two of us ran together and stood there clinging to each other for a long time. Holding her, it suddenly didn't feel like six months had gone by. I almost couldn't convince myself she was hugging me again. It felt so good, so right, like all the horrors hadn't really happened.

There was an obligatory briefing and Army crap about behaving ourselves, but it was blessedly brief. Hawaii was an R&R destination principally for guys who wanted to meet loved ones from the states. The Army figured we'd be too busy to get in much trouble. The unmarried GIs who went to Australia, on the other hand, were presumed to be looking for a wild time. Those guys were strongly admonished not to trash the place. They were told about every venereal disease and crotchrot known to man and handed supplies of rubbers to protect their government issue peckers. They were given lists of off-limit places, and threatened with time in the stockade if they were caught in any of them. Lieutenant Warren said it had taken more than an hour to clear the R&R center when he went to Australia.

I guess the brass assumed us old married folks didn't pose too much of a threat to the island. They probably thought we would head for a quiet hotel and not come out of our rooms the whole week. As horny as I felt, that wasn't an unreasonable assumption.

Linda and I caught a cab from Fort De Russy to Waikiki and settled into a nice little hotel about a block off the beach. I was in a daze, hoping I wouldn't awaken to find it was all a dream. We alternated between moments of awkward silence, staring at each other, and then both talking at once as months of pent-up news and emotions rushed to come out.

When we were finally alone together up in our room, the bashfulness that comes from a long separation lasted, oh, at least ten seconds. Then she coyly looked at me out of the corner of her eye and smiled that big smile that played my heart like a fiddle. We dove on the bed in a rush of hunger that wasn't going to be denied any longer. We tore at each other's clothes and I marveled anew at the sight of her, naked and girl-soft on the bed, looking up at me with doe eyes, waiting for me to come to her. At that instant, life was perfect. I never wanted to leave her side or be apart from her again. We were so eager for each other and I can't ever remember being so aroused. For a time, Vietnam was a very distant and forgotten place.

It was well after dark before we wearily rose from our nest, momentarily satiated from hours of exploring the look and feel and taste of each other. We had gone from intensity to frolic, to quietly and gently reacquainting ourselves with the pleasures and secrets of each other's body. We couldn't seem to get enough, and finally took a breather only when we were ravenous with a different hunger.

It was like that for six days. We made love, and ate good food, and went down to the beach, and even did some of the tourist things. One day we caught the Kodak show, with the native Hawaiian hula dancers and the colorful costumes. Another day we visited the Pearl Harbor memorial, sadly paying our respects to the remnants of a different war. The sneak attack 29 years before had galvanized Americans to mount a war effort never before seen in the world. The Japanese had truly awakened a sleeping giant and filled it with resolve. In a strange way, I envied the sense of purpose and mission carried by every man and woman who put on a uniform to fight that war.

On still another day we took a motor tour all around Oahu to see the sights away from Honolulu. We visited the crashing surf at Waimea Bay. We marveled at the colorful fish at Hanauma Bay that came up and took food right out of our hands.

We walked for miles up and down the sandy beach under

Diamond Head, and brought each other up to date on our
separate lives. I loved to walk the beach with her, holding hands.
I didn't want to lose contact with her, even for a moment. She
was so small and cute, it made me feel incredibly protective.
I noticed other guys on the beach doing double takes as they
caught a look at Linda, her lithe body draped enticingly in a
tiny bikini. Part of me rejoiced that she was mine, and I was the
envy of those beach Lotharios. But a nagging jealous voice at
the back of my mind kept reminding me of "Jody", that much-
despised symbol of hotshot punks back home stealing away the
women of guys like me stuck in Vietnam. Linda was so vital,
so alive. How could I expect to keep her while I was away and
out of her life? How could I expect her to wait for me when
there were so many hunks back there trolling for babes like
Linda? How could I expect her to wait for me when there was
no guarantee I was even coming back?

It was not a time for such doubts and unpleasant feelings.
It was time to savor being together. I pushed the troubling
thoughts from my mind.

Sometimes we were quiet, content just to be together. At
other times we talked on and on for hours. She told me about all
that had gone on in her life while I was away, and showed me lots
of photos she had brought. There were Christmas pictures of her
family and mine, pictures of my dog, pictures of my car, pictures
of friends, and lots of pictures of Linda in a variety of moods—
pensive, playful, happily smiling, provocatively vamping for the
camera.

On the morning of our second day together, I gave her
my crudely wrapped goodies from the PX. I loved her excited
reaction to an extravagant necklace and matching bracelet I
had brought her. When she opened the silk nightgown, she
immediately ducked into the bathroom to put it on and model
it for me. One thing led to another and the morning faded away,
the nightgown long forgotten on the floor.

Linda talked about how television and newspapers were
reporting the war, and told me about the discord at home
that was splitting the country into angry pro-war and anti-war

camps. She said that just the week before, National Guard soldiers had fired live ammunition into a crowd of protesting students at Kent State, killing four of them. At first, I couldn't believe what she told me. The massacre certainly wasn't getting any airplay on the AFVN armed forces radio station I occasionally heard on LZ Professional. It was just unthinkable to me that sentiment about the war had become so extreme that Americans were killing each other over it. I had no love for the students who had only disdain for me, but I certainly didn't believe in repressing dissent at the point of a gun. Most GIs in Vietnam were saddened by the lack of support at home, but not many of us would want to see students get shot for voicing opinions that many of us had, too.

Linda told me that the anti-war movement had ticked up several notches of intensity as the result of Nixon's decision to send some 30,000 troops into Cambodia. When that news broke, college campuses went nuts. After hearing so much about the war slowing down—a notion as I've said I personally found humorous—the country didn't react well to a sudden and unexpected widening of the campaign. So the students at Kent State were loudly expressing their displeasure, and the National Guard had been called out to restore order. The semi-soldiers had gotten nervous, and some nimrod had actually handed out live ammo. The weekend warriors popped some caps on the kids, and a part of America would never be the same.

The story left me very dejected, and added to the growing certainty I felt that the Vietnam War was some huge, crushing mistake. I knew more than ever that the effort had always been and still was doomed to failure.

I found it difficult to tell Linda what it was like in the jungle. It was as though words weren't adequate to convey my sense of the place, or to describe what it was like to be fighting and killing. I couldn't begin to explain the wrenching, contradictory feelings that plagued me—about the war, about the inept way we were fighting it, about platoons of amateur soldiers, about GIs dying needlessly. It was just as well, because I really didn't want her to know what my life there was like or how much I hated it. She had enough to worry about just from watching the daily dose of Walter Cronkite; it accomplished nothing for me to scare her with the unedited version. And I didn't want to add to her burden by dumping my own fears on her.

On our first night together, I slept like a dead man. I was exhausted from the trip and our marathon dance in the sheets. A sapper attack wouldn't have roused me. I began on subsequent nights, though, to find myself waking in the wee hours. I thought about how much I didn't want to go back, now even more because I'd had a taste of normal life and some time with Linda.

Only days before I had been in a hospital, a ghoulish carnival where people died from impossible rips and tears in their bodies. And not long before that I had been in Dragon Valley, terrified at the mortar barrage, and killing people. Jesus Christ, I had been *killing* people! I had blown people to bits with hand grenades, pumped bullets into enemy soldiers, and I had *enjoyed* it! No, maybe not enjoyed it. More like a grim satisfaction, a necessary outlet for overwhelming rage. Whatever the reason, I had been part of something I once would have considered unthinkable. There I was, just a few days separated from that nightmare, in a warm bed next to this beautiful little girl who was my wife, whose very face made my heart beat funny. All that I thought and felt and valued was being jerked around in ways I could never have imagined possible. I wasn't at all sure I even knew who I was anymore.

Vietnam was a hell I never wanted in the first place, and the reality of it had proven to be worse up close and personal than the stories I heard during months of training. I realized I had become genuinely afraid—of dying, of being maimed, of some new animal thing inside me that the war was creating, and of the innocence that was slipping away.

As I lay awake, I sometimes stared for long periods at Linda while she slept. Our R&R time was magical and I loved her more than ever, but every so often I had a sense that all wasn't completely as it had been. A subtle shift had drifted into our relationship, something felt just a little different than I remembered. There had been no angry words or distractions in our love-soaked time together, but once or twice I felt an uncomfortable distance between us, an awkward gulf between people a little unsure of each other. It was an unsettling feeling, particularly since she had become my primary focal point for enduring and surviving my time over there. She was my anchor, someone for whom I had to stay alive.

One morning I awoke to find her leaning on an elbow, looking down at me. For just a brief moment, I saw a flicker of sadness in her eyes. Her look sent a chill over me, waking me as surely as the snap of a twig on a night ambush. I started to ask her what was wrong, but before I could speak she transformed into a playful minx, giggling and diving under the covers where she quickly had me once again standing at attention. Her sad look later proved to be prophetic, but at that moment the chill was quickly forgotten, replaced by a tangle of tan thighs and reaching hands.

We went out to fine restaurants practically every night. We had shopped for some civvies, so I didn't have to wear a uniform and almost looked like a regular guy. It was great sitting in a nice place, with linen tablecloths and attentive waiters, eating prime steaks and fresh fish and exotic island cuisine. It was food I could only imagine a few days before while spooning cold beans and franks out of a can.

The third night we ate out, a curious thing happened to me. The restaurant we chose was really superb, and was as upscale a place as the two of us had ever been together. The menu was elegant, filled with appealing delights that left us puzzling over what to order. In a manner reminiscent of a more courtly time, the waiter gave Linda a menu without any prices listed.

After we finally made our choices, I selected a nice bottle of wine from a list every bit as extensive as the menu had been. Linda and I made a toast, enjoying a perfect night together.

I sat there, holding my glass of wine and looking at Linda in a bright yellow summer dress across the table from me, thinking what a memorable moment it was. Suddenly a cloud passed over me and I felt a frightening unease about being there. I had a sense that I somehow didn't belong in such a fancy restaurant, that I was horribly out of place. Anxiety flooded me; the impression made me feel bizarre. In a second, I had pictured myself and the rest of 2nd platoon, our column snaking through the jungle, all dressed in our battlefield finery—mud, blood, and crud on our faces and fatigues, a week's growth of beard, dullness in our eyes. Then the jungle scene was abruptly juxtaposed with the restaurant, my band of barbarians and I surrounded by silver and crystal, finery and civility.

I thought that every eye in the place must be on me, frightened and shocked that such a grotesque figure could be permitted in such a grand place. The images of soldiers faded quickly—I don't think Linda even noticed my distracted look—but I still couldn't shake the idea that I shouldn't be there, that I wasn't good enough any more to be mixing with the restaurant's refined clientele. I had a glimpse of myself as I had become, and that apparition no longer belonged with civilized people.

It was a scary moment. I told myself I was being crazy, and looked down at the table to keep from glancing at the other tables nearby to see if anyone was looking at me. I supposed that normal people who might actually see a platoon of grunts after a couple weeks in the boondocks *would* probably be a bit unsettled. We could be awfully fearsome looking. I reassured myself that I was as clean and well dressed as anyone else in the restaurant, and nobody was paying any attention to me at all. Somehow, though, my momentary vision left me thinking they had all been looking inside me, taking a measure of who I was and finding me wanting.

With some effort, I shook off the disturbing feelings. I never mentioned it to Linda. I didn't know what to say.

The memory of the restaurant episode faded as our night out continued to otherwise perfectly unfold. We walked through the city streets, holding hands. We soon found ourselves back at the beach, and took off our shoes so we could walk in the sand. The two of us strolled along at the edge of the waves gently lapping at us, pushed by a warm breeze. We laughed and talked, and pretended that our wonderful time together would never end. There was an unspoken agreement not to mention the war, or our waning time. Ever the tease, she started making suggestive comments and before long we were hurrying back to the hotel. I think it was about three o'clock the next morning when we finally slipped off to sleep.

As is true of all long-anticipated events, our week was gone in the blink of an eye and it was soon time for me to leave. Back at Fort De Russy, Linda and I held each other tightly, neither of us wanting to let go. At last she leaned back to look up at my face. "Please don't change any more, Hobie. Something is happening to you that I can't understand and that I'm not part of, and it's making you different somehow." I was shocked, and all I could think of was to swear I was going to make it through the last of my year and come home to her in one piece. "Please wait for me — I'll be back. I promise."

And then it was over. I was on my way back to Vietnam, while Linda stood and waved good-bye. It just may be that leaving her standing there alone was the hardest thing I've ever had to do.

I kept my head down when I got on the bus. I didn't want anybody else to see the mist in my eyes.

Chapter Twenty

I had a lot of time to think about Linda's parting words on the plane ride back to Vietnam. I had no idea what it was that she had sensed or seen in me, but I knew she was right. What was worse, I didn't know what to do about it. Yeah, I was seeing things and doing things I never dreamed I would see or do. And yeah, some of that Vietnam experience was affecting me in ways I didn't understand. I had no clue how to stop the process, any more than I knew how to restore Doc's lost innocence.

But I genuinely wanted to survive, not just physically but emotionally as well. I wanted to go home at the end of my year, get as far away from Army life as I could, and happily grow old together with Linda. I wanted a quietly normal, conventional life like I had grown up watching on television. I wanted to raise kids like Beaver Cleaver and Ricky Nelson. I wanted to put on a suit and tie and go to an office each day, working hard and being rewarded by a climb up the corporate ladder. I wanted to be a good husband and father. All I had to do was figure out how to prevent the war from erasing any more of who I was. I couldn't let Vietnam steal my dreams.

During the long flight, I played back the days and nights of our R&R, reliving them and fixing them in my memory like treasured photographs to carry around with me until I could go home for good. I wouldn't have given up our time together for anything, but I was struck by the cruelty of the R&R experience. It was a GI's momentary reprieve, but when the few days were over he had to go back to the war. Weeks and months in that hellhole were followed by a glimpse of normalcy, and then back to the jungle again. It was yet another unique characteristic of a most uncommon war. There sure weren't any R&R trips for grunts in World War II.

The use of air transports for shuttling troops certainly made the planet a smaller place. I made it back to my battalion trains area in Chu Lai less than 24 hours after leaving Linda standing by the bus in Hawaii. I was pretty tired after the long flight, but went over to the Headquarters Company orderly room and reported back to the sergeant major. I expected to have time for a meal, maybe a snooze if I was lucky, and then a chopper ride out to LZ Professional to rejoin Bravo Company.

But it turned out that Wilkes had other plans for me. The sergeant who ran the NCO club and the enlisted men's club in the battalion compound was about to rotate home, and Wilkes hadn't yet received a replacement NCO with the correct Open Mess MOS. He didn't have a candidate with the right MOS, but he did have a guy with the right rank passing through—me—so he decided I was going to be his temporary club manager until a more fitting replacement arrived.

Well now, who was I to argue with such insightful, practical thinking. I knew absolutely nothing about running clubs, or anything about Army open mess policies and procedures. But I knew it wouldn't involve shooting people or having them shoot at me, and I figured I could learn whatever I needed to know about pouring booze into patrons. I thought I was a reasonably quick study. Why, I even had a dim memory of going to college at some point a very long time before.

Wilkes didn't know if my assignment would be for a week or a month, but the decision had been made and I was going to be his guy, "so don't argue with me." I honestly believe he thought I would balk at the job—a seasoned combat grunt being made into a REMF—when in truth I was elated to be kept out of the jungle, however briefly. Each day spent in the rear was one day less in my tour of duty, one day less to dance with Charlie.

He took me over to the NCO club to meet the current short-timer manager, a lifer mess sergeant E-6. He already had his DEROS orders and would be going home in four days, so he had a serious case of what was called a FIGMO attitude, as in "Fuck it, I've got my orders". But he figured he could teach me everything he knew in four days.

He was right. He didn't know much. He did a brain dump for four days, teaching me what a club manager did, and then hopped his freedom bird back to The World. So began my experience as a manager of an NCO club and an EM club.

Our battalion trains area was one of the lucky units in the Americal located right on the South China Sea, and the NCO club was on the ocean side of the compound. Our area was north of the harbor and the beach, on a hill looking down at the harbor. There was a sheer cliff that rose perhaps 100 feet from a narrow, rocky beach at the water's edge. The NCO club had been built at the top of that cliff, overlooking the ocean. Helicopter gunships patrolling the ocean side of the base camp would periodically pass by the NCO club at just about eye level, and close enough that their rotor racket drowned out conversation in the club when one of them buzzed by.

The other club, the EM club, was about 300 yards away, also on the cliff overlooking the ocean. Between the two buildings was an oceanfront guard tower, which stood on the cliff facing out to sea and was undoubtedly intended to keep us secure from a fearsome amphibious assault by the dreaded Viet Cong sampan armada. The clubs were connected by a land line that had been draped along the cliff, a military approximation of a telephone to provide some communication between the two clubs. The phone in the NCO club was also hooked into the base communication network.

The two buildings were dumps, real ratholes. Panels of plywood and sheets of corrugated metal had been slapped over two by four frames by untalented carpenters, resulting in upright but rickety shacks. The enlisted men's club was just a single room with a bar on one wall, and was big enough to hold 40 GIs if they squeezed in tight. Behind the bar there was some limited space for beer and soda coolers, and shelves of bar snacks. The EM club didn't serve booze, because lower-ranking enlisted men weren't permitted hard liquor.

The NCO club had three rooms. The largest room was the bar area and held enough tables and chairs to accommodate roughly 30 people. It featured a large bar, ice maker and cooler against the back wall, and a worn pool table in a corner. Behind the left end of the bar was a door that opened to a narrow stockroom, where supplies of liquor, beer, sodas, and snacks were kept. The third and smallest room was a continuation of the narrow stockroom, separated from the supplies by a plywood wall. It served as office and sleeping quarters for the club manager, and contained a small desk built on one wall and a narrow shelf with a mattress on the opposite wall.

Hanging over the bar was the obligatory sign that GIs could find in virtually every club in Vietnam—"He Who Wears His Hat In Here Will Buy The Bar A Round Of Cheer". Next to the sign was a large bell that the bartender rang when some fool was tardy in yanking off his steel pot upon entering the club.

Maintenance over the years for both places had been practically non-existent. The buildings weren't quite ready to fall down, but that was the best that could be said about them. The floors were a disgusting green asbestos tile, probably to facilitate mopping up spilled beer and occasional barf. The tables and chairs had assorted dings, scratches, and wobbly legs, and looked like discards from a tacky mobile home park. The bar's surface was well worn, showing the years of hard use and thousands of drinks that had been dragged across it. Windows were patches of rusty screens, and had exterior wooden shutters that could be lowered if the monsoon rain blew in too hard.

Most interesting were the NCO club's walls. Cheap fake wood panels covered two of the walls in the main room and the other two were plain plywood. All four walls were completely decorated, top to bottom, with centerfolds and cut-out pictures from men's magazines. Nothing too risqué, because the Army wouldn't like having us troops being corrupted by dirty pictures. They were mostly from Playboy, and they had been accumulating on the walls for years. Early 1970 was still a time when full frontal nudity was rare, and magazines mostly airbrushed any hint of pubic hair.

Both buildings had electricity for lights and to power the compressors in the beer coolers. The wiring was primitive and shorted out every week or so. Then I'd grab a flashlight and stumble my way into the bowels of the storage area to find and reset the circuit breakers to restore the lights before the guys started groping the Vietnamese waitress.

Each club had a piss tube, its name conveying its intended purpose, prominently sticking out of the ground a few feet outside of the front doors. Common outdoor facilities on bases throughout Vietnam, piss tubes were fifty-gallon drums with both ends cut off and which were half buried in the ground. Like I said earlier, just about every place in Vietnam was somebody's toilet. On reflection, designated tinkle tubes were probably a better idea than having everyone simply whip it out to take a leak anywhere they felt like it.

The NCO club also had running water, after a fashion. The water system consisted of a discarded wing tank from a Phantom, which was mounted on a shaky wood platform adjacent to the club and elevated sufficiently to provide pressure from gravity. Connected to the tank were pipes that led to the primitive ice maker and a faucet behind the bar, in case someone wanted a splash of water in their scotch or bourbon. In addition, a pipe led to a makeshift shower, feeding through a tin can with holes knocked in it behind the small office/sleeping room.

I thought I just might have landed in heaven. My own personal shower.

A water truck came around every few days to keep the wing tank full. Every so often, green scum would start to grow in the tank and I'd have to dump some chemicals into the water to kill off the crud. And I had to periodically climb up on the platform and drive a few more nails in it to prevent a collapse. For all the hassle, running water was an incredible luxury and it was wonderful to shower and get ice any time I wanted.

The two clubs existed for the off-duty entertainment of the rear area permanent party, and for any field troops in transit. Operating them and serving drinks to a crowd of thirsty GIs was obviously more than one person could handle, and I was introduced early on to my "employees". Making up the core of my staff were three young Vietnamese women from Tam Ky, who came to the base every day to clean the clubs and serve drinks. Nguyen Ti Sen, who everyone called Sam, worked at the NCO club. (I think about half the people in Vietnam were named "Nguyen".) Tran Ti Linh, nicknamed Lynn, and another girl I only knew as Carol worked in the EM club.

Each day, the three of them would take a bus from the village to the Chu Lai main gate at 1:00, where I would meet them in a jeep that was furnished by the battalion motor pool for the NCO club manager's use. I drove them back to the clubs, where they spent time cleaning up the mess from the previous day until it was time to open for the evening. Then Sam worked the NCO club with me, sometimes behind the bar with me if it was slow, sometimes doing waitress duty for the tables. Lynn and Carol worked as waitresses at the EM club.

Sam was the oldest and the most mature of the three, and in time we became friends. She had a husband and children in Tam Ky, and the money from her NCO club job was a vital part of her family's existence. The two younger girls were single, and their pay helped them live a life that was comfortable, even affluent, by Vietnamese standards.

At first it was a little awkward for me to interact with the three of them. I had spent months hardening my attitude toward Vietnamese people in general, and developing the disdain that made it easier to kill them. I had to remind myself that there were good gooks.

As I got to know them better, I came to realize that all three girls were interesting human beings with a fascinating culture, and fun to talk with. They spoke very passable English, which probably made it easier for my by-now admittedly prejudiced mind to accept them. Their English was liberally sprinkled with GI jargon and broken French left over from the Indochina days. A single sentence might combine elements of English, Vietnamese, and French. "Beaucoup" was a commonly used word that even worked its way into GI speech. It sounded more like "boocoo" and was often paired with Vietnamese words. "He boocoo dinkidau" was a typical put-down, meaning he's really crazy.

The Vietnamese had a very uncomplicated scale they used to define good and bad. Number ten was the worst, number one was good. It was always "numba one" or "numba ten", never any other number. Nobody talked about a two or an eight or a six, just one and ten.

"He numba ten, he boocoo dinkidau." That was probably the worst thing that Sam ever said about anyone.

We didn't talk much about the war, or how it must have disrupted her life and the lives of her family and friends. She seemed very accepting of her life and circumstances, never appearing to resent the war that continued to split her land, or the politics of north and south about which most ordinary Vietnamese cared little. It often struck me that her que sera sera attitude probably helped her to cope with her current condition and with a very uncertain future. After all, if Nixon ever completed his promise and sent all the Americans home, people like Sam would have nothing between them and the godless communist hordes except the candy-assed ARVN. I guessed that South Vietnamese civilians like Sam who had worked for the Americans would not be viewed all that warmly by Ho Chi Mihn and his boys.

The other two girls were pretty carefree. Lynn was particularly cute and was popular with GIs around the compound, many of whom would have liked to get into her pants. The three of them were "good girls" though, and had no interest in picking up a few extra bucks for a roll in the hay.

One afternoon while Sam was cleaning the NCO club's main room and I was doing some paperwork back in the office, I was startled by a shrill scream from the bar. I dashed through the door, 45 pistol in hand (that probably sounds over-dramatic, but it was a war zone after all), and saw a terrified Sam standing on one of the tables. She was chattering away in Vietnamese, and gesturing wildly toward the floor in the middle of the room.

There, crawling in double-time across the floor was the biggest damn centipede I had ever seen. It was about eight or nine inches long, and had a mottled brown body covered in chitinous plates. Even from halfway across the room I could see the big sharp mandibles growing out of the sides of its head.

Sam was still screaming. "Sarga Jennings, you look out. He bad, he numba 10. He bite, you die." I had absolutely no idea whether she was right about the "you die" part, but I figured she lived in this bug-infested place and probably had some idea of which ones were poisonous. Besides, I had no intention of finding out how mean it was. I put away the gun and grabbed a long piece of iron I used to pry open crates of bar food. I crushed the flat end of it into the scurrying critter, which promptly started writhing like a hooked worm and began snapping at the bar with those inch-long mandibles. It was overmatched, though, and I soon had it tossed over the cliff into the South China Sea. I had never seen Sam so agitated, and never did again. And I fortunately never saw another centipede that big. The thought of finding something like that by accident, say in my bunk or in my boots, gave me the shudders. From that point on I took a few extra precautions, like looking in boots and under tables.

In addition to Sam, Lynn, and Carol, I regularly hired a few GIs from Headquarters Company who wanted to earn some extra cash on the side by working the bar at the EM club. Because lower-ranking enlisted men were supposedly more prone to rowdiness than us vastly more responsible and mature NCOs, I was glad to have one bartender at the EM club who was big enough to intimidate even the most belligerent boozed-up brawler. He was a spec 6 whose regular job was as a cook in the Headquarters Company mess hall. He was a big black guy, well over 300 pounds, and looked like a defensive lineman. He was always smiling, though, a cheerful bouncer. His size alone kept peace in the EM club on more than one night.

There was a standardized routine to running the clubs. Because they were open so late, usually until midnight, the manager was exempted from the bullshit of the morning formation that was mandatory for everyone else in Headquarters Company. That meant I could pretty much wake up when I wanted. It was a cool perk, because most nights I was up until two or three o'clock.

I usually got up in the morning by nine or so, showered and shaved, then walked over to the mess hall for coffee and maybe some breakfast if anything was left. Everyone else had eaten much earlier, and the only other people I met in the mess hall at that hour were NCOs and officers from the orderly room grabbing a coffee break. After breakfast I'd walk back to the NCO club to get my jeep and the paperwork for the previous day's receipts at the two clubs.

The mess hall was a short walk across a very colorless trains area. Like most places in Vietnam where lots of GIs were clustered, the compound was an unattractive place. Depending on whether or not it had been raining, the area was either a dust bowl or a mud pit as almost nothing green was still alive. The buildings were drab, characterless places, constructed simply and with whatever materials had been available. There were a few barracks for the REMFs, a BOQ for lower-ranking officers, and a couple of small one-man hootches for captains and above.

A little beyond the mess hall was the orderly room, the administrative hub for Headquarters Company and a principal communications link for LZ Professional. Next to the orderly room was a supply room, almost always manned by (he practically lived there) the battalion supply sergeant. He was a grumpy sucker who acted like every flipping thing in his charge was actually his own personal and most prized possession. It took perseverance and real creativity to pry anything out of his supply room.

Finally, at the end of the dirt road that served as the company street for the trains area, just before the street passed out into the larger reaches of the division base camp, was the motor pool. It consisted of a fenced area where the jeeps and deuce and a half trucks were parked, an open-walled shed with walk-down pits for mechanical work under the vehicles, and a small office.

On a typical morning, my first stop after picking up the jeep was a short drive down to the motor pool. I had to update the daily forms that were required in order to have the jeep checked out to me, and perform whatever maintenance was decreed by the monarchy of the motor pool. The honchos down there were a lifer staff sergeant and a warrant officer. Deebles, the staff sergeant, was an almost illiterate bald fat guy who had crawled out of a bayou somewhere down in Louisiana. He could never completely make up his mind where I fit on his scale of merit. Even though we both had the same rank, I was a product of the NCO school and consequently ranked fairly low in his assessment of worthiness. He couldn't quite decide whether he wanted to have some yuks and hassle me over the jeep, asserting his motor pool muscle by making me do unnecessary maintenance and paperwork, or if he wanted to be nice to me in potential exchange for some imagined special treatment I might give him at the NCO club. So his mood and attitude each day when I showed up to process the jeep was always a surprise—I never knew if he was going to be a good ol' boy or a prick. It was amusing.

The warrant officer's name was Martinez, and he was a good guy. Ranking somewhere between NCOs and commissioned officers, most warrant officers felt like they didn't belong with either group. In the lax setting of Vietnam, many of them could get away with going either to the officers' clubs or the NCO clubs. More often than not Martinez liked to hang around my NCO club, and I tried to make him feel welcome there. That was probably another reason why Deebles didn't diddle me around too much; he didn't want Martinez pissed at him.

After satisfactorily updating my jeep documents and maybe squirting oil on some fittings, it was off to the Chu Lai Open Mess Central Facility to turn in my paperwork and replenish the stock at the clubs. This daily trip proved to be one of the more interesting aspects of running the clubs.

The Open Mess Facility was the origin of everything that happened or was sold in every club throughout Chu Lai. It was also the central collection office for all accounts receivable.

Drinks, snacks, glassware, and other supplies were ordered from the facility at a fixed price. The food and booze were sold in the clubs, also at a predetermined price for specified quantities (one shot of booze and so many ounces of soda in a mixed drink), and the receipts were turned in to the Central Facility.

Sales volume was a measure of how busy and popular were the various clubs around the division base camp. Although the Army wasn't comparing clubs for purposes of encouraging more consumption of booze and beer, high volume did have a benefit in one respect. There were touring shows that were provided to base camps throughout Vietnam, and the Open Mess system doled out performances based on club volume. Presumably, higher sales volume translated into more GIs available to sit in an audience.

The shows were mostly rock bands, and usually not very good. They were "B" groups that might be playing in a backwater motel lounge if they hadn't been in Vietnam. The bands came from a number of different countries, but the majority of them were South Korean. Occasionally an Aussie group would pass through, and they generally sounded like English rock groups. That made them more popular than all but the very best Korean show bands.

All the groups featured a few musicians, mostly guitars and drums, who played loudly but with otherwise borderline competency. But the groups were savvy enough to appreciate where they were and who their audiences were, so they all brought along a few dancers in wonderfully abbreviated costumes. Even the bands' occasional female singers sported tiny outfits. The smaller the costumes on the babes, the more spirited the audience. And there aren't many audiences more spirited then horny GIs.

My battalion's volume managed to qualify for a show every 2-4 weeks. The guys were wildly enthusiastic when one was scheduled, and the clubs would do a land office business. Rock bands drew too many people to fit into either club, so we held the shows on a crudely built outdoor stage off to one side of the battalion trains area. Even if the band sucked, the guys didn't care much. The crowds came to ogle the prancing chicks.

It didn't take real long for me to figure out that a club manager's popularity around the battalion was greatly influenced by his ability to wheel and deal for more shows.

I usually got over to the Central Facility around 11:00 with the paperwork for my previous night's receipts and any new supply orders I needed to place. Sometimes I had to wait in line with other division club managers, and other times I could get right in. Most days, any new merchandise I wanted was small enough to haul back to the club in my jeep. A case or two of booze, some boxes of snack food, possibly some glasses to replace breakage could all fit in the jeep's back seat. If either club needed beer or soda, which happened about once a week, I'd put in an order for a pallet and the Open Mess workers would bring it out that afternoon in a deuce and a half truck. Since there was no forklift at my end, the delivery would mean a manual unloading of all the cases stacked on a pallet. It was hot, sweaty work, and every case had to be stowed in the dingy storage room.

Beer orders were simple—you didn't get to specify brand. Clubs just got whatever was in the warehouse and closest to the forklift when the operator cranked it up. Considering the primitive storage conditions, it was mildly amazing that the stuff was even drinkable. It was often skunky, but that never seemed to make any difference to the guys who came to the clubs to sit and swill it.

The Central Facility set the prices, and the size and strength of mixed drinks. For beer, soda and bar snacks, the pricing scheme posed no problems because the servings were packaged and standardized (one can of beer, one package of beef jerky, etc.). In clubs that served liquor, like my NCO club, I quickly learned that following the rules produced an unavoidable overage in receipts.

The overage resulted from pricing that intentionally underestimated the number of drinks (in standardized Open Mess glasses) that came from bottles of liquor and cans of mix.

Hard as we might try to serve generous drinks filled to the lip, there was always a little more booze and mix than the standard said we should have. That meant we would inevitably get more cash sales out of a bottle of booze than the price that was dictated to the club for that same bottle. And it meant that the NCO club always had a modest nightly profit margin. Since the Open Mess facility expected to be paid based upon the consumption of merchandise at the prices they set, the extra money couldn't even be turned in without raising questions that didn't have any easy answers. It was religiously presumed that the rules were accurate, so any manager with excess cash must be somehow cheating customers.

I might have been born at night, but not *last* night, so it was soon obvious to me that I couldn't possibly have been the first club manager to notice this profitable dilemma. It was apparent that having an open mess MOS, at least in this theater of operations, was a lucrative profession. I know, I know, there's some open mess specialist reading this getting apoplexy over the insinuation that the system might have been a little crooked. Well, you can choose any description you want, but the fact is that it was impossible to not make some extra cash running a club. Either that, or have a lot of leftover booze and mix.

I was still more idealistic than opportunistic, and decided I didn't have much interest in profiting off the backs of my fellow GIs in a margin-skimming racket. So, during the time I was there, I plowed the unavoidable extra cash back into the clubs. Sometimes it was for improvements, like a couple of tape recorders to play music in the clubs, and sometimes it was leverage to grease the palms of the lifers running the Central Facility to arrange for an extra touring show.

After turning in my paperwork and placing any stock orders, I'd head back to the clubs and put stuff away. Between noon and 1:00 I'd hop in the jeep for a drive over to the base main gate to pick up the three Vietnamese gals. On Thursdays, which were paydays, I'd make a stop at the division finance office to exchange MPC for piastre to pay the girls. MPC was "military payment certificates", kind of Monopoly money that the armed forces used in lieu of greenbacks in Vietnam. And piastre was the currency of the South Vietnam government.

Back at the clubs, Sam went to work cleaning the NCO club while Lynn and Carol walked over to clean the EM club. The clubs opened at 5:00 and closed at midnight (the Army frowned on late-night carousing). After we locked up, I'd drive the girls back to the main gate to catch their late bus to Tam Ky. Then I returned to the NCO club to finish the paperwork for the day's receipts, and then finally hit the sack.

There was always something needing attention. The first night I stayed in the NCO club after my predecessor left, I realized it had a huge rat problem. Not a huge problem, but rather a problem with huge rats. I spotted one skulking in the dark behind the club, and I swear it was big enough to herd sheep.

The morning after that first night, I found they had gnawed their way into some snack cartons for a meal of good bar food. I managed to scare up some rat traps from the supply room (the sarge was a grouch, but there wasn't much he couldn't get), and set out a half dozen in the club's little stock room. As I was nodding off to sleep that night, I heard the rimshot snap of a sprung trap. I idly wondered if the traps were large enough to do the job, or if I would instead be roused out of my rack by a miffed rat banging on the office door and dragging the trap behind him.

The traps did the job. The next morning I had four dead rats, all legitimate trophy weight. I kept up the carnage for two weeks, each day producing a little smaller catch, until a night finally came with no sprung traps. After that, I kept a few traps back there, but no longer had a rat problem. Killing rats was a whole lot easier than killing Viet Cong, and actually seemed to accomplish something.

After a week or so at my new job, I began to feel a little naked without a weapon. There was, after all, a war going on and my M-16 was still sitting in storage out on LZ Professional where I'd left it when the dysentery crew and I flew to the hospital. I went over to the Headquarters Company armory and drew a 45-caliber pistol and a few magazines of ammunition. It wasn't as good as having my M-16, but at least I'd have something to carry around with me, a cold steel security blanket. I felt a little more protected on those dark early morning trips to and from the main gate through the thinly populated areas next to the Chu Lai airbase. The armory didn't have any holsters, so I got used to the heft of the 45 in the cavernous back pocket of my fatigue trousers.

The Army 45-caliber pistol was a really powerful gun, and kicked out a sizeable slug. It was deadly accurate out to a distance of, oh, eight or ten feet. Still, I had become reasonably proficient with a 45 while I was at Fort Polk, even to the point of beating one of the drill instructors in a head to head race to field-strip and reassemble one.

I could shoot one as well as anybody, which of course meant I couldn't hit diddly with any consistency at much more distance than I could throw the gun. But, it was a gun and I had grown used to having one near me.

Once in awhile I'd stand behind the club on the cliff overlooking the South China Sea and watch sharks cruising not far off shore. I could sometimes see three or four fins breaking the surface as they swam around doing whatever shark stuff that sharks do. A couple times, for diversion, I pulled out the 45 and popped off a few rounds in the general direction of the sharks. Considering they were probably a hundred yards away including the elevation, I came pretty close. No more than two rounds hit before the fins disappeared beneath the surface. I doubt I hit anything, but I certainly shook them up.

The only other times I fired that 45 were also at wildlife. The NCO club had the dubious honor of becoming home to some sort of long-tailed wild cat, probably some variety of civet cat. There was a narrow opening between the plywood interior ceiling of the club and the slightly pitched corrugated metal that comprised the exterior roof. At the roof's highest point, there was perhaps a seven-inch clearance between the two surfaces, and it was in this crawl space that my critter chose to set up housekeeping.

At first, my only clue that something had taken up residence was an infrequent noise like a clawed foot ticking across the plywood ceiling. I was a live and let live kind of guy, so I didn't give it much thought.

Things changed. I was rudely yanked awake one morning around 4:00 to the sound of a fierce battle. In my ceiling. Some other critter interloper had decided to visit my squatter cat, and the two of them were yowling and growling and rolling around up there, separated from me by a whole half inch of plywood. I wasn't at all happy to be roused, and banged noisily on the ceiling with a combat boot. The noise stopped instantly; I had probably scared the hell out of them.

The same thing happened the following night, and I began to work up a genuine hostility toward my unwelcome tenant. The night after that passed quietly enough, but when I awoke in the morning I found that the contest of wills had escalated another notch. The little desk on the far wall from the shelf that served as my bed, and on which I had neatly stacked the paperwork I had to turn in that day, was damp with a gamy-smelling yellow liquid that was seeping through the plywood ceiling over the desk. It was cat piss.

Okay, no more peaceful coexistence. I found an engineer unit in Chu Lai, and got a fox trap and some poisoned bait. I figured if the trap didn't catch it, maybe the poisoned meat would do the trick. I set the trap just outside the opening to the crawl space, on the part of the roof where the stock room attached to the main building.

When I climbed up on the roof the day after setting my trap, I found it had been sprung. Whatever had been caught wasn't my cat. It was something smaller, about the size of a mongoose, and was no longer recognizable because my civet cat had evidently come along later and eaten it. On the plus side, the poisoned bait was also gone. Hopefully, I'd given my tenant a terminal tummy ache.

For a week or so, the ceiling hideaway was peaceful and I optimistically assumed the poison had done its thing. Late one night after closing, I was standing out behind the club taking a leak over the cliff into the ocean, when a faint sound made me glance up at the roofline. There, silhouetted against the night sky and no more than four feet from my face, was the goddamn cat! It looked at me, seemingly indifferent, as though it was wondering whether I was worth the effort.

I reached in my back pocket for the 45, and then remembered I'd left it on the desk. I tried to move slowly and calmly back into the open back door to my little room, but I couldn't help thinking how easy it would be for that stupid cat to take one step off the roof, claws first. Onto my face.

Instead (thank you, Jesus), the cat turned away. It acted completely bored, slowly stealing over the top of the roof and out of sight. Now it was war; that sucker had to go.

Later that night while I was doing my paperwork, I heard it come back to the crawl space. Its feet made soft sounds on the thin plywood, and a claw would occasionally click on the wood as it walked. No more mister nice guy. I grabbed the pistol, flipped off the safety, and heard the characteristic "snick, snick" of the slide as I chambered a round.

Standing less than two feet below the low ceiling, pointing the 45 straight up, I listened carefully for some clue that would tell me where the damn thing was standing. I moved slowly around the small room, gun in hand, focused on any sound from my furry opponent. A noise, directly above my face! I moved the pistol toward the sound and pulled the trigger.

Now, remember that my accommodations were on the small side. In fact, the room was about six feet by eight feet, max. Remember also that a 45-caliber pistol is a fairly big gun.

When the gun went off, I thought my ears had imploded. It felt like my eardrums smacked together in the center of my head. The ringing didn't stop for several minutes, and I couldn't hear a thing coming from the ceiling. Dead cat or alive, I wouldn't have known. But, I reckoned that I had, at a minimum, scared the absolute crap out of it and maybe evened the score a bit.

There was a neat quarter inch hole in the plywood ceiling where the bullet passed through. The next morning, I climbed up on the roof and gingerly peeked into the crawl space to see if I could (hopefully) spot a dead cat. No luck. But I did see the effect of the round when it blew through the corrugated metal. A four-inch hole, with splayed fingers of metal bent back from the exit point, was the outcome of my cat execution attempt. I got a hammer and banged the torn fingers back down flat.

In the weeks that followed, I took two more shots at my annoying houseguest. He was one smart sucker. He got so he recognized the "snick, snick" sound of a chambering round, and would instantly freeze in place. It was as though he somehow knew that I needed to hear him moving to get a bead on him.

A few of the PFCs and spec fours I knew from the EM club had been on guard duty in the tower down the cliff from the club on nights I went cat hunting. So there were a few jokes going around the compound about Sergeant Jennings putting holes in the roof of the NCO club again. I got real tired of cat jokes.

I never did get that SOB. We evidently reached an uneasy armistice of sorts. The critter stopped raising hell and stopped peeing on me, and I stopped blowing lead through the ceiling. That freaking cat was one of my more memorable Vietnam experiences.

The worst day I ever had as a club manager was a busy one. It started out average enough, with the usual routine working predictably. I had pallets of beer being delivered to both clubs, which meant a long hot job unloading and storing the cases from the truck.

Most of two hours had elapsed by the time the last of the beer was stowed away in the EM club. I was soaked in sweat, so I went back to the NCO club to hose off and get cleaned up just before opening time. After putting on fresh fatigues, I went back to the EM club to make sure everything was in order and discovered that the GI who I paid to tend bar hadn't yet arrived.

He was a spec 5 named Pete Deveroux, who was proving himself to be something less than reliable. He had skipped out on me once before like that, and I had to scramble at the last minute to find someone to help tend bar. I didn't much like that he was doing it to me again. I had my big cook bartender/bouncer, but it was more effective for him to be out in the club or at the door than stuck behind the bar for the whole evening.

Our battalion trains area was easy enough to cover in a jeep, so I set out to find Deveroux. I stopped by the orderly room and the mess hall to ask if anyone had seen him. Finally, someone said they had seen him with Captain Moore, a staff officer whose job nobody seemed to know much about. The captain had no command and apparently had a lot of free time, so his job must not have been too terribly demanding.

Deveroux liked to hang out with the captain and drink his booze. It was a peculiar relationship, as the Army frowned on officers being pals with enlisted men. For all I knew, Deveroux was somehow connected with the captain's job in some way.

Anyhow, I didn't particularly care. I just wanted the guy to live up to his obligations and do the job I was paying him for. So I pulled up in front of Captain Moore's quarters and knocked on the door. Sure enough, Deveroux was there and was in the bag. Way in the bag. I politely explained to the captain that I had been expecting Deveroux for duty in the EM club, and I was mildly surprised when the captain actually apologized for keeping him from his job. Deveroux, on the other hand, didn't feel like apologizing for anything. He was downright belligerent that I had messed up his little party with the captain, and he started cussing me out.

The captain told him to shut up and cool off, but by then I had turned to walk away. I didn't need a drunk working bar in the EM club, and said so. Then I drove off to find another part-time helper who might be willing to take the shift on short notice. I found an off-duty clerk who wanted a few bucks, and finally got the EM club going.

Later that night, Deveroux showed up at the NCO club, still shit-faced. He started out quietly enough. In fact, he sat by himself at a corner table and didn't say anything to anybody. Sam served him drinks, and he was reasonably civil with her. You might ask why we served him at all. Bars in Vietnam didn't have a legion of lawyers waiting to sue them if a client was "over-served". Plus the clubs were among the very few places that a guy could go and enjoy something that resembled entertainment. So we tended to cut a lot of slack for anyone (even assholes like Deveroux), as long as they remained mannerly.

His good behavior didn't last long. After an hour or so, he started talking loudly to no one in particular. He was grousing about how the Army treated him, complaining about what a rotten NCO club this was, and generally bad-mouthing me and my visit to Captain Moore that afternoon.

At first, I just ignored him. But he got louder and more irritating, even cussing at Sam, and some of the other NCOs in the place were getting annoyed at his mouth. I dropped off a couple drinks at a table near his, and he started getting on me in a really nasty way. I told him to leave, to go back to his quarters and sleep it off. He told me to go fuck myself.

Well, okay, there is a limit. I went back behind the bar and picked up the landline phone. I dialed up the division MP headquarters and told them I was a club manager with a drunk and disorderly customer and required their services. "Sorry, Sarge. The base is on alert because of reported probing at the south fence. Can't send anybody over just now; you'll have to deal with him yourself."

Now what? I didn't get any instruction book when Sergeant Wilkes asked me to run his clubs for awhile, and nobody at the Open Mess facility had ever mentioned what to do about jerks, other than call for the MPs.

I've never been much of what people would call a pugilist. In high school I had been the type to avoid fights. But I suppose that a tour of duty in a war zone might actually start making you think your stones have grown larger. Somewhat amazingly, I started thinking about throwing the bum out.

Fortunately, I was clear-headed enough to take the 45 out of my pocket and tuck it behind the bar. No point in tempting fate—a confrontation with a loud-mouthed drunk was no place for a loaded gun.

So I wandered back over to the table where Deveroux was

noisily offering up opinions on what a shitty place this was, and what a prick I was, and anything else that popped into his aggravating little head. Doc, two tables away and half through his usual fifth of vodka, looked disgusted and about ready to do a clog dance on Deveroux's REMF face. That would definitely not be good. A brawl between two drunks wouldn't win any points with the brass for the club, or for me. Better to try a surprise move, a surgical extraction.

Deveroux looked up at me with bleary eyes and ventured a comment about my heritage and my mother's sex life. If I had any reservations, that probably did them in. Without taking my eyes off his face, I shot both hands out and grabbed his fatigue jacket near his throat. In one motion I jerked him out of his chair and turned him toward the open front door of the club. Three quick steps put me at the door with a shocked Deveroux, and I used the momentum to propel him right on through it.

I had given him enough of a head of steam that he stumbled all the way over to the piss tube. He tripped and sprawled out by the tube, face down in the earth damp from the dribbles and the near misses. A little astonished at how easy it had been, I turned to go back into the club.

Doc yelled a warning. "Hobie, watch your back!'

I sidestepped to my left just as Deveroux launched himself at me. He missed me, but slammed into the wall of the club. Considering how rickety the club was and how numbed by the booze was my former part-time bartender, it wasn't clear who was hurt the most by the collision. But it obviously pissed off Deveroux even more. He bounced off the wall and turned for me.

Without thinking, I gave him a right hook smack in the face as he turned from the wall. It was like ten years had disappeared from my life and I was back on the playground at junior high school trying to keep from getting beat up by the school bully.

This time he went down and stayed down. My hand hurt. Guys were streaming out the door by this time, hollering at me to get on him and finish him off. I stood there, fists clenched, wondering what to do next, and suddenly noticed a figure approaching out of the dark.

It was Captain Moore. I will never know what prompted him to come over to the NCO club. He sure wasn't coming for drinks; technically officers weren't permitted in NCO clubs. Maybe someone had left the club earlier and mentioned to him that his buddy Deveroux was pissing off half the Headquarters Company down at the NCO club.

All I could think of was that the two of them seemed to be pals, and here I stood over a bloody-mouthed Deveroux, looking guilty. Club manager or not, I sure didn't have any rank or influence on a captain. And all the hopped-up idiots egging me on to kick his butt some more sure didn't help improve the picture.

To his credit, and to my tremendous relief, Captain Moore stopped and calmly asked what was happening. "Sir, Specialist Deveroux became drunk and disorderly in the club, and refused my request to leave. I attempted to get MPs to eject him, but the base is on alert and they have no available personnel. I ejected him myself, and he chose to resist."

Deveroux was trying to get his feet under him and was sputtering like he had lots to say. I expected the captain to turn to him and ask if it happened as I said. Instead, surprising me, he ordered Deveroux to put a lid on it and come with him. As he left, the captain said, "You won't be having any more trouble with him, Sergeant. As of now he is forbidden to go to this NCO club."

Three days later, Deveroux was transferred out to LZ Professional, doing some kind of jerk clerk duty in the staff bunker. I never found out what their relationship had been, but it appeared that Deveroux had screwed up a pretty sweet deal with an unusually accommodating officer.

As I stood watching the captain and his unhappy pal walk away, my heart was pounding like crazy and I was surging on the crest of an adrenaline wave. Getting into fistfights, even ones that were arguably justified, was just not a normal kind of thing for me. And the captain's untimely appearance heightened the guilty perception of two battling school kids being caught by the teacher.

I was getting real used to this non-combat duty, and I sure didn't want Sergeant Wilkes getting critical feedback about how I was handling it.

That night after closing up the clubs, I had the uneasy feeling that Deveroux might be drunk enough to come back for revenge. It's not very hard to get even with someone in the middle of a war zone. Stories abounded of fraggings and guys "accidentally" getting shot in a firefight by some other GI who had it in for him. Everyone, including my buddy Deveroux, had a gun of one kind or another. Not a comforting thought.

So I took a couple cans of beer over to the guard tower behind the club (I was definitely not supposed to do that, but who was going to tell?) and asked the guys on duty to watch for anyone sneaking around the club. I was nervous enough that I bunked down in the musty stock room instead of my little office. Sleeping there was uncomfortable, but I thought it was prudent given the antagonism Deveroux likely felt at being so completely humiliated.

As it turned out, he wasn't to be the problem that fittingly ended an already crappy day. Nope, instead it was Charlie, launching a barrage from the rocket pocket in the hills above Chu Lai. I hadn't been sleeping very long when the first rounds came slamming into the base. At first, I was disoriented in the pitch-black storeroom and couldn't figure out where I was. Then I remembered I was sort of hiding from Deveroux, and through the cobwebs began to realize the explosions I was hearing were incoming rockets.

It somehow just didn't seem all that threatening any more. I walked outside, and watched as rounds smacked into the long sloping rise from the harbor that housed most of the units in Chu Lai. A rocket hit near the base headquarters, another close to the fuel dump at the docks, and one even splashed down in the water. Either Charlie was shooting at boats and sharks, or that was really bad aim.

I heard one go off fairly close, maybe two or three hundred

yards away. Then another one, even closer. Still, it wasn't all that scary and I couldn't get myself very worked up about it. I don't know why. Standing out there was kind of dumb, but the rocket attack felt impersonal. Not at all like someone shooting specifically at you, bullets snapping by your ears. This was more detached. Charlie was up in rocket pocket, flinging his ordinance downrange at whatever it might happen to hit. He wasn't really shooting at me, he was just trying to mess with the base camp a little. It didn't feel like my time to die, so I stood there for ten minutes and watched the fireworks show. It was actually kind of neat.

It wasn't long before the unique red streams of iridescent Kool-Aid were marking the foothills out by rocket pocket as Puff the Magic Dragon miniguns strafed through the darkness, creeping towards the launching site. As soon as the miniguns started, the rocket barrage was over. I had seen or heard more than twenty incoming rounds. Convinced that I wasn't destined for harm this night, I went back into the club. I gave up on my uncomfortable corner of the stockroom and collapsed on my shelf bunk in the office. It had been a long day.

The next morning I drove the short distance over to the motor pool to renew the endless paperwork that permitted me to have the jeep. Sergeant Bayou-breath was in the motor pool office, frenetically twitting about, obviously worked up about something.

I asked him what had got his panties in a bunch. He frowned at me and waved me outside. I followed him around the corner toward the fenced-in lot where the pool vehicles were parked, and stopped short. I didn't know whether to laugh or feign sympathy.

There, where the neat rows of jeeps and trucks were normally aligned in carefully arranged order (motor pool sergeants tended to be a bit anal retentive), was a very large crater and at least two jeeps that wouldn't be going anywhere for a long time. One of the previous night's rockets had screamed into the Louisiana Lard-ass' precious motor pool, taking out some rolling stock. I was nice. I tut-tutted in earnest. Too bad, Sarge. Tough break.

Snicker, snicker.

In all, I had club manager duty for seven weeks before Wilkes could locate a proper replacement. During my third week there, Lieutenant Warren got promoted to captain and was brought in from the field to take command of Headquarters Company. That meant he moved back to the trains area and was responsible for all the REMFs. It probably would have been better for his career to get command of a rifle company, but I think he had his fill of combat by then. Headquarters Company was a fairly brief assignment; he only had a month left of his tour when he got promoted.

It was good to see him and get caught up on Bravo Company. I asked him who his replacement was as platoon leader for 2nd platoon. You guessed it—Lieutenant FUBAR, Marshall Courtney.

Turned out that Courtney had gotten his butt in a jam. His platoon in Charlie Company had been on patrol by itself and was ambushed. The dinks were settled into a nicely fortified position, and Lieutenant Numbnuts decided to assault it rather than call in artillery or gunships. Most commanders went out of their way to avoid unnecessarily risking their troops, and the normally available arty and air support was always preferable to sending in your people. Since ground assaults tend to leave you with your ass hanging out, Courtney's entire platoon sat down and refused his order to charge the Cong position.

Stuff like that doesn't mesh real well with the Army's image of itself as a disciplined organization. The brass fussed and dithered, but they didn't know what to do about Courtney's mutiny. It was difficult to court-marshal an entire platoon, and they really couldn't do anything to Courtney since he had given a lawful (if stupid) order. A brain transplant was one possibility that came to mind.

Later on, there were twenty-some different versions from various members of the platoon about what had happened, including one that insisted the little uprising had never even occurred. Considering the situation, it was unthinkable to leave Courtney in charge of the same platoon—in fact he was probably at risk of being shot by his own men—so the bright lights at battalion headquarters took advantage of Lieutenant Warren's promotion to rotate Courtney to another platoon in a different company.

How peachy for Bravo Company and 2nd platoon. I winced at the thought of being an NCO under his command.

Even though technically the NCO club manager was a REMF kind of job, I never really felt like I was becoming part of the cadre of clerks and supply pukes and motor pool grease monkeys. Not that it mattered. If Sergeant Wilkes had offered me any job in the rear for the balance of my tour I would have definitely stayed, happy to be a REMF. It was especially true now that my platoon leader back in the bush was a moron.

I got to know a lot of the Headquarters Company people. Most of the lower ranking enlisted men considered me an okay guy even though I was an NCO, probably because I wasn't in any kind of command position and had no reason to give them any hassle like some of the other rear area NCOs. Plus, I was the guy who brought in those shows with the fine looking babes.

They trusted me, which was flattering. I recall one night when an enterprising young PFC clerk sneaked a girl from Tam Ky into the base in the back of a deuce and a half. That was verboten; Vietnamese were not allowed on base overnight. It was also risky, driving around Tam Ky at night to pick her up. It wasn't likely that a VC or a sympathizer would do anything as overt as shoot him (although that wasn't impossible), but there were more subtle things they did that could leave you in deep doo-doo. Like fragging a gas tank, which was when the VC would drop a live grenade into a vehicle's tank with a rubber band wrapped around the spoon. The gasoline slowly ate through the rubber band, the spoon sprung loose, and the jeep or truck turned into a big roman candle. If someone happened to be driving it at the moment the rubber band finished dissolving, they had an equivalent experience to riding an airplane ejection seat. Except that it was more fatal. Even if nobody was in the vehicle, it was a tad unnerving for everyone who might ever have to drive somewhere. And if one happened to blow, it was impossible to say where the dirty deed might have been done.

Anyhow, the entrepreneur managed to get in and out of Tam Ky with himself, the truck and his little hooker intact. He set her up in a barracks in the battalion trains area, and was charging ten bucks a go for her. Although his nifty pimp business could have gotten him court-marshaled, it didn't bother him that I found out about it. He figured, rightly, that I was out of the Headquarters Company command loop, wasn't a ramrod lifer with a poker up my butt, and had no interest in pushing my rank around. Live and let live.

There was that expression we used about the limited leverage available to the Army to make guys in Vietnam behave if they didn't want to. "So what are they going to do to us, send us to Vietnam?"

I happened to wander by while the temporary whorehouse was in session and saw a group hanging around outside the barracks. One of the guys I knew told me what was going on and asked if I wanted a shot at her. I peeked in, between clients, and saw a skinny young girl on her knees, washing herself in a pan of water, getting ready for the next customer. Her face held a strange mixture of hardness and innocence. She didn't smile, but slowly looked up at me. "Hey GI, you wanna boom-boom?" She said it matter-of-factly, without much interest in what my reply might be. Her eyes had the thousand-yard look, just like war-weary combat troops. There wasn't anything remotely sensual in the situation. Somehow, it all felt crushingly sad to me, and despite weeks without a woman I felt no stirring. The prospect of a quick poke with her seemed so hollow and loveless compared to the passion Linda and I had generated in Hawaii. I thanked the guys for their offer and moved on.

The tape recorders I bought with excess club receipts went in about a month after I started the manager job. They made a nice addition, and the guys liked having music in the bars. Sound equipment was remarkably inexpensive at the PX, so it didn't take much cash to buy them.

The choice of music to play on the recorders wasn't too difficult in the EM club—anything rock and roll. Jimi Hendrix was real popular, and the Beatles. The programming for the NCO club was more of a problem. A lot of NCOs, particularly the lifers, wanted to hear country music—George Jones, Charlie Pride, Johnny Cash. The younger guys, a combination of instant NCOs and spec fives and sixes who had acquired rank through a work specialty, were more interested in rock or in folk groups like Peter, Paul and Mary.

Every night I had to make sure we played some of each. Sam and I would pay attention to the mix of people in the club, and try to match the type of music to the majority in the club at any particular time. We didn't have to guess what they liked; most were quite vocal about their preferences, and my shit-kicking Louisiana lug from the motor pool was the loudest of all. Despite being a dyed-in-the-wool racist, the guru of grease was crazy about Charlie Pride.

There was also a television in the NCO club. Armed Forces Television had one station, active several hours a day with shows from the states. It was usually turned on during club hours. It wasn't watched much. Most patrons preferred listening to loud music.

The one show most guys did want to see was Johnny Carson. It was usually good for a few laughs, always nice considering where we were, and was a familiar slice of home. The night that Tiny Tim married Miss Vicki was a real howler in the NCO club. None of us believed anybody could be as big a wimp as that ukulele-plucking pansy.

Doc was in the club every single night. Sometimes he sat with the other Headquarters Company medics, sometimes by himself. Once in awhile if it was slow, I'd sit with him. He drank vodka and orange juice, and would often personally kill an entire bottle of vodka. He never was able to drown his demons, though, and I had no words that could get him to think about what he was doing to himself. He never caused any trouble, so I didn't have any reason to keep him out or deny him the booze.

It was hard to watch. For all his tough veneer, he wasn't

much more than a kid. He had enlisted right out of high school. I tried talking to him about it once, but all I did was make him mad. I went back to minding my own business.

Doc rotated back to the states while I was there, about a week before Captain Warren went home. He never said so long, or even mentioned that his orders had come through. One day he was there, the next he wasn't. It was like he had disconnected from everything and everybody. Nothing mattered to him any more. He had crawled back inside himself to a place only he and the booze could reach, and was indifferent to anything that went on around him. I never heard from him again.

On the Monday morning at the beginning of my seventh week in the rear, Sergeant Wilkes strolled into the club to tell me that he had an NCO with an open mess MOS arriving that afternoon. He asked me to show the new guy the ropes, and then rejoin Bravo Company at the end of the week. I had about three and a half months left in my year and, although I sure wasn't thrilled at the prospect of going back to the jungle, I figured I could get through the time. I had to admit I was pretty lucky getting seven weeks of unexpected time in the rear. Including my R&R and hospital time, I had been out of the field for the best part of eleven weeks. Hard for me to feel sorry for myself. I could have been slogging through the boonies all that time.

Wilkes himself was real short, and had orders to go home the following week. For him, going home also meant retirement after 30 years in the Army. He had one last trip to make, out to LZ Professional at the end of the week for some administrative stuff.

The new club manager turned out to be a thoroughly unpleasant lifer mess sergeant, another fat guy with a well-nourished beer belly and huge, Dumbo ears. (I am personally convinced that there was some kind of secret incentive to encourage mess sergeants, motor pool sergeants, and supply sergeants to be plump. Almost all of them were butterballs.) The incoming guy knew all there was to know about running an NCO club, and damned sure didn't need any input from some two-week wonder instant NCO like me. I think he was really shocked to find out I had been running the club for awhile, like it was somehow not permissible for a shake and bake to be part of the lofty inner circle of the open mess brotherhood.

The funny thing was that the guys down at the Open Mess Central Facility had actually grown to accept me, despite having been a bit aloof when I first started managing the clubs. I had made it a point to be very respectful and frequently asked their advice about club operations, and I think they saw me as a hard worker. I had even succeeded at increasing club revenues, the true measure of accomplishment for a club manager.

I introduced Sergeant Fat Guy to the Vietnamese gals and to the part time staff who tended bar at the EM club. I could tell that Sam took an instant dislike to my replacement, but she had seen them come and go for years. It was only a couple days before one of the GI bartenders decided he didn't need to work for extra spending money any more. GIs, even in the rear, were picky about working for someone they disliked if they didn't have to. Interestingly, my new guy hit it right off with Deebles, the bayou birdbrain down at the motor pool. They were two fat-assed good ol' boys who had been popped out of the same mold. The new club manager wasn't likely to get much chickenshit hassling over the jeep.

The last night I spent in Chu Lai was a show night. I had booked a group through the Central Facility the prior week, and it would be a good chance to let the new guy get a feel for running it. So for the first time, I got to sit out front in the audience and enjoy the show. Normally, I had to station myself outside the little closet behind the stage where the dancers changed costumes. Otherwise, legions of horny GIs would have surrounded the place in hopes of a peek inside at the undressed cuties.

The show featured a Korean group, and they weren't as bad as many of the touring groups I had seen. The band played the usual compliment of current rock hits from the states. While they played and sang, four nicely built dancers pranced around in bras and G-strings. I recognized a few Turtles songs that had been big in The World the year before, and the band did *Crystal Blue Persuasion*, which had been a favorite of Linda's and mine when we got married.

Their final number was a song that had taken on the status of an anthem for grunts doing tours of duty in Vietnam in those days. The entire audience, which by then was mostly hammered on EM club beer, roared its approval and sang along.

Well it's one, two, three what are we fighting for?
Don't ask me, I don't give a damn,
Next stop is Vietnam.
And it's five, six, seven open up the pearly gates.
Well, there ain't no time to wonder why,
Whoopee! We're all going to die.
Country Joe and The Fish

Chapter Twenty-One

The chopper ride out to LZ Professional was shorter than I remembered it being. I hadn't ever been eager to take the ride, but this time felt worse than any of the previous trips. I guess sometimes the devil you know really is worse than the one you imagined. Please Mr. Custer, I really, REALLY don't want to go.

By coincidence, I rode on the same slick with Sergeant Wilkes, who was making his last trip to the hill as acting battalion sergeant major. For a quiet, normally unemotional guy, he was really getting excited about going home. I envied him, and longed for my own still distant homecoming, but I was glad for him, too.

The loud rotor noise and rushing wind discouraged conversation, and I found myself daydreaming. I imagined family and friends, and Linda welcoming me home, alive and well—at least physically anyhow. I wasn't so sure about all the mental aspects. Despite the more normal few weeks in the rear, I still felt like I was screwed up in a lot of ways, sliding down some greasy slope into a nightmare and unable to stop. I kept reassuring myself that going home would end those disturbing feelings. And I thought about being done with the Army, discharged, military obligation completed and behind me. No more bullshit, no more meaningless drills and mindless orders, or people telling you what to do, how to act, what to wear, what to think. No more bullets and bombs, no more gooks, no more killing. Back to civilian life, with most of my future ahead of me, still mine to plan and live and enjoy.

I was absolutely certain that homecoming would be the

most memorable day of my life. Out of Vietnam, out of the Army, and back to my wife. All at the same time. It didn't get any better than that.

My reverie ended as the Huey sat down near the dump on LZ Professional. I was back to the assault on the senses that was a battalion firebase. In a relatively short time away, I had put out of my mind how ugly and depressing a place it was, and had become spoiled by my comparatively cushy club manager life. Time for a return to reality. I parted company with Sergeant Wilkes, and wished him well on his retirement and homecoming in case we didn't see each other again before I left to rejoin my rifle company.

I went to reclaim my gear from a musty storage area near the Operations Bunker. Fortunately, most of my stuff was still there and intact. My rucksack was so completely intact that it stunk to high heaven from being closed up and unused for so long. The last morning before I'd left on the medevac, I had rolled up my dirty, wet poncho liner and stuffed it into the rucksack on top of some C-rations, dirty socks, a sweat-crusted fatigue jacket, old letters from home and a couple extra bandoleers of M-16 magazines. The pack hadn't been opened again since I left. It had been sitting in the hot, dark bunker, cooking like a crock pot, getting astonishingly ripe and truly fragrant. Despite my clean fresh uniform from Chu Lai, when I put that rucksack on I was instantly a jungle grunt again, a REMF no more.

My M-16 was okay, but in dire need of cleaning and oiling. Most of the ammo I discarded in favor of new issue. No point in tempting fate by carrying bullets that had spent weeks in the slow cooker.

I ducked into Operations to let them know I was back and ready to be sent out to my unit. Bravo Company was out on patrol, and the chopper that had brought Wilkes and me from Chu Lai would be taking a resupply flight out to them later in the day. I would be aboard. So I spent the next few hours reloading magazines with fresh ammunition, cleaning up my rifle, and scrounging for grenades and C-rations. It felt a little peculiar to be holding an M-16 again after so long. I hung my poncho liner from the top of a bunker to air out a little, but it was hopeless.

Bravo Company had been working the AO southwest of LZ Professional for the previous week. It had been charged with a somewhat unusual mission, over and above the usual hunt for Chuckie. The captain was evaluating potential new sites for the battalion firebase. Apparently, brigade brass had decided that the Burlington Trail was no longer used much as a supply route from North Vietnam, and it was felt that our battalion could be put to more effective use elsewhere in the Americal AO.

It was no small matter to move a firebase. In addition to the complex logistics and countless details of a physical move, and those were daunting, there were critical issues about the location and topography of a new site. Although American firebases were formidable challenges for an enemy foolish or frenzied enough to attack one, ground assaults still did happen from time to time. The better fortified a firebase made itself, the less likely it might be overrun. And taking advantage of terrain features when deploying a firebase was an important consideration in how well fortified it could be made.

So the business of fortification actually began with site selection. Elevation was good; you always opted for the highest hill around. High ground has been an element of military advantage since people started fighting one another. It also helped if the area around the firebase was reasonably open. Triple canopy jungle was a real inconvenience when defending against an assault, since you couldn't see shit more than a few feet away. The idea was to have enough clear area surrounding the base so that you could spot the bad guys when they were still too far away to hurt you, and then drop all sorts of nifty fireworks on their heads. Places that had all the ingredients for a suitable firebase were not all that abundant in the battalion AO. LZ Professional was a rathole, but it was a reasonably secure rathole.

So I was mildly surprised that afternoon when I rejoined

the company and learned about the search for a new home. The resupply flight was routine, and in the wrenchingly short span of seven hours I had gone from a clean bed and a shower in Chu Lai back to the muck and the leeches of grunt heaven. There were no gradual transitions in this war.

Lieutenant Courtney, looking a little more like a seasoned leg soldier than the last time I had seen him, welcomed me back to 2nd platoon and filled me in on our firebase search activities. Living in the jungle could make even a dweeb like Courtney look like a fighting man; time would tell whether he had actually become one.

I wasn't terribly surprised to learn that no new E-7 had arrived to assume platoon sergeant responsibilities. That meant, as an E-6, I was still ranking NCO in the platoon and consequently the default platoon sergeant. Chief had been stuck with it during my absence. That's how screwy it got—I had the rank of a squad leader and was acting as platoon sergeant. Chief had the rank of a fire team leader and was filling in for *me*. It seemed the only people who could do the job their rank called for were privates. Somebody had to be at the bottom of the pecking order.

Chief caught me up on events while I had been gone. Four more soldiers in 2nd platoon had reached their DEROS dates and gone home, and we'd received three fresh-faced FNGs to replace them. Dee was one of the four sent home, leaving us temporarily without a squad leader for his old squad.

Contact with Charlie had been intermittent—nothing new there—and there had been just four casualties in the time I was gone. Two of them were fairly minor wounds, superficial hits from shrapnel in a close call with a booby trap. The other two were Gibson and Sheppard, two guys in Dee's squad, who had both been killed by an RPG in an ambush. They had been first and second in the column and never had a chance. I had known them both pretty well and the news left me shaking my head, wondering if it would ever stop.

The war hadn't really wound down a whole lot while I was gone. Nixon was getting popularity points from the media for "getting our boys out of Vietnam", but the people I knew were still dying.

Bravo Company's search for a new firebase was fairly simple. Lieutenant Courtney told me the captain had been ordered to examine a number of possible sites, locations that looked good on topo maps, or places that had been reconnoitered from the air. There were a half dozen spots he needed to check out and the rest of us were sort of along for the walk while he did his survey, possibly doing some searching and destroying as we went.

Hey, it was better than another trip to Dragon Valley.

That first night back in the jungle was more of an adjustment than I had expected. Back at the NCO club, I had gotten used to sleeping through the entire night without having to stand a watch. I hadn't worried about putting claymore mines around my perimeter, or had to keep my boots on, or kept an M-16 close along my leg in my poncho liner. There were no leeches crawling on me back there. Darkness didn't bring an end to useful activity. I'd had electricity and could read, visit with people, or watch TV when I wasn't working.

Most important, the only people trying to kill me back in Chu Lai were the gooks in rocket pocket, and I had concluded that their aim was pretty bad.

Being jerked awake in the middle of the night to stand watch was a huge treat. First there's a moment of disorientation and the feel of your body protesting its denial of sleep, followed by several minutes of trying to get your eyes to work in the darkness. All the while you're wiping the clammy night dampness and the odd leech off yourself. Grope around in the dark for your gun and the claymore trigger, and steel yourself for two hours or so of fighting to stay awake while listening to the sounds of the jungle night and of sleeping men all around you.

I decided I'd rather be snoozing in the stockroom hoping Deveroux wasn't drunkenly sneaking around with a gun than out in the jungle night laager. I tried not to feel sorry for myself. I'd had relatively good duty for several weeks while the guys sleeping near me had been out here humping the boonies the whole time I had been enjoying the rear. Time was passing and I was getting close to three quarters done with my year. Just keep crossing the days off, one by one, and keep on living.

That same night, while I was feeling a tad depressed about going back to work as a grunt, Sergeant Wilkes died.

I didn't even hear about it until Bravo Company went back up on the hill ten days later. As the acting sergeant major, Sergeant Wilkes had been responsible for most of the minor disciplinary problems in the battalion. He was involved in a number of Article 15 actions, small-time penalties for soldiers who had committed petty infractions. Although I had always found Wilkes to be a fair and evenhanded guy, it's probable that some people in the battalion didn't care much for him.

Maybe because of the NCO school program, there seemed to be a line drawn between the ranks of E-6 and E-7. A sergeant first class E-7 like Wilkes could only attain that rank through many years in the Army, while instant NCOs like me were definitely not lifer types. So a lot of enlisted men had a general perception of E-7s and above as part of the Army establishment, therefore to be disliked and distrusted. Sergeants and staff sergeants like me were often just draftees who had a little extra school, and were more likely to be one of the guys.

Whatever the reason might have been, some dopehead, his brain clouded by too many Chu Lai 101s, had decided to frag Wilkes. The sergeant major had to spend an extra night on Professional because he couldn't get a chopper out after finishing his business. There was a small bunker near the Operations staff that was reserved for overnight guests who had some rank. Since he was sergeant major, Wilkes got the bunker.

The dopehead was a spec 4 who Wilkes had busted to private E-2 a few weeks before. He came creeping around, and rolled a hand grenade into the bunker while Wilkes slept. Top never had a chance, and probably didn't even know what happened. Of course, hand grenades make a rather noticeable racket, and the fragger was the only person around when people came running after the explosion. He had been hauled off to the stockade in Chu Lai to stand trial for murder, and would likely spend a good part of his life in Leavenworth. Small consolation that the perpetrator got caught; most fraggings were never solved.

And the fact that they got the asshole didn't help a dead Wilkes one bit. He wasn't even 50 yet, and he'd had big plans for his retirement. Instead of happily welcoming her husband back from his last duty assignment, his widow would get the flag off his coffin and a survivor's pension. No small hobby ranch for the two of them as he had planned. No cruising the country together in a motor home, no holidays with all the grandkids, no summer afternoons watching baseball and drinking beer, no vacation to a Caribbean island for two aging lovebirds celebrating their golden years. God, how I hated what this war was doing to good people.

Bravo Company spent just six days on the hill and then was sent back to the southwest again to keep looking for a new firebase location. Much of the routine of being in the jungle came back to me quickly, but it felt a little different from when I had previously been with 2nd platoon. Certainly the jungle was the same, and I hadn't lost any skill with the equipment we carried. Part of the difference came from the constantly changing face of the platoon, the new guys who kept arriving and the familiar ones who were gone, either sent home in a brand new uniform or in a body bag. I missed having squad leaders whose abilities I knew and trusted. Dee was gone and Buzz Gallagher, too, his broken leg having proved to be a ticket home. Chief was the only squad leader holdover from the first part of my tour, and he was getting short. So the lieutenant and I just had to make do with what we had.

Two weeks after I rejoined the platoon we got a brand new sergeant E-5, fresh from NCOCS training, and made him squad leader in Dee's old squad. His name was Bill O'Hara, a redheaded Irish guy from just outside Chicago. It wasn't long before people were calling him "Rusty", and it stuck.

Rusty was a gentle soul. He was smart, and it was the kind of intelligence that enabled him to readily acknowledge how little he knew about this war stuff. His self-effacing attitude helped him get accepted by the skeptical grunts in his new squad, one of whom had been temporarily handling the job and all of whom were wary of having another FNG in charge. Rusty went to them admitting he needed their help to learn the ropes, and promising to live up to their expectations. I liked him right off the bat, and went out of my way to guide him along.

We talked, and learned about each other. Rusty had gone to Northwestern, and was engaged to a girl he had met there. He had studied to become an insurance actuary and hoped to go to work for State Farm or Allstate, both headquartered there in his home state. The Army had put his plans on hold for a while, as he was drafted right after college.

Rusty was a self-described pacifist who hated being in Vietnam even more than most of us. By the time he was drafted, the whimsical and unpredictable draft board decisions on who got picked and who didn't had been replaced by the national lottery. Each year, a list was published of the birth dates that would be subject to the draft in the following year. The list was ranked according to the likelihood of being called up. The system was intended to be fairer than the unaccountable decisions made by individuals on local draft boards, and allowed each year's crop of potential raw meat a chance to see whether they would be tapped on the shoulder to help out their Uncle Sam. Rusty's birth date was number twenty on the list, a certainty for the draft.

Much the same as me, Rusty had seen NCO school as a delaying tactic to postpone an overseas assignment to Vietnam. By the time he was going through infantry AIT, the daily news had as much coverage about winding down the war as reports on actual fighting and body counts. He hoped it would all be over by the time his NCO training was done, and possibly avoid getting sent. I thought ruefully about how I made the same judgment, about a year before Rusty did. That's how long the politicians had been talking and arguing about ending it. To us grunts in the jungle, the concept of a stretched out disengagement was black humor. Nothing really ever changed—we were still out there doing the mambo with Chuck.

So I was empathetic to the feelings of anxiety and inadequacy I knew Rusty was having, and tried to reassure him that most of us were more interested in surviving the war rather than "prosecuting the war", as the brass loved to say. "You'll be okay. Just stay cool and keep your eyes open. Your guys know what to do—watch them."

As the days went by and the firebase search progressed, it was becoming evident that one of the first sites we had visited after my return from REMF-ville was somebody's preferred site. The company had climbed up on at least eight possible places over the course of the search, and we kept coming back to one in particular. I'd heard conversations that suggested the battalion commander was partial to it, a hill in a shallow valley about four miles from Professional.

That was unfortunate. The hill itself was adequate enough. It had roughly the same elevation as Professional, and it sat almost in the middle of the valley and had relatively open ground on three sides. It was kind of an anomaly; one lone hill tucked into what otherwise was a valley.

Which was precisely the problem. There were other hills around the prospective firebase—two lines of hills that made up the sides of the valley. A few of those hills in the valley ridgeline were higher than the proposed firebase, meaning the new site would be unnecessarily susceptible to mortar and rocket fire from those hills. And the one side that didn't have open ground was choked with thick brush almost to the base of the hill.

Our captain tried to convey his concerns to battalion, but he wasn't having much success. The Lieutenant Colonel who was battalion CO, a guy whose combat experience had largely consisted of issuing orders from his operations bunker or flying over battle areas in his LOH, was insistent. He had seen the firebase site from the air and for some reason liked the idea of that one lonely hill in the middle of a valley. It somehow seemed more secure to him than the alternatives the captain tried to pitch.

So began the laborious process of moving from one LZ to another. First came the engineers, to survey and blade the hilltop for bunkers and the permanent structures a battalion would need. Then came the building supplies — sandbags, two by fours, corrugated metal, empty ammo boxes (you could fill them with dirt and build more stable walls than with sandbags) — and the day-by-day grind of building a new base. Labor wouldn't be a problem. Grunts worked cheap and were good at digging ditches.

In all, it took a month to construct the new LZ Professional. Because the 1st of the 46th had adopted the battalion name "The Professionals", our leaders didn't want to name the new firebase anything different. So for a time, we had two separate LZ Professionals.

During the building, we were spread pretty thin around our area of operations. Because the new site was more vulnerable while under construction, there was always a rifle company on or around the hill. The old firebase still needed a company to ensure its defense, particularly since all the artillery and mortars were still located there. That left only two companies out in the bush at any time, and it was difficult to cover the entire AO with just two companies.

Fate was kind to us while the construction was going on. Although there were numerous little skirmishes with VC here and there — an occasional ambushed column, a tripped booby trap, a cache happened upon — it was generally calm. No new NVA sightings had been reported, and best of all the brigade planners had enough sense to leave our battalion alone while we were building the base. The one major operation they initiated was happily assigned to some other lucky battalion.

As you might imagine, there was a constant grumbling debate among the lower ranking GIs about which duty was worse, roaming through the jungle or digging bunkers and filling sandbags on the new LZ. Even the occasional week on old Professional wasn't as much of a respite as it had once been. There were endless work details like cataloguing and packing equipment in preparation for the final move.

Bravo Company spent one week on the firebase while it was being built. Each platoon was given a list of construction tasks to complete, and the whole effort was being coordinated by a unit of engineers from Chu Lai under the command of a captain. They were good, and their design made the most out of what was, after all, only a hill in the jungle.

The top of the hill had been flattened and rearranged by a bulldozer flown in early on hanging from a Chinook. Most of the natural vegetation was long gone, and the hill was beginning to take on the familiar muddy look of a real firebase. Bunkers were slowly forming on the perimeter, spaced carefully for maximally effective interlocking fields of defensive fire. The highest point on the hill, the part that had been bulldozed, was being prepared for artillery batteries. You wanted artillery at the top, so the guns could execute fire missions in any direction.

A command bunker and operations bunker were under construction. Unlike the defensive positions which were dug into the ground and then fortified with sandbags and beams, the command and operations facilities started out as above-ground buildings that were later encapsulated in layers of sandbags, ammo boxes full of dirt, and corrugated metal. Both the above and below ground bunkers looked like they could take some heavy punishment and still protect their occupants.

Recalling the rat-infested and often fragrant trash dump on the original LZ, battalion brass made the wise choice to locate the new dump almost at the base of the hill. A little further to take out the trash, but it would be a whole lot more livable on the hilltop without the aroma of a dump so near at hand.

While we were on the construction site, the squad leaders and I typically spent our days supervising work details. Lieutenant Courtney wandered around, supervising the supervisors and overseeing the big picture. It was typical Army. In the service, there was always so much manpower available for a project that the Army rarely made an effort to do work of this sort with anything like the organization and efficiency of a civilian construction business. Nonetheless, the place was slowly becoming a firebase. I noted with some relief that emplacements had been developed to a point where we could defend it if we had to.

Rusty O'Hara was really trying hard to fit in. He was so earnest and so openly decent and likeable that many of the guys were warming up to him and stopped treating him with the indifference accorded to most FNGs. He had a natural leadership ability, and earned his squad's respect by getting down in the mud and working just as hard as his men. Maybe harder. I liked having him in the platoon, and was impressed by his adaptability.

After weeks of rotating construction teams on the hill, it was at last moving day. For most of the battalion, the move was a non-event. Two companies were out in the jungle searching and destroying, and weren't affected. The company on old Professional was responsible to load into a constant stream of helicopters all the stuff that was going to a new home. Once the old place was cleaned out, the company doing the loading simply walked down into the jungle and headed out on patrol until their cycle came around to show up at the new firebase.

The company on the new firebase probably had the toughest duty, and it turned out to be us. Everything that arrived on new Professional had to be taken somewhere and stowed. Supplies, ammunition, all the mess gear and food, the operations bunker radios and equipment, the artillery pieces, and a bunch of other stuff I hadn't even realized had been on the old LZ started arriving by helicopter.

When the moving day arrived, the sky was dark with choppers. The air was filled with the scream of the turbines and whopping noise of big rotors. As the day went on, it wasn't unusual to see a Chinook dangling a 105 artillery piece over the top of the hill, another with a water blivet on its hook, Hueys setting down on the landing pad near the new dump, a slick hovering near the operations bunker, and two more birds coming down the valley. In addition to all the stuff pouring in from the old LZ, a lot of supplies were being flown in from Chu Lai to equip a newly established firebase.

It was a scramble to keep up, and details of sweaty GIs were hustling up and down the hill with loads of equipment. The decrepit old truck had been flown over from the former Professional on one of the first flights, and it was grunting up the slope from the pad laden with boxes of ammunition and howitzer rounds. I think if Charlie had been in the area, he could have walked right on the base and not even been noticed. We were too busy to be diverted by anything as trivial as security. On the other hand, the extent of chaotic activity probably would have discouraged any VC watching the show.

The busy pace went on all day, but by late afternoon we actually had a working and reasonably well-stocked firebase. The gun bunnies had been surprisingly quick in setting up their batteries, and had already boomed out a fire mission to help Delta Company knock down some sniper fire they were getting somewhere off to the west of the LZ. I didn't particularly like the ear-numbing racket of the big guns any more than I had at the old base, but it was reassuring that they were up and working again.

Night began settling into the valley and shadows grew long on our tenuous new hilltop sanctuary. It didn't really feel all that much like a new facility, not like the clean unworn feel of a new house. No, this place already felt like any other raggedy-assed firebase. It had the mud and the dirt, the smoke already coming off the burning shit drums from the latrine, the miles of coiled razor-edged concertina wire strung in waves around the girth of the hill. Dozens of claymores nestled in the concertina, each with its wire snaking back to a bunker. All of the claymores had a daub of yellow paint smeared on the back to provide a visual assurance that sappers hadn't crawled in to turn them around toward our own positions.

All the comforts of home.

Chapter Twenty-Two

Spec 4 Roger Lynch died on a Sunday. He was the first one to get hit, but he wound up at the head of a body bag parade. I remember it was a Sunday because a chaplain had flown out to Bravo Company's overnight position on a resupply chopper to provide a non-denominational service for us while were still set up in our laager. It was an upbeat occasion, because the flight also brought a hot meal and a couple of FNGs for 1st platoon. Although it wasn't unusual to see a chaplain on a firebase, it was a little out of the ordinary for one to visit a company out in the boondocks. Even chaplains aren't bulletproof, and many of them probably preferred a little less hazardous duty. But we had a pretty secure position and there hadn't been any contact for a while, so he might have felt reasonably safe coming to see us.

It was a nice little service, complete with a few hymns sung off-key and a short inspirational sermon intended to reinforce how important our efforts were to preserving a life of freedom for the South Vietnamese. He wanted us to know that God was on our side. That was comforting.

Most guys, except for a few watching the perimeter, attended the service whether they viewed themselves as religious or not. In war, you play all the angles you could to improve your odds of surviving. Since God was on our side, we all wanted Him to know we were paying attention.

The Huey came back for the mess gear after the service and the meal, and our Sunday sky pilot scampered aboard to hitch a ride back to Professional. No dummy was this man of God; he had no particular interest in hanging around out in the bush with the rest of us fools.

Our captain, bless his little OD heart, wasn't in any hurry to move out, so we all sort of lulled around for a couple hours, enjoying a fairly protected location and a full stomach. Some guys cleaned weapons, some wrote home, some tried to catch up on sleep, a few played cards.

I sat on the ground, leaning back on my rucksack, and tried to write a letter to Linda. There had been one from her on the chaplain chopper and I wanted to get a start on answering it before we headed back out. You always wanted to have a letter ready to go, because helicopter visits were unpredictable. I hadn't heard from her in several days, and I was searching for diplomatic words to tell her I didn't think she was writing as much as she used to. I lived for her letters, and I tried to convey how important that regular connection was to me.

I began by writing about how the two of us were on the downside of my year away, and that it wouldn't be too many more months before my tour was over. I wrote about the little Sunday service we'd had, and the hot meal. I told her how much I missed her, and that I thought about her a hundred times a day.

I hadn't figured out how to mention the declining frequency of her letters by the time the CO decided it was time to get moving. So I folded up the half-written letter in a piece of plastic sleeve and tucked it in the thigh pocket of my fatigues to work on later. I packed up my gear and was just shouldering my rucksack when Lieutenant Courtney walked by to tell me the company was splitting into platoons. Second platoon was heading north.

Chief's squad had the lead. Roger Lynch, a spec 4 in Chief's squad who had about eight months in country, was walking point. He was dead, but just didn't know it yet.

Less than a klick from our night laager, the terrain opened up some. The jungle thinned into long stretches of marsh grass and elephant grass punctuated by frequent clusters of trees every fifty or hundred meters. Within the clusters of trees it was still thick, but mostly free of the choking vines and impenetrable bamboo that slowed our pace in so many other places in the AO. The periodic stands of trees gave us cover to move, but they also provided lots of places from which to observe our column when we left one cluster for the next.

Since we had broken the company night position so late, we were already well into the heat of the day. It was stifling. The sun pounded on us with a physical weight and no breeze stirred the elephant grass we walked through. Canteens moved back and forth from web gear to thirsty mouths and the sweat ran in rivers.

I was in my usual spot at the rear of the column. I had just taken a drink of warm water and was chewing on a salt tablet when the last of us in the platoon came out of a thicket into the open. I could see ahead where the middle of the column was winding into the next cover of trees, and further ahead where the point element was coming out of that same small cluster. The column was changing direction, swinging the line of march to the right. I was looking right at Lynch, distantly leading the file, when he pitched forward on his face.

That sight was followed an instant later by the unmistakable crack of a rifle, a sound like someone smacking two boards together.

That was it. Nothing else happened, no other noises broke the quiet. The men close behind Lynch, including Lieutenant Courtney, looked at him in disbelief and belatedly dropped for cover in the tall grass. Still in the tree line from which the point squad had just exited, the middle of the column was spreading out to return fire. If only they had something to shoot at.

I scanned the thickets of cover to the front and around the point of our column, and saw nothing. No movement, no glints of sun on metal, no puffs of smoke, nothing to give away the location of Lynch's executioner. And he was definitely dead. There had been no instinctive arm movement to break his fall. I watched as the platoon's new medic, a Florida kid named Bobby Carter, duck-walked up to the front. He took one look at Lynch, then turned around and scuttled back to the safety of the trees.

The soldiers directly in front of me who had been in the

open between the two groups of trees had taken cover, some
moving forward and some coming back to the thicket I was in.
As the last guy reached the trees near me, a branch splintered
just above his head. Everyone ducked, and we heard the two
boards smacking together once again.

Whoever was sniping at us was far enough away that the
bullets were arriving before the sound. And we still had no idea
where he or they were located.

A few minutes went by. Emboldened by the lack of
shooting, I stuck my head up high enough to see over the grass
to the next stand of trees where the rest of the platoon was
pinned. I still couldn't see any sign of the bad guys. Someone
in Chief's squad was peering out of the other tree line, like
me looking for the source of the sniping. He turned to say
something to the man next to him, and abruptly dropped to the
ground. I heard the delayed report and understood why he had
fallen. I couldn't tell at that distance who the GI was or how bad
he was hit, but he had definitely been shot.

John, my RTO, and I heard Lieutenant Courtney radio for
a gunship to help us find the bad guys. That was fine with the
eight of us in the rear stand of trees. We didn't much care to be
walking around in the open with a sniper popping off rounds.
Let the rotor rangers find them. I said a silent thank-you that
our good lieutenant had learned it's better to ask for help than
to needlessly feed ground troops into Charlie's shredder.

It took twenty minutes for a Huey gunship to arrive, trailed
by a medevac. In the intervening time, Chief and his squad
had cautiously retrieved Lynch's body from the open grass and
moved it to the far side of the trees, furthest from where he
had been hit. I overheard on the radio that the other man hit
was a relative newcomer named Stedman. I had barely gotten to
know him, he was so new. His wound wasn't life-threatening.

There had been no additional incoming fire, which left
all of us wondering whether Charlie had hightailed. The other
option was that he was still out there, maybe hoping for a shot
at a helicopter.

The medevac stood off while the gunship gingerly edged

out in front of the lead part of 2nd platoon. The lieutenant was doing everything right; he remembered to mark his position with smoke so the chopper wouldn't mistakenly open up on his bunch of guys. And, yes, you can bet your butt I had also popped smoke in the cluster of woods where my little band was laying low.

For fifteen minutes or so the gunship traced a box pattern over the various clumps of trees and high grass where the ambushers might have been hiding. The Huey didn't draw any fire and evidently saw no signs of bad guys, even with the advantage of its altitude. Twice the ship hovered over questionable spots, blasting grass and tree limbs with its rotor wash, getting a better look at the ground.

While the gunship was searching, the medevac ducked in quickly to fetch our casualties. The pilot of the unarmed dust-off was taking a risk, but he probably assumed any bad guys still around wouldn't expose themselves to a gunship by shooting at the more distant medevac.

Not long after the dust-off faded in the distance, I heard the gunship tell Lieutenant Courtney that it couldn't stay on station any longer because of low fuel. It made one last pass, opening up with its guns on several suspicious areas out in front of the lead squad. A little recon by fire before departing.

And then we were on our own again, still faced with uncertainty about what might be waiting for us. We couldn't even call in artillery, because we had no legitimate target.

I got on the horn with Lieutenant Courtney. Since the platoon was already divided, I suggested that the two groups move out separately and parallel rather than closing up again into one column. I had two reasons, one practical and one selfish. The practical reason was that keeping the accidentally split platoon in two pieces might facilitate a flanking action if one group ran into sniper fire again. It was even remotely possible that the gooks might not realize the platoon was in two parts. The selfish reason was that I had little interest in crossing the open area into the stand of trees where the rest of the platoon was waiting.

Surprisingly, the lieutenant thought it was a reasonable suggestion and decided we would give it a try. So, when I saw the front of the column start to move out of the trees ahead of me, the eight of us in the rear thicket moved back into the trees, headed off to our right, and finally broke out of the trees about 60 meters away from where we had been waiting, in a line of march that was a little behind and almost parallel with the other group.

The platoon's two groups were separated by roughly 150 meters. Movement was slow and exceptionally cautious. Everyone was hunched over in a crouch, and heads were panning back and forth as all eyes searched for suspicious signs in the trees and high grass to the front.

Ten minutes went by, and the tension began to ease a little as we grew more confident that Charlie had decided to di-di when the gunship flew in. I stood a little straighter to ease the cramp I was getting in my back from walking in a crouch with a heavy rucksack on my shoulders.

A sudden volley of shots, a terrible scream, and I was on my belly in a flash. Chuck was still there. He must have dropped back along our line of march, and waited for another chance at us.

I stayed on the ground for a minute, trying to figure out what the heck we should do, and perversely enjoying the respite from the discomfort of walking hunched over. The scream had come from the direction of Courtney's piece of the platoon, so I was fairly sure the eight of us in my group hadn't taken any fire. Most strangely, I didn't feel frightened, just annoyed that Charlie was being so goddamned persistent. John Fournelle crawled over to me and reached out with the handset. "The El-tee wants to talk to you."

Lieutenant Courtney told me that someone in Chief's squad had taken a bullet in his arm. It was broken, but still attached and the bleeding wasn't too bad. That meant it wasn't critical to get him out right now, and gave us some flexibility for dealing with the gooks.

The lieutenant said Chief thought he had seen muzzle

flashes straight in front of their column when the shooting had started. Still, they were presently seeing nothing to shoot at, and the incoming fire had again paused. Courtney wanted me to know that Chief and two other guys were going to attempt a low-crawl forward while the rest of the lieutenant's piece of the platoon threw out covering fire. He asked me if I could move my group up and over to the left to flank the bad guys.

When I heard what Chief was attempting, I thought to myself, "That crazy fucker really thinks he's part Indian."

Since I hadn't taken any fire, as near as I could tell, I thought it was possible Charlie still didn't notice that the platoon had broken into two pieces and that a group was to his left as well as in front of him. So I told the lieutenant we could do it. I wasn't really eager to sneak up on snipers, but our odds of getting there undetected were better than Chief's. Besides, I couldn't leave Chief with his ass hanging out while he attempted to crawl up on Charlie's position.

Rusty O'Hara and most of his squad were the guys who had been cut off with me. I motioned them together in the tall grass, and whispered what we were going to do. I wanted them to form a single file line with about ten feet of separation between each man. Then we would crawl forward about 100 meters, turn 90 degrees to the left, and crawl in a skirmish line toward where I thought the snipers were hiding. If I was right, we could bring eight guns to bear on the bad guys, maybe before they knew we were there.

All of us shucked off the clumsy rucksacks, as we sure didn't need the extra weight on our backs during a long crawl. I kept my pistol belt with two grenades and a canteen on the back. Finally, I put a single bandoleer of M-16 magazines on backwards, so it draped across my back instead of my chest. John killed the volume on his radio to keep it from betraying us when we got close. Then we started crawling. I took the lead, because I had a pretty good idea where we needed to go.

The grass both helped and hindered our slow approach. Helped, because the long stalks bent over as we passed and we slid over it more easily than if we had to crawl on bare earth.

Hindered, because it was cutting the piss out of our uncovered skin, and the agitated tops of the stalks unavoidably signaled our approach to anyone attentive enough to be watching the movement of the nearby grass.

After painfully crawling for what seemed like a very long time, we came to a point to the right and fifty meters or so from a thin stand of trees I thought the VC might be using for cover. I gestured to let the man behind me know it was time to wheel left, and he passed the signal back down the line. Pausing momentarily, I wiped the sweat out of my eyes and noticed that my arms were covered with blood from sliding over the sharp-edged grass. I listened for any sound, good guys or bad guys. And I heard nothing. The lieutenant's people weren't putting out any covering fire after all, probably because they couldn't be sure where Chief was, or where I was.

Worried about Chief's progress in his effort to close up on the snipers and unable to use the radio to get any more information, I started my line of grunts sliding again toward the trees. Now, instead of one column of men moving single file in the grass, we were all making separate wakes through the waving sea of green. I kept expecting bullets to whiz by, or a grenade to come arching down on top of us.

A shot! Directly to my front, and close. More shots, this time from the left where the lieutenant's group was, and where Chief probably was. I tried to judge how far away the return fire had been, to gauge whether it had been Chief or the lieutenant, but more shots were going off right in front of me and drowning out the more distant gunfire.

Every instinct in my body screamed at me to stay down on the ground. But I couldn't see anything in the tangle of grass, and I sure wasn't doing anything to help out Chief and the other two grunts who were coming up on Charlie's front. The gunfire was sustained now, but didn't appear to be directed at us. I swallowed hard, and rose to my knees. It was still too thick; I couldn't see through the grass. So I stood up.

Right in front of me, partially hidden in the trees, were four VC intently firing at something to their front. The closest one was no more than fifty feet away from me. Out of the corner of my left eye, I saw Chief and his two men shooting back at the VC. Chief was up on one knee, shooting bursts from his M-16. The other two guys were a little behind him, to his left. The snipers were concentrating on the three GIs in front of them, and still weren't aware of me on their left. My M-16 was against my shoulder, my finger starting to squeeze the trigger, the men in my skirmish line beginning to stand up, following my lead.

When the bullet from one of the VC rifles smashed into the middle of Chief's face.

I went absolutely stone crazy berserk.

I was only dimly aware of what happened. I heard a strange noise, almost like a growling, and realized without thinking it peculiar that the noise was coming from me. Feeling almost disembodied, I was vaguely conscious of muzzle flashes coming from my own M-16. The gook immediately in front of me turned toward me in sudden alarm, and was greased before his head was far enough around to see me. The next one, the son of a bitch who had fired the shot into Chief, was shifting his attention to the other two grunts out to his front.

My feet hadn't stopped moving. I was in the tree line and almost on top of him. The dumb shit never knew what ended his life, as I cranked five shots into him at point blank range and watched him twitch as each one of the hits opened wet holes in him. I hated, and it felt good.

The third gook, recognizing that something was very wrong on his left, turned and saw me. We were practically face to face in the trees, and I could see the terror in his eyes as he tried to get a round off in my direction.

Crack, crack, crack. One in his face, two in his chest. Dead before he hit the ground.

All this seemed to be happening to somebody else, not to me. It was as if I were an observer, watching dispassionately, unaffected by the mayhem. I was on autopilot, and I wasn't even thinking about the skirmish line behind me.

There had been four VC. I turned to my right, and saw the

fourth one aiming his rifle at me. As I looked at him and tried to swing my M-16 around, his chest erupted in red and he was pushed backward like a huge fist had struck him.

I spun around. There stood Rusty O'Hara, just finishing off a whole magazine on automatic. He had saved my life. He looked like he was going to puke.

There used to be a science fiction television show, at the end of which the announcer would say, "We now return control of your TV set to you." That's how I felt, like something had taken control of me and I was just getting it back.

Rusty had sat down on the ground and had his head between his legs. I walked, a bit rubber-legged, over to Chief. The other two guys who had been with him were standing over him, one of them with a limp forearm dripping blood. Chief was face down. He had fallen forward when he was shot, and part of the back of his head was missing. I didn't turn him over.

Lieutenant Courtney and the rest of the platoon hurried up as we stood there, looking down at Chief's body. Nobody said anything. I felt an incredible emptiness inside me, and I couldn't shake the feeling that it was all some kind of a cruel dream.

The lieutenant put his hand on my arm. "I saw what you did back there. I'm putting you in for a Silver Star." I turned and looked at him. Right then, a decoration for being a contributor to the gore that surrounded me was the farthest thing from my mind. I can't begin to explain the senses I was experiencing. I wanted to walk away, I wanted to quit, I wanted to howl in pain, and possibly wanted to smack the lieutenant upside the head. I felt denial—this couldn't possibly be happening, and I *definitely* couldn't be part of it. And I felt incredibly frustrated that there was apparently no force on the planet capable of ending this insanity.

I finally spoke to the lieutenant. "I lost it, pure and simple. They shot Chief, and I wanted them dead." I walked away, thinking that a Silver Star should mean something. It should stand for heroism. Was there anything heroic about having so much hate and fury that you want to kill? I didn't think so.

I was practically sleepwalking. Chief was gone. It wouldn't be strictly accurate to say I had been his friend—nobody was really friends with Chief. But he had been a good guy, and I had liked him a lot. He had less than a month left before he was to have gone home.

And now some little slope prick had shot his face off. My world was upside down. The inmates had taken over the asylum.

It was late afternoon, and we needed another medevac. There were two wounded, and Chief's body needed to start its long journey home. We moved a short distance to a decent landing zone, Courtney's RTO putting in the call as we walked. The platoon set out a perimeter, and we settled in to wait for the chopper. Rusty still looked wobbly, but he had a little color back in his face and didn't look like he was going to barf any more.

As usual, I heard it long before I saw it. Someone popped smoke to let the pilot know where we were, and I watched as a Huey with a big red cross on a white background flew into sight over a stand of trees to our north.

And I watched as green tracers ripped into it, sending it into a spin and an instant later into the ground. The chopper had been low and flaring when it was hit, so it was moving somewhat slowly. It hit on one skid, then momentarily skated along the ground as it turned into a shattered pile of shrieking, protesting metal. Even after it stopped sliding, its broken rotor was still turning and banging into the remains of the tail. One moment the helicopter was flying gracefully toward us, the next moment it was an unrecognizable pile of junk on the ground.

I suddenly felt very weary. I didn't want to play any more. I wanted to take my ball and go home.

Two of the Huey's crew struggled out, and looked intact. I could see at least one other person in the cockpit, not moving. Around me, the men on the north side of the perimeter were firing into the stand of trees from which the green tracers had climbed. The VC we had killed earlier evidently hadn't been alone, and their buddies simply waited for the vulnerable dust-off to arrive. We had screwed up.

There were three M-79s in the platoon, one in each squad. It took awhile to get them all to the right place on the perimeter—we didn't need any more casualties. While the grenadiers were moving, Patterson's pig kept cranking out bursts to keep Charlie's head down.

Once we had the M-79s on line, I told them to start firing white phosphorous grenades into the trees. No more low crawls and dead GIs; I wanted to burn them out. The first three rounds looped into the trees, and the bright flash of burning phosphorous lit up the thicket. Charlie shot back.

Three more rounds arched downrange, floop floop floop. Then more, as fast as the grenadiers could reload and pump them out. The stand of trees was dazzling with phosphorous blasts. We heard a scream over the exploding grenades, and two gooks suddenly bolted from the trees, brushing wildly at their clothes. Rifles and machine guns opened up in unison, and two VC did the dance for us as dozens of bullets smacked into them.

It got quiet. Wary of yet another unseen gathering of bad guys, we stayed put for ten minutes. Then we took our time carefully maneuvering toward the trees. Not far into the thicket, we found another dead VC, badly burned from the exploding willie peter.

Lieutenant Courtney talked to battalion back on LZ Professional and got yet another medevac inbound. One of the crew on the downed Huey was dead, another slightly wounded. The two who jumped free were shaken, but unhurt. Chief was still dead.

The sun was barely hanging on above the top of the elephant grass when the replacement medevac lifted off with its disagreeable load. The lieutenant and I moved a subdued 2nd platoon into the nearest stand of trees that didn't have any dead VC cluttering it up, and set up a night laager.

After the perimeter was set and the claymores out, I sat down in the center command position with the lieutenant, shedding my gear as I sank to the ground. Mechanically, I pulled the poncho liner out of my rucksack. Just as mechanically, I took off my boots and put on a pair of socks slightly less filthy than the ones I peeled off.

I looked into my rucksack for something to eat, and then decided I really wasn't hungry. I thought about finishing my letter to Linda before the light was completely gone. Didn't feel very much like writing—to her, or to anybody. I lit a cigarette, and sucked the smoke down deep. As I exhaled, my whole body felt slack, exhausted.

It had been a very tough day.

Chapter Twenty-Three

The war went on, a huge living thing indifferent to the mood of a world which had lost interest in it. There was an ebb and flow to the war, like music in a classical symphony. Sometimes it was quiet, almost peaceful, with relatively few participants playing their parts while the rest of the musicians waited for a cue. At other times, the stage was filled with bombast and percussion, many players all contributing to the thunderous noise.

More people went home. Patterson and Costellano were both gone, back to stateside duty for the last six months of their two-year draft obligation. New faces arrived, some astonished that there was so much fighting still going on. The platoon changed almost weekly, but it stayed always depressingly young and inexperienced. Sure, the guys who had been around for a while and lived through combat had the eyes of old men, but kids we were. I had been there for at least a lifetime, and I still didn't see myself as a seasoned veteran, much less a professional soldier. I was, however, a young man who had learned how to kill—without hesitation. And I spent much of my time being afraid.

Days and nights went by, each endlessly repeating the routines of all the ones that had come before. The closer I got to the end, the slower time passed. I marked the days off on a ragged, wrinkled short-timer's calendar I had been carrying for a long time. It was a picture of Snoopy the beagle, surrounded by a line of boxes each containing a number representing the number of days left in my year. Time was measured in the number of days left plus a wake-up. Each day another box was crossed off my calendar, one less to endure, and brought me one sunrise closer to leaving this awful place.

My battalion had settled in on the new LZ Professional. It didn't exactly feel like a home. No firebase ever did, especially to the leg soldiers who endlessly wandered off it and on it, taking over a bed made out of empty ammo boxes on the floor of a muddy bunker from the grunt in another company who had just left it to head back into the jungle.

But it no longer seemed like the new place we had built. I was still uneasy about its potential vulnerability, but my concern faded as days and weeks went by without incident. The brush on the overgrown side had been cut and sprayed with defoliant, providing a much better approach view. The recon guys had placed motion sensors on a few of the surrounding hilltops, hopefully to alert Operations if activity was detected. And whatever company had firebase duty routinely sent out daytime patrols to check the area around the hill for any sign of Cong mischief.

The former LZ Professional had no further value, and was rarely visited. Once on patrol we crossed the Burlington Trail and passed by the old hill. It looked like most any other hill around, and vegetation was already spreading over the slopes where concertina and claymores had ruled not so long before. The flat part at the top where the 105s had fired so many rounds was covered with green, a strange sight for a place once so barren.

There was no need to climb it, even for old time's sake. You learned to conserve energy when humping through the bush. It was always too damned hot and the load too heavy to be hiking up every hill you happened upon.

We had occasional firefights, found some caches, and tripped the odd booby trap. Walked for miles though thick stuff and thin, wandered through forgettable rice paddies, burned off countless leeches. Sweat gallons, and drank gallons more from rivers, streams, and muddy rice paddies. Ate C-rations and malaria pills and salt tablets. Spent some time with a platoon of ARVN, even more useless than the bunch I met when Lieutenant Courtney was still an FNG. Killed a few gooks. Same old shit.

A heavy lassitude had settled over Bravo Company. Not a single man, I don't even think the newly arrived company commander, believed there was any point to what we were doing any more. No longer was there any question of whether the U.S. would be leaving Vietnam, there was only the question of when. It was one thing to accept that fact and simply bide your time living like an animal in the jungle, just to get to the end of your year and out of Vietnam. We could rationalize, could handle a little discomfort. But when people were still out there fighting and getting killed while the country slowly dithered its way out of the war, that was an entirely different thing than just enduring an uncomfortable jungle life. The thousands of American lives already lost were going to be meaningless once we walked away, and continuing the carnage—knowing we were going to leave—was genuinely immoral. The continuing exodus of body bags, that was the point where acceptance and rationalization ended, and discontent and muttering began. There was a lot of muttering going on.

I'm sure there are folks who believe some of the deaths in Vietnam were meaningful deaths, that people accomplished something there by dying. I suppose that might have somehow been true earlier in the war, but I sure had a tough time seeing anything meaningful in the waste of the guys I had personally watched die.

Once, somewhere in the blur of days, we stumbled into a firefight with a couple of VC who were as surprised at the chance meeting as we were. I was way in the back, and the fight was over in seconds. None of our guys was hurt. One gook was dead, the other wounded. A Huey picked up the live one for interrogation back at an ARVN compound, and we learned later that he sang like a canary back at Chu Lai. (The ARVN were pretty good at making people talk—they weren't constrained by the rules we followed.) The captured Cong had information on a large VC force gathering to our west, roughly six miles from LZ Professional. Since brigade headquarters had lately been in the dark about which units of bad guys were in the neighborhood, our captured VC proved to be a popular fellow.

I continued getting letters from home, but it was becoming more and more apparent that Linda wasn't writing nearly as often as at the beginning of my year. I found that unbelievably frustrating, because there wasn't anything I could do about it and I couldn't understand why it was happening. It could take two to three weeks for a letter to make the journey to or from Vietnam, so you always had multiple conversations going on with any correspondent. You found yourself responding to things in any letter you wrote that they had written to you several weeks before. I never felt I could push too hard about the frequency of her letters, beyond continually asking if everything was okay back there. It was a refrain I repeated in every letter I wrote. I think I was afraid of the answer I might get if I came right out and asked her why she wasn't writing as often.

Lieutenant Courtney got progressively better at his job. He was still not my candidate for a leadership award and would never be a Tom Warren, but then I suppose I wasn't all that much of a prize my damn self. The lieutenant had avoided any further bonehead plays like the one that got him "rotated" out of his first assignment, and the grunts in 2nd platoon had grudgingly accepted him as adequate to fill the platoon leader's role.

Bravo Company was split in platoons playing chase the Charlie when orders came for us to get ready for an eagle flight. The company was to reunite and would be flown west to the area believed to be a gathering point for a large VC force. Intelligence gleaned from our wounded prisoner had led to a series of overflights, and brigade headquarters now suspected something was going on out there. My battalion was elected to go take a first-hand look.

The company's three platoons spent the next day linking up. We had about four klicks to cover in order to reach the rendezvous site, so it was almost dark when we found the rest of the company, already in a night laager.

Once 2nd platoon had filled out its part of the perimeter and we had checked the squad positions, Lieutenant Courtney and I went to a briefing by the captain of our insertion plans for the following day. He was a fairly new guy; our previous CO had been sent home two weeks earlier. Captains had one-year tours, too, just like the rest of us.

I was very interested in hearing his mission orders and his plan. Recalling how inept was my first air assault when the brass falling from a Cobra gave me a moment of terror, I was determined to get as much information as I could about objectives, support, anticipated resistance, and individual unit responsibilities. Plus I couldn't muster a huge amount of confidence in either my platoon leader or a brand new and untested company commander. It really wasn't the place of platoon sergeants to do much more than listen when participating in a gathering of officers, but one way or another I was going to make sure all the right questions got asked.

The meeting at the command position in the middle of our perimeter lasted twenty minutes, and I was pleasantly surprised at how thoroughly this eagle flight had been thought out. The captain wasn't strictly an FNG. Although he was new to commanding a rifle company, he had been a platoon leader in Vietnam on a previous tour. He had learned a few things his last time through, and my confidence in him went up a notch.

Bravo Company was being inserted near an untended rice paddy roughly a klick from the suspected VC build-up, and Delta Company was being placed a half mile or so to our south. Cobra gunships would be along for the festivities, although LOH choppers probing earlier that day hadn't spotted any enemy activity around our intended LZ.

There would not be any artillery prepping the LZ ahead of our assault, as the brass thought that might be a signal to Charlie of our plans to pay a visit. Still, the VC knew this countryside much better than we did—they lived there—and would be familiar with every place that helicopters could set down for miles in any direction. If Chuck saw a bunch of choppers, you could bet he would be able to quickly determine where they might land. And he could just as quickly di-di to the LZ, or send a message to some friends, inviting them to meet us with a warm welcome.

Each platoon was to be responsible for a one-third arc around the LZ. Lieutenant Courtney and 2nd platoon would take an arc on the north and east. Although I wasn't tremendously excited about flying out to look for bad guys, especially now that I was getting short, I was happy that this time I at least knew where the hell I was supposed to go when the birds landed.

I had first watch, and was glad for it because I was too wound up to sleep. Even after my watch was over and I had awakened the next guy, I couldn't get to sleep. I kept thinking about the coming eagle flight. Short-timers often developed a kind of paranoia about getting into a pissing contest during the last weeks of their tours. Nobody wanted to get wasted when the end was in sight, after managing to survive so long. I was a tad anxious, wondering if I had made it this far only to buy the farm on some dumb helicopter assault.

Sometime around two o'clock I dozed off. It seemed like only minutes had passed when I was being shaken awake again. It was first light, and the company was coming to life and preparing for the insertion. There was the usual low murmur of morning in a company laager, of men rolling up poncho liners and making coffee in canteen cups over fires made from a pinch of C-4, of rifle bolts snicking shut as final checks were made to M-16s, of GIs retrieving claymores and wandering outside the perimeter for a morning constitutional.

I saw Rusty O'Hara checking over his new machine gunner, Costellano's replacement. Rusty was becoming a decent squad leader, and I thought again that I was glad to have him. Finishing our coffee and a morning butt, the lieutenant and I took a walk around the platoon positions to look over the guys and their equipment. It probably wasn't necessary—the squad leaders knew to do that every morning we were in the jungle—but it gave us something to do. Wouldn't hurt to double check, since our destination could be lively. It might also help convey to the newer guys who hadn't yet been on an air assault that this could be serious stuff.

The sun had barely made it above the nearby treetops when the thudding rotors of twenty-odd helicopters sounded their imminent arrival. We had moved to the pick-up point, a large clearing less than half a klick from the night laager, and waited in the thin cover around the clearing for our rides. As soon as the rotor racket interrupted the still-quiet morning, GIs in groups of five began edging into the clearing to await the slicks. The noise grew louder, and suddenly the first birds came into view low over the trees at the south end of the clearing.

It was always an awesome sight when so many helicopters flew together, and I felt my pulse pick up as they drifted overhead. When the lead Hueys reached the north end of the clearing they flared, tails down, and settled on their skids in the long grass. Instantly, the closest groups chugged through the grass toward the first ones down, shoulders hunched under the loads, heads down to avoid the main rotor. They piled on board and grabbed for any handhold. The rotors never slowed, and in seconds the choppers were leaning forward and pulling for air to lift off. Throughout the clearing, the same scene kept repeating as each Huey fetched its load.

I watched the ground fall rapidly away beneath me as my helicopter gained altitude. By then, my heart was hammering. If anything I was more apprehensive then I had been on my first eagle flight. I looked around at the other guys who had loaded with me, and realized not one of them had ever been on an insertion before. Great. I'm stuck with a bunch of virgins. Lordy, I was the role model.

According to the plan, the Hueys closest to me would all be carrying other groups of 2nd platoon people. That was a whole lot smarter than indiscriminately mixing the platoons, and would allow us to quickly regroup and set up our arc to the north and east of the LZ. I hoped someone had told the chopper pilots where each load was supposed to go.

About two miles out from the LZ the crew chief leaned over to holler in my ear that we were getting close. I saw two pairs of Cobras flying just ahead of us, linking up with our flight to provide air support. I signaled to the grunts with me to lock and load, and I released the bolt on my own M-16 to hammer a round into the chamber.

The LZ was visible out in front of us, maybe 500 meters away, and the choppers were already slowing for the drop-off. My hands automatically took inventory, touching and checking grenades, bandoleers, canteens, rucksack straps, smoke canisters. The Cobras were slightly ahead of the slicks, and directed their miniguns at the LZ as soon as they were in range.

My helicopter floated in toward the LZ, barely above tree level. I saw other slicks all around us, similarly slowing for the insertion, gently dropping their tails to bleed off airspeed. The buzz of the Cobras' miniguns was drowned out by the engine and rotor noise of my chariot, but I could see the red tracers slashing into the grass and trees in and around the LZ.

And then I saw the green tracers, too.

Hot LZ! Hot LZ! It's a fucking hot LZ! The crew chief was yelling something into the mike on his headset, and the door gunners swung their pigs around to begin laying down fire toward the source of incoming fire. I turned my head to look out the open door on the far side of the Huey and saw green tracers climbing toward us on that side as well. The other four guys with me were wide-eyed.

I kept hoping somebody would decide to abort the insertion, but the choppers all continued their descent toward Charlie's welcoming committee. The green tracers were everywhere, like swarming bees. I felt the crew chief shake my arm and turned just in time to see a Huey off on the opposite side drop sickeningly to the ground, tail first. The day was not starting off very well.

And then we were down, sliding along on the skids, piling out of the slick as fast as our legs could move, lurching and stumbling toward the edge of the LZ that my compass said was the northeast. I could see Lieutenant Courtney way off to my left, and Rusty O'Hara with his squad close on my right. John, my RTO, was right behind me and struggling to keep up as the radio bounced on his shoulders.

Because of the irregular shape of the landing zone, I found myself with a lot of ground to cover in order to reach our assigned part of the perimeter. We were in chest high grass and thinly scattered trees, running toward a more dense line of trees. The footing was treacherous, half slippery mud and half tangled deadfalls. I felt like my chest was bursting from the exertion, and my lungs screamed for air. For all our effort, though, the progress was painfully slow. The cover we wanted at the edge of the jungle seemed to take forever to reach.

The incoming fire, first so occupied with knocking down the landing helicopters, was shifting to the ground troops as the surviving slicks departed. I had no idea how many had landed intact. It had been a lot easier to see the whole picture from up in the air, and I couldn't tell if I was now taking fire or not. I heard the buzz of miniguns and saw Cobras slicing by as they worked the edges of the LZ, trying to help us out.

Looking back on that day over the distance of time, it's difficult to say what I was feeling. We were so preoccupied with getting to cover and aching from the hard run, I don't think anyone thought much about what he was experiencing. I know I was scared, and I remember thinking how cruel it would be to get to this point and get greased on this damn insertion. And I was getting mad again.

Our line was pretty ragged as we advanced toward the trees, but it was a line. I glanced to my right, and saw someone go down hard on his face about 50 feet away. Curiously, my reaction to the sight was dispassionate. I thought of it as confirmation that, yes, we were indeed taking fire, and not that someone I probably knew had just been shot. I heard somebody yell for a medic.

Less than a hundred meters to the tree line. Lungs on fire. Rucksack bouncing and painfully chafing on my shoulders. M-16 up at port arms, safety off, round chambered, set on automatic. Leg muscles burning and threatening to go on strike.

Suddenly, the tree line in front of us erupted in flashes and smoke. An explosion went off somewhere close by. I didn't see it, but my ears rang and I almost fell as I was pushed forward as though someone gave me a shove in the back. A man near me was lifted off his feet, gracefully floating, a ballet dancer. There wasn't anything graceful about his return to the ground.

I could see the goddamn green tracers again, coming right at us. It was like being stuck inside some large and very loud machine. One of the Cobras had seen that the northeast sector was taking fire and roared overhead, closing on the tree line with guns blazing and rockets pouring from its racks. On the ground, we were all diving for what little cover there was and trying to put some return fire toward the bad guys. And those guys in the trees kept cranking out a wall of metal in our direction. The noise level was astonishing.

The lieutenant had managed to get one of our M-60s working on the left side, and its volume of fire began to distract the VC to my front. Rusty's squad and I were cautiously darting between the scattered trees in the open LZ, hoping to get close enough to the thicker growth to get some better shots at Charlie. My hands were squeezed tight on my M-16. I was trying to keep them from shaking.

I dashed, as low as I could hunker myself down, across an area that was a hell of a lot more open than I cared for, and flung myself at the base of a sturdy tree, still short of the main tree line. Up on one knee, I looked slowly around it through the grass in the direction of the bad guys. And saw three of them, about forty meters away, all shooting at the machine gun near Lieutenant Courtney.

They hadn't seen me. Remember to take careful aim and squeeze off bursts. I sighted, and then fired. One down. Then another. The third one had turned toward me and was firing. A bullet thunked into my tree. I held my finger on the trigger while my M-16 spit out bullets like a faucet.

I don't know how many shots hit him before my magazine was empty, but it was sufficient. I could see the blooms appear on his body as the rounds slapped into him.

I didn't feel a thing, not even hate. Every fiber in me was racing, and I was tighter than a drum. I was just another gear in that big, noisy machine, grinding up anything unfortunate enough to be in the way.

My fingers weren't working very well. I had a hell of a time getting another magazine out of my bandoleer. One finally came loose, and I promptly dropped it. Cursing, I bent over to pick it up, the heavy rucksack sliding uncomfortably up my back. I heard the crack of bullets passing right above me.

Jesus! If I hadn't dropped that magazine...oh shit! Some days you eat the bear, some days the bear eats you.

I slammed the new magazine into my rifle, stayed real low, and kept my feet moving toward the tree line. It was getting closer.

Another automatic weapon was firing up ahead and to the left. A final dash and tumble, then we had made it into the heavier trees. I motioned the people around me to form a skirmish line, and we started to push more deeply into the thicket. Slowly, in a crouch, we moved forward. I reached and passed the three gooks I had shot. They looked...dead. They were meat on the ground, not people. Simply obstacles between me and the end of my tour.

I could hear the automatic weapon, probably a Chicom machine gun, in front of us. In the thick stuff, we couldn't see very far and I was losing sight of the GIs in my line as we crept forward. The only people I could still see were Swint and Harrison, two PFCs in Rusty's squad. They were on my right, intent on the shadowy tangle of growth in front of us.

Straightening up for a better look over a deadfall, I flinched at the sudden "tick" of bullets smacking the leaves near me. Down low, shooting back. Off to my left I saw Swint on the ground, holding his leg and yelling in pain. A flash of something in front of me caught my eye, and I tossed off rounds until the magazine was empty again.

I rolled a quarter turn onto my left side so I could get at a magazine with my right hand. I still could see Swint, but Harrison was no longer in sight. My fingers closed around a fresh magazine and I rolled back on my stomach, looking to the front again.

And saw a frightened VC holding an AK-47. Aimed at me.

He was tentatively walking toward me, not more than forty or fifty feet away. He saw the magazine in my hand, frozen halfway to the rifle. The fear went out of his face, replaced by a smile. The little son of a bitch actually smiled.

He knew he had me. I knew it, too. I thought about Linda, and the only thing that came into my head was that I would never see her again. My mind raced, weighing options—do I try to reload even though there was no chance, do I raise my hands and hope he doesn't blast me?

Off to my left, Swint was not in direct view of the VC. He must have seen the gook step toward me, and he managed to fight through his pain to fire off a burst.

The VC wheeled toward Swint, shooting. It was the distraction I needed. One thousand, one—I pounded the magazine into my M-16. One thousand, two—I flicked the bolt loose from its locked rearward position and started shooting as soon as it snapped forward. One thousand, three—the gook wasn't grinning any more. One thousand, four—he wasn't doing anything any more. I had me a nice new AK-47 trophy. Smiling Jack, no, make that Smiling Nguyen, wasn't going to be needing it any more. Don't grin at me when you're fixing to shoot me, you little fuck. I wasn't smiling.

Swint was okay. That is, my VC had missed him. He still had the bullet in his leg and wasn't having much fun, but his effort on my behalf hadn't worsened his situation. I yelled for a medic, and started moving forward again.

I saw Harrison, rejoined with Rusty, ahead of me taking cover behind a couple of trees. They were firing at something slightly to their left. I didn't need to look in order to tell what they were shooting at. It was the Chicom machine gun and it was a lead-spraying garden hose streaming rounds at them.

Staying low, I worked my way to the left, hoping I wouldn't attract the VC gunner's attention. I carefully chose a very large tree to nestle myself behind, and managed to crawl there without being noticed. Hoping mightily that I was in throwing range, I plucked a frag off my pistol belt. I pulled the pin. With my thumb holding the spoon, I slowly peeked around my tree to get a look at the VC position.

It was damn near invisible in the thick jungle, but I spotted it because of the muzzle flashes. The gooks were directly in front of me, and they were within my range. Up on one knee, release the spoon, snap out from behind the tree (overcoming a fiercely held instinct to avoid exposing my fragile body to a machine gun), and let the grenade fly. I threw myself down behind the tree and pressed my face in the dirt just as the bullet stream traversed toward my suddenly revealed presence. I heard the angry snapping as the rounds punched into the heavy tree. A second later, I heard the whoomp of the exploding grenade.

Ever so timidly, I peered around the tree. I might never get a job pitching for the Tigers, but I had thrown a strike with my frag. The machine gun position was history, and the two unfortunate VC who had been there were seriously dead.

After risking a look to make sure there weren't any more bad guys by the machine gun, I got up and joined Rusty and Harrison. The three of us started moving forward again, further into the trees. A few more minutes went by before we realized that it had turned quiet—no guns, no explosions.

My RTO came stumbling through the trees behind us, busily talking on the radio. The LZ was being reported as secure, and all platoons were to return and regroup. I hollered to unseen grunts on my left and right to turn around and go back to the LZ.

Getting organized took awhile. We had casualties, three of them from the crashed chopper in addition to the guys who went down as we assaulted the VC positions. Incredibly, that was the only Huey to go down. The others managed to dump their loads and get out of town with only a few bullet holes.

Dust-offs, and more gunships, showed up after a half hour to haul away Swint and the rest of our casualties. We kept a perimeter around the LZ while we waited, and two fire teams scouted for a body count. Twelve VC, an even dozen, had concluded their war while grinding away at our eagle flight. Another grease pencil entry for the acetate chart at battalion headquarters, another step forward in the Lieutenant Colonel's quest for a promotion to full bird.

Shortly after the medevacs came and went, I glanced at my watch and was astonished to see that it was already 2:30 in the afternoon. The assault had taken more than six hours. It felt like a lot less. Or maybe a lot more, depending on your perspective.

Bravo Company wasn't likely to do much more searching and destroying on this day. We were pretty ragged. So the captain had us saddle up and head toward some higher ground that we could see on the topo maps.

It was less than a two-hour walk to the hill, and it proved to be a suitable place for a company night laager. I was surprised at how tired I felt, and was grateful both for the early stopping time and the absence of any further harassment from Charlie. And, after looking at the wrong end of Smiling Nguyen's AK-47, I was grateful to still be alive and feeling anything.

The hill was just about perfect for a company position. It was the highest spot around, and the terrain was reasonably open. (If Charlie didn't know you were around, you might want thicker foliage to help stay hidden. But since the Indians knew we were in Indian country, more open approaches worked in our favor.) There were scattered trees, but not the thick triple canopy we often confronted. Grass and scrub bushes covered the sides and interfered with some lines of sight from the top, so it wasn't perfect. But it was as good as we were going to find out there.

We set up, four men to a position, and put out every last claymore we had in the company. It was remarkable how a little firefight cranked up everybody's pucker factor. One of the guys in my position, an E-2 named Randy Surtees who had only recently shed FNG status, pulled off his rucksack and rummaged around for a can of C-rations. The other two guys, Cassidy and Brooks, started a card game. I opened up a bag of LRRPs and poured a generous slug of canteen water into the freeze-dried gunk. In about five minutes, the stuff was reconstituted enough to heat up over a piece of C-4, and I had supper. Truly a culinary delight; Army gruel.

It was still light enough to see, so I started writing a letter. It was tough thinking of things to say in the letter, because my mind kept wandering back to the morning insertion. It dawned on me that I had killed once again, and felt practically nothing at having done that—positive or negative. No sense of victory, or remorse. Didn't even feel a need to rationalize that I had only done what was necessary. Just another day on the job.

I remember thinking now nice it was going to be when the time came to write that last letter home during the final days of my tour, a letter that would arrive only a day or so before I would. That was the last thought I had—I nodded off, the letter on my lap, unfinished.

I had third watch. The writing paper was still on my lap, night-damp, when I felt Randy nudging me awake. As always, I felt the momentary disorientation that comes from being wrestled back to wakefulness at night in the middle of a jungle. One of the strongest memories most grunts have of the war is lack of sleep, and how much your body rebels at being awakened when it's really tired. We were always tired, and sleep was forever being interrupted. This night was no exception.

Once he was sure I was awake and had the detonators for the claymores in front of me, Randy curled up in his poncho liner and quickly went to sleep. It was 1:00, and my watch would be two hours.

The time passed at a crawl, just as it did for every guy on every sentry rotation. I kept glancing at my watch, and each time the faintly luminescent hands had barely moved. The night was fairly bright, a thin sliver of moon providing a low wattage light bulb in the cloudless sky.

My mind wandered. I looked out at the brush and the silhouettes of a few trees in front of me, trying to stay alert and, by way of incentive, reminding myself of the fun time we'd had the previous day. Charlie was possibly still around, and I was damn sure not going to do something as stupid as falling asleep.

The faint moonlight splashed images on the hillside. Shadows rippled like smoke tendrils in the night-mottled brush, ghostly figures drifting and flowing through the trees, playing tricks on my eyes and imagination. I had learned not to look directly at something on night watch. You can see better at night with peripheral vision, turning your head a little. So I moved my head, back and forth, trying to sort the shadows from...from other shadows, I hoped.

Maybe an hour and a half into my watch, I was having a hell of a time staying awake. My eyelids were impossibly heavy. It was actually painful to force them to stay open. I knew I would nod off if I didn't do something to jog myself. I pinched my leg, hard. It worked, but not for very long. Then I was drifting again.

So I stood up. We weren't on ambush. It didn't matter whether I moved around a little because any bad guys who might have been nearby were already aware of a company of snoring GIs on the hill. It seemed reasonable, then, to force myself awake by some sort of physical activity. I just had to be careful not to wake the other guys, or catch the attention of some nervous watcher at another position on the perimeter who might mistake me for a sapper coming up the hill.

Standing up changed my perspective of the hillside. The shadows still were there, some moving around as a gentle night breeze nudged the brush. But they looked different from a slightly higher viewpoint. Less sinister, I thought. More fully awake, I yawned and stretched. And froze.

There was a figure by a tree about halfway down the hill. Foolishly, I stared right at it, and then it disappeared. I rubbed my eyes and tried again to look a little off to the side of the tree. Nothing there but the tree.

I was suddenly *very* much awake and feeling like I was probably a bit too visible, standing on the hill silhouetted against the night sky. I slowly settled back down to a sitting position, telling myself it had just been another shadow, a hint of mist floating near the tree. If only we had starlight scopes, something to brighten the night. But they were exceptionally rare, at least for leg infantry, and we hadn't seen one in months. Right then I would have traded my grandmother for a starlight scope.

I tried hard to resist watching the spot where I thought I had seen something. If you stare long enough at one night-cloaked place, two bad things happen. First, you convince yourself something is there, whether or not something really *is* there. Second, you aren't paying enough attention to the rest of the arc in front of your position, possibly missing a real threat.

So I scanned, and wrestled with indecision over whether to wake someone else, just in case. No longer having any difficulty keeping my eyelids from drooping, I peered intently down the shallow slope of our hillside looking for any indication something was out of the ordinary. I was looking to my left, and abruptly sensed motion back to my right. My head jerked back to the right, but all I saw were undulating shadows.

I told myself I was being jumpy, unreasonably imagining evil Cong killers slithering up the hill to do me in. I was getting close to the end of my year, and conjuring up thoughts of bad things that would keep me from making it out alive. Just the same, I reached out in the dark and touched the detonators for the two claymores set up some fifty feet down the hill from my position. The cool metal handles felt comforting and I placed them close to me, one on each side.

There was a full magazine in my M-16, a round in the chamber, the safety on. I halfway wished I hadn't stood. If Chuck was out there he would have undoubtedly seen me and marked my position.

I had that thought just as something clearly moved out in front of me on the left, less than a hundred feet away. Alarmed, but still not entirely sure there were bad guys in the weeds, I reached for the detonator by my left hand. Just as my hand closed around it a bright flash and the explosion of a grenade came from the far side of the night laager, one of the 3rd platoon positions, followed quickly by the unmistakable blast of a claymore.

My heart was in my throat, and the guys in the position around me were trying to make the groggy transition from the unreal worlds of their dreams to the greater unreality of loud explosions in a Vietnam night. The blasts behind me had briefly illuminated the hill to my front, and gave me a fleeting glimpse of figures moving outside the perimeter. I shut my eyes to preserve my night vision, and squeezed the left detonator.

The blast was deafening, and I could see the flash even through my closed eyes. Randy, awake now and unaware that I was tripping a claymore, hadn't closed his eyes. I heard him scream, "Gooks on the right!" I hit the right claymore.

Another blast, this one accompanied by an awful shriek from somewhere to the front. By now, all four of us were pressed flat to the ground and putting out M-16 fire. Muzzle flashes played hell on my night vision, but I could see Charlie's muzzle flashes now, too, further down the hill. It looked like a whole lot of muzzle flashes, and they were coming closer. To my right I saw several together, blinking fire at us.

I grabbed a frag and lobbed it down the hill in the direction of the apparent cluster of bad guys. A blackly humorous thought popped into my mind, a memory of some infantry training instructor reciting an uninspired reminder that GIs should maintain separation and never cluster together—"One hand grenade'll get you all".

Charlie had evidently forgotten his training. Whoomp! The grenade ripped open its piñata of lethal steel candy, and the grouping of muzzle flashes suddenly ceased.

Someone in the next position to our left fired a willie peter M-79 grenade out in front, and the fiery concussion lit up the night, a baby sun momentarily strobing and backlighting an uneven line of gooks scrabbling up the hill toward Bravo Company. When I saw how many of them were out there, I actually felt the hair on the back of my neck stiffen. I kept squeezing off rounds, changing magazines, throwing grenades.

I heard an M-60 grinding out a long belt on my right, and could see red tracers lazily drifting down the hill. I wondered about the first explosion I had heard, over on the far side of the company. It meant we were being attacked on at least two sides, perhaps all around the hill. Could Charlie have breached the perimeter somewhere?

There wasn't time to think about it or to worry that bad guys might be behind me. There were more than we could handle right out in front of me.

I normally carried four hand grenades, and they were

quickly gone. Both our claymores had been fired. I had emptied a bandoleer of magazines, started a second bandoleer, and was trying to recall where I had set my rucksack which contained a third bandoleer. At the rate we were expending ammo, it wouldn't take long to run through the entire company's supply. What normally seemed like a wealth of ordinance, and a heavy load to carry, started to feel laughably inadequate. I yelled at the people around me to choose their shots, to conserve ammo.

There was almost a metronome quality to the sound of grenade launchers flooping rounds into the brush around the perimeter. Most of them were HE rounds, flinging out jagged shrapnel just like hand grenades. Occasionally one of the explosions would be white phosphorous, catching the whole battleground in a flashbulb freeze-frame, VC down in crouches crabbing their way toward us and GIs flat on their bellies pumping out everything they had at the approaching mob.

One of the willie peter grenades went off near me on the left, and I clenched right up to pucker factor nine when I realized there was a VC coming up the hill at most twenty feet from my position, carrying a carbine and a satchel charge. In unison, Surtees and I cranked off a half dozen rounds that mangled the place where the VC's face had been and sent him tumbling backward into the dark.

A Vietnam vet who had been an instructor at Fort Polk told me about pucker factor nine. It was when you got so scared "They couldn't drive a nine penny nail up your ass with a sledgehammer."

Up to that point it had been a humorous, if colorful, expression, the kind of macho bullshit remark some guys like to throw around. But it took on new meaning for me when Charlie suddenly materialized out of the shadows right there in front of me.

I wasn't at all sure what time it was or how long we had been fighting. The firefight settled into a pattern, quieting for a bit and then surging somewhere around the hill as the gooks probed for a weak spot. It was unusual for them to be so persistent. They were too close for us to call in artillery, and we couldn't get close air support at night—too risky, they might grease us instead of the bad guys.

Charlie, normally a hit and run kind of fellow, had decided for some unknown reason to stick around and mess with us. Perhaps the VC figured they had us where they wanted, and that there wasn't another American unit near enough to do anything to help, especially at night.

A chaotic swell of gunfire, explosions and yelling around the perimeter to the right made me wonder if the gooks had made it to our line. Then it faded, and I found myself again preoccupied with muzzle flashes to the front.

A sudden burst of shots came out of the dark directly below us on the hill. I heard the characteristic sound that a bullet makes when it hits flesh—kind of like a cleaver thunking into a beef roast—followed by a soft sigh on my right. I looked at Surtees. He was dead.

I don't know how long it took before some nimrod in some safe rear area office decided that the war effort could spare a little illumination for us. I heard a plane approaching—no clue what it was—and within a minute flares began popping open in the sky. It lit up an eerie scene of combatants, bodies and devastated foliage.

I could see a half dozen VC bodies scattered in front of my position, one of them badly mangled from what must have been one of the claymore blasts. I could also see too damn many bad guys still on their feet coming toward us. They were suddenly hesitant, more than a little surprised to be caught in the revealing light of the flares. Chuck, my boy, your shit is hanging out. Real bad.

As flares turned the night into a surreal, artificial day, our dicey situation was turned into a turkey shoot. All of the ordinance we had flung down the hill had further thinned out what had been fairly light cover for the approaching horde, and they were hopelessly exposed. Bravo Company fairly erupted with a wall of lead.

I had no shortage of targets. I just started shooting at the closest Cong. It was like being back at Tigerland, out on the M-16 range going through the qualifying course. The range had automated man-sized targets that would pop up at varying distances in a thirty-degree arc in front of the trainee taking the test. They stayed up a few seconds while the trainee tried to sight and shoot to knock them down, the impact of the bullet registering a hit and releasing the target back to its prone position. On this Vietnam hillside range, the targets fell just as fast, but they didn't bounce back up again. I felt little more emotion as I sighted and squeezed off rounds at the real life targets than I had when I qualified so very long ago at Fort Polk.

Noise and gunsmoke and guttering flares filled the bizarre night landscape, a horrible nightmare out of control. We were ripping them to pieces. I hit at least four, and could see the will of others further down the hill start to crumble. A few had intelligently dropped to the ground for what little cover they could find, and a few others were clearly uncertain about trying to continue in the face of withering, and now accurate, fire from our night laager.

Cassidy threw his last frag. It landed between two gooks, one on his belly, the other starting to inch his way backwards down the hill. The explosion obliterated my view of the one standing, very likely obliterating him as well. And it lifted the prone VC off the ground like a rag doll, twisting his leg unnaturally sideways in the process.

That did it for the bad guys on our side of the hill. They turned and ran, rabbits bounding in terror from the hunter's shotgun. M-16 rounds and machine gun tracers followed them all the way down the hill until they disappeared into the gloom at the far edge of the flare illumination. We dropped a bunch as they raced away.

We fired until there was nothing to shoot at. Two or three desultory rifle shots from the far side of the perimeter, and then it was over.

The last couple flares sputtered out, and darkness settled back over Bravo Company. People were yelling, radios crackling. I heard a call for a medic on the right side, and took a quick check of the guys in the positions on either side of me. The only casualty for the three positions was Randy, and that was utterly amazing.

The captain was worriedly trying to find out what condition his rifle company was in, and platoon leaders were scrambling to check their people. I told my RTO to advise Lieutenant Courtney that Surtees was dead and the rest of the guys in my part of the perimeter were okay. Then I told all three positions to give me an ammo check. I figured the next thing the captain would want to know was how much ordinance remained. We would likely need an emergency resupply. Finally I settled back to smoke a cigarette while the officers flitted around like nervous chickens.

Right about then there was a frightened little kid somewhere down inside me who wanted nothing more than to pull the covers over his head and withdraw from the world. Since I couldn't do that, I sat with my guys and chained smoked, our eyes staring off at some unseen thing in the distance, all of us one step short of catatonic. All that killing can have a strange effect on you.

It took almost half an hour to get a handle on the company's status, and by that time the sky was preparing for another sunrise. We had three dead and five wounded, mostly in 3rd platoon where the gooks had gotten close enough to toss a satchel charge.

Sprawled out around the hillside below us were forty-one VC, all dead. If there had been any wounded VC, they either hobbled away or had been converted from wounded to dead in the wall of bullets we put out when the flares started. It was a gruesome early morning sight, and it wouldn't take long to become a gruesome smell, too.

The company needed medevacs, and a major ammunition resupply. Almost all of the machine gun ammo was gone, and we were completely out of claymores and hand grenades. Only a handful of M-79 grenades remained. I had four magazines of M-16 rounds left, 72 bullets. That used to feel like a lot of ammo, but no longer. It could disappear alarmingly fast.

Looking back, I honestly believe that, if we hadn't been given illumination support when we did, the company might have exhausted its ammunition and possibly been overrun. Not a thought I particularly cared to dwell on.

Just as soon as there was enough daylight, the sky was buzzing with aircraft. The medevacs came first, uncontested, with a pair of Cobras for escort. The two Cobras stood off while the dust-off Hueys came in for our dead and wounded. I saw one of the 3rd platoon casualties climb aboard, in shock. His arm looked like somebody shoved it down a garbage disposal. If his life wasn't over—like TC pretending to be alive for a few days after he was shot—then his war certainly was.

When the medevacs were safely airborne and out of range, the captain radioed the Cobras to head west, the direction we believed Charlie headed after departing our hill. If stone killing machines like Cobras could catch the hapless gooks out in the open, they could deal out some hurt that would make our overnight firefight look like a church social. A minigun weenie roast. I hoped the gunships would find our VC, but suspected Charlie wasn't stupid enough to get caught in the open.

Following the medevacs into our position was a slick carrying a resupply load. It was a hell of a load. Rope-handled wooden crates of M-16 and machine gun ammo came off first, each quickly carried from under the spinning rotor by a pair of grunts. Then the Huey crew handed off boxes of grenades, claymores, M-79 rounds, and a couple cases of C-rations.

Bravo Company spent the next hour reloading magazines and packing gear. As I gathered up my scattered empty magazines and stuck bullets in them, every so often I could hear a distant burst from a minigun. The Cobras were probably reconnoitering by fire, trying to flush the VC by shooting at places they might be hiding.

I could also hear a jet or two, high above us, and I caught periodic glimpses of the battalion commander's LOH. Rounding out the air traffic was an artillery forward observer. Comforting to know we were attracting so much attention and air support. Or rather, I reminded myself, the gooks who traded the nighttime pyrotechnics with us were attracting attention. Bravo Company was simply one of the tools available to grease the bad guys, just like the helicopters and airplanes.

The heat of the day was on us before the company had reorganized, resupplied, and repacked enough to move out. To no one's surprise, we headed west—after the VC. Our column snaked its way down the hill, picking through the gore that had been VC fighters just hours before. Although the real stench of death was still a day or so away, the bodies were already starting to get ripe. I was glad to be leaving.

We covered roughly three klicks during the balance of that day, finding no trace of Charlie. In deference to the long night we had just gone through, the captain ended our patrol early and let the guys catch up on their rest a little. I realized I was exhausted, and was grateful for the early stop. Even better, the VC left us alone all night.

There was considerable speculation about what enemy force we had scrapped with. The talkative Cong prisoner from a couple weeks before had identified some VC units that were part of the reported buildup, but we still had no idea who had greeted our eagle flight or come to visit us in the night. And to be perfectly honest, I hoped we would never meet them again.

About halfway through the second day after the night firefight, a vigilant pilot in a scouting LOH spotted something in heavy jungle to our west. He went lower for a look, and took fire for his efforts. Evading, he managed to avoid getting shot down. But he got close enough to report that he had found a main body force. Charlie was located.

Christ, all hell broke loose. The radio was filled with constant traffic as multiple artillery fire missions were called, jets and helicopter gunships were dispatched, and Bravo Company got orders to close on the reported position. Delta Company, still a couple miles to our south, was also ordered to the site.

We had five klicks to cover, but we soon heard the racket. Phantoms screamed overhead carrying 500-pound bombs and napalm. Cobras ferried back and forth from their home bases, expending their lethal loads on poor Chuckie and returning for more.

And, oh my, the artillery. We were too far away from LZ Professional to get 105 support. But eight-inchers were coming from somewhere, passing over us and off to our right, and sounding like bulldozers flying through the air.

The VC had themselves a real bad situation. A fight was, for once, happening on our terms, not theirs. Charlie had the bad luck to be spotted, his location revealed, and the stupefying firepower of the American war machine was bashing the piss out of him. That was just fine with all of us. We hoped there wouldn't be a single gook still alive by the time we got there.

All day long the pounding went on as Bravo Company pressed nearer to the VC base camp. We heard the distant thumps of bombs and eight-inch shells and, as we got close, the buzz of miniguns.

By mid-afternoon we were close enough that the air and arty boys had to call off the barrage. Everyone knew that we couldn't be certain whether any bad guys were still around. Once the first salvo had slammed into the camp, Charlie might have melted into the jungle or dived into tunnels. He could be miles away, or simply waiting for the pounding to end.

Even so, the blitz had kept up for hours in the hope that some, perhaps a lot, of the VC force might have been caught in the open and annihilated.

Long before our column reached the camp we began seeing the signs of bombardment. Broken and blackened trees were the marks of short rounds, and torn foliage showed how far shrapnel could be thrown to rip and slice.

Delta Company was still en route, but the battalion commander was eager to have us go in and assess the situation. Our captain ordered his three platoons on line in squads, nine columns of GIs closing the last half kilometer to the camp. I was, as usual, toward the back of the platoon, but not feeling all that secure at the prospect of another tussle with Chuck.

Cautiously approaching point men still hadn't drawn any fire when they reached the edge of the camp. The company fanned out into a semicircle, enclosing about half of a partial clearing where Charlie had hidden his base. Our perimeter was intentionally only halfway around the compound. If there was a fight, we damn sure didn't want to be all the way around the camp and shooting at each other.

The devastation from the daylong pounding was purely unbelievable. What few buildings, hootches really, had been in the compound were flattened and reduced to splinters. Cooking fires were scattered and extinguished. Busted weapons littered the ground. Bodies, and pieces of bodies, were everywhere. Dozens of bodies, broken and burned. Some had blistered skin peeling away from bone, roasted by the intense heat of napalm. Blood formed wet spots on clear patches of earth, and was splashed dark red on the remnants of the hootches.

It was like a scene out of a Hieronymus Bosch painting, a macabre panorama of lost souls descending into hell, tormented by demons spearing and tearing at them.

I glanced over at Rusty O'Hara. He was pale, and abruptly leaned over and barfed. And barfed some more. Poor guy, still a little less hardened to this crap than many of us. A sensitive guy, hopelessly out of his element, over-matched by this ugly war. An image of Doc rose in my mind. He would have been grinning from ear to ear at such a pleasingly grisly sight of bad guys brought to an untimely end. I turned back to the morbid spectacle spread out in the VC compound, and mentally shrugged my shoulders. It was disgusting, but I didn't feel the horror that I suspected Rusty felt. Or like I might have once felt, way back when I was just Hobie Jennings, decent midwestern college kid.

No longer. Like the man said, I'm not really apathetic. I just don't give a shit.

And that's how the operation ended. A company of grunts, standing around what had been a camp for some still unidentified VC force, staring at bodies, blood and destruction. There was no battle, no bunkers of bad guys waiting to trade bullets with us, no further contact at all. The VC had the sense to di-di when the roof started falling in, at least the ones who didn't get toasted right away.

First platoon got the unpleasant task of counting dead

gooks while the rest of us kept an eye for any VC stragglers. There were 53 in all, give or take an extra arm or leg. Another grease mark on the chart at battalion headquarters, another bunch of Vietnamese families missing a member, another vivid memory in blood-red Technicolor to awaken me years later, shaking on sweat-soaked sheets.

The body count detail found two caches of food and ammunition, hidden underground. Chunks of C-4 soon reduced it to the same rubble as the rest of the camp.

After counting the corpses and checking the area for anything intact enough to be useful or informative, the company turned around and headed back the way we had come. We started the long trek back to LZ Professional.

Nobody looked back.

Chapter Twenty-Four

I've often thought of my mental state in Vietnam as analogous to a neutral gear on a transmission. Even that isn't quite right. It was as though I discovered in myself some capacity to disassociate, to put my mind into some stepped-down state where the slow crawl of time and the unrelenting images of pain and hopelessness couldn't completely reach me.

It wasn't denial, and not truly an escape from the unpleasant circumstances of a grunt in a jungle war. It was rather a mind trick of not noticing or feeling or caring quite as much—sort of a self-numbing process; brain Novocain. Those who couldn't find the switch to throw inside themselves turned to other numbing agents like grass and booze.

I was vaguely aware that I did it, and recognized that it made me think and act differently from the person I had been such a long two years before. I told myself it was temporary, a passage through an ugly time, and that I would somehow automatically revert to a normal, connected and fully engaged person after it was all over.

The mental withdrawal hadn't been something I consciously set out to accomplish, but the "skill" had grown progressively stronger during my tour. I was not as obsessed and frustrated as I had once been at the painfully unhurried passing of days. I was still as eager as ever to be done with it and going home, but oddly more accepting of the slow pace. And it no longer bothered me very much to look and feel like some troll from under a bridge, unwashed for weeks at a time, indifferently picking off leeches, wiping sweat and mud off my face with the filthy towel that hung around my neck under the rucksack strap.

Perhaps the best consequence of my psychological neutral gear was the thicker skin I had grown somewhere along the way, an apathy to the portraits of war. Rusty O'Hara had puked his guts when he saw the result of an extended fire mission on the VC base camp. The scene hadn't troubled me nearly as much. Tough guy. Strong and silent. Keep it to yourself. Sure.

I couldn't help wondering if whatever it was Linda thought she had seen in me during our Hawaiian fairy tale might be related to this trick of disconnection, or whatever the hell it was. I found that thought a little annoying. Wasn't she supposed to cut me a little slack? Didn't a year in this cesspool deserve some understanding, some compassion?

Bravo Company and Delta Company never did rendezvous. There was no need since Charlie had slinked away to lick his wounds. Bravo Company was on the way back to Professional, and I didn't much care where Delta went.

It took several days to get back to the hill. I don't know how many, none of us were counting. The company was just a big balloon that our experiences had deflated. We were flat, and I was as deep into my neutral gear as I had ever been. Nobody talked. We all simply trudged along in the column, enduring the hot sun, each of us with our private thoughts and unanswerable questions about what on earth we were doing out there.

I was angry, but now not at the gooks. I was angry at the entire impossibly absurd situation, a supreme catch twenty-two. The American public didn't want us to fight in Vietnam anymore, the politicians didn't want us to fight anymore, and most of the rest of the world didn't want us to fight anymore. I sure as hell didn't want to fight, and never really had wanted to. The South Vietnamese didn't seem to care about fighting. About the only folks who wanted to fight were the North Vietnamese, and some might argue they had a reason. So what the heck were we doing out there piling up gook bodies?

I guess I was mad about everything that trapped me into a farcical state of affairs that I, and any of my comrades, could not influence. It defied logic, and I was a very logical person. Oh yeah, that mental neutral gear did nothing to mute anger.

Neither did it have much effect on fear. It just helped you to not give a shit.

In time we made it back to LZ Professional and climbed up the muddy slope to the relative comfort of its bunkers. Back to maintenance details, shit-burning, maybe a new pair of boots if your size was available, and a few hot meals.

The battalion S-3 had been increasing the frequency of close-in patrols, typically conducted by the resident company on the firebase. They were intended to watch for and discourage any flagrant probing by the bad guys. Just about the first orders our captain received on our arrival was a schedule of daily platoon or squad sweeps the battalion people wanted us to maintain while we were on the LZ. It wasn't like me to say I told you so, but it struck me that other folks might be starting to share my earlier concern about the security of our new location.

I was getting real short. With less than a month left in my year, I could get orders almost any time. DEROS orders (date of estimated return from overseas) were notoriously unpredictable. Some guys got drops of a week or two and went home early, others humped the bush right up to their 365th day.

Each night as I fell asleep, I thought about going home and fantasized about how it would be. That first night on new LZ Professional, tired from a long day of walking, I finally drifted off to dreams of all the people and things I missed. Most of all, Linda.

Bravo Company spent six more days on the firebase, filling sandbags, inspecting concertina wire, roaming through the nearby jungle to see if Charlie was scouting the hill's defenses. I wrote letters to everyone at home, and I know my growing excitement at the approaching special day must have shown in my words.

When our time on the hill ended and we cycled back to the bush, I don't mind admitting I was anxious. Nobody ever liked wandering around in the jungle, pretending to be a target. But grunts were especially nervous when they got short. When the tour is almost over and you're still alive, your thoughts are dominated by all the horrible things that could happen during those final ticks of the clock.

When new guys got hit, all the veterans nodded sagely about how it was good to get it early in your year if you were going to get it at all. Better that, than to last through a whole year of the sweat, crud and horror, and then get nailed at the end.

Bravo Company had orders to go south and look for bad guys. The captain wanted to cover as much territory as possible, so shortly after working our way through a camouflaged passageway in the wire around Professional's perimeter, we broke into platoons and headed in separate directions.

Lieutenant Courtney had continued to mellow. He had stopped sounding like quotes from OCS textbooks and seemed willing to take advice from the rest of us in the platoon. He was still a dork—he knew it and all the guys knew it—but he wasn't walking around like he had a ramrod shoved up his ass anymore, and the platoon was tolerating his command more and more.

Our medic, the guy who replaced Doc when he moved to Headquarters Company, was a quiet and gentle guy—a far cry from his predecessor. He had no interest in walking point, a job from which as medic he was legitimately exempt. He carried a standard 45-caliber pistol like most other medics, and was an unlikely candidate to charge an enemy ambush or tote an AK-47. In some ways, he was a welcome change from Doc. Of course, he was called "Doc" too, just like every medic in the country.

The lieutenant's new RTO was a skinny Alabama kid, no more than 18. Dave had gotten a bad number in the lottery and was drafted right out of high school. He was an odd choice for a radioman. His southern accent was so thick he could be difficult to understand, especially on the radio. His nickname was "Weasel", and he said it like "Weeso". He was asked to repeat an awful lot of radio traffic by folks who couldn't understand what the heck he was saying.

Lieutenant Courtney had given him the job during my time in the rear, after Tom Warren's old RTO went home. Weasel worked at it, and seemed to enjoy some status in carrying that heavy radio. So I learned to understand him, and asked him to be sure he used the phonetic alphabet for important messages that we didn't want misinterpreted.

Now that I was in the eleventh hour of my tour, most guys who had been in 2nd platoon when I first arrived were gone. There had been a half dozen FNGs just since my return from Chu Lai club duty. There was a different feel to the platoon. Attitudes were a lot more sullen, soldiers even less spirited than when I came over. Replacement troops coming into Vietnam were still mostly draftees, but many had become wrongly persuaded by the war-is-almost-over-and-our-boys-are-coming-home rhetoric that they would never see a tour of duty.

They believed the hype, were convinced the risk of a visit to Vietnam had passed, figured they would get some safe stateside assignment or maybe a trip to Germany to keep an eye on the Russians, and they crashed back to earth when the orders for Vietnam came around. The mood back when I trained had been a sad and disappointed compliance with inescapable orders to a controversial war. The mood of these new guys was bitterness, and some of them came close to open rebellion.

What an irony. The U.S. began its involvement in Vietnam with a professional military, committed to what was then an apparently justifiable conflict. Over time, the professionalism waned as Army training facilities churned out less and less willing infantry soldiers who possessed ever fewer skills. Finally, with the end in sight, many of the new guys were close to useless and were completely unmotivated.

As a consequence, the position in which I found myself was very awkward. On the one hand, I was (astonishingly) a seasoned veteran and a logical person for those green troops to look to for guidance. On the other hand, a lot of those green troops were uninterested in anything to do with the Army or Vietnam, even if what they didn't know might kill them. And I had reached a point of considerable empathy with their views, since I had long sensed the pointlessness of it all. Still, I didn't want anyone unnecessarily croaking on my watch.

I began to notice that drug use was up, both in the numbers of grunts who were doing it and in the openly unguarded way many of them toked up. They kept it away from Lieutenant Courtney, but I could see what was going on. I was too short to get into any disciplinary crap, and I really didn't want to set myself up as a fragging target by pissing off some dopehead. So I focused on letting people know my limits, and that I expected alert troops in the jungle. I put the word out that people better not smoke any grass in the bush or do it in front of me on the firebase, but if they wanted to take their chances with the officers on the hill, it was their own business.

It made me uneasy to think of GIs standing watch in a night laager or even up on LZ Professional, sucking on Chu Lai 101s and jiving with a transistor radio. I had visions of VC sappers, cutting their way through the concertina and crawling up to bunkers, hurling satchel charges and slaughtering a bunch of my guys because some feel-no-pain pothead was too high to notice bad guys in the wire. Those thoughts later proved prophetic.

Second platoon was sent to patrol furthest to the south. The lieutenant formed up a column, and we struck out on our own. I had no idea how good or bad the guy on point might be. He had only been in country a couple months and I didn't know if he had walked point before. But it was Lieutenant Courtney's platoon; he presumably knew the kid and his capabilities.

On the second day out, still within three klicks of Professional, we walked into an ambush. In most ambushes, unless he had a big force, Charlie's usual tactic was to pick off the first few guys in the column, then disappear. This time the ambush came from the side, well after the point element and the first third of the platoon column had passed by.

I heard at least one automatic weapon and what were probably carbines. Only a handful of M-16s were shooting back.

The squad in the middle, likely getting the brunt of Charlie's incoming fire, was Rusty O'Hara's. The trailing squad, with me at the rear, had all burrowed as close to the ground as they could get, and none of them, including their squad leader, was holding up a gun to shoot back. Apathy—waiting for your buddy to fight back first—in a firefight is often a fatal error in judgment. Sometimes, nobody is the first to fight back. Then the VC can have their way.

I had no more interest in sticking my head up than anyone else. My thoughts were consumed with getting through the last few days of my year and getting out alive. But what are you going to do? I had no idea what the lieutenant was doing up front, and my RTO couldn't raise Weasel—Alabama Dave. Can't just lie there and let old Charles leisurely pick off targets. Sooner or later, you'll be one of the targets.

So I angrily ordered the squad leader to get off his ass and get his people into a skirmish line toward the point of ambush. And I started working my way up to Rusty's squad, dodging from tree to tree, wondering when the bullets would start tracking me.

I kept hoping that the "thocka thocka" of the Chicom weapon would stop, but it continued to spit out small bursts every few seconds. The gooks must have recognized how pathetic our return fire was, and decided to hang around for some extra kills.

Veteran or not, I hadn't gotten any better at pinpointing the source of fire just from the sound. As I crawled and dodged, I wasn't completely sure where I was in relation to the ambush site, until I came upon two wounded GIs. Doc was working on one of them. He had a sucking chest wound, just like the ones they taught us about in basic training. The poor guy was making a strained wheezing noise, laboring hard to breathe with a lung threatening to collapse. I couldn't tell where the other man was hit, and he wasn't moving.

Rusty was the only one shooting back. He had crawled behind a tree and was putting magazine after magazine of M-16 rounds on a deadfall about 60 meters away from which the automatic weapons fire seemed to be coming.

I didn't question his nerve. He saw what had to be done

and he was doing it. Unfortunately, he was a squad leader and should have been kicking butts to get the rest of his people to lift their heads far enough out of the dirt to shoot back.

It really pissed me off. Everybody in the platoon was acting as though Charlie would go away if they just ignored him. I got a little crazy and started cussing out the motionless lumps around me to shoot at the goddamn gooks. I must have sounded pretty frightful; they were evidently more scared of me than the ambush and within a minute we had a heavy suppressing fire going back at Chuck.

One of the wounded guys had been the M-79 grenadier in Rusty's squad. I grabbed his grenade launcher and a few rounds, and then crawled up beside Rusty. "Where are they?" He pointed at the deadfall, and at a clump of trees next to it. I fired an HE round into the deadfall.

For a moment after the grenade exploded, the automatic weapon quieted. But then it cranked up again, clearly looking to find the GI with the grenade launcher. So I tried a willie peter round. White phosphorous is really evil stuff. The flash blinds, and the shrapnel is burning phosphorous. Even if it doesn't penetrate, it sticks to you and burns.

The round was on target. Someone shrieked, and a VC jumped from behind the deadfall slapping at his chest. Rusty dropped him within three steps with a burst from his M-16.

And that was it. If the dead VC had any friends with him, they just faded into the jungle. We were left with a dead gook and two wounded grunts needing a dust-off.

It was a little troubling that bad guys were operating so close to the new firebase. I supposed the brass would conclude a contact of this sort was evidence of the need for more concentrated patrol activity in this part of the AO, and that probably made them feel they had made a good choice in the firebase's location. I looked at it a little differently. To me it suggested that Professional might someday be in a world of hurt.

I was apprehensive about the firebase. The old place had

been well established and hadn't experienced any serious enemy activity, let alone a real ground assault, in all the time I'd been there. I couldn't help thinking the new base was a tempting target for the VC.

Chapter Twenty-Five

A week went by. Then another. Much to my relief, there were no further contacts. I was within days of my DEROS, and still had no word on going home. It was obvious I wasn't going to be among the lucky guys who got a drop. Then, on a hot and clear Wednesday morning, the word went around that a resupply chopper would be coming that afternoon.

Lieutenant Courtney sought me out. "Sergeant Jennings, you got your orders. You'll be going out on the resupply bird."

It's almost impossible to describe how I felt when I heard his words. Sure, I had known it was coming, and had certainly anticipated the elation that the news would bring. But you can never really know in advance just how wonderful it feels to get to the end and know you made it. Alive.

I couldn't stop grinning. I had waited a year for that moment, marking off time by days and sometimes hours. A year is an incredibly long time, especially a year in a place like Vietnam. Jubilation is not a strong enough word to capture the surge of joy at knowing it was over. Not one single night more in the jungle, no more bullets and bombs, no more dead comrades and dead gooks. Home soon to loved ones, home to a life put on hold so long ago, and now almost forgotten.

The jubilation was followed quickly by paranoia. What if we run into a firefight before the chopper comes? What if something happens to the chopper? What if...what if...? I had to settle myself down. You aren't safely out of Vietnam until you're looking out the window of your jetliner from several thousand feet, back at a country you hope to never see again.

The day dragged on forever, teasing and taunting me. I kept

checking my watch, now hopelessly clouded by condensation inside the crystal from a year's worth of heat and humidity. The hands barely moved.

The platoon was still on patrol, and had a lot of ground to cover before the resupply would arrive. More of the much loved "search and destroy". (I could never understand why someone didn't come up with a catchier mission description.) We had continued moving south, and found ourselves in a reasonably open grassy lowland area. It would provide any number of perfect places for a helicopter to land, drop off supplies, and pick up an eager short-timer.

It was also excruciatingly open, and I spent most of the day nervous as hell that something bad would happen. I tried to keep my head as low as possible. No point in tempting fate.

Good-byes were not a big deal. Despite the fact that most GIs knew they would never again see a buddy who was heading home, departure was typically low-key. It was some of the same psychology that kept people from getting close to each other. Death was the great uncertainty, and we avoided confronting it by refraining from promises of getting together back in The World for some grand reunion. And the guy on his way home tried not to be too demonstrative about it because all the guys around him had to stay out there until their turn came up. Not very becoming to rub it in.

Besides, the guys I knew the longest and had been closest to were long gone or dead. This new and different platoon included a lot of grunts who were still mostly strangers to me. Nice enough guys, but still in many ways unknown.

So the day slowly ground on. A few people who heard I was leaving wished me well when the column stopped for a break. One new PFC actually said he had been glad to have me for a platoon sergeant. I didn't know what to say—I wasn't sure *I* was glad to have had me for a platoon sergeant.

Rusty O'Hara made it a point to find me once he learned I was leaving. He was uncomfortable, and both of us felt a little awkward, but he wanted to thank me for helping him and teaching him a few things along the way. I told him I thought he was a good NCO and that I hoped the balance of his tour would go by quickly. And I thanked him again for dropping the VC who would have nailed me. We swapped home addresses; I thought that he was one person I'd met in Vietnam who I actually might contact post-Army.

The rest of the afternoon somehow eventually passed. And then the resupply arrived. An uneasy chopper pilot, idling his Huey on the ground and worried about taking fire, had no patience for prolonged good-byes. If you planned on leaving in *his* bird, you got your butt on board in a hurry 'cause it was time to di-di mau. I saluted Lieutenant Courtney, something you normally didn't do out in the bush, but I figured it wouldn't hurt to set a respectful example for the rest of the guys. He snapped a salute back to me with obvious pleasure. Then I jumped into the cabin and the Huey was biting for air.

From the time that chopper lifted off, my life got blurry. I spent a night on LZ Professional going through the usual administrative BS and turning in most of my gear. I felt a little naked that night without my M-16, especially because of the uneasy thoughts I continued to have about the new firebase's vulnerability.

About noon the next day I caught a ride into Chu Lai. A long shower and a clean set of fatigues made me feel a little less of a crudball. Then there was more paperwork to begin my separation process, an effort I didn't mind because it meant my freedom. I went through the typical Army out-processing crap, this time from an all-new cast of characters. There was a new battalion sergeant major, a new Headquarters Company CO, a new quartermaster. Even the Louisiana lump from the motor pool was gone and a new fat guy was in charge of the wheels.

None of that mattered to me or even held my attention very long. I was going home! They could have made me clean the latrines or scrub the grease traps, and I wouldn't have cared.

The World was waiting for me. Fast food and slow dancing, hot cars and cold beer, civilian clothes and rock groups that weren't Korean and beds without leeches and so much more.

A real job, one that didn't require me to carry a gun and shoot people.

And my family. And most of all, Linda, my wife of one year, less than a month of it spent together.

It seemed so incredibly wonderful; it almost hurt to anticipate it all. It was total, absolute joy. But there was apprehension creeping into my thoughts as well. What would going home be like? What would *they* be like, my family and friends? How would I handle a reunion after so long away? Perhaps most important, what would they think of me, how would they react to me?

Had I really changed so much, as I uncomfortably suspected? Would I no longer be the person they knew and loved? Had *they* changed, had they gone on with their lives, growing and transforming in a world no longer obsessed with far-off Vietnam, while those of us who were still here marked time in suspended animation, living like animals and absorbed by distracting details like surviving?

The questions were troubling, and they tempered some of my exhilaration at the prospect of going home. The three best things ever to happen to me in my young life were about to occur simultaneously: going back to my wife and family, getting out of Vietnam, and getting discharged from an Army I really hadn't wanted to be a part of in the first place. I tried not to let my apprehension about who might have changed rain on this parade.

Practically sleepwalking, I compliantly went about out-processing for a couple days. Go here, sign this, go there, turn in form number such and such, get some other form stamped by fourteen REMF Remington Ranger clerks on the third Tuesday of a full moon.

I remember hanging around with dozens of other short-timers on the baking tarmac at Chu Lai airport, waiting to board a bulky C-130 for a flight to Cam Rahn. We shuffled up the massive tail ramp into the stifling cargo belly, sitting on bench seats and webbing that ran down both sides of the fuselage. The temperature inside was over 120 degrees, and in five minutes we were dripping sweat.

When the plane finally took off and climbed to altitude, the air temperature plummeted as the colder outside air rushed in the open cargo bay in the tail, and we were soon shivering in sweat-soaked fatigues. It didn't matter—nothing mattered. I was going home. Roast me, freeze me, numb me with paperwork, make me do pushups. I had already survived the worst they could dish out and the end was in sight. Nothing could faze me now.

Two days at Cam Rahn brought more out-processing, boredom, and impatience. If you appreciated massive logistics, it was an interesting place. The process of winding down the war was beginning to squeeze Vietnam like a sponge. As the Army down-sized and decommissioned units, soldiers were flowing into transfer points like Cam Rahn to be funneled back to the U.S. or be reassigned to surviving units elsewhere in Vietnam. It was no small operational challenge to receive and process the flow, and to fill up a daily train of jetliners taking troops back to the states.

There was more paperwork at Cam Rahn. They put us in barracks for our two-day stay, and kept the lower ranking guys busy with make-work details. I was glad to be an NCO, as I avoided most of the harassment.

There was a final shakedown inspection, each of us individually checked for stuff we weren't supposed to take back to The World. GIs about to go into the inspection area filled up a lot of wastebaskets with marijuana, loose bullets, and any number of other items frowned on by the brass. I had been carrying a few loose rounds in my pocket for so long I almost forgot about them. No longer were we cleared to carry ordinance.

We had to go to a finance officer and turn in all our MPC and piastres. It was strange to have a pocket full of real American greenbacks again after using the Army's play money for so long.

At the end of the second day waiting in Cam Rahn, my number at last came up and I boarded a 707 emblazoned with the logo of an airline I had never heard of and have never again

seen. It didn't matter; it was an airplane. A cabin full of worn
and tired GIs, at once both euphoric and subdued, settled in for
the long ride home.

A hundred heads turned in unison as pretty flight attendants
busily went about their pre-flight chores. These were the first
round-eyed girls many of us had seen in months. Still, we were
a respectful bunch, no whistles or suggestive leers. We couldn't
take our eyes off them, but it was a quiet awe—a symbol of
something to be glad we survived for—respect rather than the
spirited lusting of boisterous young men.

The flight was a little shorter in distance than the trip over,
because our destination was Fort Lewis, Washington instead of
New Jersey. Most of the flight I spent trying to sleep. When
I couldn't sleep, I stared out the window and thought about
the coming reunion. We refueled in Honolulu, and I replayed
my R&R of a few months before while waiting for the journey
to continue. The stop was only an hour, and they let us off to
stretch our legs. As I wandered around in the Honolulu airport,
it felt like years since I had been there for my week with Linda.
And I happily recognized that Honolulu meant that I was back
in the good old US of A.

When we finally arrived at Fort Lewis, the bullshit of the
stateside Army quickly reappeared. I was thinking about kissing
the ground, but was interrupted by our greeting. It had been
customary in Vietnam to wear the shirtsleeves of our jungle
fatigues rolled up. It was a hot climate, and nobody—including
all the officers—ever wore their shirtsleeves any other way.

So imagine the surprise of a planeload of Vietnam veterans,
many of us only days removed from killing people, when we
were met by a prissy, dickhead lieutenant. "Get into formation!
Get those shirtsleeves rolled down and buttoned. You're back
in the states, now. Start looking like soldiers!"

I saw astonished looks being exchanged among the people
who had been on the plane with me. The lieutenant was a skinny
little shit, and had nothing but a National Defense ribbon on
his summer khakis (the Army passes those out in basic training).
The guys around me were all wearing CIBs, the mark of walking

in harm's way and taking hostile fire. And our welcome back to The World wasn't a big brass band or a hearty thank-you from a country grateful for our sacrifice. No, it was a whiny, adenoidal dweeb ordering us to roll down our sleeves. Go figure.

The buck sergeant standing next to me leaned over and spoke quietly to me. "You want to frag the little cocksucker, or should I?" Someone in the back muttered in a stage whisper, "Go fuck yourself", which made Lieutenant Jerk look a little nervous. But we all meekly complied, slowly rolling our sleeves down and buttoning them like good little soldiers. It was important, after all, to be aware of the things that really mattered, to look sharp and know you were valued by your superiors.

The three days I spent at Fort Lewis were a little like basic training, at least in terms of the mindlessness and bureaucratic paper shuffling. For those of us who were getting out of the Army, there was more out-processing, a final physical, a final accounting of pay and leave time not taken, and a fitting for a new set of dress greens to wear home.

They reviewed our orders for medals we had been awarded and made sure we had ribbons for each of them to put on our dress uniforms. I found myself with a chestful of junk that made me feel ambivalent. I had to admit to myself there was some pride there. But the medals said I was some kind of hero, and I sure didn't feel that. There were no heroes.

Most like basic training during my waiting time at Fort Lewis were the dozens of make-work details. Here were GIs just home from a war, and they had us doing things like walking in a line through the compound, shoulder to shoulder, picking up cigarette butts for hours. These were guys who only days before were ducking bullets, and we were being treated like raw recruits. Even NCOs weren't exempt from the BS, and I picked up a lot of cigarette butts.

I was genuinely astonished. I knew there was no love of Vietnam veterans by most of the civilian population, but I never would have imagined being treated so shabbily by the Army itself on my return. I was a little pissed, but with the end so close I could taste it I damn sure wasn't going to make waves.

There wasn't a single thing in the entire out-processing experience to make us feel appreciated, nothing to acknowledge that the war we fought was of any consequence to anyone. I had no expectations of ticker tape parades or anything like that, but I was really struck by the Army's total indifference to our return from overseas. I didn't feel like a soldier, a combat veteran. Whatever pride I felt was at having survived the ordeal, at having stepped up to be measured and found to be capable. I couldn't manage any pride in being part of that Army, not the one that placed so little value on its combat veterans. I felt like a goddamn commodity, just another stock unit off the shelf of some OD-pissing supply sergeant. And, despite my total focus on being finished with all of it, I confess I felt a little resentful at the shabby treatment.

I suffered the final days quietly. A lot of the crap really couldn't reach me, because I was still benefiting from my neutral gear. And I had the "FIGMO" attitude—I had my orders. At least a dozen times I heard guys say, "What are they going to do, send us to Vietnam?" Keeping your head straight like that tended to keep the little indignities in perspective.

And so my Army days wound down fairly uneventfully. I called Linda and my parents, to let them know I was safely back in the U.S. It was a little unreal to be talking on the phone with them. My mother cried. Strangely, I couldn't think of much to say other than I'd let everybody know when I had a definite arrival time.

Four of us who had been on the same plane struck up a friendship, and when the processing at last was over and we were released late on the third day, we got a cab together to the Seattle-Tacoma airport. One of the guys was carrying a Chicom carbine he had taken as a souvenir off a dead VC. It was legal, all tagged and marked, with the firing mechanism removed.

When we arrived at the airport, it turned out that all of us had to go through Denver to get to our various destinations. A Denver flight was leaving in one and a half hours from Portland, and a shuttle flight from Seattle to Portland would get us there in time to catch it. The only catch was that the shuttle was leaving in five minutes.

So four GIs in dress greens, one holding a VC carbine out in front of him at port arms, went running like crazy men through the Seattle-Tacoma airport. Back then, someone with a gun in an airport didn't attract a lot of attention. People simply watched us dash by and shook their heads—either because of our unseemly behavior, or because we were just another quartet of those baby-killers who had been doing bad things to the poor folks in Vietnam like Jane Fonda said. In today's world, with much of the country's innocence lost to violent zealotry, I'm reasonably certain that running down an airport concourse with a gun would get you shot.

It took three plane changes and several hours of hanging around airports enduring the disapproving stares of people who assumed anyone in a uniform was amoral, but at last I made it back to Detroit. I was a nervous wreck for the last hour of the flight, anxious about how it would go and undecided whether to rush off the plane or wait for everybody else to get off first. I waited.

A small crowd was there to greet me. Every relative for miles around had come, and the attention was almost overwhelming. I felt awkward and embarrassed, but incredibly happy. Linda was beautiful, and beaming her fantastic smile. I didn't want to let go of her hand. My year in hell was over. I was home. Life was good.

Memories of momentous occasions are often hazy, and that night was truly a blur. I recall being shepherded around by enthusiastic family members, receiving hugs and kisses and slaps on the back. There was a party at my parents' home, attended by friends and relatives. I heard "Welcome home" at least fifty times, and liked the sound more every time I heard it. I held Linda's hand tightly. And through it all I wore a silly grin that wouldn't go away.

It was dreamlike. I was floating, and not completely sure I could trust that it was really happening. I thought I should pinch myself. When the party finally wound down enough for us to leave, Linda and I went back to our apartment—a home I hadn't seen for exactly one year. In less than a week I had gone from humping through the jungle to standing in my own living room looking at the woman I had thought about virtually every hour I had been gone. I walked over and wrapped my arms around her. Neither of us slept at all the rest of the night.

I think the first few days home were the happiest of my life. It was just like I had dreamed it would be, only better. I had successfully negotiated an unpleasant detour in my life, and now the future was filled with promises of wonderful things. I was back in control of who I was and what I would be.

Linda took a couple weeks off from her job so we could spend all our time together. The days were filled with exploring and shopping and fixing up the apartment. The nights, when we didn't just stay home and fool around, were devoted to getting back together with old friends and partying. Bobby, my friend and roommate pre-Army, and his wife lived about five miles from us. The four of us really hit it off, and there were a few nights when we all drank too much and raised some hell.

And all of the time was for Linda and me to share—time to hold hands and talk, time to stare at each other like we couldn't believe it was finally over, time to make love and hold each other so we would never be pulled apart again.

My PX stereo was there at our apartment, the components waiting to be wired up. Linda was a self-admitted electrical illiterate, and hadn't even taken the stuff out of the boxes. So I hooked it all together, and we sat for hours listening to the marvelous sounds that came out of a 150 watt Sansui receiver and a pair of four foot high speakers.

My civilian clothes were in sad shape and two years out of style, so Linda hauled me off to the mall for an extended shopping trip. We bought mostly informal stuff, in keeping with the laid-back life we were living. Shirts, slacks, shoes, belts, underwear—a complete remake from top to bottom. It seemed strange to be wearing bright colors again instead of OD. We even picked out a suit, in deference to the recognition that I would eventually have to go looking for a real job.

Between the pay I had designated to be sent directly home and the cash I had received at Fort Lewis, there was enough money for us to buy a new car—a shiny red Camaro convertible with a big, throaty V-8. We cruised around like a couple of high school kids in that car, having a ball and catching up on time denied us the previous year.

Whenever we were with them, my family and a lot of my friends wanted to hear about Vietnam. They wanted a first-hand accounting of what it was really like to be there. Most of the news stories by late 1970 were negative, unflattering reports of "Vietnamization". It was the word Washington was using to describe our hand-off of the war to the South Vietnam government. All of them had ideas, mostly shaped by network television, of what it was like in Vietnam, and wanted to try their ideas out on me.

I really didn't want to talk about it. And I didn't know what to tell them, either. Should I describe what it felt like to blow somebody's brains out, or how it felt when TC wasn't there any more, or my rage when Chief's face was smashed in by a Chicom bullet? I didn't think anyone really wanted to hear that kind of stuff. So maybe I should tell them about the little boy in the middle of nowhere who drew pictures of helicopter gunships shooting at him. Or tell them about the backwards peasants whose homes got burned because they were too stubborn to move away and because GIs had a tough time telling good gooks from bad gooks.

I suppose I could relate the stories of drugs and racial tension and fraggings. And I certainly had some interesting first-hand examples of casualties by friendly fire.

Maybe I could tell them what it was like to think of an entire country of people as "gooks", a life form sufficiently insignificant that it didn't matter too much if we blew them away.

No, there wasn't a hell of a lot to talk to them about, even if I tried to sanitize my stories. Their interest was understandable, if a bit too much like the people who slow down as they drive past an auto accident. But I wanted to put it all out of my head. I didn't want to freshen the memories by pandering to people's fascination with war stories.

Life was almost perfect for maybe two weeks. Then I began to sense something shifting. So much had changed while I was gone, it was really hard to catch up. Sort of a Rip Van Jennings, I expected everything would be pretty much as it had been when the bus took me away to basic training. Plus I had aged a lot more than the two years I had spent in the Army, and some things I had once viewed as cool now looked juvenile to me.

Linda and I went to see the Woodstock movie at a drive-in theater. I had a hard time with it. About a half hour into the movie I found myself thinking, "I've never heard of these groups—who are these people?" Most of the music was good, but who was this Joe Cocker guy doing an imitation of a spastic? I liked the warm harmonies of Crosby, Stills and Nash, but where did they come from? What happened to the groups I used to listen to?

And all the drugs. They were everywhere, and they were being glorified in music and pop culture. I wasn't a drug prude by any means, but it seemed like the drug thing had really gone overboard. Part of me still saw drugs as a threat, something you didn't want people using when a moment of carelessness or inattention could get a lot of grunts killed. Linda had a little grass in the apartment, and I surprised myself at how disapproving it made me feel. I wanted to let my hair down and get stoned, but inside me was a platoon sergeant who had seen how messed up it could make you.

I was hung up somewhere between military and civilian life, and struggling to figure out who the hell I was.

At a party one evening, I wound up with a group of people in a conversation that bounced around from one current event to another. I wasn't talking much—I had become more and more guarded since I came home. But I stood and sipped my drink, and listened as my companions offered up opinions on all that was going on in the world.

One particularly assertive pair of conversationalists, a young husband and wife, evidently had a strong view on anything the group talked about, and it wasn't long before the Vietnam War came up. I started to get a little uncomfortable and was trying to slip away, when someone commented that I had just returned from overseas. Mrs. Opinion immediately turned cold. It was real clear that she didn't have much use for me. I heard her mutter something about baby-killers (you know, that really got to be an overworked term back then). It pissed me off, but I held my tongue. But then Mr. Opinion turned to me and said something about what an exciting adventure it must have been, how being in the Army was probably good for me, and how "neat" it must have been to be part of the glory and do the battle thing, and did I ever kill anyone.

I saw red. I wanted to hit him, to knock him down and put a Ranger stomp in his face. Even as my blood was rising, I suddenly felt Bobby's hand on my arm, gently restraining me. I looked at Bobby, took a deep breath, and got a grip.

When I turned back toward Mr. Opinion, he was grinning. I suddenly felt out of place, just as I remembered feeling in the restaurant in Honolulu. I didn't belong with these people. I was spoiled goods, tainted by an experience they would never understand. I should be hidden away from civilized folks, off in a sweltering jungle far from this stupid party.

In a low, flat voice that made his grin disappear, I told him that until he had walked across a blood-smeared battlefield, littered with broken bodies and moaning wounded, until he had looked someone in the face and shot him dead, he had no business flapping his lip about the "battle thing". There wasn't anything glorious about death, especially purposeless death.

I got a lot of blank looks. We left the party early.

Over time, I began to realize that Linda and I had both changed, perhaps more than either of us wanted to admit. There were little signs, a few petty disagreements, some misunderstandings. There had been a time, despite the brevity of our relationship, when we both seemed to know what the other was thinking. Communication had been simple, and sometimes unspoken. No longer. It was clear there were things we didn't see eye to eye about, and neither we nor our marriage had matured enough to provide the depth we needed to work them out.

My little paradise was slipping away, and I was powerless to stop it. The realization that all was not right made things worse, because it frustrated me. This was subtle stuff, and I was used to correcting problems with an M-16. Helpless and unable to fix what I couldn't see or understand, I sometimes let my anger show. That only worsened things, and brought out a wrathful side of Linda I didn't previously know existed.

Eventually it came out that Linda had met someone while I was gone, and had found in him the comfort and attention that I couldn't provide from a far off jungle. Her sense of responsibility to our marriage made her want to give it a chance when I came back, but I think we were doomed before I ever stepped off the plane. Rebuilding a relationship that has been strained by a year apart takes effort and commitment, a discouraging prospect for a vibrant young woman who had found an apparently more kindred spirit. He was waiting for her, and eager to resume where they had left off. Good old Jody could chalk up yet another conquest of a Vietnam grunt's girl back home.

But, in fairness to her, I was probably not an ideal mate right then. I was confused and puzzled by the wrenching changes in my life. I had gone from jungle killer to young civilian, and was wrestling with my new role. I was troubled by changes in my world, and by surroundings that should have been familiar, but that I frequently didn't recognize. Terrifying images occasionally awakened me in the middle of the night, memories that gnawed at me and kept me from going back to sleep. Once, Linda found me in the morning, sitting by a window staring out at nothing. She didn't know how to deal with it, and I didn't know what to say to her.

So, within a month of my return, it had all crumbled around me. Linda moved out with almost no warning, taking half the stuff in our apartment and our new car. She filed for divorce, and resisted my pleas to try to work it out. I didn't even know where she lived. I think she didn't want me to know, because she had resumed her thing with Mr. Jody.

It was a crushing punch to my emotional center. In one

month I had gone from the most ecstatic I had ever felt to the most despondent. I withdrew from friends and my family. They all had their own lives to lead, and I suppose some of them felt uncomfortable being around me. After all, I was home safely and wasn't quite the same concern to many that I had been while I was still in Vietnam. I started to drink too much, trying to erase the growing depression.

Money was rapidly running out, so I unenthusiastically went out to find a job. It wasn't difficult, since some businesses preferred veterans to fresh college graduates. Another "management trainee" position where you don't have to know anything to get hired, this time with a bank.

I was living my life in a trance, going to work during the day and drinking like Doc at night. I had ridden an emotional roller coaster from the highest high to the deepest low, and felt little motivation to do much of anything beyond what was necessary just to exist.

The job was okay, but it didn't give me the life-centering anchor I had hoped to find with Linda. I wore a suit to work, really another type of uniform. The people around me were nice enough, but I didn't feel as though I fit in all that well. I still had an unsavory self-image, the unwashed grunt doing things my new colleagues couldn't begin to imagine. Although they knew I was recently in the Army and even asked me about my experiences, I refused to talk about it for fear they would see what I was and be horrified by it. It didn't take them long to peg me as a loner, and I was left pretty much on my own.

I realized that my head was still in that neutral gear, still marking time as my life passed by. I didn't know how to stop it, and wasn't sure I cared enough to want to. The routine of my wartime life had been replaced by the routine of an unfulfilling new day job and too many drinks at night. The empty feelings and unhappiness I had felt in Vietnam were replaced by an entirely different emptiness, but I was as powerless in dealing with it as I had been over there.

The final event—the last time the Vietnam War reached out to hurt me—may have been the point I hit bottom and began to turn my life around. I didn't recognize it as the bottom at the time. It was just another way Vietnam found to mess me up, even after I had left it behind. Yet another smack to the head for a battered young guy who had more demons than he could handle.

I had picked up a news magazine along with my evening beer supply, something to read while waiting for the numbness to set in. I was idly paging through it, hardly conscious of what I was reading, when I came across an article about Vietnam.

"*Firebase Overrun In Ground Assault*" was the article's heading, but what caught my eye was a caption under one of the accompanying photos that identified the place as LZ Professional. It was that one word, that silly name of a mud hill in the jungle, which leaped off the page at me. The beer can slipped out of my hand and fell to the carpet.

In what would prove to be the last major Viet Cong ground assault of the war, LZ Professional—a place whose muddy bunkers had been my home only four months before—had been attacked and overrun. The story described a night assault, VC sappers sneaking through the hill's defenses and tossing satchel charges into bunkers. The VC were eventually repelled, but not before considerable damage was done. A lot of guys were killed or wounded.

The story recognized a hero of the fight, a Sergeant Bill O'Hara, who had led a determined counterattack and battled the intruders in hand to hand combat until he was cut down by enemy fire. He was being awarded a Silver Star, posthumously.

The same Rusty O'Hara who had been one of my squad leaders. The same guy who had once saved my life. The gentle, self-effacing sergeant who didn't want to be there, but tried so hard to do a good job. A quiet, unassuming pacifist, another reluctant warrior. He had been my friend. And he wasn't going to be coming home.

I thought about all the people who had been part of my life for a year. Mike Keene, Tom Warren, the Chief, Doc, TC, Brady, Dee, Murphy, Kenny Whitman, Buzz Gallagher, Sergeant Major Wilkes, Marshall Courtney, Gibson, Sheppard, Patterson,

Costellano, Roger Lynch, Rusty O'Hara, and all the rest of them who lived and died in that godforsaken worthless country. What an incredible, obscene, unforgivable waste.

The magazine lay open in my lap. In my mind I saw the blood and the gore, the bodies bloated to twice their size in the hot sun. I remembered the first time I killed another human being. It was an event that increasingly weighed on me, but one I still hadn't been able to share with another person in civilian life. I suddenly saw with perfect focus how I had grown not to care about the killing. I recognized in myself how war subtly and seductively draws its participants to some lower plane that makes no room for sensitivity and morality. I wasn't at all sure I had returned from there, and I still found my tortured thoughts more confusing and disturbing than I could handle.

I thought about the ungrateful and uncaring country that had sent so many of its scared but trusting young men to a forgettable place on the other side of the planet to thrash around in the jungle and fight a purposeless war. Many of those lucky enough to return were greeted by neighbors turning their backs on them as though they were infected with a disease.

All the frustration, all of the anguish that had been buried in me welled up from the hidden place where I had locked it away. I realized, with painful clarity, that I had been a casualty, too. The fresh-faced, optimistic college kid from two and a half years ago was irretrievably gone. He had been replaced by an angry, cynical loner who didn't sleep very well, who didn't know who he was, and who didn't like himself very much.

I stared, unseeing, at the magazine. At Rusty's picture. I cried, sobbing like a little child.

There was nobody left to hear.

ABOUT THE AUTHOR

George Chute is retired and living in Green Valley, Arizona. George worked in the insurance industry, most recently as an underwriting vice president for a large property-casualty insurer. He grew up in the suburbs of Detroit and went to school at Western Michigan University. Following graduation from Western, George was drafted and spent two years in the Army. He served a tour of duty in Vietnam and was discharged in 1970, a decorated infantry NCO. George lived in Illinois, Ohio, and Minnesota before moving to Arizona. George and his wife Kathy have discovered a variety of interests in retirement, including travel, golf and hiking in the southern Arizona mountains. George has always been an avid reader, and had considered writing a book about Vietnam for a number of years. Retirement afforded him the opportunity to finally do it.

ABOUT GREATUNPUBLISHED.COM

www.greatunpublished.com is a website that exists to serve writers and readers, and to remove some of the commercial barriers between them. When you purchase a GreatUNpublished title, whether you order it in electronic form or in a paperback volume, the author is receiving a majority of the post-production revenue.

A GreatUNpublished book is never out of stock, and always available, because each book is printed on-demand, as it is ordered.

A portion of the site's share of profits is channeled into literacy programs.

So by purchasing this title from GreatUNpublished, you are helping to revolutionize the publishing industry for the benefit of writers and readers.

And for this we thank you.